Nina Stibbe's acclaimed novel *Man at the Helm* was shortlisted for the Bollinger Everyman Wodehouse Prize for Comic Fiction. She was born in Leicester, and now lives in Cornwall with her partner and two children.

You can discover more about the author at www.ninastibbe.com

PARADISE LODGE

It's 1977, and fifteen-year-old Lizzie Vogel is working in an old people's home. The place is in chaos, and it's not really a suitable job for a schoolgirl — she'd only gone for the job because it seemed too exhausting to commit to being a full-time girlfriend or a punk. She's also distracted by her family's financial troubles, keeping up with schoolwork, and deciding which brand of shampoo to use. When a rival old people's home opens, offering better parking and daily 'chairobics', business at Paradise Lodge takes a turn for the worse, and everyone must chip in to save the home before it's too late — from the crazed Matron, to the assertively shy nurse who only communicates via little grunts, to the very attractive son of the Chinese takeaway manager . . .

Books by Nina Stibbe
Published by Ulverscroft:

MAN AT THE HELM

NINA STIBBE

PARADISE LODGE

Complete and Unabridged

CHARNWOOD
Leicester

First published in Great Britain in 2016 by
Viking
an imprint of Penguin Books
London

First Charnwood Edition
published 2017
by arrangement with
Penguin Random House UK
London

A catalogue record for this book is available
from the British Library.

ISBN 978–1–4448–3178–8

Published by
F. A. Thorpe (Publishing)
Anstey, Leicestershire

Set by Words & Graphics Ltd.
Anstey, Leicestershire
Printed and bound in Great Britain by
T. J. International Ltd., Padstow, Cornwall

This book is printed on acid-free paper

Grateful acknowledgement is made for permission to
quote from *Uneasy Money* by P. G. Wodehouse.
Published by Everyman Library, 2004. Copyright ©
P. G. Wodehouse c/o Rogers, Coleridge & White Ltd,
20 Powis Mews, London W11 1JN; and from
The World is Full of Married Men by Jackie Collins,
reproduced by permission of Simon & Schuster UK,
222 Gray's Inn Road, London, WC1X 8HB

For Victoria Goldberg

At the age of eleven or thereabouts women acquire a poise and an ability to handle difficult situations which a man, if he is lucky, manages to achieve somewhere in the later seventies.

P. G. Wodehouse, *Uneasy Money*

PART ONE

Paradise Lodge

1

Linco Beer Shampoo

May 1977

The job at Paradise Lodge was Miranda Longlady's idea. I happened to bump into her outside Pop-in stores one day and she pointed out a card on the noticeboard.

Paradise Lodge — nursing home for the elderly.
Non-unionized auxiliary nurses sought for part-time duties — 35p per hour.
Ideal part-time position for outgoing, compassionate females of any age.

Miranda wanted to apply and was hoping to talk her sister, Melody, into going with her. But when Melody came out of the shop with a loaf of Take 'n' Bake and read the notice she said it wasn't for her. She'd gone into a punk phase around then and had pierced her upper ear with a needle and an ice cube and had intellectual obscenities felt-penned on to her T-shirt.

'Go on,' Miranda whined, 'I don't want to go on my own.'

While they bickered, I read the card again closely and realized that I wanted the job. I was

3

fifteen and I loved the idea of being professionally compassionate. I was longing for something
that might blossom into a new phase that didn't
involve horses, or school or becoming a punk like
Melody, or having a full-time boyfriend — all of
which seemed too exhausting to commit to —
plus 35p per hour would work out at almost £3 a
day — a huge amount then. You could practically
live on it. Plus it was a walkable distance and I
was a hater of bus travel.

'I'll go with you,' I said, and Miranda spun
round and looked at me gone out. We'd never
been particularly friendly. Actually, I hated her
and ditto she me, but for the reasons above, I
ended up walking with her to the next village to
'apply in person forthwith' as per the card.

The walk to Paradise Lodge was fascinating.
Miranda opened up to me about her reason for
needing the job and it was so compelling and
romantic and unlike the Miranda of old, I
changed my mind about her. I still didn't like
her, as such, but she seemed interesting, which
was more than could be said for most people.

Miranda and her mother were at loggerheads
regarding her boyfriend, Mike Yu. Miranda had
gone on the pill to be poised to have intercourse
with him — when the time came — and Mrs
Longlady had twigged it because of Miranda
suddenly going up two bra sizes in spite of a
recent switch from real bread to low-calorie
Slimcea. Mrs Longlady had stopped Miranda's
pocket money and was now refusing to give her a
penny until she stopped seeing Mike Yu.

The real problem was that Mrs Longlady

4

preferred Miranda's ex. A boy from Market Harborough called 'Big Smig' who was posh but tried to play it down by swearing and whose dad worked for British Leyland on the admin side and whose mum did charity work for Princess Anne with a horsey connection and was single-handedly arranging five interconnecting street parties for the Queen's Silver Jubilee.

Miranda's mother was offensive about Mike Yu, calling him 'Buttercup' and saying he was Japanese. This infuriated Miranda because Mike wasn't, he was from Hong Kong and the people from there are British or Chinese — unless they're another nationality. But they weren't usually Japanese for some reason. Miranda had researched the whole thing thoroughly with an encyclopaedia and had even asked Mike Yu about it, even though that had been awkward and intrusive.

Miranda had recently had a bad dream in which her mother made a voodoo doll of Mike and stuck a pin in it. While poor Mike writhed in agony (in the dream) Miranda had shouted at her mother, 'Stop doing voodoo on Mike, I love him.' And it was via the dream that Miranda was first aware that she'd actually fallen in love with Mike.

Since then, Miranda's relationship with Mike Yu had become so serious she'd been to dinner twice with the whole Yu family (Mike, his parents and an old granddad). On the first occasion they'd had food sent up to their flat from the Good Luck House takeaway, which they owned and was downstairs — and it had been very nice.

The second time, though, it was disgusting. Mike Yu's mother had attempted to cook in the English style, in her honour, and though it was a kind gesture Miranda had very nearly been sick at the table. Mike Yu's mother had served great big onions as if they were a vegetable, just cooked whole and plonked at the side of the plate — next to a slab of pork. Miranda had struggled with the pork (chewy/salty) and the onion (slimy/sweet) and had literally gagged and only just managed to cover it up with a pretend coughing fit. Plus it hadn't helped that Mike Yu's old granddad had sat there with his plastic face and glued-up eyes, eating hard-boiled eggs with his fingers.

In spite of all this horror, Miranda was so keen on Mike she'd tried to learn Chinese so they could chat in his language. It had come to nothing, though. Just learning Tuesday (*tinsy-waah*) had taken her a week and then no sooner had she learned Wednesday (*tinseeteer*) than she forgot Tuesday. Miranda had expected it to be a doddle, her mother having become semi-bilingual (English/Spanish) within a matter of weeks when attending a night class.

Miranda had thrown in the towel and just spoken in English and signs. She did learn Mike Yu's mother's name (Yu Anching), which meant 'Quiet', and his father's (Yu Huiqing), which meant 'Good Luck', but hadn't bothered with the old granddad because she didn't want to have to look at him.

She thanked God for Mike having an English name, otherwise she might not have been able to go out with him.

'But he must have a Chinese name,' I said.

'No,' Miranda assured me, 'Mike's Mike in Chinese.'

Anyway, Miranda needed the job for money to buy clothes and cosmetics to look trendy and attractive for Mike Yu, especially as she had outgrown all her clothes with her new bigger bust. She had given away her Dorothy Perkins bras to her sister, Melody, who wasn't on the pill and needed the padding and had gone a bit manly in puberty.

My reasons for wanting a job didn't seem anywhere near as exciting or romantic as Miranda's, nor as straightforward — which was just as well, since there was no time. Her story had lasted the entire forty-minute walk.

'There,' said Miranda, pointing, 'Paradise Lodge.'

I flicked my fag into the drain and we tiptoed over the cattle grid.

Miranda — being in high-heeled shoes — was cautious and had to watch her footing. Looking down, I saw a walking stick lying in the oily water in the pit underneath.

'Jesus,' said Miranda, wobbling a bit, 'there's no way the old cunts are escaping from here.'

We knocked and while we waited I gazed around and saw a lady at the window above the door. She wasn't looking out but had both hands and her cheek on the glass — a thing my brother Jack used to do when he wanted our mother to come home. He'd have to keep rubbing his breath off the glass. Eventually, the front door was opened by an old nurse who took us through

7

to a large, steamy kitchen.

A woman in an apron introduced herself as the cook and announced it was almost teatime. She gestured us to sit and she began ladling hot stringy fruit from a great copper pan into bottles lined up at the other end of the scrubbed table. By the look of it I guessed it was stewed rhubarb.

We were joined then by a woman of around forty called Ingrid who was very tall and obviously the boss. 'Shall we have some tea?' she said, looking at the cook, and the cook smiled and said, 'Yes, let's. And a scone, perhaps?'

We were interviewed there, together, at the table. Trays of tea foods were lined up along a dresser and a little gaggle of nurses appeared and took the trays, and the cook filled two catering teapots with boiling water and it was like the nicest tea you've ever seen from days gone by or a royal palace. The whole thing was delightful, except I noticed Ingrid had very red eyes and had either been crying for ages or had something wrong with her. If I'd been her, I'd have said, 'Sorry about my red eyes, I've got a bit of hay fever,' whether I had or not. But she didn't say anything about it.

It's strange now, calling her Ingrid, because after that first meeting she was only ever known as the Owner's Wife, and though this seems wrong now, that's how it was. Also, I'm not 100 per cent sure now her name was Ingrid, it might have been Inga, or Irena. I only know it began with a vowel and meant 'Divine Strength' in Old Norse. You can look it up.

The interview was brief. She told us the golden rules for working with the elderly and asked if we'd had any experience with an Aga, which she said was the heart of the house. Miranda hadn't but I had and was able to speak intelligently about riddling and raking. The cook, particularly, looked pleased to hear it.

The Owner's Wife then asked us why we wanted the job. I answered first, explaining that my family couldn't afford two types of shampoo or two types of coffee so I was stuck with Vosene and Woolco's econo-coffee (which was half coffee, half chicory extract). And since my sister had begun bringing home all sorts from a part-time job at Woolworth's, it had become my ambition to progress on to Linco Beer shampoo in its little barrel and Maxwell House coffee with its fresh-aroma promise.

The Owner's Wife was intrigued. 'It sounds as if you've been seduced by the advertisements on the television,' she said.

'I've tried the products and they are actually nicer than the cheap brands,' I assured her.

Miranda butted in to explain her reasons for wanting the job. She was eager to work in a caring setting because she was a compassionate person who had experienced illness but was now in full good health. It sounded very impressive and I felt slightly outdone.

The Owner's Wife smiled and nodded at Miranda and turned back to me. 'Linco Beer shampoo?' she said.

'Yes,' I said, and I described how Linco Beer shampoo made your hair feel. 'It contains real beer and makes it all bouncy, thick and healthy-feeling.'

'Well, I shall remember that, Lizzie,' she said, 'it sounds marvellous.'

And that was pretty much it. I forgot to mention my outgoing, compassionate nature but it must've come across because we both got the job and were to report for our induction the following Saturday at 8 a.m., in sensible footwear.

★ ★ ★

After the interview Miranda and I walked home. I felt quite comradely towards her now we were workmates and thought it right to share *my* reasons for wanting the job, since I'd heard hers in such detail and because the things I'd said in the interview will have seemed shallow and childish. I was keen to present myself in a more philosophical light.

'It's not just the money,' I said, 'I want my independence.'

It was true. I didn't want another year of trying to cheat the vending machine, relying on handouts and lifts and third-hand information, medicated shampoo, sugar sandwiches and scrounging cigarettes, babysitting for neighbours just to steal a pot of jam or some good quality tea bags from their cupboard, another year of being in the way of other people, trying to make ends meet. I felt like a great big, grown-up nuisance.

I started on this, but Miranda wasn't the least

bit interested so I changed back to the subject of her and Mike Yu, which was lovely to hear about anyway.

Miranda immediately confided in me that Mike was so good at kissing, it made her pelvis twang. He had three different types of kiss. The first type was barely a kiss at all, just his mouth hovering close to hers, almost touching but not, and blowing hot air from his nostrils on to her upper lip. 'Like a friendly dragon?' I suggested but Miranda ignored me.

The second type was to cover her entire face and head with hundreds of tiny kisses while she just sat there — eyelids, earlobes, the lot, and one time he removed her birthstone earring (sapphire) with his teeth and spat it gently into her hand as a surprise finale.

And the third type of kiss was to poke all round the inside of her mouth with his tongue, including where she'd had a molar removed and the gum was shrunken and half numb, half sensitive.

The kissing was all they were doing for now, apart from erotic hand-holding. Mike Yu didn't want to go all the way because he felt it wrong and undisciplined and said that there was so much more and that having intercourse was like galloping through the forest on the Emperor's best horse — which was a tremendous thing but shouldn't be experienced until you've walked slowly through on foot a hundred times and noticed the drops of dew on the leaves, the moss in the bark and all the shafts of light coming through the trees etc. Which was annoying,

11

seeing as Miranda had gone on the pill specially and was gaining weight by the day.

At the edge of the village Miranda went into a phone box and told me to come in too. She rang Mike and told him that she'd got the job, she described the interview and added a few details that I'd missed, like the Owner's Wife telling Miranda she was exactly the kind of candidate she was looking for. For some reason she told him I was in the phone box with her and put me on to say hello. Then the pips went and Miranda grabbed the receiver back and shouted, 'I love Mike Yu!'

Walking home, Miranda continued on the theme of Mike. He was a size seven in shoes, she told me, which was smaller than average but meant she could borrow his slippers when she was with him at the flat. This really appealed to me. I told Miranda I'd love to wear a man's coat or shoes, just to show I could, and she said that was one of the tragedies of coming from a broken home, I'd forever be wanting to wear men's clothing. She herself could take it or leave it, having had a full-time father in residence since birth.

Mike never ate puddings, except for tinned lychees and the occasional plum. He wrote poems — including one, dedicated to her, called 'The Snow-Fairy and the Sun' which was hopeful but realistic, and one which was quite porno called 'Chick Penis' about a half-man, half-woman, half-hen and was really about identity and mercy, but had a sad ending.

As we reached the edge of the Sycamore

Estate Mike Yu pulled up in his Datsun Cherry.

'Look, it's Mike,' said Miranda and ran across the road.

I recognized him but he looked completely different, now I knew so much about him.

Miranda jumped into the passenger seat and kissed Mike's cheek. They spoke briefly, then Mike shouted, 'Hey, Lizzie!'

I went over.

'Can I give you a lift?' he said.

Miranda answered, 'No, she only lives on the Sycamore Estate.'

'Thanks, though,' I said.

'I thought you lived the other side of the village,' said Mike.

'She used to,' said Miranda, 'but her family went bankrupt.'

Mike looked alarmed. 'God, so sorry,' he said.

'It was ages ago,' I said.

'Bad luck,' said Mike.

2

The Comfort Round

I was shown the ropes at Paradise Lodge on day one by Ingrid, the Owner's Wife, the authoritative, red-eyed woman who'd interviewed us a few days previously. I could tell straight away that she was the linchpin of the place. She noticed everything, from a tiny stray thread on the day-room carpet to a patient lying flat out on the floor after tripping on a loose tile. She was eagle-eyed and always on the alert.

I noticed that day, the patients liked her a lot — because of the above, I expect — and they followed her around the room with their eyes to see what sensible or wonderful act she might perform next — say, putting a jug of sprigs on the mantel, or scooping up a spider and freeing it out of the window into the pretty shrubs which flanked the patio. I'd actually go as far as to say they loved her.

The staff were just the same. It wasn't just her tallness, it was her niceness — or probably the two things together. The staff went out of their way to share her opinions and nodded in agreement when she said a thing. One minute a nurse would be saying how rotten some old man was and what a fucking old bossyboots and a typical German and how she'd like to shove the broom handle up his backside, and the Owner's

Wife would gently mention that that old man had renounced Hitler, had a high IQ and had been runner-up for the Max Planck Medal, and the nurse would say she supposed so and what a clever old thing he was.

It was Miranda's first day too and she was shown the ropes by a peculiar old woman wearing Foster Grant's called Matron, who was supposedly a senior nurse but could easily have been an over-indulged patient with delusions and a nurse's outfit. Matron was the opposite of the Owner's Wife. She was short and squat, the patients ignored her and the staff liked to contradict her.

At morning coffee break that first day, for instance, when everyone else was playing with Nurse Hilary's brand-new Crazy Baby curling tongs and setting Farrah Fawcett flicks into their fringes, Matron suddenly announced she'd seen Gordon Banks washing his Ford Granada wearing Marigolds and she had lost all respect for him because of it.

The staff rounded on her.

'Why shouldn't he wear Marigolds?' they asked.

Even Miranda, whose first day it was, chipped in saying it was impressive of Gordon Banks to wash his own car and not get his wife to do it for him. I was surprised at Miranda ganging up on her day-old mentor like that. And though I didn't care a jot about the Marigolds it put pressure on me to contribute, so I said, 'True,' in a mature way, which is always a safe bet, yet non-committal.

15

Matron said we spoke as if he was the *real* Gordon Banks.

'He is,' said one nurse.

'No, he's not,' said Matron.

'Yes, he is,' said another nurse.

'*Is* he?' asked Matron.

And the tableful of nurses laughed.

The staff all had their quirks — I can't list them all here (the staff or their quirks), it'd be a whole chapter — but I was struck that day by Nurse Hilary, who drank her coffee through a straw, and Nurse Sally-Anne, who was assertively shy and communicated via little grunts that the others seemed to understand. I found out later that Hilary had unusually pitted teeth that stained easily and, even worse, that Sally-Anne had just had twins who she'd named after the show-jumping Schockemöhle brothers and who'd been adopted by a couple in Scotland. I wished I'd known that then and I might have been nicer to her. Also, there was Nurse Gwen, who had a diploma in advanced geriatric nursing and worked to the principle of keeping the patients comfortable and happy but not necessarily alive. Nurse Gwen spoke almost exclusively in swear words and I realized for the first time how aggressive swearing could sound.

There was Nurse Eileen who was very pretty and had graceful movements. She cocked her head to the side when she lit up and made a hell of a lot of smoke with endless small puffs and hardly inhaling. Also, she hated feathers.

Finally, there was Nurse Dee-Anna, who seemed completely normal in every way. She had a nice voice and honey-coloured hair and sang 'Take Me Home, Country Roads' while she went about her business. Her name was Diana but she pronounced it Dee-Anna. If I write it Diana, you'll not say it right in your mind. It being Dee-Anna is important. Somehow. She was so normal I suspected she was hiding something like a crime in her past, or a love affair with someone in the room.

As time went by I met assorted other staff, but for the first day it was just the above.

★   ★   ★

After coffee break Matron, Miranda and I followed the Owner's Wife and went off for a tour of the house. I'd already heard from Miranda that it had been quite grand until the owner's family had been forced to turn it into a business due to complicated money difficulties. The owner had hoped to start up a boarding kennels for dogs but his wife had insisted on a nursing home for elderly gentlefolk. According to Matron, they'd arm-wrestled for it in the Piglet Inn and she'd won 2–1 in a best-of-three contest and thought up the name 'Paradise Lodge' on the spot — being a huge fan of the poet John Milton — and they raised their glasses, 'To Paradise Lodge!' and laughed like posh people do in times of great uncertainty, and the landlord had rubbed his palms together at the thought of all the future nurses coming in for vodka and orange and KP Nuts. Which they did.

None of this was mentioned on our tour of the

house but the Owner's Wife did tell us that Paradise Lodge had previously been called The Old Grey Hall and they'd had to apply to change it to something more upbeat to attract old people. They soon found out that changing a house name is quite a complicated business but they changed it anyway, having had all the advertising and headed paper done.

True to its ex-name, Paradise Lodge was a big, old, L-shaped, grey, stuccoed house. The front door was at the side and you could tell it always had been because a thick old wall ran right across the front, with no gap for a gate, and all sorts of ancient trees and climbing vines. The rooftop was the most attractive feature — dramatic, big and steep, and a mass of little windows in the gables where the nurses' quarters were.

The house was grand, but not beautiful. You wouldn't walk past and say to yourself, 'Ooh, I'd like to live in that house,' like you would about the tall red farmhouse opposite, or the modern box with slitty windows the other side where the German film director lived with his mother (and whose father was a patient). But once you were inside, Paradise Lodge was lovely and in some ways beguiling. There were backstairs and front stairs and secret stairs and doors hidden in the panelling that the owner had had put in so that he could go about his business without ever having to bump into a sick old person who might need help. There were outhouses, including a stables and a summer house. Next to the brand-new laundry was the tack room which was supposed to become the salon for hair and chiropody but never had, and beside that was the boot room which was now the morgue and had a bench, a candle, a cross and a Bible and, for some reason, a little brass bell. I imagined ringing it like mad if ever I was in there and a dead body came back to life. Next to that was the larder.

The Owner's Wife pointed things out along the way and always Matron would chip in, trying to be helpful but sounding like an idiot. The Owner's Wife showed us the main bathroom. I commented on the pretty Victorian bath with little dog's feet.

'Yes, it's very pretty,' said the Owner's Wife, 'but not ideal for bathing the infirm.'

I watched Matron and Miranda dawdle ahead and noted they made a ridiculous pair: Matron as previously described, and Miranda teetering on a pair of high wedges and constantly picking her pants out of her bottom. After a short but serious talk about the laundry, particularly the importance of adding a lidful of Dettol to the wash and even more so the adding of soda crystals to help combat the effects of hard water on the element, we went away in pairs.

The Owner's Wife led me out into the hall and we stood for a while and she ran through the daily routine.

'So, the day begins at about six thirty when the night nurse takes the breakfasts round . . . ' she began.

I had to gaze about to avoid looking at her (me still not comfortable with one-to-one chats). It would have seemed rude in any ordinary hall but luckily this one was genuinely fascinating with ornate cornicing and decorative dados and two different colours on the walls. There was a curving banister rail in gleaming mahogany and, on the floor, patterned tiles in approx ten different colours. And the furniture — delicate matching consoles with inlaid wood and shapely legs — was topped with all sorts of urns and bowls and antique china dogs etc.

' . . . and that's the day-to-day routine,' the Owner's Wife was saying, 'now, let us go and meet the patients.'

I'd been dreading this bit. I had imagined them all bedridden in dimly lit wards with the Vicar sitting, reading from the Bible, and a nurse feeding them drips of watered-down honey — like you do with baby birds that you know aren't going to make it. But as we approached the day room I could see they were mostly sitting bolt upright in chairs. Before we entered, the Owner's Wife gave me a few pointers re meeting them. One was on the subject of communication — tone of voice and vocabulary.

'Not that I'm suggesting you should come over as condescending,' she said, 'just don't speak too quickly, try to be clear and try to avoid slang words.'

'I understand,' I said. And I did. She was really talking about Miranda, who used endless slang, such as 'right on' and 'nope' and 'bog' and other words that the elderly wouldn't be at home with. God knew how they coped with that sweary nurse with the diploma, though.

The day room was really two large, adjoining reception rooms with the big divider doors pushed as open as they could go. We went to the smaller room and the Owner's Wife introduced me to the male patients, one by one. There were five of them. One of them, Mr Greenberg, said, 'Well, bless my soul! A new chap.' And then muttered something about cheese upsetting his stomach.

They were extremely old — around a hundred years, I guessed — and it was like being at the aquarium and thinking the amphibians looked like old men (only the other way round). But they were very alive, one of them was reading the *Daily Mail* and another was fiddling with a transistor radio.

The Owner's Wife flung an arm towards the adjoining room. 'And all our lovely ladies tend to sit in there,' she said.

The ladies — about thirty of them — sat in assorted chairs in a ring around the edge of the room. A few looked unbelievably old and frail, but somehow healthy. Some were just oldish but quavery. Others were extremely sprightly indeed. One wore bright red lipstick, a couple had blue-rinsed hair, and one was wearing a silky turban. Overall they looked more human than the men.

'Ladies, we have two new carers starting today,' the Owner's Wife called out, 'this is Lizzie, you'll meet Miranda in due course.'

A few of them smiled or nodded. One old lady close to us repeated, 'In due course,' and then another said, 'What did she say, dear?'

21

And I said, 'In due course.'

It was like the beginning of a horror film.

'Should I go and introduce myself?' I asked.

'No need, you'll meet them by and by,' said the Owner's Wife, 'when we do the comfort round.'

We strolled back out to the hall.

'I thought they'd all be in bed,' I said.

'We do have two bedridden ladies,' said the Owner's Wife brightly, as if not wanting to disappoint me. And she took me into a long room containing eight beds. Two, side by side, were occupied, a skull-like head on the pillow and a basic human shape draped in softly pleated white linen. It reminded me strongly of the stone tomb effigy of T. E. Lawrence in a Dorset church. His head, in Arabian headdress, resting on the saddle of his favourite camel — which, our mother told us, was called Faisal. I've always remembered it. The smooth coldness of the stone, and the idea of the camel and everything.

Strange, unsettling noises filled the ward — loud snoring and some awful gurgling, as well as a gentle motorized hum which, I found out later, came from the electric ripple mattresses used to prevent bedsores.

Back in the hall, the Owner's Wife stood for a moment to let an old man pass. He was tall and a bit wobbly and because his sandal buckles were undone he jangled slightly as he walked.

'Morning!' he said as he drew close and he stood, looking at the Owner's Wife, and she did a small cough and said, 'This is my husband,' and then, gesturing to me, 'Lizzie is one of the new auxiliary nurses, Thor; I'm showing her the ropes.'

'Oh, jolly good,' said the owner (I realized he was the owner). 'How are you getting along?'

I said I was getting along fine and commented on the hallway. 'It's like a stately home,' I said, thinking it a complimentary thing to say.

'Yes, yes,' he said, 'the floor tiles are knockout, aren't they? You won't see better in the Alhambra — Euclidean geometry and whatnot.'

I said, 'Brillo Pads!' which was a normal thing to say in those days, meaning 'brilliant' (I'd picked it up from Miranda), but the owner misunderstood and became anxious. Some of the tiles were loose, he explained, because previous staff had used Flash, which had eroded the grouting (he tapped at the floor with his sandal to demonstrate).

The Owner's Wife groaned. 'Off you go now, darling,' she said, and he shuffled off, but called back, 'Take her up to meet Lady B.'

'Yes, yes, all in good time,' said the Owner's Wife.

I felt sorry for the Owner's Wife. It was always embarrassing seeing people's husbands; especially the idiotic sort, and you seldom saw any other. Also, I was at that age where you can't stop yourself imagining the couple having sexual intercourse. And it was really awful.

'The tiles are lovely,' I said to the Owner's Wife after he'd gone, to make her feel a bit better about him.

If it had been up to her, she said, they'd have

been covered with a practical, non-slip linoleum years ago, and she went on to list the many ways the building was unsuitable for its elderly residents. The flooring in particular, which she said was unstable, and the driveway and paths, which were ever changing, like a dry riverbed. And there was no passenger lift, even though there was nothing to prevent the installation of a small one — only the owner's unwillingness to compromise his living quarters. Talking about it seemed to upset her but she pulled herself together and gave me a recap on the golden rules of working with the elderly, which we'd been through at the interview.

The most important thing seemed to be (a) that I appreciate the huge privilege of being among them and remember they had a lot to teach a young woman like me. And (b) that I must take them to the toilet frequently and regularly, but do my utmost to avoid calling it 'the toilet', suggesting 'comfort area' and 'spend a penny' if I absolutely had to say anything.

The comfort round had to be done after breakfast, coffee, lunch and tea, and carers had to be ready to help at all times in that respect above all others.

It was a bit like looking after a toddler, I said, and started to talk about my tiny brother, Danny, who'd just gone into pants, but that was obviously a very wrong thing to say and the Owner's Wife told me never, ever to say it again.

We were silent for a moment and I was about to apologize and explain when a car clanked over the cattle grid and sounded its horn. The

Owner's Wife rushed away to investigate and reappeared a moment later in a controlled fluster.

'A convalescent patient has arrived, we weren't expecting him until tomorrow, we're not quite ready,' she said, 'you'll have to do the comfort round.'

So, I was thrown in at the deep end — as it were — and though I hadn't had the proper training (only the theory), when it came to it, the comfort round was only a matter of escorting or wheeling the patients to the sluice across the hall, waiting outside and helping with corset hooks and stockings and trying to avoid saying the word 'toilet' or 'wee'. I noticed the shy nurse plucking her eyebrows in the mirror above the vast butler's sink while she waited for her gentleman and even when he called out, she carried on.

It was nice to get to know the ladies without the Owner's Wife watching my every move and word, especially since running into her husband in the hall had put her in a 'blue funk' (her words). And though it was a simple endeavour, it still took me over an hour to get the thirty-five-odd patients all to the conveniences and back into their chairs. Some of them said they didn't want to go and had to be forced, literally, to get up and walk across the hall. Sometimes my euphemisms must have been too vague so I was resorting to nods, hand gestures (raindrops) and pointing. Some walked incredibly slowly and others had walking frames which, in my opinion, slowed them down. Some took ages in the cubicles (one fell asleep) and others insisted on washing their hands afterwards. Some had to go twice, one did it on the way and I had to drag a cloth round with my foot and hope to God the Owner's Wife didn't appear and notice the area of brightened tiles.

★   ★   ★

After I'd finished the comfort round I joined the Owner's Wife and the patient who'd arrived unexpectedly. He was called Mr Simmons and lived locally. He had reddish, greyish hair and not a single eyelash. The Owner's Wife was asking him very specific questions about his health and his breakfast preferences but kept interrupting herself to say how delightful it was that he'd been discharged early from hospital, and she wasn't being sarcastic — even though anyone could see the chaos it had caused. Mr Simmons was in good health except for a gammy foot and whatever operation he'd just had, which wasn't discussed — presumably it was made clear on his medical notes or was too personal for an auxiliary to know about.

He had been scheduled to have something done to his gammy foot but the surgeons had found this other more pressing (undisclosed) thing and had switched to that instead. The Owner's Wife said that was a common occurrence and probably quite right under the circumstances. But it was obvious Mr Simmons was fed up — so fed up he made a little fist of crossness. That was the thing with private hospitals, I supposed (privately), it being in their interests to find extra things to do. Ditto vets, hairdressers and car mechanics.

Apart from guessing what his breakfast preference was going to be — porridge with cream (I'd guessed Grape-Nuts) — I could hardly stop myself from groaning out loud with boredom.

Mr Simmons waited in the Owner's Wife's office while she and I prepared his room. Room 8 was a bright, sunny room with its own little bathroom and, instead of parquet and rugs, had a bristly carpet on the floor. The fireplace with overmantel gave it a comfy, sitting-room feel and from the leatherette Morris recliner you could see the reservoir and, in theory, you'd be able to chuck a sugared almond at Prince Charles as he trotted past to tackle Mr Oliphant's cross-country course (which he was rumoured to do occasionally).

Signs of the previous incumbent were still very much in evidence (that's what the Owner's Wife was so flapped about) — a square, silver-backed hairbrush and a tortoiseshell comb sat on a shelf in the bathroom and a pair of grey trousers was still sandwiched in the press. These had all belonged to Mr Cresswell who'd passed away the Thursday before, the Owner's Wife explained. I gazed at the talcy outline of two enormous feet on the cork bath-mat and felt a wave of anxiety.

'Now, Lizzie, Mr Simmons' stepdaughter is a tricky one,' said the Owner's Wife, 'tread carefully if you have dealings with her.'

'In what way?' I asked.

27

'She'd rather Mr Simmons wasn't here — she thinks it unnecessary,' said the Owner's Wife.

'And is it unnecessary?' I asked.

'Well, we don't think so, but I suppose it's her inheritance being spent.'

The Owner's Wife gave the room a final blast of Haze and sent me downstairs for a tray of coffee and biscuits while she went to fetch Mr Simmons and his tricky stepdaughter, who had just arrived.

At the bottom of the stairs we separated and I went to the kitchen for the refreshments. I almost caught up with them, a few minutes later, approaching Room 8. Mr Simmons shuffled along slowly and the Owner's Wife walked behind with his relative. I followed behind at a distance and, as she turned to take the bend on the stairs, I saw to my dismay that Mr Simmons' relative was a teacher from my school. Not any old teacher but Miss Pitt — the Deputy Head.

I turned on my heel and strode — tray and all — back to the kitchen. It was troubling in the extreme to see Miss Pitt in this context. I hadn't been doing anything wrong, I wasn't smoking or skiving, but having been respected all day I really didn't want to be humiliated in front of my new mentor/boss and a convalescent patient.

Miranda and the old Matron were now in the kitchen with Nurse Sally-Anne. Matron was wiping the edge of a tiny china cup with a piece of kitchen paper.

'You're to take this to Room 8,' I said to Sally-Anne, thrusting the tray at her.

'Why can't you?' she mumbled.

'She wants someone more senior,' I said.

Sally-Anne took the tray.

Miranda and I groaned at the thought of Miss Pitt and I told Matron what a tyrant she was and gave her lots of examples, like the time she'd given me a detention for saying 'For coughs and colds take Veno's' and her absolute horror of anyone having the odd day off school for their real life, even in an emergency or for a funeral.

★   ★   ★

At the end of the day, the Owner's Wife gave us little brown wage packets, thanked us and said we might as well go and get changed out of our uniforms. Then, just before I'd left the kitchen, the cook asked me if I'd mind taking Mr Simmons his teatime sandwiches, cake and pills which had been forgotten due to him being a day early and not getting on to the lists. I had no choice, so I took the tray and prepared myself mentally for an encounter with the Deputy Head. When I got to Room 8 I was relieved to find Mr Simmons was alone. He'd fallen asleep in his chair, bent over like a hoop, with his head almost in his lap. I placed the tray on the little table beside him and he sat up, startled and disorientated.

'Where am I?' he asked.

'Room 8,' I said, and again it was like the start of a Hammer Horror.

It was my first proper encounter with a patient — not just a natter on the way to the toilet

— and I could tell Mr Simmons was in some discomfort. I pointed to the little cup of pills on the tray and he gulped them down.

'Shall I put the telly on?' I asked, thinking he might not have noticed the portable set on the chest opposite. 'It might be *The Two Ronnies* or *Des O'Connor.*'

'No thank you. I'm a bit tired for television this evening,' he said, then quickly added, 'but do put it on, if you'd like it.'

It struck me that Mr Simmons seemed very young to be here and not at all like the other patients. And as I was thinking that about him he was thinking the same about me.

'You seem rather young to be working here,' he said, 'if you don't mind my saying.'

'I'm still at school. Actually, I'm a pupil at Devlin's School — where your relative works,' I said.

'Oh,' he said, 'bad luck.' And we both laughed.

'You seem much younger than the other patients,' I said.

'Yes, well, I'm not all that much younger, but I suppose the others here are mostly Victorian, whereas I'm from the modern age — that's the difference.'

'Oh,' I said.

'I'm aware of Elvis, for instance,' he said, 'Elvis Presley.'

And we chatted more about the modern age.

By the time I got back down to the kitchen the day was over. The Owner's Wife was warming milk on the Aga for the bedtime drinks, I'd missed my lift home with Miranda in Mike Yu's

30

car, and the day nurses were getting ready to go to the pub. It was like watching a *Play for Today* where the actors are that good you can't see the acting and though nothing's actually happening, story-wise, you want to watch.

The Crazy Baby tongs were passed from one to the other and newly formed curls sprayed with Harmony hairspray. Tubes of mascara bobbed in a Pyrex jug of boiling water, cigarettes were lit from other cigarettes and the room filled with smoke, eau de cologne and the sound of chatter, laughter and scraping chairs.

The Owner's Wife spoke to me while she arranged teacups on to trays. She told me that the nurses' dresses in small sizes were like gold dust. 'I should hang on to that one, if it fits well, and put your name in it.'

'I'll keep it on and surprise my mum with it,' I said.

'Good idea,' she said, 'and I'm definitely going to give your shampoo a try.'

'Linco Beer shampoo,' I said, just to make sure she'd got the name straight in her head.

'Thank you, Lizzie, I know you're going to be a real asset,' she said, 'I'm just so glad you're here.'

And, not knowing quite how to respond, I said, 'And I'm so glad *you're* here.'

I wished I hadn't said that because it seemed to choke her and later I couldn't think why I'd said it at all.

On the way out, through the corridor at the back, I took another peek into the morgue. This time there was something on the bench. I peered in and gasped as I realized it was a body covered with a sheet. A bluish foot poked out. The paper luggage tag hanging from the big toe read: *Cresswell*.

3

Home Life

It was true about the Linco Beer shampoo — it really did make your hair feel lovely — and of course I was going to get my own little barrel at my earliest convenience, and other items previously mentioned. But now, knowing I could just walk into Boot's the Chemist and buy it and have enough change for a Bronnley lemon soap-on-a-rope, it seemed less urgent. And then, acknowledging that somehow led me to face up to the fact that things weren't going terribly well, school-wise. I'd got into a bit of a mess and no amount of decent coffee or shampoo was going to help. I'd taken a few days off — for personal reasons — and found myself irretrievably behind in some subjects. Being behind at school is an uncomfortable place to be, especially if you're not used to it. The eagerness to please that had spurred me all through primary school seemed to evaporate every morning — either as I had my first cigarette of the day in bed, or on the nauseating bus ride.

The teachers were mostly too busy with the day-to-day to single me out for practical help. My exceptionally nice tutor, Mr Mayne, was exasperated by my seeming lack of ambition. He did his best to encourage me but was busy in the extreme with a handful of tricky tutees — who needed him just to get through the alphabet — and I imagine he looked at me and thought, 'Lizzie Vogel will be all right in the long run,' which was a huge compliment (if that was actually what he thought).

My mother and Mr Holt were too busy — driving vans and running a laundry depot, trying to make ends meet with a new infant and trying to launch a pine-stripping venture — to notice I was struggling. My sister was gearing up to leave home for university. An anglepoise lamp and a striped cotton rug in a Habitat carrier waited in the hall for her departure and acted as a daily reminder that she'd soon be gone. In the meantime, she worked odd hours in Woolworth's and hung around with a girl from Mauritius called Varsha. And had no idea what I was doing. Or not doing.

My sister's smoking ban in our shared bedroom had ruined our relationship. She made the far-fetched claim that I was poisoning the air and giving not only myself deadly diseases, stunting my growth and dulling my skin and brain, I was inflicting all that on her too — as she slept. This had driven her to make a permanent bed in the living room and take away all her records except one. 'The Killing of Georgie (Part I and II)' by Rod Stewart. Which she couldn't bear to listen to because (a) it was sad (Georgie gets killed by a New Jersey gang) and (b) she couldn't stand the image it conjured of Rod prancing around in a white suit. I loved Rod in his white suit and was glad when she gave me the record but then listened to it so often I stopped liking it too.

All in all, I was ready for a new place to be, to start again and be wanted and needed. If I wasn't going to be fussed over by doting parents or singled out by an intuitive teacher — who saw something unique in me — urging me to go for Oxbridge, I'd settle for doing the minimum at school — attending just often enough to get through and not have my mother arrested by Mrs Hargraves, the truant lady. I'd pop in for science and maths and when I needed to attend, and at other times I'd help old ladies fasten their corsets and thread their embroidery needles and I'd earn enough money to buy an ongoing supply of John Player tipped in the blue pack with a matching lighter, a bottle of Paco Rabanne, and seven pairs of new knickers in pastel colours with the days of the week printed on them — like a woman in an Edna O'Brien.

I thought all this through as I walked and skipped home in the nurse's dress. These were my reasons for wanting the job. Not as exciting as Miranda's but more complex than wanting nice shampoo.

Approaching my house, I straightened my cap and hoiked up my Pop Sox and made an entrance through the back door. My mother was playing a Clementi sonata on the piano while Danny chewed a crust in his Babygro. I wanted her to look round so I coughed. She turned and saw me in my uniform and burst into tears.

It wasn't that she was sad (or angry or happy). She was *moved* and she told me not to get changed until she'd found her camera, which she

35

never did. But I had to not get changed until Mr Holt got home, and when he did he smiled and said something about Florence Nightingale and hoping I wasn't going to start skiving off school again.

⋆ ⋆ ⋆

It was strange being at school the following Monday. Being treated like a child again after having been treated like a twenty-year-old at Paradise Lodge — having seen an ancient, naked lady with a bedsore, who might die any minute, and having taken an emery board to a lady's upper denture, where it was causing an ulcer.

I ran into Miranda and a couple of her followers in the toilets — applying kohl to their inner eyelids — getting ready for the lunchtime discotheque. Miranda mentioned Paradise Lodge and before I knew it I'd said it was a privilege to be among elderly people and them having a lot to teach young women like us.

Miranda frowned at me via the mirror (this obviously wasn't the line she was taking in the group) and was clearly annoyed to hear me talk like that.

'You're joking, aren't you?' she said.

She didn't really like being among elderly people. Seeing them all so sad and old, struggling along, clanking their walking frames, made her want to scream and push them over, she said — not to hurt them, and not that she didn't like them, just that the feelings they provoked in her were so at odds with the feelings she had about Mike Yu (a company director aged only nineteen) and life in general. The patients were contaminating her mind, she said, and making her hopes and dreams seem pointless.

'I mean, how fucking depressing at our age, spending all day with people who are just around the corner from death, and you know it and they know it,' she said, 'and having to pretend everything's normal.'

I reassured Miranda that they didn't see themselves as around the corner from death. They saw themselves as around the corner from a nice cup of milky coffee and a Lincoln biscuit or a trip to the lavatory. And actually, was that any different from us here now, in these toilets, me having a cigarette and her around the corner from a vending-machine Kit Kat and the lunchtime discotheque?

Miranda tutted and said she'd never use the vending machine. She then cheered herself up by describing a three-piece trouser suit she was saving up for from Richard Shops — halfway between the boardroom and the bedroom, taupe chalk stripes, halter-neck waistcoat with plunging neckline and trousers you couldn't wear pants with. It was going to blow Mike Yu's mind.

It sounded quite nice, except I wasn't so keen on chalk stripes and would always want to wear pants.

'If my mother wasn't such an old bag,' said Miranda, 'and yours wasn't such a mess, we wouldn't need this grim fucking job!'

I don't think I blamed my mother for my

needing the job. I blamed her at school for my truanting but I didn't want to be the sort of idiot that gives up on their academic career because their parents don't give them enough attention — I hated kids like that — but I couldn't deny that my lack of direction coincided with our mother breaking an agreement with our newish stepdad, Mr Holt.

Mr Holt had been gently training our mother to be careful with money — after years of frivolity (hers) — but in spite of the two of them making a 'no more babies' agreement, our mother had deliberately got herself pregnant and had a baby in 1976. She denied she'd done it deliberately and denies it to this day, but of course she had.

I felt sorry for Mr Holt. He was a clever and intuitive man and had taught himself much about the world. He knew more than most people learn at even the most expensive school just by using his brain and reading. The one thing he'd failed to understand, though, was that our mother was never going to stop wanting to have babies — however many agreements she made. She couldn't help herself.

My mother didn't tell Mr Holt about the pregnancy to begin with and then, just when she thought perhaps the time had come, he accidentally saw her in the nude, sideways on, and he'd said 'Jesus H. Christ' under his breath.

He hadn't intended to hurt her feelings but he had, and she'd cried in dismay and said what a bad person she was — relying on the fact that when you tell someone you're a bad person, the other person tends to say, 'No, no, you're not!' etc.

But this wasn't Mr Holt's style. He agreed (yes, she was a bad person) and went on to remind her she already had plenty of children, and very little time and even less money and about the 'no more children' agreement they'd made at the outset.

And of course that made my sister and me think he was a bad person for not rejoicing at the idea of his very own, imminent little baby and we all ganged up on him behind his back and called him hard-hearted and uncaring. And our mother said what did she expect, taking up with someone called Harry? (Which was Mr Holt's first name.) And she recited William Blake's 'Infant Sorrow'.

My mother groaned! my father wept.
Into the dangerous world I leapt:
Helpless, naked, piping loud:
Like a fiend hid in a cloud.

Struggling in my father's hands:
Striving against my swaddling bands,
Bound and weary I thought best
To sulk upon my mother's breast.

But to be absolutely truthful, I wasn't overjoyed myself. The whole thing had surprised me — the pregnancy and then the not being overjoyed. Some of the most joyful times in my life up to then had been when our mother was pregnant, it always seemed as though everything

39

was going to be all right. And the saddest, most awful times had been when she suddenly wasn't pregnant any more, for whatever reason.

I'd reached that self-conscious age and, to me, my mother seemed a bit on the old side to be having a baby, so I kept the news to myself. Even our mother kept it quiet.

Compared to her others, this pregnancy was joyless. Her pregnancies with our biological father in the 1960s, with my sister and me and our little brother, had been cause for great celebration: the ordering of a private midwife and blankets from Harrods, the housekeeper's husband asked in to paint the nursery in a neutral, rich cream, new maternity smocks in Liberty prints and the borrowing of the Benson swinging cradle that dated back to the birth of Tobias H. Benson in 1812 — which had such ornate carvings it had to be polished with breath and a feather and certainly not Pledge and a yellow duster — and the thinking ahead to the christening, the godparents, the engraved glass and birth mug. And the names.

And the pregnancies after her marriage to our father had — as previously mentioned — been intense and joyful and sorrowful.

This one, though — in 1976 — was half hidden, it was disapproved of, ignored, made light of and cried about. Even our mother who'd deliberately caused it was so sad she'd spoon Horlicks straight into her mouth from the jar and, because she didn't smoke a single cigarette and drank nothing but econo-coffee with tons of sugar, she ballooned in weight and had to put her feet up on the piano stool to soothe her veins and when she stopped work she could hardly fit behind the steering wheel of the laundry van.

Mr Holt was so disappointed, anxious and despondent he could barely bring himself to speak to her.

And then, at dawn on the day after George Best's birthday, our mother's waters broke just as Mr Holt was making himself a cup of tea and listening to the 5 a.m. news on the wireless. She asked if he would mind driving to work via the Royal Infirmary. He nodded and waited while she put her shoes on. He watched her struggle for a moment and then bent down and did up her laces for her. She thanked him and put her hands on his shoulders and smiled for the first time in weeks, and he said, 'Well, we'd have been here all day.' And off they went.

My sister and I got up for school and found a note: *Gone to the Royal to have baby.* And on the note she'd drawn a baby and a horse's head. She always drew a horse's head because it was the only thing she could draw and it showed she was happy.

In spite of the horse's head, I was upset that she'd gone off on her own. But my sister said, 'We'd only be in the way — and would you really want to see the baby come out?' which were both good points.

We went to school on the bus as usual and none of us mentioned it. Then, in my last lesson, for some reason I told a girl called Julia Dwyer that my mother might have had a baby and she said, 'Yuk! How old is she?' and I shaved two years off her to make it seem less revolting. And regretted the whole thing — the telling and the pregnancy.

Back at home my sister, my brother Jack and I sat watching telly and had forgotten all about it when the phone rang and it was our mother calling from a phone box.

She'd had a baby boy called Daniel John Henry Holt but we had to promise not to shorten it to DJ or Danny. He was Daniel. And they came home that evening in the Snowdrop van with Mr Holt.

That was the start of Danny, who — after being so faintly drawn — burst into our lives in full colour, like the sun shining through expensive curtains. We all sat around that first evening kissing his tiny hands and feeling the perfect little weight of him and I realized the world would go on and on forever. Everything was exactly the same — Mr Holt telling us to put our shoes on the rack, and our mother tutting — and yet everything had changed.

This little baby — who'd been deliberately got but then regretted and slightly denied, who was the embodiment of irresponsible, selfish actions and the reneging on an agreement, and the cause of so much sadness just by existing at all — was held aloft and adored by everyone, and chuckled at and dandled. Quite rightly so, as he was pure delight.

His hair was black and wavy and his brown eyes were so kind — he was half-puppy, half-boy. He looked like Mowgli and Aladdin and Richard Burton all rolled into one, only prettier, and he just got nicer by the day, and all the people who had pronounced another baby ill advised — my mother's relatives — would see him in his pram or, later, in his stripy pushchair, holding a little ribbon in his fist and sucking his thumb, and they'd smile and feel happier than they had before. The only time I ever knew him disliked was by a springer spaniel called Turk and even he came to love him. Our mother had got away with it by having the nicest baby it was possible to have.

There was no denying we were badly off, though, and having Danny had made things considerably harder, and Mr Holt — who was already very careful with money — tightened up further and put a lock on the garage where we kept the tinned foods and a lock on the phone that prevented us dialling.

'Can we actually afford this baby?' asked Jack, that first evening.

'Good question,' said Mr Holt. 'No, we can't, and we were stretched to the limit already.'

'But he's worth it, though,' our mother said, worriedly, 'isn't he?'

And Mr Holt lifted Danny into the air in front of him. 'He's all right,' he said, but he was almost bursting with joy and had to get his hanky out.

'What's it like to have a baby?' I asked my mother — I meant how did it *feel*, emotionally.

'It's like shitting a football,' she said.

'I meant, emotionally,' I said.

'Shitting a football,' she repeated.

4

Opportunity Knocks

Early one morning, soon after my first day at Paradise Lodge, Nurse Hilary telephoned me at home to remind me I was down on the duty rota for Friday — a split shift starting at 8 a.m. It was news to me and I said I'd be at school on Friday and couldn't work.

'But you're needed here,' she said, 'we've a bit of an emergency.'

'But Friday's a school day,' I said.

'I understand that,' said Hilary, 'but we're short-staffed.'

'OK, then — see you on Friday,' I said and hung up.

What could the emergency be? I imagined all the pretty hall tiles adrift and a spate of tripping accidents, but decided in the end it was more likely there'd been a sudden rush of new patients with special medical needs. It had been strange being phoned at home and it not being one of my friends saying they hated their dad's guts or did I want to go into town for chips and beans in Woolworth's café and have our photos taken in the booth? It was a coming-of-age call. I stood in the hall and pondered on that for a while and then had to run for the school bus.

★   ★   ★

Miranda had been asked to do the Friday too. We walked up to Paradise Lodge together. She was dreading it. She was in school uniform and furious that I hadn't phoned to tell her I'd be in my nurse's uniform with a snake belt and white cap with bare, shaved legs. I was forced to tell her about our phone being 'incoming calls only' and she groaned and made remarks about my family being on the breadline. In self-defence I bragged about my rapport with the Owner's Wife and Miranda said how repugnant she'd found the Matron in the Foster Grant's. I felt I had the upper hand, but arriving at Paradise Lodge I could sense change.

The little Matron was suddenly acting as though she was in charge and had put earrings in — hoops — not the sort of ear-wear you'd expect in a medical setting.

She greeted us as we entered the kitchen and said that due to our superb performance on day one, she would like to interview us with a view to being promoted to the 38p per hour pay band.

I asked what the promotion would entail. She explained it would be 'a more responsible role on the teatime shift' plus ad hoc hours to suit (them). We went, one at a time, to the owner's office, me first. The owner's office was a doorless nook with a pretty view over an old orchard. Though still small, Matron seemed slightly taller than I remembered and was rectangular-shaped — approx 20 inches wide. As we reached the office she invited me — with a hand gesture — to go ahead of her but then changed her mind and barged past me to beat me to the better

45

chair. I wondered if the race for the better chair was all part of the assessment. I hoped not because I'd let her have it out of good manners and it occurred to me that it might be construed as unambitious. She was rock solid.

'So, Lizzie, what can you tell me about the elderly?' she asked. 'And don't just trot out the Owner's Wife's golden rules.' She sounded sarcastic.

I paused for a while because I was a bit confused and because I had heard something recently that was highly relevant to this question. Matron drummed her fingers on the desk while I searched my mind for the thing. It seemed to go on for a long time — her finger-drumming and my mindsearch.

Then it came to me. 'Old people are not suited to granary bread,' I said, triumphantly, 'they dislike it.'

It was worth the wait, she looked at me wide-eyed, as though I'd surprised and impressed her.

'Yes, and they're right to dislike it — it's evil,' she said emphatically. And we went off briefly at a tangent and seemed to bond over our mutual hatred of the stuff. Matron said she didn't know a single person who liked it. Then she remembered someone who did but said that person was nothing but a fool and not to be trusted. Getting back to the point, the elderly were particularly at risk from it, she said, and the bakeries were all jumping on the granary bandwagon, and the dentists and doctors were all in cahoots.

'Folk are putting their stoppings out on bits of

grain like gravel and blocking their internal tubes with the seeds and what have you,' said Matron. 'And who gains from that?' she asked.

It was rhetorical so I just nodded and said, 'True.'

'OK,' said Matron, moving on, 'what experience have you for this role?'

'I'm an expert beverage maker. I know the imperativeness of pouring freshly boiled water on to the bags and that only constant agitation prevents the forming of tannin and the telltale metallic skin and bitter taste.'

We'd just done this in chemistry, but I wasn't entirely faking. I did love tea.

Matron was clearly pleased to hear this and said she'd be in touch forthwith. She followed me out of the owner's office nook and, to my annoyance, Miranda sat there — applying roll-on lip-gloss using a hand-held ladybird mirror — listening.

'See you anon,' Matron said and ushered Miranda into the owner's nook. I watched as Matron barged her into the archway, exactly as she had done with me. Miranda barged her back, though, and flopped into the better chair.

I walked away.

I doubted even Miranda would have the nerve to bring up granary bread, as if she'd thought it up herself, or that she'd get through the interview without unwittingly revealing her hatred of old people.

I stood around the corner and listened. Matron asked Miranda what she knew about the elderly and Miranda came straight out and said

47

she found them difficult to comprehend and a bit depressing but would do her absolute best to help them not wee everywhere or drop their food. Far from being cross with Miranda for this negative attitude, Matron agreed and said in her opinion the patients were a bunch of spoilt old bastards and not one of the ladies had done an honest day's work in their life — apart from Miss Tyler, and even she'd had the life of Riley since retiring and having bread and marmalade brought to her every morning on a tray.

★   ★   ★

Later on, Matron called Miranda and me into the office nook. First she told us we'd both been successful in our application for promotion. And then she told us she had news.

'I have good news and sad news,' said Matron. 'Which would you like first?' she asked.

'The sad,' I said.

'It's the Owner's Wife,' said Matron, 'I'm afraid she's gone.'

'What, dead?' asked Miranda.

'No, she's left Paradise Lodge and gone to start up an art school, if you please,' sneered Matron.

'Oh, no!' I said.

'Ah, but the good news is, I've been promoted,' she said. 'I have taken her place as General Manager — as of yesterday I'm Queen Bee.'

'Congratulations,' said Miranda, 'that's great news.'

I was speechless but managed a smile.

I could hardly believe it. The Owner's Wife — the linchpin, my mentor — gone. Ridiculously, I wondered if I was partly to blame for it, the way my sister had felt when my father left (blaming herself, not me). Matron was now Queen Bee. It didn't make sense.

In the kitchen at coffee break we discovered not only had the Owner's Wife gone but she'd also taken Dee-Anna, the very normal nurse who I'd suspected of having something to hide on day one (and now I knew what it was). Also gone was Lazarus, the golden retriever — but not the owner's Rembrandt self-portrait. The owner wished it had been the other way around, for Lazarus meant more to him than Rembrandt and had been by his side for the previous five years. He'd telephoned his solicitor to see if he could arrange a swap but the answer had been no.

Nurse Eileen, Nurse Gwen and Nurse Hilary were still there, though, and you could feel something, maybe resentment, betrayal, abandonment. But mostly, the staff were furious with the owner (apart from Matron, who he'd put in charge). Nurse Gwen told us that the Owner's Wife had been trying to modernize the place for years — she'd had plans drawn up for new wards, hospital bathroom facilities and everything — but the owner had forbidden it, due to not being able to cope with change or dust or builders, and he'd threatened to leave or slit his wrists or go and live in the Volvo if she covered over any more tiles with lino.

It was difficult to get on with the daily routine with this cloud hanging over us, and because I'd not actually been fully trained except vis-à-vis the comfort round. We all sat at the table smoking and saying how awful the owner was, driving his wife, the linchpin, away.

Even the cook, who was a known friend of the owner, called the Owner's Wife 'the beating heart of the place'.

'She ran this place like clockwork,' said Nurse Eileen.

'The owner has let us all down by driving her away with his drunken cuntishness,' said Nurse Gwen.

'She must have been at the end of her tether,' said Miranda.

I couldn't add anything so I just said, 'True.'

Everyone agreed it was a disaster, the home wouldn't survive without her and Dee-Anna, and the owner himself wouldn't survive and would probably take the coward's way out. It seemed they'd said all these things before and were just reiterating them now for my and Miranda's benefit.

By lunchtime they'd become more philosophical, partly because the owner himself was sitting at the table sharing his thoughts about what had happened. His wife hadn't been happy since she was thwarted in her ambition to desecrate the house with linoleum. She'd succeeded in laying vinyl flooring in the ladies' ward while he'd been in hospital having a simple male procedure and she had been about to have the hall done too but he'd arrived home and put a stop to it.

And Nurse Hilary, who'd called him all the names under the sun earlier, poured him a glass of Tio Pepe and massaged his slumped shoulders and eventually he shuffled off and we could talk more freely about the doomed marriage and the bleakness of the future.

★ ★ ★

The Owner's Wife leaving Paradise Lodge wasn't the only thing that hadn't turned out as I expected.

When I first joined the staff, for instance, I imagined that I'd be the cheeky-but-wise one. The one who said clever, witty things that made the others gasp-but-chuckle. But somehow Miranda took that role and she wasn't quite as good at it as I'd have been — her cheekiness being a bit on the mean side. To be fair, she didn't mind being slightly disliked — which I would have. An example of this was that Miranda kept lording over us that she was a non-smoker and loved saying negative, disparaging things about smoking — which was an odd thing to do when all the rest of us delighted in it and did it as much as humanly possible, me included. She'd say things like, 'Hey, you lot, I've made a bonfire outside with a load of swept-up leaves, why don't you all go out there and stand around it and inhale for free?' in a sarcastic way. And everyone would laugh at the wise-but-cheeky thing she'd thought up.

It was particularly annoying for me since smoke rings were my non-verbal catchphrase

51

— either a stream of tiny ones or a large, thick quivering one that hung in the air. I'd practised in the mirror in my bedroom since I was eleven and could even do rectangular ones and ones which shot out and then stopped. And I'd received many compliments. Nurse Gwen, who was usually unsupportive, said my smoke rings were like a modern art phenomenon and I should go on *Opportunity Knocks* with them.

One day, when Miranda complained that the air in the kitchen was like a London fog and dramatically opened a window, Matron commented that it was odd and unnatural for a nurse not to smoke. 'All nurses smoke, it's their prerogative,' she said, and she repeated it because it was the run-up for one of her jokes. And then she said a nurse not smoking was as odd as a Chinaman who didn't like tea or a nun who didn't like sex. No one really noticed the joke but I'd started to notice how many times people said 'Chinaman' in jokes. I felt offended on Mike Yu's behalf and looked at Miranda to see if she was. She wasn't.

She was busy telling the saga of her Great-Granddad Norman who'd had a lung pack up on him due to tobacco smoking. He'd had it removed in touch-and-go surgery, and was now living his last days on the dodgy remaining lung.

'It doesn't even look like a lung any more,' said Miranda, 'more like a dog's ear in a pound of tar.'

'How do you know?' Eileen asked.

'He keeps it in a piccalilli jar on the sideboard as a deterrent.'

If we'd been at school, everyone would have been snorting with laughter by now, but this was the adult world and you had to sit through all sorts of manipulative rubbish and pretend to be interested. We all fell silent and none of us took a puff until the story was finally over, and wasted at least half a cigarette each that break time.

It was exactly the kind of psychopathic effect Miranda was after.

5

Certificate of Secondary Education

The previous year at school, work had suddenly got harder. We were expected to listen, take notes, study at home and demonstrate our understanding of subjects with endless little tests. This new climate coincided with the arrival of baby Danny and my having the odd day off and, for the first time in my school life, I found myself struggling to keep up — as previously mentioned.

My chemistry teacher, Mr Mackenzie, spoke to me one day after I'd scored 8 out of 50 in a test.

'It's all the lessons you've been missing — you've fallen behind,' he said, 'way behind.'

'I know, I'm sorry,' I said.

'I had you down as a scientist, Lizzie,' he said.

It sounded like he'd given up on me. I was heartbroken. I quickly, slightly tearfully, reminded him of my idea to invent a strongly scented talcum powder, which would mask odours but be completely see-through and invisible, not white. And therefore could be used liberally all over — on the occasions when bathing isn't an option — and no one would be the wiser.

'You need to get your skates on and catch up,' said Mr Mackenzie, 'otherwise you'll fail the end-of-term exam.'

I confided in him about the birth of Danny and my mother's despondency since a friend, who lived opposite, had seen her weeing in the kitchen sink and suggested a net curtain if she was going to make a habit of it and how this had caused the friendship to end and thus my mother had been friendless at the most vulnerable point in her life.

Mr Mackenzie had seemed sympathetic and showed me — in my textbook — the sections I particularly needed to work on at home. And I really meant it when I said I would.

It was the same in French. In the third year I could name every building and business in the city, I could get you to the park and the cinema and buy a three-course meal in informal and formal French. I had invented an alternative French family whose complications and quirks demonstrated my verbal and written linguistic skills and delighted Madame Perry. I had twin brothers who played the accordion and rode a tandem, and triplet sisters who loved roller-skating. Our granny, an ex-trapeze artist, lived with us and our five English sheepdogs, a donkey called Raisin and a cow called Noisette. By halfway through the fourth, I couldn't follow even the slowest conversation in class and kept asking 'Voudriez-vous ouvrir le fenêtre?' (masculine) instead of 'la fenêtre' (feminine).

Working at home wasn't easy — which was why Mr Holt used to stop on the way home and do his paperwork parked in a field gate. I tried to work, but honestly the stuff on the pages looked like Egyptian when I opened the book at home.

One day, after chemistry, Mr Mackenzie spoke to me again; he seemed less sympathetic this time. 'You're disrupting the class with your questions and chatting,' he said. 'I have reported it to Miss Pitt.'

'Oh, no,' I groaned and tried to explain my predicament, using the kind of scientific language he'd understand.

I was like a sandstone rock with a tiny crack in it, I told him. And water had got in and when the sun went down and the night froze, so the water had frozen and expanded and pushed the crack further apart and then, when the sun had come back, the melted ice had crept further into the crack. And so it had gone on and on, making the crack bigger and bigger, until a whole piece of me had fallen off into a fast-flowing river which had transported and deposited that piece of me into a lake where I languished under layers of sediment. My analogy began to break down and Mr Mackenzie interrupted.

'You'd better tell all that to Miss Pitt, she's a geography specialist.'

I went to Miss Pitt's office in the Victorian part of the school and knocked. She called me in and I started to speak, half-heartedly, about limestone.

'I didn't ask you to speak,' she said, which was actually a relief. And she told me, in no uncertain terms and at length, that she would not tolerate truanting. I tried to butt in — to blame baby Danny — but she really didn't want to hear me.

'You were a perfectly good pupil and now

you're absent half the time,' she said, taking a deep breath and looking at a register. 'You're aware of the 1960 Beloe Report, are you, Lizzie . . . ?'

'No,' I said, 'I wasn't born in 1960.'

' . . . marking the introduction of the CSE examinations — for the less academic pupil.'

'No,' I said.

'It explains the criteria for regarding pupils as academic or less academic,' she said. 'It states that a pupil with erratic attendance should not be entered to study or sit the GCE 'O' Levels, but the CSE examinations.'

I couldn't think of anything to say. I shrugged. I disliked her too much to ask for clemency or try to explain again.

'Off you go, Lizzie,' she said, 'and please bring me a letter from your mother to explain your recent absences.'

As I opened the heavy door, she said, 'By the way, how *is* your mother?'

It seemed a personal and somehow nasty thing to say and, even though I was continually trotting the baby out as an excuse for my doing — or not doing — a thing, I felt under threat. I looked at her.

'I mean with the baby,' she said.

'She's fine,' I said, and just thinking of Danny made me smile.

Miss Pitt smiled too. 'Well, just as long as that clever sister of yours doesn't disappear off to university and leave you holding it — so to speak.'

It was puzzling. Was she being nice, or not?

57

'I mean, your mother might consider one brilliant daughter sufficient and quite like the second one to stay at home and help,' she said.

'No, my mother wants two brilliant daughters,' I said.

'Let's not disappoint her, then,' she said.

6

Jackie Collins

The live-in nurses weren't all that interested in me. I suppose I seemed so much younger and had nothing to offer. So I was forced to let Matron befriend me, and a vicious circle started. Not that there was any viciousness. Just that the more I sampled Matron's different tea leaves — including Lapsang and pink Darjeeling — and watched *Stars on Sunday* with her instead of going home to do normal teenage things, the less normal I seemed.

It seemed my role was to do things none of the others could face, from talking to unpleasant relatives, answering the upstairs bells or feeding a patient who was very hungry but toothless and incredibly slow — and it taking half an hour — to sometimes taking a pinch of snuff to cheer everyone up with a funny sneezing fit, and being nice to Matron. Being nice to Matron became more important than almost anything. Matron was like another patient — to be chatted to and listened to — but I soon realized the only way to be friends with her was to try to understand the heart of her. It was my English literature class and she was the baddy who's had a tough past.

First and foremost Matron was tired, she didn't sleep well. Her eyelids were puffy and if you looked up close, when she wasn't looking, you could see she was very, very old. You could see it in the papery skin, the brown marks, her milky old eyes and the very awkwardness of her bones. You could hear it in her breathing and the crackle of her old dyed hair. She was deep in old age but hadn't made the arrangements for it. She hadn't any savings and, due to tax avoidance or some kind of bogusness, she wasn't eligible for the state pension or the health.

She envied the patients their carefree lives, their breakfast trays and the certainty that there'd be someone to help them with their stockings for as long as they lived. Whereas *she* worried day in, day out that she'd end up at St Mungo's homeless shelter. Like her dear friend, who owned nothing but her name — but whose name she couldn't remember.

Matron told me all this one day as we sat on a bench in the drive. I asked her what she planned to do.

She told me she'd always banked on landing a live-in companion situation to a nice solvent gentleman, which was what women in her position did and had always done. It was a tit-for-tat thing where the live-in companion was like a friendly slave but ended up with a small bungalow.

'Does it have to be a gentleman?' I asked — gentlemen being that much harder to come by than ladies.

'Oh, yes, it has to be. Ladies leave their bungalows to the cats' home or church,' she said, 'whereas a gent likes to pat the coin into your palm, it makes him feel important, even after he's dead. A gent is like a Labrador — you just give him a titbit, rub his shoulders and pat him, engage and play.' She paused. 'Ladies don't want to be Labradors.'

Matron had let two gents slip between her fingers just that year and had known a handful over the time she'd worked at Paradise Lodge who might have been, but had come to nothing. But there had been one gent who she had moved in with — Mr Arthur Minelli, from Barrow upon Soar. He'd shortened the name to Minell without the 'i' at the end to make it sound English but Matron hadn't known it, and not knowing it had been her downfall. When Mr Arthur Minelli's nieces had swooped in, they'd been able to say, quite rightly, 'You're just his nurse, you don't even know his real name.'

And she'd got nothing. Not a bean, not even the little egg pan she'd paid for with her own money. And she'd looked after him and lived in the tiny spare room in his house and done up his buttons and rubbed his shaggy old shoulders for more than three years. And he'd been happy every day until she'd found him one night, standing in a corner, his brain gone, and she'd taken him to his day bed and lain with him, singing Irish songs, until the new day came and he was dead.

'Why did he die?' I asked.

'They do, they just do,' said Matron. 'That's why you need the paperwork done. I meant to tell him I was in need. I always planned to. I had three Xmases with him — not that I had any better offers — but we never saw hide nor hair of the nieces and only got a card and a box of biscuits each year from the two of them together,' she rambled.

The Xmas Days had been just like any other day, except they'd cooked chickens and had tins of gravy. She and Arthur had amused themselves every day the same, reading funny books, watching telly in the evenings and making up nicknames for the people who wandered in and out of their lives: the butcher 'Beaky' — on account of his nose — and the doctor 'Sprout' — on account of his hair — and the two nieces 'Gert' and 'Daisy' — which was hilarious, except Matron never knew why.

'I never knew who Gert and Daisy were, but hadn't the heart to ask,' she said.

'My mother would know,' I said, seeing a way out. Jumping up from the bench, I said, 'I'll phone her.'

And we went up to Lady Briggs' room and I helped Lady Briggs on to the commode, since we were up there, and we whistled 'To Be A Pilgrim' until our lips ached because Lady Briggs always said whistling hymns helped her go.

While we waited, I rang my mother and she explained Gert and Daisy were two gossiping women from *Workers' Playtime*, which was on the radio during the war — blah, blah. And then — can you believe it? — Matron began telling Lady Briggs the whole tale of Mr Minelli and I snuck away so as not to have to hear her tell it again only slightly different.

★　★　★

Matron kept putting me on the rota but no matter how much I liked being at Paradise Lodge, I had my future to think of vis-à-vis school and catching up and not ending up being deemed 'un-academic'. I was very keen to put in a decent attendance, especially as the end of term approached and that was when all the totting up would be done.

It wasn't long after my meeting with Miss Pitt that Nurse Hilary phoned to ask me to come into work the following morning. I said I was sorry, but no, I couldn't because it was a school day. Immediately afterwards Matron phoned to tell me I was down on the rota for the next day — to do a split shift — and could I please confirm I'd be in?

I said I couldn't — I was being monitored by the Deputy Head regarding my attendance, and it was imperative that I go to school. Matron begged. She'd been offered the chance to go on a tour of the Weetabix factory, she said, with a convalescent patient, Mr Greenberg (proprietor of Greenberg's Bespoke Tailors on Granby Street), and she believed he was on the brink of asking her to become his live-in companion.

'We've got an auxiliary nurse off with impetigo,' she said, 'and I might not get this opportunity again — I was counting on you.'

I stuck to my guns and hung up before she could wear me down. The phone rang again but I flung my brother's parka over it and ignored its muffled tinkles.

I felt strong and proud to be on the way to school the next day as we sailed through the villages. I was doing the right thing. We were about to go past Paradise Lodge when the bus stopped suddenly. Matron had flagged it down. She clambered up the steps and spoke to the driver. He called me to get off the bus. 'There's an emergency at the old folks' home,' he said.

I ran ahead of Matron up the drive, thinking I'd find Miss Brixham stuck in the cattle grid, or something like that, but there was no emergency, only Mr Greenberg sitting in his Austin with a no-cheese packed lunch and a hat on his head — waiting to go off on his excursion.

I was annoyed and started to walk down the drive, back on to the lane. I drew level with Matron. 'You mad cow,' I said, but she pulled me by the sleeve and then forced me backwards, up against the wall and held me there by my collar. She was surprisingly strong.

She told me in a hoarse whisper that Mr Greenberg had practically asked her to become his live-in companion, and she just needed this excursion to tip him over. She reminded me she was facing a penniless retirement with no state pension or health, unless she could find a companion position and have a bungalow bequeathed to her.

It was a major rant and all the time she held me under the chin, like a school bully. She said that the departure of the Owner's Wife would result in Paradise Lodge going to ruin and if she ever got an interview for a new job — which was unlikely, due to her age — she'd be tainted by its failure under her command. 'I thought I'd explained all this,' she said.

I knew Matron had had a tough life. She often talked about the bad old days wherever it was she'd grown up — when you weren't allowed to eat a bag of crisps in the street and they probably didn't even have crisps anyway, but even if they did, she couldn't afford them and people's parents were always drowning themselves or drowning kittens or leaving in the night or whipping the children.

I agreed to work her shift. 'Not because you deserve it,' I said, sullenly, 'but because I want to buy a floppy mackintosh.'

'Good gel,' she said, 'a floppy mac covers a multitude of sins.'

'But you'll have to drive me to school first, so I can register.'

We got into the Austin, I sat in the back and Mr Greenberg drove. It was the oddest thing I'd ever done. Matron kept laughing and eating sweets out of a tin and pointing at cows and horses. 'You're like our very own little gel,' she said.

They waited outside in the street while I ran to the school office to register as a late arrival and then snuck back out of the gates. It was all ridiculous and I felt really annoyed.

Back at Paradise Lodge Matron thanked me and said she was much obliged and then, as they were driving away, she shouted through the window, 'Keep an eye on Granger.'

⋆　⋆　⋆

In the kitchen, I read the Day Book to see what Matron had meant about Miss Granger.

65

O/B+++ black stool. Agit'd, ref. Food.
NOK informed by tel.

I asked Nurse Hilary what it all stood for.

'She's coming to the end,' said Hilary with a sniff.

It seems so obvious now, but at the time I wasn't entirely sure what Hilary meant. And daren't ask. I spent the day obsessively creeping in and out of the ladies' ward looking at Miss Granger.

Between chores, I offered her sips of water, dabbed her forehead with a flannel and talked to her about any nice thing I could think of. I'd been told by my mother that old people liked being read to, or spoken to, especially when they were dying or close to dying — that it was soothing and the next best thing to having a lullaby.

So I talked to Miss Granger just in case. I talked about Jackie Collins, ex-pupil of Miss Tyler's, who'd written a bestselling book that some of the staff had read and loved. I fetched the book and read her an excerpt:

'All right, I'm sorry I spoke. I just don't know why you want this stupid career of yours. Why don't you — '

'Why don't I what?' she interrupted coldly. 'Give it all up and marry you? And what do you suggest we do with your wife and kids, and all your other various family entanglements?'

He was silent.

66

'Look, baby.' Her voice softened. 'I don't bug you about things, so why don't we just forget it? You don't own me, I don't own you, and that's the way it should be.' She applied lipgloss with a flourish. 'I'm starving. How about lunch?'

After that it got a bit saucy, so I switched to chit-chat. I told her that Matron had gone out for a tour of the Weetabix factory and that I actually disliked Weetabix since having it one time with slightly sour milk. And for some reason I told her my favourite word was London.

'London,' I said, 'London.'

And that was the only time she opened her eyes, and it occurred to me that maybe London was the only word she'd understood all day. 'London,' I said again, 'it's such a nice word, and exciting.'

Just before I went off duty, things seemed to have taken a turn for the worse. I could see from the doorway. She seemed to be breathing — but only in-breaths and not out. I stood a while and then she took a breath in . . . and then nothing but a gurgling noise . . . and then another breath in . . . and so on.

I looked from the doorway for quite a few minutes, hoping someone would just happen along and take over. I had no intention of going any closer but I told myself I had to do something, there were two other ladies already in the ward beginning to get ready for bed. One of them, Miss Boyd, saw me and was about to speak. I turned and walked as quickly as I could without rattling the floor tiles, and bumped into Nurse Hilary.

'Whoops-a-daisy,' said Hilary.

'It's Miss Granger,' I said, 'I don't think she's very well.'

Hilary strode to Ward 2. I followed and noticed she was cow-hocked. I felt sorry for her, it being such an unattractive walk — especially as the outsides of her pork-pie shoes were worn right down. Maybe the two things were connected. Maybe it was another defect, like the pitted teeth.

Hilary stood by the bed and looked at Miss Granger.

'She's Cheyne-Stoking,' she said, 'or, to use the vernacular, she's got the death rattle.'

'Does that mean she's dying?' I whispered.

'Yes, she'll be gone in a few minutes — she's slowly drowning in her own bodily fluids — it's how most of us go.'

And Hilary walked off on her cow-hocks to telephone Miss Granger's great-niece who lived locally but hadn't shown up yet.

I felt I should stay and not let this woman die alone. Not that I could be of any comfort, but I'd be in the room and that must surely count for something. I couldn't bring myself to get close enough to dab her brow, or wet her parched lips, so I just spoke some more gibberish on her favourite subject. 'I've been to Madame Tussauds in London twice,' I told her, 'they've got Kevin Keegan in there,' and I listed other famous names that I thought she might know.

I stood and waited, feeling as if I might faint. I

think I was half expecting her to rise up, clutch her chest, groan dramatically and flop down again, at which point I imagined I might say the Lord's Prayer. In fact, the gurgle grew softer and then nothing until her bottom denture popped out like a candy pipe, and her chin dropped into her neck and her eyes stared off at nothing and she didn't look like herself any more.

Hilary returned and marched up to the bed, took Miss Granger by the chin, calmly twisted the denture back in and pulled the sheet over her face.

'Is she dead?' I asked.

'No, I just can't stand to look at her,' said Nurse Hilary, and she laughed and pulled a face at me. 'Only joking — yes, she's gone to Heaven, Lizzie.'

Hilary flicked the switch on the ripple mattress to 'off' and the slight hum died away and the two ladies called out, 'Is she dead, then?' and, 'Thank goodness!' etc.

I couldn't help but make a tiny cry sound. I was sad about the death. I always was. Even the merciful ones. I still had silly ideas about people miraculously recovering and laughing about it the next day over a hearty breakfast and all the nurses and relatives saying what a close thing it had been.

'Go and get yourself a cup of tea and a fag,' said Nurse Hilary.

★　★　★

In the kitchen, Matron had literally just breezed in and still had her headscarf on. They'd had a

69

lovely time, her and Mr Greenberg, at the Weetabix factory and she was extolling the virtues of a cereal breakfast in place of bread and marmalade and praising the countryside. I didn't want to spoil it with the sad news straight away but Nurse Hilary came in behind me just as Matron was telling a tableful of staff about Northamptonshire's gently undulating hills.

Hearing this, and seeing Matron all smiles with a sample box of Weetabix and a tin of sucky sweets, Hilary put her hands on her hips.

'Sounds as though you've had a lovely day, Matron, I'm so glad.'

'Yes, we did, thank you — ' Matron began.

'Well, the news here is that Granger's dead,' she snarled. 'Died with her fucking teeth in and no relative.'

'Another eighty quid a week gone,' said Nurse Gwen. 'I thought she had another year in her.'

There was a general sadness but no one reacted philosophically. None of them imagined it being their granny, mother, sister or themselves. No one seemed to care that this woman — who'd once been someone's baby girl, who'd seen Captain Scott leave for the Antarctic, whose favourite colour had been peacock blue and whose dressing gown had caught fire on a candle one winter's night when they still had candles — was dead and gone. And the last image in her mind having been the waxwork model of Lester Piggott.

Hilary and Sally-Anne left the kitchen to do whatever you have to do to a recently deceased person.

'By the way, Brixham's shit the bed,' barked Hilary from the door, 'Lizzie had better come and sort her out.'

I followed them to Ward 2. A screen had been put round Miss Granger's bed and Hilary and Sally-Anne went behind and clanged around a bit.

I laid an inco-pad across the seat of the communal wheelchair and helped Miss Brixham out of bed.

'Where are you taking me?'

'To the bathroom,' I said. 'You've had a little accident.'

Matron appeared in the bathroom and said quietly to me, 'It's a bad omen. I bet Mr Greenberg's going to go and die on me. I bet you he's next, and I need to get out of here before this place closes down.'

'No, he won't,' I said, just meaning to shut her up.

'I'll give you a pound note if he's not the next to go,' she said, looking gloomy and folding her headscarf again and again, into a tiny, tiny square.

'He won't die,' I whispered.

'Ah, something'll go wrong,' said Matron.

'What could go wrong?' I asked.

'He'll either die or, worse, get better and leave,' she said. 'I'll give you a pound note if he doesn't.'

'Right,' I said.

'And you give me one if he does,' she said.

After cleaning and powdering and putting Miss Brixham in a clean nightie, I began

71

wheeling her back to the ward. On the way, a traffic jam had developed in the corridor behind Hilary and Sally-Anne struggling to carry Miss Granger in what looked like a cricket bag. They'd not secured her properly and it looked as though she might tumble out. She didn't, but an arm flopped out and the owner, who was drifting along with a large Campari and soda, looking for Lazarus, let out a high-pitched scream.

7

A Rival Concern

Paradise Lodge, for all its faults, started to feel like home — the comings and goings, the bickering, smoking, eating, laughing — and with no one guarding the biscuits, and only Miranda telling me smoking would stunt my growth and poison the air. There was all the hair-curling, making-up and bathing, and I was being paid.

I loved the feel of the place, the big sunny windows, and the height of the ceilings, the space, the smell of fruit pies baking and talcum powder in the air, the sound of the owner's sandal buckles as he mooched drunkenly about, the endless perfect denture smiles and the dreamy niceness of the old ladies, their constant murmuring, their gladness to see me and their tales. And that the simple act of singing 'Play That Funky Music' while I dusted caused such happiness among them.

I loved the continual, ongoing gossip. Eileen telling us her technique for relieving her boyfriend in the cinema without their seat-neighbours suspecting. Not in a rude way, or to be aggressive or showy-offy, but to have an amusing conspiracy against men and their keenness to be relieved in cinemas. She told us about one boyfriend of hers who'd unexpectedly begun relieving himself during the film *Jaws* at the Odeon, Longston. Eileen had been so shocked she'd had to leave before the end (of the film).

I very much liked hearing this stuff (the relieving of men etc.) but only in a group scenario and not if the speaker was looking at me. I used to listen intently but look down and sharpen the end of my lit cigarette by twirling it round and round in the ashtray. To this day a full communal ashtray reminds me of Nurse Eileen spitting into her hand during *Airport*.

★   ★   ★

But things were not getting better at school. The next time I turned up for classes Miss Pitt sent for me. She had a spiteful manner.

'How are you, Lizzie?' she asked.

'Fine,' I said.

'I gather from your tutor that you're frequently absent from school,' she said. 'I shan't beat about the bush, Lizzie, I *am*, as warned, going to have to remove you from the 'O' Level group starting from the autumn term unless you make dramatic and immediate improvement, attendance-wise.'

She talked in paragraphs, like teachers sometimes do. It wasn't a conversation.

I'd been ready for a little row with her, but hadn't expected this full-blown threat. I told her straight away I'd turn over a new leaf, attendance-wise. And I meant it.

'I have never seen a letter explaining your absences,' she said, 'so I would like a letter of commitment from your mother — stating that she will support your getting to school, every day.'

'OK,' I said and left the office.

Later, I wrote a letter of commitment — from my mother (blaming herself for my absences) — I made her sound like a busy mother with sore gums and breasts and signed off like this:

Anyway, I hope you'll accept my sincere apologies for asking Lizzie to take the occasional day off school. The thing is, I have had mild periodontal gum disease due to having a baby recently (an afterthought) as I think you know (much against my fiancé's wishes) and Lizzie has very occasionally had to look after it while I am at work or at the dental hygienist's etc. but all the while reading a wide range of literature with a view to taking her 'O' Levels next year.

She will turn over a new leaf, attendance-wise, from September. You have my assurance.

Yours, etc.
Elizabeth Vogel (Mrs)
PS: I have found a childminder.

I dropped the letter into the Deputy Head's office the next day and, instead of going home from school, I called in at Paradise Lodge. I needed to ask Mr Simmons for advice on the mind of his stepdaughter.

'Your stepdaughter has threatened to chuck

75

me off the 'O' Level course,' I said. 'Do you think she means it?'

'Yes,' said Mr Simmons, 'she is quite hard-hearted.'

And by 'quite', he meant 'very'.

'I hear she would prefer you to be at home, and not here,' I ventured.

'Yes, and yet the harder the wind blows the tighter the man holds his coat around himself,' he said and laughed.

★ ★ ★

Mr Simmons had made a speedy convalescence after his operation and though I disliked his stepdaughter, I had to agree that his prolonged stay at Paradise Lodge was probably not entirely necessary, medically speaking. In fact, Paradise Lodge seemed like an expensive social club.

It suited us well, though, and Mr Simmons soon became an important member of the team. He'd get up early and help with the breakfasts and then he'd go for a little walk in the village and come back with the newspaper. He'd help out with assorted day-to-day duties, such as cooking and pie-making, and did his best to keep on top of the paperwork. He was especially helpful in handling the owner when he was sad or drunkenly ranting at the poor patients — a thing he'd started to do since his wife left. Mr Simmons seemed more like a friend than a patient, diverting the owner from his various troubles and preventing him slipping further into depression via trips to the Piglet Inn, games of backgammon, and talks about how difficult marriage could be, and business. Mr Simmons would say, 'The show must go on!' and things like that to gee him up.

One morning, Daybreak, the owner's gelding, came trotting into the courtyard without the owner on board. He didn't try to tell us anything with his hoof, he just went to his hay net, tripping a bit on his trailing reins, and munched away, regardless of his poor owner.

It was Mr Simmons who searched for and found the owner and helped carry him home on a plank of wood, because, in spite of a hurt back, he wouldn't agree to an ambulance. Mr Simmons had known where to look for him because he'd listened to all his mumbling nonsense about the places he liked to go for quiet contemplation. And that had saved his life. Later that day the owner called us all into his quarters and gave a gloomy talk from the chaise longue, warning us that we were 'on the skids'. I put it down to his general discomfort.

★   ★   ★

Almost every day the staff talked about the owner's state of mind. We also talked about the Owner's Wife and wondered what had become of her — whether she'd ever come back and whether that would be a good thing. Or not. Had she started up the art school? And if so, where? Some said St Ives in Cornwall because of its associations with the arts. Others felt it more likely she'd gone to Italy to run watercolouring holidays — where you might paint an olive grove in the morning, have a bottle of wine and a knees-up by the pool in the afternoon, followed by lasagne, then bed.

We were careful not to tell the patients that the Owner's Wife had gone — and to fool them, the owner would dress up occasionally in his wife's old Dannimac and headscarf and dash past the day-room window with a trug of something.

And then one day we had news of her. And if it hadn't come from Miss Tyler — our most able-bodied and mentally reliable lady — we shouldn't have believed it.

It was teatime and Miss Tyler began on an anecdote about her favourite hat, a solid turban in duck-egg and ruby shot silk.

We all knew the hat — she almost always wore it and, if truth were told, it was getting a bit raggedy. Everyone had something to say about this hat, for it was extremely handsome and had a touch of something exotic. That day Nurse Eileen picked it up and put it on. She looked amazing, like Elizabeth Taylor. I couldn't try it because my nurse's hat was pinned on too fiercely, but everyone else did and all looked equally fetching in it — it suited everyone, patients and staff alike. The turban was declared a 'wonder-hat' and we all vowed to steal it away etc.

'Well, I almost lost it this week,' said Miss Tyler.

'Oh, no,' we all said, not being able to imagine her without the duck-egg turban.

'Yes, I was visiting a friend at the new nursing

home — Newfields, in Longston — and I forgot to pick it up when I left, and I was just getting into my taxi when I saw the Owner's Wife — our dear Owner's Wife — running out into the car park with it in her hands. It was most definitely she. She asked me how we were all getting along.'

'What?' we all said.

'She has taken over the nursing home. She's bought it with a business loan and refurbished it with council grants. She's the owner,' said Miss Tyler. 'And Nurse Dee-Anna's there too.'

'So who is it rushing past the window in the Owner's Wife's mackintosh, then?' asked Miss Boyd.

'That's the owner pretending to be her so we won't know she's run off,' said Mr Freeman. 'Either that or the chap's lost his marbles.'

And it was true. The Owner's Wife hadn't gone to start up an art school at all. It was much more exciting and treacherous than that. She'd opened Newfields — a rival, purpose-built nursing home with all mod cons, including safety flooring and corner-to-corner handrailing. Plus being situated on the outskirts of Leicester (Longston side) and on both the County Travel and Midland Red bus routes, making it handy for frozen food supermarket Bejam, the Pork Pie Library, the Odeon and a huge Co-op that sold everything from tinned peas to toilet seats.

As soon as the truth was out and confirmed, everyone could suddenly see what an utter bitch she was. And they stopped blaming the owner for making her life hell. They blamed her and

79

only her and they devised all sorts of versions of how she'd planned it all along. How she'd let Paradise Lodge slip into a state of near collapse before abandoning ship with her lesbian lover (Nurse Dee-Anna) and how they'd set out to ruin us with their perfect nursing home with all its sly and spiteful extras that would appeal to anyone with a relative to dump and shopping to do.

Miranda snatched the news for herself and, gasping, suddenly remembered that the Owner's Wife had tried to recruit her for the dastardly new venture. Miranda was lying, though — I could tell because she did a false yawn afterwards.

The badness of the Owner's Wife became the number one favourite thing to gossip about. Some stories were mundane: she fertilized the raspberry bushes with urine-soaked horse manure, and this caused the owner chronic one-year-long tummy-ache and meant him constantly having to dismount Daybreak to go behind a bush on long hacks.

And some were wild and vivid: she was a nymphomaniac who used her vagina to gain power over the owner, only to brush him aside once he'd begun to suffer with brewer's droop. She wasn't just sex mad like a normal nympho — with her it was a sickness of the mind and all to do with power and control, expressed via refurbishing the house to make it like a hospital.

It sounds unkind but it was understandable — the staff had all loved her so very much before she left and their feeling of abandonment turned that love sour. It always does. All the tiny tales of evil made them feel better about being left behind. My little brother had felt like this about our divorced father. He hadn't wanted to hear how great he was, why would he? He was the head of a whole new family now and someone else's father. It's always better to think the thing you lost is worthless.

Secretly I still liked the Owner's Wife. Other tall women I'd known had always stooped slightly to bring themselves down an inch or two. She didn't, though — she had stood up straight as if she intended to fill the horizon, which she did, like a soldier trying to unnerve the enemy or a goalkeeper flapping his arms about to make the goalmouth seem smaller, or a bird puffing its feathers up to look bigger, and so on and so forth. I tried to remember this — her occupying of the space — because it was honestly one of the most powerful things I'd ever seen, woman-wise. And it was the reason I'd gone into high wedges. Not because I was copying Miranda.

My loyalty to the Owner's Wife had influenced the way I went about my day-to-day work from day one. Before she left, she asked me to keep a particular eye on Lady Briggs in Room 9. It had seemed like nothing at the time.

'You will make sure Lady B isn't forgotten — up there — won't you, Lizzie?' she'd asked.

And I'd said of course I would make sure.

I soon understood that she'd said it because she was about to leave and that in itself was strange and troubling. The burden of it — on me alone.

And so it was that, right from the start, I'd been up to Room 9 numerous times every day and waited while Lady Briggs tried for a wee in her commode — which she often didn't manage. There was something a little bit spooky about her. Partly it was her long, cobwebby hair, rheumy eyes and ghostly demeanour, and partly it was a click that came from her mouth — not a side-of-the-mouth click that might go with a wink of the eye, but a hard click as if the tip of her tongue was striking the very centre of the roof of her mouth and it was made of brass. The click was regular and intermittent like the tick of a clock. But mostly it was the knowledge that Lady Briggs had been at Paradise Lodge for seven years and had never once left her room. She'd had no visitors except occasionally the owner (or so she claimed) and once a bogus window cleaner who'd tried to steal the antique ablutions jug from her washstand in 1975 but had been caught by a nurse sunbathing on the fire escape. Lady Briggs saw hardly anyone — unless they'd come to put her on the commode — she never listened to the radio or watched telly or read a book or a newspaper. She'd just sat there, for seven years, clicking and thinking. She was a recluse. And they're always spooky.

Anyway, we were supposed to be keeping the Owner's Wife's departure a secret from the patients, so as not to unsettle them, and even though the true facts behind her departure had now been blurted out, over tea, by Miss Tyler, we'd been asked to keep mum. On one particular day, though, I'd gone up to see Lady Briggs after coffee and she'd been trying for a stool and we were having our usual commode-side chit-chat, and she'd said such intuitive things about the atmosphere at Paradise Lodge — a sense of things not being entirely all right. And even though I knew I wasn't supposed to, I told her that the Owner's Wife had left and opened a rival nursing home with all mod cons in a better spot etc.

'There's a strange atmosphere, Nurse,' Lady Briggs had said.

'Well, it's probably because the Owner's Wife has left,' I said.

'What?' she gasped.

'The Owner's Wife, Ingrid, or whatever her name was, she's left.'

'No!' said Lady Briggs, horrified. 'When?'

'Yes,' I said, quietly, 'a while ago.'

'But why didn't anyone tell me?' she asked.

And I told her the whole sorry tale, from my point of view, but swore her to secrecy.

'She's opened a brand-new nursing home called Newfields and it's taking all our prospective patients,' I said. 'That's why there's a funny atmosphere.'

'Oh dear, oh dear, that is very bad news,' said Lady Briggs and she gazed around the room and clicked and moaned slightly. 'And what about Lazarus?' she asked, meaning the owner's golden retriever.

'Lazarus has gone too,' I said.

And then Lady Briggs brought her hands to her face and started to cry and I knew she'd have no chance of going after that so I pulled up her pants and tried to cheer her up by blowing a gum bubble. I'd blown an enormous one the day before that had had her in stitches, but just when I needed a result, my gum was too old and it blew into holes and stuck around my lips, so I just helped her back to her chair. She dabbed herself with 4711. I wondered briefly if she might have had a mini heart attack and was about to ring for help, but she recovered her composure after a few sips of water and asked me to fetch her boxes down from a shelf. The boxes were packed with old papers and photographs, which she always liked to leaf through at times of stress, when the doctor was due, or she'd had a senna pod.

I'd unsettled her and now I was unsettled. I lay down on her bed for a moment to gather myself. It was a normal thing to do. Lady Briggs never minded us nurses having a rest up there. She used to like it. Ditto making the odd phone call on her extension.

Obviously telling Lady Briggs about the Owner's Wife leaving and so forth had been a mistake. And, though I wasn't a believer in honesty being the best policy, I went downstairs and straight away told the others around the table what an idiot I was.

'Lady Briggs was very upset to hear about the Owner's Wife and all that,' I said.

'We're trying to keep it from as many of the patients as we can,' said Eileen.

84

'I know, I'm sorry, I thought she'd be fine about it,' I said.

'Don't worry,' said Eileen and she smiled.

'The owner won't want her knowing,' said Matron, 'you should've kept your mouth shut, Lizzie.'

Apart from Matron, I must say, there was a very compassionate attitude to mistake-making at Paradise Lodge, especially the tangible, funny kind you'd imagine might be frowned upon in a semi-medical setting, but they really weren't. The nurses and seniors were mostly very understanding and actually found mistakes quite amusing — however inconvenient. And when an amusing mistake was made, everyone would laugh and then queue up to tell us about their own. Like the time Nurse Gwen had called the bingo numbers too fast and caused two funny turns and an accident.

Apart from almost giving Lady Briggs a heart attack, my biggest mistake at that time concerned the dentures. I have heard people — over the years — tell this same tale, so it's obviously an easy mistake to make and I don't feel too embarrassed about it.

I'd collected all the teeth in the little initialled plastic pots and taken them on a tray to be cleaned. Except for Mr Simmons and Miss Tyler, who had their own teeth and cleaned them with a brush and Euthymol.

When I got to the sluice I ran a big sink full of water and dropped the teeth carefully into the water, so as to avoid chipping them, and put in one quarter of a Steradent tablet, gave them a good stir with the end of the broom and left them to soak overnight. As instructed.

It took a very long time in the morning to reunite teeth and patient and though nothing else got done, not a single person didn't find it amusing and charming. Nurse Hilary wet herself and had to go and change. The funny thing was seeing the patients trying to speak with the wrong teeth in. It really was a revelation how unique each human mouth is, shape-wise. Like a fingerprint.

Mr Simmons turned out to be very good at matching the pairs of dentures by aligning the bite and matching the colour and wear and tear of the bite surfaces on actual teeth and guessing whose they were. 'Who's got a huge jaw?' he'd say and we'd shout, 'Miss Steptoe!' And he'd start there.

I made other mistakes too. A couple that were quite upsetting (and not funny, as such). I once wiped a lady's bottom too soon and, as I did, I said, 'Shit!' which was awful and upsetting for both of us. But the worst, by miles, was when I told Miss Mills that Zebedee the stripe-less zebra — she'd seen him in 1926 at Paignton Zoo and so loved remembering — hadn't been a stripe-less zebra at all, only a white horse with its mane cut all stubby. It was a swizz. Miss Mills had fallen silent when I'd said it and took a long while to recover.

It was strange, the teeth mix-up seeming so bad at the time — all the patients having to try each other's teeth like Cinderella, with Mr Simmons peering into their mouths and saying,

'Say 'Isle of Wight',' and then wrenching them out again and popping in another set to try — being nothing but fun and everyone laughing until they wet themselves. And the thoughtless clever-clogs comment about the stripe-less zebra being heartbreaking. I'd stamped on a magical memory and I still think of it now.

And there was the time I hadn't known what 'carnal' meant.

8

A Dog Named Sue

My mother felt lonely. It was quite common for women to feel lonely after having a baby, especially one they'd had deliberately after breaking an agreement (spoken or unspoken). Being a mother was an extremely lonely thing to be in those days when you had to do it a certain way or be judged. And so, as soon as I'd got my feet under the table at Paradise Lodge, I would invite my mother up for lunch. Even on the days I should have been at school, and even though my mother was as keen as anything that I attend and succeed, I'd sometimes ring her from Lady Briggs' secret telephone and ask if she fancied a walk up. And she always did.

She'd wheel Danny up in his pushchair in time for the staff's after-lunch lunch break, it being the perfect distance for Danny to nod off after *his* lunch and for her to use up 300 or so calories. That was another thing about motherhood that was difficult for women (like my mother), it being all about gaining weight, eating, feeding, having a hungry dependent and feeling hungry yourself, and then dashing about desperate to burn off a few ounces of the fat you'd gained in pregnancy by not taking stimulants.

The first time she came up to Paradise Lodge

she ran all the way. Not that she liked running but she'd forced herself to run by pretending that someone evil was chasing her and if she let him catch her, she'd die and Danny would be alone in the lane and in the world. She arrived exhausted (but glad to be alive) and spent the next half-hour encouraging everyone to try 'running away from a murderer' and other calorie-burning strategies. My colleagues around the kitchen table — all calorie counters — thrilled at this kind of talk.

Eileen was addicted to butterscotch-flavour Ayds, the hunger-suppressing candy that you were supposed to eat between meals (to stop you wanting meals), and she recommended these to everyone, but not the Limmits calorie-controlled diet (which she believed to cause water retention). And Hilary swore by Energen starch-reduced rolls with St Ivel low-cal cottage cheese with chives.

My mother — who had dashed over a mile, uphill, to burn 300 calories and admitted to preferring thinness to chubbiness — suddenly said, 'I've a bloody good mind to stay fat forever just to annoy my mother and Nancy Mitford.'

And a cheer went up.

She kept touching the biscuit plate but not taking one and I bet myself 50p she wouldn't, and she didn't. 'I don't see why I should starve myself and smoke and go back to taking speed just to look nice in a bikini?'

The staff laughed.

'I mean,' she said, 'who the hell am I staying thin for?'

'All the men you might fancy,' Sally-Anne mumbled.

'Exactly,' said my mother, 'and they can sod off.' And with that she lit a fag and pushed away the biscuit plate.

I could tell Miranda was pleased my mother had shown up. Probably thinking her eccentricity cancelled out her mother's racial prejudice. But she was wrong. The staff liked her and the patients quickly picked up on her being a Benson of the Knighton Bensons. Many had had dealings with her father, who was a saint, a good cricketer and an all-round good egg. In fact, my mother brought them alive with talk of old Leicestershire and all the folk she knew from her former posh life and would often recite bits of poetry with them, including a favourite of hers about a bloke who asks God for immortality but forgets to ask for eternal youth to go with it and ends up getting more and more decrepit but unable to die. It seemed a bit near the knuckle, to be honest, but the patients loved it — its author being an old Laureate.

★   ★   ★

Around this time my mother brought an adorable collie puppy home from a farm with an unwanted litter — not the usual kind of farm collie, who might have wanted to do the right thing (like rounding up sheep or warning its owner of danger), but a collie mixed with less well-behaved breeds, such as Labrador and corgi.

To start with the puppy was called 'Sue' because the previous owner had called her Sue from birth. She'd named all the puppies after her siblings. Sue knew her name already and came to the call, but my mother wanted to change it — she'd known two really mean Sues and a rotten Susan. She told the previous owner she was going to change the puppy's name. The previous owner advised against it. She told my mother that she'd soon forget the two mean Sues and the rotten Susan but my mother doubted it — they really were exceptionally mean, the two Sues.

The previous owner said it might be just about OK to switch to a close-sounding name, like Susu or Lou. I suggested we try Suzy with a 'z' — us knowing a dear Suzy. Our mother considered all the options and held Sue's pretty little face, saying Sue, Suzy, Blue and Lou.

At home later with Sue, away from the previous owner and her draconian rules about name-changing and puppy-recall, we relayed all this to Mr Holt and my mother said, 'I mean, really, she's our dog now and it's not up to the previous owner to tell us what we can and can't call her.'

'Naming's half the fun,' I said.

'Exactly,' she said, 'and this dog just isn't a Suzy or a Sue. I'm going to call her Jeanette.'

I'd had a feeling it was going to be Jeanette because Danny would have been Jeanette if he'd been a girl. It came from a Virginia Woolf story, or maybe a song, but anyway, she loved it. Sadly, though, Jeanette didn't catch on for Sue — it was too long and Sue was already Sue. As hard as we tried, we couldn't call her Jeanette. I kept calling her Sue, Mr Holt and my sister kept calling her Sue, Jack kept calling her Sue, and in the end my mother gave up and officially named her Susan Penhaligon — after the actress from *Bouquet of Barbed Wire* (but who she'd first seen playing Juliet in *Romeo and Juliet* at the Connaught Theatre while on holiday on the South Coast in the 1960s). Sue for short.

You might think Mr Holt would have been cross about the extra expense of a dog but people in those days — even sensible ones — didn't see dogs like that. Dogs weren't seen as an expense.

Sue was very naughty indeed, she chewed Mr Holt's slippers and woke him up at night licking his cheeks and one time swallowed a sock and had to be rushed in the Snowdrop van to Mr Brownloe — who was like a vet, only unqualified due to dropping out of vet school for ethical reasons, and very cheap (if not free). Both of the qualified vets in the area were to be avoided because our mother had had sex with them in 1973 — before she'd got together with Mr Holt and had stopped being lonely in that way.

Mr Brownloe gave Sue a soda tablet and jiggled her stomach and said it would either fetch the sock up or send it down, or she might just die. Mr Holt was so worried about Sue he lost a whole night's sleep waiting for the sock to come up or go down (it did the latter). And although he was really tired in the morning (and accidentally buttered both sides of his toast) it showed how much he loved Sue, and that on its own made my mother cry with joy at the knowledge that they were in it together. Sue slept all the next day and never ate another sock.

A thing I'd noticed, over the years, was that however much people (men) said they didn't want a baby or a puppy, if/when it came to it, they usually fell in love with it quite soon (around the time it could catch a ball or laugh). And it struck me as a very handy way to go about things. It meant they got all the babies and puppies they might want but with none of the infinite, yawning responsibility that comes with wanting one. And this reluctance giving them the option of saying, quite reasonably, 'You wanted the fucking thing!' whenever they didn't want to help.

*   *   *

My mother was great fun and adventurous when it came to getting puppies and getting pregnant, but she could be stern and serious at times too. For instance, the day she got the letter from Miss Pitt informing her I'd finally been chucked out of the 'O' Level group. I'd been keeping my eye out for correspondence from school, as I was keen to keep Miss Pitt and my mother very much apart, but a letter had snuck through in the second post.

According to my colleagues, the van roared over the cattle grid and screeched to a halt at the back door. My mother stomped into the kitchen and asked for me. I was at the age when the sudden arrival of a parent — or any adult — could be quite terrifying. Especially if you'd heard they were in a hurry to find you and were foaming at the mouth.

I came into the kitchen and saw her standing there. She read the letter out, in front of a few others, and asked me what it meant 'in essence'. I thought of peppermint essence, as I always did when she said essence — which she did a lot.

I said it seemed to be saying — in essence — that I'd been entered to study for the less academic examinations, the so-called CSEs. And again she asked the actual meaning of this.

'It means,' I said, knowing she'd wail at what I was about to say, 'I shan't study Shakespeare but a challenging modern alternative instead.'

She did wail, like a cartoon. 'You cannot NOT study William Shakespeare,' she said, 'you know *Hamlet* backwards, you've seen a nude *Twelfth fucking Night* with me playing Malvolio in a body-stocking.'

'I know,' I said, 'but let's talk about it later.'

'You called your first guinea pig Queen Mab,' she said.

'No,' I said, 'you called it that, I called it Rosie.'

'But soft what light through yonder window breaks . . . ' she said, looking at me. 'Lizzie! But soft what light through yonder window fucking breaks?'

'It is the east and Juliet is the west?' I struggled.

'Juliet is the SUN!'

The other nurses all looked agog. Miranda

sniggered but the owner appeared suddenly in the doorway and said, 'Arise, fair sun, and kill the envious moon.'

And before you could say 'exit pursued by a bear' (and before I could warn her about the 'letter of commitment' she'd apparently sent) I was on the way to school, moving at speed in the Snowdrop van, with her ranting.

'I don't need this, Lizzie, just when I'm trying to get Danny off the breast.' And she gestured to her front.

In no time at all, we were standing in Miss Pitt's office. My mother, with Danny chewing on an Afro comb on her hip. Me, in full nurse's uniform and hat. Pitt, seated, looked calm compared to my denim-clad mother who, I now noticed, had damp coin-sized stains on her bra area. The room stank of Barleycup but my mother's smell (cigarette smoke and Je Reviens) did its best to mask it.

'I want an explanation,' my mother was saying, 'Lizzie is bright.'

It sounded strong until she rambled, 'We are a Shakespeare family, Lizzie's seen *Midsummer Night's Dream* in the round at Wicksteed Park with Joss Ackland and Ronnie Corbett.'

'That's most commendable, Mrs Vogel, but Lizzie fails to attend school on a regular basis and I'm afraid that is the criterion.'

'Well, she will attend from now on,' she turned to me, 'won't you, Lizzie?'

'Yes,' I said.

'Well, let's see how it goes between now and the summer holidays.'

'OK,' I said.

'I seem to recall we've been here before,' said Pitt, 'but I shall keep an open mind since it seems to mean so much to you.'

★ ★ ★

My mother drove back from the school like a maniac and yelled at me. She'd been so keen to yell at me she'd forgotten to leave me at school.

'A modern alternative to Shakespeare! No, Lizzie, you cannot study a modern fucking alternative.' She banged the steering wheel with the heels of her hands and went on, 'Why have you fucked up? I trusted you, I had faith in you — why have you done this?'

I wanted to tell her I hadn't fucked up. I wanted to remind her that secondary school was pure hell, it was dog eat dog, and I could barely survive, let alone thrive, in that atmosphere and that my reason for not attending was that I was at WORK, earning money for coffee and shampoo and other essentials that we couldn't afford because *she* had fucked up. She had been expelled from a good boarding school because she was combative with the house mistresses, secretly met boys in the town for sexual shenanigans and — as a last straw — threw fruit out of a dormitory window (wasting food in the 1950s was about as evil as you could get without murdering someone). Had she worked harder and achieved dazzling results she might have been able to demand the chance to go to university — like her brothers — instead of being

96

married off like a brood mare.

We bounced along the curving lanes between school and Paradise in silence for a while and I thought hard about my situation and how it had come to the point where I was probably on my way to fucking up.

I first began to not want to go to school around the time Danny was born. School suddenly seeming ridiculous and pointless if it just came down to this — conning a bloke, shitting a football and ending up with a gorgeous baby who needed every second and every ounce of you, all day, every day, and sometimes kicked his blanket off and had the coldest little feet and sometimes did a hiccup so strong he'd sick his milk up. And I skived off school a bit to be with them, partly to make sure everything was all right, but mainly because doing anything else seemed, as I say, ridiculous.

My mother didn't notice — the way a baby-less mother might have — probably because it was so nice having a teenager around. Danny would wake and I'd say, 'I'll go.'

I became expert at baby care quite quickly. I taught myself how to smoke without removing the cigarette from my mouth, for changing Danny's nappy — like my mother had for doing yoga.

'You're an endurance athlete, Lizzie,' my mother would say when I'd produce Danny all bathed and changed and chewing a crust. And it was like that. It was important work and I felt needed.

And then, when she went back to work the

first time — after having him — and would go off in the van at seven with a flask of econo, a packet of Ryvita and Danny in a tot-box, and the others would traipse off to school and the house would be empty and warm, I'd make toast under our tiny grill and have to shuffle the slices around to get an even toasting. And I'd spread it with Blue Band and the tiniest scrape of Rose's lime marmalade.

On my first day home alone I ate my way through a loaf of Sunblest and had to search all the nooks and pockets in the house to scrape together the change to replace it. I knew our opposite neighbour, Mrs Goodchild (my mother's ex-friend who'd seen her wee in the sink), would be able to see me going about my business in the kitchen, so I kept the strip lights off and stayed low. I had the whole week off.

Being alone was a strange new thing after fifteen years of jostling and barging, and silence was a mysterious luxury. I can't say I enjoyed it as such — I was lonely, and I didn't know myself in solitude — but school was worse somehow and every minute I wasn't there made it harder to go back.

On the Friday of that week, my mother decided she couldn't cope with being back at work after all and walked in the front door swinging the tot-box and saying she'd had it with the Snowdrop Laundry — they showed no support for working mothers — and she was going to start a pine-stripping business. I helped her drag a painted blanket box and a small varnished desk in from the back of the van and, after Danny had had a bottle and nodded off, she applied a thick layer of Nitromors to the blanket box and asked why I wasn't at school. I'd had plenty of time to think up an excuse but decided to tell her the truth.

'I couldn't face it,' I said.

She got us both a cup of econo-coffee and, while the Nitromors went to work dissolving the layers of gloss paint and filling the house with strong fumes, we discussed the world: people, life, babies, dogs and school.

'Don't screw up, Lizzie,' she said that day, 'please don't screw up.'

'No, I won't,' I said.

'Promise me I can trust you to have a great life.'

'I promise,' I said.

And, at the time, I'd meant it. But then only a short while after that I'd bumped into Miranda Longlady and we'd walked up to Paradise Lodge together and got the job.

My mother dropped me at work in time for me to start the second part of my split shift. I should have been doing double biology. Later she read me a short story she'd written entitled 'The Modern Alternative' about a girl on her way back in time to Ancient Greece, with only a Peter and Jane for guidance.

9

The Baby Belling

Mr Simmons was suddenly taken away. He wasn't fully officially convalesced (paperwork-wise) but the horrible Miss Pitt came and took him anyway. He hadn't wanted to go and there was quite some struggling and shouting and, if you believe Matron (and you couldn't always, as you know), Pitt darted him, and she and her pal, the family doctor, took him off. I watched as they helped Mr Simmons over the rickety tiles and down the steps, partially dragging him. She and I locked eyes and although it wasn't school time, and I was doing nothing wrong, I knew she had it in for me. I shrank away out of habit, and then — realizing that it was her doing something despicable, not me — I stood up straight and watched with my hands on my hips as she protected Mr Simmons' head before pushing him into the passenger seat of the doctor's car.

'Drive on, Roger,' she called. Then she got into Mr Simmons' Rover and drove away herself.

Matron was quite heroic and stood in front of the cattle grid with her arms out like Gordon Banks in his heyday. And only jumped out of the way at the last minute.

Later I was ordered to Room 8 to collect up all Mr Simmons' bits and bobs. As I folded that day's paper I was relieved that it wasn't me who had to break the dreadful news to the owner.

As well as being sad and disturbing, Mr Simmons' departure was part of a negative trend — to use the business parlance — because he was by no means the only patient to go. Three others also left around that time. All had gone to Newfields, and the gloomy talk the owner had delivered from the chaise longue began to seem less ridiculous.

This made the staff furious with the Owner's Wife. 'She's stealing our patients,' they said. And in a way, it was true. The patients' relatives would have seen the home's glossy leaflet and read about all the nice features that I've already mentioned (such as the close proximity of Bejam and the giant Co-op) and the less advertisable benefits (such as being permitted to leave your car in the car park free of charge for up to three hours). Previously, patients leaving Paradise Lodge (alive) had been unheard of, so this negative trend was extremely worrying. Especially as no new patients seemed to be forthcoming.

The departure of Mr Simmons had an immediate impact on everyone. He wasn't there to keep an eye on the Aga, check we had sufficient tins of grapefruit segments in the larder (and if not, drive down to Flatstone in his car to get some) and keep the kettle hot for tea and coffee at all times of the day.

Nurse Gwen gave the owner some home truths. 'The place is going to wrack and ruin,' she said, or something of the sort. 'Either you promote me to run the place properly or I have to leave, I can't work in this chaos.'

The owner called Gwen's bluff. He didn't think she'd really go and he wanted Matron in charge because her relaxed style suited him. So Gwen resigned and then left straight away without working her notice.

There had been over fifty patients in the home's glory days, apparently, when almost every day one of the local GPs might refer a male convalescent patient for a six-week post-operative stay and, nine times out of ten, the patient might stay a bit longer — or even forever — because they hadn't quite bounced back to their former state. Or, in some cases, because they liked the view of the reservoir, the idea of the view and all the goings-on and the scones and the pub and the nurses and *The Val Doonican Show*.

Plus, there was a seemingly endless supply of isolated elderly spinsters who hadn't married. Who, consequently, had no devoted daughter or son willing to help them remain in their own home or to take them in. So, lonely and vulnerable, they came for the views and the setting and the grandness of the old house with its creeper and its chestnut trees and the history and the tiles in the hall and the swirling banister posts and the smell of Pledge in the air. And all the promises of sketching and dominoes and bingo and fresh fruit daily.

And, as patients aged and died away, they were replenished with new Misses and short-term Misters — until now, until they started to go to Newfields.

And then, to make matters worse, Miss Boyd suddenly got ill and looked as if she'd need lots of nursing care and maybe the bed with a ripple mattress — which the owner had just sold and would now have to hire back, at great cost, from the cottage hospital. And Nurse Gwen, who had always nursed the very ill patients through their last days and hours, was gone.

And, as if the house knew something was wrong, the Aga went out and the fuel man wouldn't give us any coal until we paid the bill and Mr Simmons wasn't there to speak to him in his BBC voice, which was much prized for its unusual vocal creak and worked well for persuasion and broadcasting sad news.

The kitchen was cold and we had to cook on a Baby Belling.

10

The Pound Note

No one liked Matron very much; I think I've made that clear by now. No one saw the sad old woman that I saw. The main problem being that she was an ugly, fat, spiteful bitch and wore a girdle that felt like armour. Also, she was a snob — this was obvious and unhidden. She couldn't bring herself to use the communal coffee mugs and couldn't even bring herself to wash her own china teacups with the communal washing-up brush or dry them with the tea towel. She wiped them after use with a piece of kitchen paper and put them in a special corner of the mug cupboard.

She looked odd, and what a person looks like is the first thing you have to go on. She wore sunglasses inside and said strange, troubling things.

Her lying was the main problem, though. She thought no one could see her if she covered her eyes, and that made her think it was all right to lie and lie and lie. To be absolutely fair, telling lies in those days was more common. People lied more than they do today. I lied. People were deceitful, like my mother deliberately getting herself pregnant against the 'no more children' agreement with Mr Holt and thinking nothing of it and expecting him to think nothing of it. It was before people really believed that honesty was a good thing in a relationship. No one said to a newly-wed woman, 'Tell him you don't like the necklace, be honest, tell him you'd like to change it for something else.' And, 'Build the relationship on a solid foundation of trust and truth.' No one said that. It was thought better to smooth things over with a layer of fibs and just wear a necklace you hated.

Back then, people who didn't lie were known for it and seemed oddly honest and eccentric, or aggressive.

Matron's lying took the biscuit, though. Her lies were like the lies of a child — pointless and self-aggrandizing and without any sign of shame and never showing any planning or forethought.

But for all Matron's dishonesty, untrustworthiness and snobbishness and nastiness, I believed a few little snippets of what she told me and I couldn't help liking some bits of her flawed nature, and I liked that she liked me.

When Miss Pitt had me chucked out of the school netball squad for poor attendance, Matron offered to telephone Miss Barnes, the PE teacher, on my behalf — to say what a great player I was, which I was. And before that — when Miranda and I had played an important match against Longston School — Matron had turned up in her navy Matron's dress and all the accessories and cheered and cheered, whistled like a man, with her fingers, and called the opposition idiots and cheats. And though her being there spurred us on to win, it was never spoken of afterwards.

I liked that she *always* wore the Matron's dress and never anything else, because why would she when it really suited her? The navy blue and the white piping went well with her Irish eyes and no other colour was so flattering and no other style so easy to wear. And the pockets so handy for cigarettes and lighter and, of course, it took away the uncertainty of what to wear every day.

'Vicars wear their dresses every day and at the shops,' she'd said, 'so why shouldn't I?'

When Matron had told me on the drive that Mr Greenberg had invited her to become his live-in companion, I'd been pleased for her but felt it likely she was lying. It seemed implausible that this dear old man with his watery eyes, papery hands and his slightly shaky *Times* newspaper would want anything to do with Matron and her cussing and fag breath and hoop earrings. But something rang true and I hoped it was, because it would be the answer to Matron's prayers (literally — I'd heard her) and would mean once and for all that she could stop worrying about ending up in St Mungo's like her strange poor friend — who she never stopped referencing — who'd owned nothing but her name but whose name she could never remember.

Plus it would get her out of our hair. Also, it was well into the summer holidays by then and Matron's absence would guarantee more work for me — and Nurse Eileen would surely be promoted to Queen Bee.

I brought it up with Mr Greenberg on bath day — the subject of his imminent departure. To my surprise, he corroborated Matron's story fully. He said he was leaving on Friday-week and, yes, a nurse was going with him but he was confused about any more details. Nurse Hilary arrived with a jar of emollient after-bath cream and we heaved Mr Greenberg into the bath. Hilary hung around, which was awful because she told Mr Greenberg to wash his 'soldier'. And Mr Greenberg didn't realize she meant his thing.

'Make sure you wash your soldier, Mr Greenberg,' she chuckled, 'he's not going to wash himself.'

Afterwards Hilary commented on Mr Greenberg's seeming unreadiness to go home. 'How's he going to cope, on his own?' she asked. 'He's never going to be ready in less than a fortnight's time.'

'Oh, but Matron's going with him,' I blurted out, 'she's going to become his live-in companion.'

Nurse Hilary had been busily picking the hairs and flecks out of the Imperial Leather as we chatted but, hearing what I'd said, she froze — except for her eyes, which slowly rolled up and locked on to mine.

'How lovely. I am pleased about that,' she said, smiling broadly, 'but, Lizzie, I think we should keep this to ourselves, OK? I don't think Matron would want this broadcasting just yet.'

I agreed with Hilary. I mean, as soon as I'd blurted it, I had a feeling I shouldn't have and was mightily relieved by Hilary's sensitive response.

'Yeah, you're right,' I said, 'better not say anything yet.'

'No, we wouldn't want to jeopardize it,' she said, 'with things the way they are, financially.'

Which was exactly right. And though I'd always had a lack of respect for Hilary, I felt a nice bond between us and imagined us becoming friends, chatting, listening to her Jasper Carrott LP, flicking ash into her Betty Boop ashtray-on-a-stand. Which she'd found at the indoor market and had to bring back on the Midland Red and the driver had made her pay a full fare for it — it being so tall and lifelike and needing a seat of its own.

* * *

One day we'd run out of coffee, butter and Tio Pepe. The owner was drinking up the dregs from every bottle in the cabinet and had finished the gin and only had a half-bottle of crème de menthe left to go. It shouldn't have mattered because the catering grocer was due to call. He had been expected in the morning but arrived late — just after lunch — and then, he parked in the drive and didn't bring our order to the back corridor as he usually did. He tooted and looked at a clipboard and tooted again.

The cook went out and came back saying unless the bill was settled right then and there, in cash, he wouldn't let us have our order.

Matron stormed out and spoke to him through the driver's side window. 'We have upwards of fifty folks here, are you telling me we can't have our order?' she bellowed.

The catering grocer said that was exactly what he was telling her.

Matron went to the back of the van, opened the doors and heaved herself up. It took him a moment to realize she was in there and then the catering grocer jumped out of the driver's seat and up into the back. After a lot of shouting, the owner appeared — ashen-faced, with his transistor radio to his ear. He went to the back of the van and spoke to the pair inside. The catering grocer jumped out and gently helped Matron down and the three of them leant into the radio and looked as if the world had ended.

Elvis was dead. That's what it was. They came into the kitchen and one of them told the cook and she made a jug of coffee with tears dripping into it. Elvis had died and though the owner preferred Wagner and Schubert, music-wise, he said he wasn't sure he'd be able to survive in a world without Elvis and launched into a sort of Elvis lecture which included the revelation that he and his wife had bought a bunch of Elvis LPs for romantic purposes — her being a bit put off by German operatic song — and although the owner wasn't a fan of popular music (at all, and didn't even like David Bowie or the Beatles), Elvis had been the soundtrack to his love-making for twenty years and after his wife had left, and taken the LPs, he'd gone to the Esso garage and bought two Elvis cassettes, *Fun in Acapulco* and *Elvis for Everyone!*

The catering grocer sat at the kitchen table, leaning on his elbows, hands covering his face. I thought he might be trying not to laugh

109

— imagining the owner and his wife having intercourse to Elvis (like I was) — but he was actually moved to tears.

The owner paused to sip his drink but it was empty and he called out, 'O happy dagger! This is thy sheath; there rust, and let me die.' Which is the bit in *Romeo and Juliet* where Juliet kills herself. I couldn't quite see how it was relevant — being au fait with the play — but I didn't say anything and soon the catering grocer broke the silence by half singing, half speaking 'Love Me Tender' in a Brummie accent (which was highly relevant). The cook, Nurse Hilary and the owner joined in with the 'song' and were all choked up. It was honestly one of the worst moments of my life, worse even than my uncle's wedding where a woman sang an Italian solo to the bridal couple in front of the congregation. This was much worse because I was being paid to be there and is the closest I've come to prostitution. It wasn't that I doubted the sincerity of their grief, or mocked it. Far from it; it was precisely because I believed it. I quietly and respectfully did the washing-up from lunch so I could turn away and try to block it all out. I gazed out of the window and saw Matron by the grocer's van having a moment of private sadness and helping herself to groceries at the same time. All day people wandered in to talk about Elvis. Villagers went into the lanes in the hope of meeting someone and to be able to say they couldn't believe it. 'Only forty-two,' they'd say, and, 'The 'King' is dead.' And so forth.

110

The following day, I was dawdling through the
village, early for once, and pondering on the days
of the week. I'd come to terms with Elvis quite
quickly, not being a fan. I noted that Wednesdays
had always been my favourite day of the week.
Partly the name and partly afternoon games and
partly because of something to do with Winnie-
the-Pooh that I can't remember now. Anyway, it
was a Wednesday and I was just arriving at Paradise Lodge to start my shift and, walking into the
courtyard, I saw a troubling sight.

Mr Greenberg's Austin didn't have its car
jacket on. And had a whole load of stuff
crammed into the back. That wasn't troubling in
itself. It simply meant that today was going to be
the big move day for Matron and Mr Greenberg.
What worried me was that the stuff in the car
included Nurse Hilary's Betty Boop ashtray-on-
a-stand and a crate of Tio Pepe. It wasn't even
that Matron had stolen Betty Boop — I could
see why one would, it being an iconic,
once-in-a-lifetime possession — but she hadn't
even bothered hiding it with a stolen towel or a
counterpane. It was blatant.

There was a strange atmosphere and then, at
coffee break, you could tell Nurse Hilary was on
edge. She kept twizzling her bangle. She made sure
we were all together around the kitchen table
before she blurted out her shocking news. I thought
she was going to say, 'Someone has stolen my
Betty Boop ashtray-on-a-stand.' But she didn't.

'I have given the owner notice of my

resignation,' she said.

There was a gasp.

'I'm leaving Paradise tomorrow, to become a live-in companion to one of our gentlemen.'

Matron, who had been wiping her teacup with a piece of kitchen paper, looked up. 'Please God, not Mr Greenberg — proprietor of Greenberg's Bespoke Tailors?' she said.

'What other gentleman could it be?' said Nurse Eileen.

No one was that surprised — well, no one except Matron and me.

'But Mr Greenberg isn't fit for discharge until Friday,' said Matron, clutching at straws.

'He'll be with me — a State Registered Nurse,' said Hilary, blowing smoke through a tube she'd made out of her tongue.

'State Enrolled,' said Matron.

'State Registered,' shouted Hilary. 'Do you want to see my certification?'

'Yes, actually, I do,' said Matron.

'Well, I'll see yours first,' said Hilary.

And Matron backed down like an idiot who had no certification at all.

'I'd like to see your certification,' I said, more to show Matron I was on her side than an actual desire to see Hilary's papers.

'Well, you can fuck off,' said Hilary with a horrible sneer.

⋆ ⋆ ⋆

Then, on the actual leaving day, all morning Hilary kept nipping over to Mr Greenberg's

112

bungalow to take her bits and bobs and get it all nice before Mr Greenberg was there, bothering her. I saw her in Mr Greenberg's Austin with a heart-shaped floor cushion squashed against the passenger-seat window (*Love is . . . never wanting to be apart*) and a load of cuddly toys, plus a long lacy dress, draped across the back seats, like a dead princess.

Matron was very upset but crashing around trying to act normal, and then she gave up trying to act normal and turned Mr Greenberg out to wait for Nurse Hilary on a bench outside in quite a breeze. She stood over him and shouted that she couldn't stand to have him in the building. He'd already settled his account and the paperwork flapped around in his lap. He'd obviously noticed the black-stamped 'includes breakfast on day of departure' and he was in a bit of a tizz about his lunch.

'Shall I be taking lunch here, Nurse?' he asked.

'No, you won't be taking your lunch here, you'll be taking it at home with that immoral woman and good luck to you,' she said. 'I hope she fucking poisons you.' And with that she waddled quickly away before he could see her tears. Not that he'd have noticed.

I went out and told him that his new companion would be back soon and would arrange his lunch. And he asked which one it was going to be.

'Which nurse?' he asked.

'Nurse Hilary, the one with the funny legs,' I said.

'Oh, not the one with the dark blue dress?' he asked.

'No, the one with the white dress and the funny legs,' I said.

I went inside, got some coffee and biscuits on a tray and was about to go back out to him, but Matron called me back and asked who the tray was for.

'No!' she shouted. 'His live-in companion can sort out his food and drink from now on.' She flung the tray into the sink and turned to me, furious. 'And you owe me a pound note,' she said.

11

Egg Fu Yung

Now, four patients had left plus a couple of convalescent patients who'd been expected to stay on had gone home early, and Miss Granger had died. So the departure of Nurse Hilary and Mr Greenberg was a huge blow. Not for the patients, who found Hilary a bit brusque, but it was heartbreaking for Matron, of course, and a setback in her retirement plan. It was sad for the staff too, losing Hilary's nursing know-how, especially after losing Dee-Anna and Gwen. Mostly, though, it was extremely bad news for the owner, losing Mr Greenberg who — due to his superior views and incontinence — had been on the highest tariff.

It was obvious that without the Owner's Wife running it like clockwork, and Mr Simmons doing his bit, Paradise Lodge was going downhill rapidly. The staff shortage was getting worse and the laundry wasn't getting done. Also, because the catering grocer had stopped calling due to unpaid bills, and the cook was working only sporadically and to suit herself, we were having a lot of 'pudding only' days. On these days lunch would be just a hot fruit pie, such as apple and raisin, with custard, due to there being hundreds of catering tins of apple and raisin pie filler in the larder, plus endless custard powder and milk

115

always being available. If a patient asked awkward questions about the savoury first course, they were told they'd just had shepherd's pie and peas but must've forgotten all about it. And none of them seemed to mind, the pudding pies were that delicious.

Just one or two days after Mr Greenberg had left, we had an acute meal crisis. There was nothing for lunch except ginger cake and tins of marrowfat peas. This hadn't been noticed until gone 11.30 and the patients normally had their lunch at 12. We couldn't give them apple pie again — we'd had pudding-only days twice running already, plus we'd run out of Trex and flour.

We found some ancient tins of oxtail soup but the patients couldn't manage soup with a spoon and couldn't face drinking it from a cup — we'd tried before and it was just cruel to put them through it. Only Mr Simmons had ever coped with soup and he wasn't there any more.

Miranda uncharacteristically took charge. She phoned Mike Yu at Good Luck House, in Kilmington, and spoke to him on the telephone in the hall with us crowded round, listening.

'We've run out of food, hun,' she said.

We could hear a garbled phone voice, which must have been Mike because why else would she have said 'hun'?

'We've only got some ginger cake,' she said.

More garbled Mike phone voice.

'Could you?' she said, nodding vigorously and smiling at us. 'Oh, hun, would you?' And then she placed her hand over the mouthpiece and said, 'Mike's going to come over with some egg fu yung and Chinese chicken legs and chips.'

We all cheered and Mike must have heard and Miranda swelled with pride.

'OK, see you in a minute,' she said and hung up.

'Mike's going to come over with some egg fu yung and Chinese chicken legs and chips,' she said again and we cheered again.

Sally-Anne set the table for lunch in the day room and the patients were all pleased to see her. 'Is it lunchtime, Nurse?' they asked, and Sally-Anne mumbled back, 'Nearly.'

And then we all waited in the driveway and we cheered again when Mike Yu's Datsun Cherry clattered over the cattle grid. Miranda swelled with pride again and we all chased the car into the courtyard. Matron said it was just like wartime when the baker took a wheat delivery or someone arrived with sugar or chocolate. And it was a lesson to us that a little bit of hardship could cause brief, intense joy. Mike Yu came across the courtyard loaded, arms to chin, with boxes of hot food. You could smell it straight away. Mike couldn't quite see where he was going with his chin tilted up like that. He felt his way forward with his little feet and peered over the boxes. In the end I took his elbow and guided him over the cobbles and then I said, 'Mind the steps,' as we went inside and I continued guiding him over the flags. I can't describe how it felt — slightly pushing Mike along by the elbow — and, knowing of his subtly sexual repertoire, I wondered if I was doing

117

something erotic. We served the food quickly on to warmed plates, with a few marrowfats on the side, and carried them through to the day room like silver-service waiters and Mike shouted after us, 'Tell them it's omelette, they'll love it.' And they did.

After the patients had had theirs, the staff had theirs and it was really delicious. Mike Yu couldn't stay and enjoy the wonderful atmosphere because he had a statistics exam that afternoon and he drifted away almost unnoticed as the staff chattered and ate and laughed. He kissed the top of Miranda's head and grabbed his car keys.

As he passed me, I looked up and said, 'The egg fu yung was delicious.'

And he said, 'I'm really glad, Lizzie.'

I watched him go and accidentally smiled after him a bit too long. Then, glancing at Miranda, I saw that she'd seen. She looked at me as if to say, 'I saw you looking at Mike and now I know something.'

★   ★   ★

The laundry became a huge issue. It's funny how it always does. Laundry really messes people's lives up — you'd think they'd have come up with a solution by now. The laundry woman had left suddenly when she saw the owner in the nude after his wife had left and she took it badly (both things). She truly believed the owner had targeted her with his nude walk-by outside the laundry room. Which was nonsense, he'd just

118

wanted a top-up of Bath Olivers, that was all, and he'd taken the obvious short cut from his quarters to the larder — in the nude, because it was so hot.

The rest of us had seen him in the nude numerous times and hadn't taken it personally. He was genetically Scandinavian and nudity means nothing to them — ditto suicide, which was more of a worry.

The patients' dirty clothes had ended up in a huge, damp wee-smelling pile in the corner of the laundry — by the time we discovered the pile, and realized it included pretty much all of the ladies' dresses, they were too smelly to fish out and reuse.

For a couple of days the ladies had to stay in their nighties, which they hated, and Miss Brixham had cried and insisted on wearing her coat just in case the Vicar came to call, which he didn't. Anyway, after that, I volunteered for laundry duty to tackle the backlog and had to let Sally-Anne do the teas, which I'd taken over with much success. I wasn't happy about it because I'd come to like doing the teas, and I especially worried that Sally-Anne's teas wouldn't be soft enough for the patients on a soft diet. Or nice enough in general — the tea being the highlight of the day for almost all the patients. I worried even more that her teas might be better than mine and that the softs might eat even more of hers. She was a dark horse.

One of the reasons I volunteered to do the laundry was because I'd had some experience and knew the pitfalls. Twice, as a child, I'd flooded a whole house, I'd discoloured whole baskets full of clothing and I'd been barred from a launderette in Longston for over-soaping. Anyway, my early experience paid off because it wasn't long before I'd got it under control and began to find a great sense of satisfaction. I taught myself many tricks. For instance, if you ironed before the garment was dry, that made ironing it so much easier. Soon I was ironing straight from the wash and hanging to dry after ironing. It was controversial for a while, because of all the steam, but soon I learned to open the windows.

'Your pores are really going to open in this humidity,' said Miranda, popping her head in one day. I didn't know whether or not that was a good thing so I shrugged.

At home I told my mother of my laundry triumphs — her being a laundry van driver and yet temperamentally unsuited to *doing* laundry. I told her about the ironing-when-wet trick and about the hard-shake folding technique and about washing smalls in a stocking. To begin with she was disappointed and dismayed to hear me talking like this. She said I was getting caught up in what she called 'washing line syndrome' — a thing where a woman's immense pleasure from seeing her family's sheets and shirts pegged up on the line, billowing in the breeze, blots out proper ambition or desire for equality. But hearing about adding soda crystals to prevent 'heater build-up' sent her rushing for her notebook, wherein she scribbled SODA CRYS-TALS and underlined it twice. And later wrote a

120

beautiful poem about limescale and women, which included the lines:

It's not the son nor the daughter
Not the limescale in the water
But the line of dancing sheets
That will please her, then thwart her.

On a very hot day, at the tail end of the laundry crisis, a car tooted in the lane. I looked out. It tooted twice more. Then the driver came to the door and said he wasn't prepared to bring his much-loved car into the drive — not liking the state of our cattle grid.

He told me he'd picked up a senior citizen from the Royal and needed to offload him asap. I followed him out and saw Mr Simmons fast asleep in the back seat, a hospital tag on his wrist, beside him a small canvas bag and two framed pictures sticking out of a carrier, plus a polythene sleeve containing his medical notes in his lap.

I was overjoyed. I whooped and clapped my hands.

The taxi driver looked gone out. 'D'you know him?' he asked.

And I said, 'Well, he's just a patient who left, and now he's back,' and felt like a fool because my eyes filled with tears.

I woke Mr Simmons gently and he immediately tried to struggle up out of the car. The driver was eating a box of TUC and wiping his salty hands on his trouser legs, and had no intention of helping. Knowing the rule about not lifting patients on my own, I asked Mr Simmons to wait a moment and rushed indoors for help.

Matron was in the day room totting up her Embassy coupons — Miss Brixham (our best concentrator) was helping. She was a quarter of the way towards a mini picnic table with foldaway legs. I congratulated her and told her a convalescent patient had arrived in a taxi outside. I didn't say it was Mr Simmons because I didn't want to excite Miss Brixham and the coupons.

Matron said we weren't expecting anyone. 'Tell the driver to dump her somewhere else, or failing that, back at the Royal,' she said.

The taxi driver had come to the door and heard and yelled back that he couldn't take the patient anywhere else because he was due to deliver a box of Hamlets and some After Eights to Engelbert Humperdinck's mansion on the Oadby bypass. Matron doubted it. She couldn't imagine Engelbert smoking — what about voice care?

And the taxi driver said they weren't for Engelbert himself but for some of his international superstar pals who were all over the place timezone-wise and couldn't get down to the corner shop. And he stomped off back to the car.

I followed him. Mr Simmons was fully awake now but looked grey and ill. 'It sounds as though there's no room at the inn,' he said.

'No, there's loads of room,' I said, 'it's just that the place is still in turmoil — worse since you went — and Matron's counting her fag coupons.'

He leant back into the headrest. I smiled and

asked if there was anything I could do. He closed his eyes and said quietly, 'Do you think I might have a glass of water?'

I dashed inside. Matron was securing little bundles with elastic bands. She frowned at me. 'I'm just getting him a glass of water,' I said.

'Him?'

'Yes, the patient — it's Mr Simmons,' I whispered, 'remember him?'

'Of course I remember him — you told me it was a woman — for God's sake bring him in, Nurse,' she ranted. 'I thought it was a lady.'

The taxi driver was there again. 'What difference does it make whether it's a bird or a bloke?' he asked.

'We've plenty of room for Mr Simmons,' said Matron with a sniff.

Nurse Eileen helped me get Mr Simmons into a wheelchair and we tried to wheel him in via the French windows, but the wheels were too weedy to take the ramp and, after a few attempts, Mr Simmons got out of the chair and entered on foot. Matron pretended to go through his paperwork. Mr Simmons was her first patient admittance and I could tell she was all at sea.

'So, Mr Simmons, it says here in your notes you're a broadcaster,' she said. 'Is that something to do with farming?'

'No. Radio and television broadcasting,' whispered Mr Simmons in his poorly voice. Tiny, perfect white flowers decorated his hair from where I'd wheeled him slightly into the shrubs flanking the drive.

'Ooh, that's good,' said Matron.

'I've had an inguinal hernia repair,' said Mr Simmons.

'Do you know Val Doonican, at all?' asked Matron.

'I know of him,' stammered Mr Simmons.

'But you don't *know* him, as such?' asked Matron.

'Not personally,' said Mr Simmons.

Nurse Eileen and I went upstairs to prepare Room 8 for Mr Simmons. No one had been in it since he left, so it only needed a quick freshen up. The sheets looked fine, so we turned the pillows over and got busy with the Haze and fly spray. I wiped the leaves on the weeping fig and gave it some water and soon Mr Simmons was sitting in the Morris chair by the smaller window (his choice). I took down the two pictures belonging to the room — a woodcut of Blue Boar Lane and one of Leicester Guildhall — to make room for the ones he'd brought with him. One a sketch of a Sopwith Camel, the other a dauby oil painting of a shifty-looking, cross-eyed spaniel sitting beside a small table.

'This is nice,' I said, holding up the spaniel. It was awful really but I wanted to be nice after all the confusion and upset. It actually reminded me of the dog called Turk that had bitten my baby brother for no good reason. Although I didn't recall Turk being cross-eyed.

'It's entitled 'Olaf with Cracker',' said Mr Simmons. 'It was painted by my late wife.'

'Lovely,' I said.

'So what's been happening here?' Mr Simmons asked.

I told him the catering grocer had given up on us and we were living off apple and raisin pies, and the owner had apparently been slipping in and out of a mild coma. Mr Simmons grimaced and said as soon as he felt up to it he'd resume quartermaster duties and he'd run errands to the wholesale supermarket. Meanwhile, we could scrump some of his early plums for the pudding pies to give everyone a break from apple.

I told him about the laundry crisis and my having been taken off the teatime duty, and I mentioned the death of Elvis but he already knew about it, which I thought a good sign until he asked what room Elvis had been in.

12

Mr Freeman's Parker Knoll Recliner

One of the golden rules I'd learned on day one was the importance of not making it obvious who your favourite patient was, nor your least favourite. Nurses must be like parents towards their offspring and never let it be known or felt — by anyone, not even the favourite. I was dubious because I could always tell whose favourite I was — or wasn't. There'd been a teacher at my primary school who'd liked me best in the class and I could tell by her little soft-eyed giggle after everything I said, and there was a riding instructor we'd had whose favourite I definitely *wasn't*. I could tell by a tiny hard-eyed sneer. Ditto our first piano teacher.

I knew instinctively and fundamentally and totally that I was my mother's favourite, not by any facial giveaways but just by the fact that I knew her so well. She'd never admit it, of course, and was adamant that she liked us all the same. She often said that if we all fell into the river she'd be really stuck as to whose life to save first. In fact, it was a constant worry for her.

Anyway, however imperative it was not to have favourites, I couldn't help liking one patient above the others. In spite of her age and difficulties Miss Mills was fun-loving and sweet, and even had a Leicester accent — and for that reason seemed ordinary, as well as normal. She was on the ball and had a keen interest in Mr Callaghan and the trades unions and so on. All in all, she might have been an old woman you'd meet in the street, or someone's granny. Her legs were set hard, bent at the knee due to some joint-seizing condition — like arthritis, but permanent and constant. Miranda used to say it looked as though she'd been squatting for a wee and the wind had changed direction.

I'd first met Miss Emma Mills on day one when I'd been asked to do the comfort round on my own. Miss Mills had been snoozing in a wheelchair with a crochet blanket over her knees. As I'd leant over to ring her bell for assistance, she'd woken and clapped her hands to her heart.

'Fanny-Jane!' she cried. 'Well, I never did,' laughing a calm little laugh, 'Fanny-Jane!' And she scrabbled her knobbly fingers through her hair, fished out two kirby grips and patted her hair.

'Hello, Miss Mills, I've come to take you to spend a penny,' I said. 'I'm just waiting for help to come.'

'Oh, Fanny-Jane, you still look like Miss Moppet the wide-eyed kitten.' And saying it made her chuckle. It was the kind of joke old people made — completely unfunny but a bit personal. And for all the time I knew her, she fully believed me to be her sister, and to begin with I used to tell her I wasn't Fanny-Jane, but every time she saw me she'd light up and say, 'Ah, Fanny-Jane.'

At first I hadn't known whether or not I

should go along with the Fanny-Jane thing. Nurse Eileen said it was kindest not to contradict her, but not to enrich the delusion either. So, as time went on, if Miss Mills said, 'Oh, Fanny-Jane, look at the summer moon,' which is the kind of thing she'd say, I'd gaze up at the moon and say, 'Oh gosh, it's lovely tonight.' I never went 'into role' as Fanny-Jane, though Fanny-Jane became my nickname for a while.

★ ★ ★

After Nurse Hilary and Nurse Gwen left, the staff shortage at Paradise Lodge got considerably worse — obviously. Matron, being too chaotic and gloomy to sort the problem out properly, simply put Miranda and me on the rota more and more often. Miranda started to feel at home at Paradise Lodge, and as long as she kept patient contact to a minimum, she was happy. Mike Yu — after the egg fu yung success — had started to be a sort of unpaid helper and hanger-around too, which was very nice.

It all suited me down to the ground. Paradise Lodge was where I liked to be and the more I went there, the less I liked the idea of going back to school after the summer — back to being patronized and belittled and asked to spit out your Mint Imperial in front of the class when, the day before, you'd powdered a lady's under-bust area with Cuticura to prevent fungal infection and earned £2.80 towards a quirky mechanic's boiler suit — with Castrol GTX and

128

SPT badges — you'd seen in Chelsea Girl for £6.99.

However much I liked Paradise Lodge, I never fancied doing a night shift, and knew my mother wouldn't like the idea of it either, but one day a crisis arose and there was apparently no one else available.

'You'll not mind doing a night shift, will you?' said Nurse Eileen.

'On my own?' I asked.

'Yes, well, except we'll all be upstairs in our quarters watching telly or doing whatever we all do,' she said, 'or at the pub.'

'Perhaps I should do it with someone first so I know what I'm doing?' I said.

'No, you'll be fine. Just do the milky drinks and collect the teeth and then the night's your own,' she said. 'You can watch *The Streets of San Francisco* or whatever's on.'

'*The Streets of San Francisco* isn't on any more,' I said.

'The night's your oyster really,' Matron butted in.

So it was that the following Saturday night, when Nurse Eileen had gone off to the pictures with her boyfriend — who was trying to grow a moustache and looked vile — and the others had spilt out into the lane to go to the Piglet Inn, I was standing on a low stool stirring a cauldron of milk on the Aga (which we'd got going again thanks to Mike Yu sourcing some coal) to make the Horlicks and cocoa.

The 5 till 8 staff had put everyone to bed who needed putting. The sprightly patients were

129

watching *The Val Doonican Show* with Matron — who was mad on Val Doonican and said he was the most relaxed television presence she had ever encountered and that was down to his having confidence and pride in his hair. Or they were relaxing out of bounds in the owner's conservatory with an Ulverscroft Large Print.

Doing nights was like starting all over again. I went round with the bedtime drinks and realized I should've made them that bit hotter because I had a few complaints about them being lukewarm.

I had to feed Miss Lawson with a spouty cup and that took ages because she was lying down already and I didn't want to choke her. In the end I had to fetch Matron to help me lift her up on to her pillows.

Afterwards Matron was annoyed. 'I don't want you bothering me when I'm watching my programme just because you're too puny to lift a patient,' she moaned.

And I didn't say anything but felt helpless and told off.

Mr Simmons could tell I was a bit anxious and downcast and followed me into the kitchen to offer some clear and sensible advice, a thing he was very good at.

'You want to get the spouty drinks done before you start the main drinks. Then you get the milk good and hot and then take the upstairs drinks round and then the downstairs. And then you have a drink yourself,' he said, 'that's how the real night nurses do it. Then you collect the cups, wash them up and get the breakfast trays

130

ready for the morning.'

Matron had come back into the kitchen and seemed irritated by Mr Simmons' advice-giving, and took over.

'I thought you were convalescing, Mr Simmons,' she said in a snippy tone, 'off you go now.'

She tapped the breakfast tray list that was stuck to the side of the big fridge. The list detailed exactly what each patient had requested for breakfast when they'd first arrived. One patient, for instance — Miss Tyler — had asked for a kipper and a cup of Earl Grey. But Matron was only showing me the list to tell me to completely ignore it.

'Just give everyone the same and make life a lot easier for yourself,' she said.

She suggested a small dish of tinned grapefruit segments, bread and butter with marmalade and a cup of tea. She even helped me butter and marmalade the bread, ready for the morning.

'Now go and get settled in the lounge, Nurse,' she said, 'I'm off to bed. Night, night.'

★　★　★

At about 10 p.m. I was helping Miss Mills with her corset. We'd forgotten to take it off before getting her on to the bed and it had twisted round the wrong way and she was stuck on her back with a hundred tiny corset hooks all grabbing the counterpane.

'Keep still,' I said, 'I have to roll you over a bit.'

After I'd released half of the hooks an upstairs bell rang and rang. I sped up the job in hand but the bell still rang and rang. I hurried out to see who was ringing. It was Mr Merryman in Room 7, a convalescent patient in a private room. I couldn't ignore him — him being quite normal and with a broken wrist in plaster and a telephone by his bed. It would be just my luck if he ended up ringing the police. Which he'd done once before — apparently mistaking Matron for an assailant — and a constable had arrived and we'd had to explain it was a false alarm.

I asked Miss Mills to hang on and took the stairs two at a time. When I got to Mr Merryman's room the door was locked. I knocked and called and knocked again. Eventually, the door opened a bit and there stood Matron looking like something out of a *Carry On* — all flustered and as if she'd been having sex under the covers — while Mr Merryman lay in bed looking as if he'd seen a ghost.

'Thank you, Nurse,' said Matron, trying to block my view of the room. 'Mr Merryman is fine now, he just needed some help with his cot-sides.'

Matron reminded me of my mother briefly and I gave her a slightly puzzled look — not deliberately, but while my mind sorted out what I was seeing.

'Go on, fuck off, you nosy little bitch,' she whispered.

I went back down to the ladies' ward to untangle Miss Mills and got another telling off.

'You go running upstairs, Fanny-Jane, like

132

they're royalty up there,' she moaned, 'and I'm left here, stuck on my back like a cast ewe.'

A while later Matron came down to make herself and Mr Merryman cups of Ovaltine. She apologized for swearing at me. 'I'm sorry, Nurse,' she said, 'I'm suffering from terrible mood swings, it's the change. No hard feelings?'

'It's fine,' I said and left her to it.

I settled back in Mr Freeman's corduroy Parker Knoll in flat-out mode and watched telly for a while . . .

*   *   *

. . . and woke to see Mr Simmons looming over me.

'You're cutting it a bit fine, Nurse, if you don't mind my saying.'

I jumped up and saw the telly flickering and the clock showing nearly seven; I'd had a full night of uninterrupted sleep. Mr Simmons, seeing I was a bit groggy, switched the telly off and opened the curtains.

He continued to be exceedingly helpful and, between us, we got the breakfast ready. I was surprised at how easily he lifted the ten-pint catering teapot, walked across the kitchen with it and filled the cups, not all at once, but dipping and lifting and in full control without a single drip.

'I fell asleep,' I told him, 'I've been asleep all night.'

'Yes, so I gathered,' he said.

'I feel so guilty,' I said.

133

'It's all right, you'd have woken if a bell had gone,' he said.

'Yes, I would,' I said. 'I definitely would, I'm a light sleeper.'

I felt relieved to have been honest and then so reassured. It was an unusual feeling for me.

We took the trays round to the wards and rooms together but Mr Simmons didn't like to come into the ladies' ward because of them being ladies, in their nighties, and because Miss Brixham had taken a shine to him and would call out obscenities and do her smutty laugh, which embarrassed him.

I took a tray to Miss Mills first — her being my favourite — and she was in a very grumpy mood. She said they'd been ringing their bells on and off all night. They'd had night creatures in the ward — two foxes, she reckoned — scampering around and rummaging through her corsets.

I said it must have been a dream but Miss Boyd had had the same dream and I couldn't deny there was a foul smell in there and the French windows were wide open.

I decided I hated night duty. I suited daytime shifts, when other people were around and nothing could go wrong.

13

Bubble Writing

On my next day shift, Matron — who was supposedly in charge — had gone off to an agricultural show with a convalescent patient called Mr Dallington, and that left just Miranda and me on duty with Sally-Anne on call upstairs with the telly and a cucumber face pack on.

During the second part of my split shift, around 7ish, I was getting the upstairs patients ready for bed — and particularly helping Lady Briggs, who'd got a hairbrush tangled in her hair — and the downstairs bells were all ringing like mad. I ignored them for a while but eventually had to go down and investigate. All hell had broken loose in the ladies' ward. Miss Mills had been left on the commode — she said for over an hour — and was wailing and shrieking that the pot was cutting into her buttocks and she was in agony. Half her insides were hanging out, she said, she'd been there so long, and there was a fly buzzing around her. Some of the other ladies were telling her to be quiet and others were trying to lift her off and she was hitting them with her handbag.

I rang for help and waited. I rang some more and then went to look for help. There was no one around. The owner was either asleep or dead on his settee with some awful choral music on the

135

gramophone. Sally-Anne wasn't in her room. I finally tracked Miranda down but she was on the drive in Mike Yu's Datsun Cherry doing the face kissing. I was too embarrassed to approach and interrupt. To be fair, it was that time between bedtime and when the night nurse came on duty — the thirty minutes or so when nothing much happened, usually.

Miss Mills was heavy (maybe twelve stone) and unwieldy but in spite of this I decided to lift her off the commode single-handed. I knew it was against the rules but I didn't feel I had any choice. I'd tried to find help, I'd even run over to the pub to see if Gordon Banks was available. He was playing a darts match.

In my defence, Miss Mills looked smaller and less heavy in her chair, all held in with corsets, and it wasn't a lift so much as a chuck from commode to bed. I put the screens round her bed, waited until the other ladies were in bed and whispered to Miss Mills, 'I'm going to lift you on to the bed.'

I rang the bell a few more times just on the off chance and waited, but still no one came. I hooked my arms under hers.

'Oh, Fanny-Jane, you can't lift me,' she said.

'I thought half your innards had fallen out, I've got no choice,' I said.

And she said, 'Very well then, Fanny-Jane, but I'm damned heavy, don't hurt your back.'

I took a deep breath, I lifted her forward and slightly up and swung her round so that her bottom was on the very edge of the bed, and we remained like that while I got my breath. I tried to slide her back on the bed, to safety, but the little tufts on the counterpane worked against me.

Her great big knickers were tangled around her ankles and her hard, bent legs wouldn't let her sit down properly. It was like working with Action Man or Sindy — she didn't quite fit the real world.

'Just, shuffle your bum back, if you can,' I panted.

'I can't shuffle it,' she said, 'I'm crippled from the waist.'

And then she toppled forward and her face was up against my face and I was holding her weight but my feet were slipping and we both went down and even though I cushioned her fall, she took it badly — not that she shouted out or cried, but I could tell.

We lay together on the floor, her pinning me like a wrestler, and she said quietly, 'Oh, oh, I'm a goner, Fanny-Jane,' and I said, 'No, you've got years yet.' And she said she wished I were right because she longed to see the mauve lilac tree just one more spring and smell its lovely scent in the evening air.

And her wishing about the lilac was unbearable because I had no idea what she was on about but thought it meant she was going to die and the lilac was a heavenly vision before death.

I tried to wriggle out from underneath her but she did cry out then and I saw her leg was at a funny angle — sort of the wrong way round — and the words from a hundred telly

137

programmes rang in my head, 'Don't move the patient.'

'Are you all right, Nurse?' called Miss Boyd from the far end of the ward.

'Yes, thanks, Miss Boyd, the hot drinks will be through soon.'

'Shall I ring my bell?' she asked.

'Yes, yes please, that would be good,' I said.

I knew not to try and get up but I grabbed hold of the bell cord and pulled the bell to me and rang it and rang it. I held my finger on it and heard it tinkling weakly from the bell board in the hall. We lay there for what seemed like hours.

Miss Mills didn't cry or call out. I spoke soothing words to take her mind off the situation and I waited. I looked at the room from this new angle. The leggy metal-framed beds on their knobbly casters. The underside of the mattresses and the erratically tucked-in sheets — some tucked, tightly, all the way under, others bunched up and messy. I saw Miss Lawson's waffle blanket dripping off the bed and, in the other direction, I saw a dry triangle of bread and marmalade under Miss Mills' bedside cabinet. Miss Mills saw it too, 'Ooh,' she said, tutting, 'look at that, what a clumsy old thing, I must have dropped it, I *am* sorry, Nurse.'

I saw where the floor covering ended under the skirting and noticed a long tear in it. All this chaos bothered me. I ran my finger underneath and prised the khaki lino away; I pulled hard and tore it more and lifted it up to see the floor beneath. Underneath were the most beautiful tiles. I think I went slightly mad and wanted to

138

see the tessellations, so I ripped it further. Miss Mills' eyes swivelled in their sockets and I thought she'd died but she hadn't, she was just trying to see the tiles and, like me, she'd gone mad.

'Look at the tiles, Miss Mills,' I said, 'you won't see nicer in the Alhambra.'

'Fanny-Jane,' she groaned, 'fetch that old piece of bread out that I've dropped down there, I'm so ashamed of it.'

'I'll get it as soon as we're up,' I said.

The screen shielded us from the other ladies, except for Miss Lawson who grinned at us. The bell tinkled weakly in the hall and Miss Mills stopped looking at the tiles. Nobody came.

Miss Mills was in a bad way and getting worse. I could feel the drops of perspiration on her frozen skin and her mouth was shaking so much her teeth were clacking together; she was like a cold little child. Her cheek against mine. At one point her teeth fell right out of her mouth and lay on the floor like a joke in front of us — not together neatly but wide apart like a Monty Python cartoon.

After a while, I realized I'd stopped ringing the bell, so I began ringing again. I'd pulled the counterpane off the bed and arranged it over us as best I could, and I cushioned the side of her head with her pretty crocheted blanket all bundled up, but she was cold.

No one came. I paused and then started ringing again. Eventually, Miranda's voice came from the doorway. 'What!' she snapped in an angry and annoyed voice.

I was so frightened I just said, 'Help.'

She came over and peered at us and asked what had happened. I told her to call an ambulance. Miranda looked horrified, she dragged another blanket off Miss Mills' bed, flung it over us and dashed away. I started to cry.

'No, Fanny-Jane,' said Miss Mills. 'It'll be all right, I promise.'

Miranda came back. 'Shall we try to lift her?' she wondered.

I said, 'No, definitely not, let the ambulance men do it.'

And Miranda was wonderful then and started chatting like you do when something awful has happened and you want to take a person's mind off it. She said she was so sorry she hadn't answered the bell but she'd been kissing Mike Yu in the car (at least she was honest) and after that she'd been making him a birthday card and just needed to get it finished, and the problem was she'd committed herself to bubble writing.

She chirruped on and on and it was perfect.

Mike hated shop-bought things, especially the fake greetings in shop-bought birthday cards, but really appreciated a gesture. She'd drawn the card herself — a horse rearing up in a heart meadow — and had written: HAPPY BIRTH-DAY MIKE YU. ALL MY LOVE MIRANDA X.

All in bubble writing, each letter a different colour and coloured in with shines and shadows. It did sound impressive and I pictured it in my mind, but I wished she'd answered the bell before Miss Mills' teeth had dropped out of her

140

mouth. And then I wondered why she hadn't done it in Cantonese or Mandarin or whatever his language actually was.

'Keep talking,' I said, 'please, keep talking.' Because it was true, it did take your mind off the situation.

Miranda continued, quite like a maniac, and it was perfect and much needed and the best thing she could possibly have done and I'll never be able to repay her for it.

She told us that she'd offered to have sex with Mike for a special birthday treat but that he'd turned her down. Not because he found her unattractive, far from it (they'd had numerous dry rides and kissing marathons), but Mike Yu didn't believe in sex before marriage because he was afraid of losing something. Something long term, important, philosophical and possibly Chinese.

I wondered briefly, out loud, if he might have that phobia where the man imagines the vagina has teeth like a shark's mouth, or even a hamster's. Miss Mills murmured 'vaginas'. And Miranda said she'd heard of it but didn't think Mike had it. He was phobic about cows and daren't go for a country walk in case he got trampled, but he seemed fine with vaginas.

I agreed with Miranda. I couldn't see Mike Yu having a phobia of vaginas either. Why would a man with that particular phobia keep picking a girl like Miranda up in his Datsun Cherry? Surely you'd keep away from girls in short nurse's dresses, wouldn't you?

After some time, the talk got less interesting. I

mean, no one could keep it up forever and soon Miranda was dredging up stuff about her family. The time her mother tried to kill her father with a Flymo and once, when her father had accidentally unplugged the deep freeze, she'd called him a 'bandit', which made me rock with laughter, and that had hurt Miss Mills and that made me cry. Miranda carried on, though, like a hero. About her sister, Melody, my ex-best friend who'd gone manly in puberty, as previously mentioned, and thanked God for punk arriving so that she could join in with fashion and feel she belonged without trying to look girly.

Eventually, we heard the telltale clanking of the cattle grid and knew the ambulance had arrived. Somehow Matron appeared at the same time and acted professional. Miss Mills was lifted off me by two big men and strapped on to a stretcher on wheels.

Miranda helped me up and I leant on her as we watched Miss Mills being wheeled away — one of her bent legs sticking up, as usual, and the other not — and heard the clanging of the doors and then the clanking of the cattle grid. No one went with her in the ambulance. She went on her own. I was relieved not to have been asked to go but soon became troubled at the thought of her alone without her teeth or her blanket. I think I ranted about it for a while.

'She's not alone,' said Matron, 'she's got the medics with her.'

'But she doesn't know them and they don't know her. And what about her wheelchair,' I whined, 'and her teeth?'

'She won't need a wheelchair at the Royal, she'll go straight on to the ward,' said Matron. And because I was worrying, it was decided I must be in shock so they poured me a large glass of sherry, and lit me a Consulate.

Later, someone rang from Leicester Royal Infirmary to inform us that Miss Mills had a suspected fractured femur and concussion and would be staying in hospital for the time being.

'I'll go and visit her in the Royal on Saturday — I'll take her teeth,' I said.

'I thought we were going roller-skating Saturday?' said Miranda.

Matron butted in. 'She'll be dead by Saturday anyway.'

★   ★   ★

I didn't want a lift in Mike Yu's Datsun. I walked the mile and a half home — slightly downhill all the way, until you got to my actual road and then it was a short, sharp uphill climb.

I tried to keep my mind busy. I noted that the hawthorn and blackthorn hedges along the Collington Hill for a quarter of a mile, which had been brutally layed the winter before — when the sap was down — now looked wonderfully thick, neat and safe. The village had been shocked by the loss of so many trees in the lane but it had worked well and the animals were safe from the road. You had to admire the farmers.

'She'll be dead by Saturday.'

I hated Matron. Why did she say things like

that? Miss Mills was going to be fine — she'd only broken a leg. We'd talked about lilac and lino and she'd seemed intrigued by the vagina phobia. But Matron saying that had frightened me. It seemed so true-sounding.

At home one of my mother's relatives had called in. It was most unusual for him to be at our house; relatives never called on us and we only ever saw them at family occasions. I didn't feel up to seeing him. He was one of those over-educated, soft-spoken types who don't seem to mind that everyone's uncomfortable around them just as long as they're always in the right — like a killjoy kid who won't jump on the furniture even though there's a wonderful game in full swing, and it spoils the fun for everyone.

I crept upstairs, lay on my bed and smoked two cigarettes, one after the other. Then, looking out at the empty space behind our house where three beautiful elms used to be and the line of greyish washing that had been there, hanging from mildewed pegs, since Monday, I prayed and prayed that I hadn't just killed my favourite old lady.

I must've been in shock or, more likely, tipsy from all the anti-shock sherry, because I crept downstairs into the hall and did the most extraordinary thing. I took the telephone out on to the front step — as far as the lead would reach — and vandalized it swiftly with a boot heel, until the dial-prevention lock fell off. And then, sitting on the step, I dialled Good Luck House — whose number I knew by heart.

Mike Yu answered. 'Good Luck House,' he

said, in a busy voice.

I stayed quiet.

'Good Luck House,' said Mike again. 'Can I help you?'

I hung up, replaced the phone and listened at the sitting-room door. My sister was awkwardly talking to the relative about her various holiday jobs.

'I worked on Easter Day this year,' she said, chirpily, 'but Christmas Day is more important than Easter, so I didn't mind.'

'Whaaat?' said the relative, laughing. 'More important?'

'I mean, in terms of having to work,' said my sister, now uneasy.

The relative laughed more and louder. 'Christmas Day is more important than Easter, is it?' he said. 'Try telling that to Christ!'

I burst in.

'Telling what to Christ?' I asked.

'Oh, hello, Lizzie,' said the relative, startled.

'Try telling what to Christ?' I said again.

'That Christmas is more important than Easter.'

'No one gives a shit about Easter round here,' I said.

My mother gasped (not at my swearing, at my anger). 'Are you all right, Lizzie?' she asked and put her palm to my forehead, pretending to be concerned.

'I just miss the elm trees,' I said. I hung my head and stood there in the middle of the little room. The relative coughed and said he'd better be off and I didn't even look at him.

When he'd gone I apologized. My mother said it seemed as if I'd gone insane. My sister said it was as if I'd turned into my mother. My mother had to agree. I told them about Miss Mills. My mother told us about the time she'd helped at a donkey derby and the donkey she was in charge of had gone berserk and kicked the Lord Mayor's wife in the head and it had ended up in the *Mercury*.

'Did she die?' I asked.

'No,' said my mother, 'but she never liked donkeys after that.' As if that was almost as bad.

★ ★ ★

The seriousness of Miss Mills' accident caused the owner to give one of his pep talks. Attending pep talks was always awful. It was like watching a foreign film and being obliged to respond normally to abnormal, confusing things. This pep talk, however, was more straightforward than usual. He told us we must be careful not to injure the patients and that losing Miss Mills really would be the last straw.

'We must make every effort to prevent losing the patients,' he said. 'Quite apart from the unpleasantness and suffering caused to Miss Mills, frankly we cannot afford it.'

He paused as if he'd only just thought of it himself and was taking it in for the first time.

'The death of a low-maintenance patient who might very well have years more,' he said, 'is terribly vexing.'

'She's not dead yet,' said Matron.

146

'True,' said the owner, 'but she's no longer here at Paradise Lodge and in all honesty we have to accept that we have — in effect — dropped below the bank's required minimum income. And, unless Miss Mills returns within a week, I think I will have to contact her solicitor and have her fees frozen.'

He was looking at me as he lectured. I didn't flinch or say, 'What you looking at me for?' as I would have at school or home. It would have been inappropriate in the circumstances.

Nurse Eileen spoke up and said that Miss Mills' accident was a result of the staff shortage and under-trained auxiliaries basically running the place. She told him it was now time to face the music and take on a senior nurse.

The owner said he'd asked Nurse Gwen to come back but she'd got a job working for his wife at Newfields and was doing a further diploma in palliative care just to add to the home's catalogue of wonderful features.

The owner told us that the two prospective convalescent patients who'd been to look round earlier in the week had decided to go to Newfields.

'So, please, let's all pull together and try to keep our existing patients alive,' he said, finishing up, 'and let's hope Miss Mills is back with us soon.'

I nodded along with the others and puffed away on Nurse Eileen's duty-frees, but in all honesty I couldn't have sworn I'd do anything differently. The owner then launched into a lecture on money-saving and was commending

Mr Simmons (who had joined us for the pep talk) for making trips to the wholesale grocers where he had discovered boxes of oatmeal soap which worked out at a staggering 3p per bar and a perfectly good sherry that was less than half the price per bottle of Tio Pepe and certainly more than half as good. Just then Lady Briggs' bell went and everyone looked at me. I excused myself and trotted upstairs.

'What's going on downstairs?' Lady Briggs asked.

'Nothing, we were just having a pep talk from the owner,' I said.

'But you look so upset — what's it about?' she said. And I told her about the accident with Miss Mills. Lady Briggs seemed shocked and angry. It was a strange thing — telling an old lady I was about to help on to the commode that I'd dropped and seriously injured another old lady doing that exact thing.

'It was an accident, she was very heavy,' I said, 'I shan't drop you.'

'But you shouldn't have been alone,' said the sensible Lady Briggs.

'I know, but I was,' I said.

'This place is going to the dogs,' said Lady Briggs, which had been said many times before but sounded strange and serious coming from her.

'We're doing our best,' I said.

★ ★ ★

It was Mike's birthday. Miranda had handed him the birthday card that she'd done all in bubble

148

writing and Mike had seemed really pleased. I wished Miranda hadn't given it to him in front of me — it seemed a bit intimate. They kissed on the lips but hardly touched lips. It could not have been more sexual but gave me no pleasure at all. I just felt a wave of nauseating jealousy and wanted to punch Miranda in the face.

Many evenings after work I got a ride home with Miranda and Mike Yu in his Datsun Cherry. Knowing how private he was, I felt a bit uneasy knowing so much about him — his kissing skills, hand-holding eroticism and the size of his feet etc. — I felt guilty, looking at his eyes in the rear-view mirror as he checked for vehicles behind before indicating to turn or pull in and stop. I felt sleazy. But it was better than walking.

Mike and Miranda often stopped in a lay-by on the way home before he dropped Miranda off at home because of her mother not approving. Usually they'd do that barely-touching kissing — unless I was there, in which case they'd just chat and maybe kiss once or twice while I had a cigarette outside the car and monitored the progress of various hedges. And I'd puff away and make up names for a pop band or my children or imagine what I'd do if I won the pools.

* * *

I went into town as planned with Miranda and her egg-twin, Melody, on the Saturday morning. They were going roller-skating first and then to look at clothes and lipgloss. My plan was to visit

149

Emma Mills at the Royal Infirmary while they skated and meet them for shopping afterwards (I was thinking I might look in C&A at macs and berets). I'd got with me Miss Mills' little crocheted blanket in a carrier bag and, though I knew hospitals were like furnaces, thought she'd like to have it. And I'd taken her teeth wrapped in damp kitchen paper to avoid shrinkage.

When we got off the bus near Granby Halls the Longladys got into the queue for a skating session and I jogged across to the Leicester Royal Infirmary.

On the way in, on the bus, I'd not believed in Matron's words. Emma Mills wouldn't be dead; it was the sort of deliberately unsettling, ghoulish thing she liked to say. She'd be on the mend and pleased to see me, and she'd hold the blanket to herself and ask if I'd brought any New Berry Fruits. But entering the hospital I started to think the worst, that she would be dead and she'd had no one there to speak soothingly in her last hours and minutes. I cursed myself for not coming before.

I went to Odames Ward and spoke to the nurse in charge. She was pretty with red hair and blue mascara.

'Miss Mills, Emma Mills,' I said, 'she came in on Wednesday evening.'

The nurse in charge leafed through a book and looked up at me.

'Are you a relative?' she asked.

'Yes,' I said.

'What relation?' she asked.

'Friend,' I said.

The nurse stood up straight then and closed the book. I had to be related, she said, before she could look at the book for me.

'But I'm a good friend, I'm her only friend,' I said.

The nurse shuffled papers and looked at her upside-down fob watch.

'I mean, not everyone has relatives, so does that mean they can't have visitors?' I said. 'Or people knowing how they are or if they'd like a blanket or fucking something?'

I shouldn't have said 'fucking' because then she slammed the desk with her hand and said she wouldn't be spoken to like that.

'The thing is,' I explained, 'I work at Paradise Lodge where Miss Mills lives and she thinks I'm her sister and she'll be wondering where I am — I've got her teeth.' I held out the little pink pot to prove it.

'Oh,' she said, softening right down, 'you're Fanny-Jane?'

'Yes, yes I am!' I said.

'Hold on here a minute,' she said and clipped off.

Soon a different nurse popped her head out of a doorway and peered at me as if the other nurse had said there was a clown in the corridor.

'Are you Fanny-Jane?' she called.

'Yes,' I said.

The new nurse came out and walked towards me, lips pressed together.

'I'm afraid Miss Mills died yesterday afternoon,' she said.

'Oh,' I said.

'I'm terribly sorry,' said the nurse, 'she did ask for you, but, I, we thought — '

'It's OK,' I said, 'I've got to go.' And I strode out into the street. I put Miss Mills out of my mind. Gone. Dead. Over. No one would be surprised. Matron had predicted it. There was no need to think about it again.

I crossed the road and stood at the entrance to the Granby Halls where I could see Miranda and Melody and a few others skating anti-clockwise, laughing, shrieking, red-faced. The song, 'Sugar Baby Love', and the thumping on the boards were so loud you couldn't hear the laughing and shrieking, you could only see it. They looked wonderful, they were good enough skaters to move along quite nicely, and they knew the song and mouthed the words and did a kind of routine.

I waited at the bus stop on Welford Road for the County Travel to take me back to Paradise Lodge. I didn't feel like trying on macs and berets after all.

I wish I could say I went to Miss Mills' funeral and tossed the crocheted blanket into the grave. But I didn't — we never went to the patients' funerals. I don't know why we didn't, we just didn't. It wasn't the done thing.

I found Mr Simmons reading in the owner's conservatory. He was engrossed and didn't notice me. Strictly speaking, the room was out of bounds for patients because there were no bells out there and, in theory, the staff weren't able to properly look after the patients out of bell reach. But he was there and I sat down opposite him.

'Hello,' he said.

'I've been to visit Miss Mills,' I said, 'at the Royal.'

He shifted round to look at me full on and the wicker squeaked horribly. 'How is she?' he said.

'She died yesterday,' I said.

'She died?' he said.

'Yes,' I said and I did a bit of sniffly crying. And he blinked rapidly and shed a few tears.

Without eyelashes, tears look different. Mr Simmons' tears started in the corner of his eyes and welled up in his baggy old eyelids and then they overflowed, in slow motion, on to his cheeks. He pretended it wasn't happening, stayed calm and didn't wipe or rub his eyes at all.

'I dropped her,' I said, 'it was my fault.'

'You did your best,' he said, 'you mustn't blame yourself.'

To change the subject I asked about his book. He lifted it to show me the cover. It was a business book called *The Naked Manager* and, in spite of the sexy title, looked boring as hell.

'Any good?' I asked.

'Very,' he said.

On the way out, I popped into the ladies' ward to pick up the dried-out triangle of bread and marmalade that we'd spotted under Miss Mills' bedside cabinet. As I was under the bed, reaching an arm underneath, I heard footsteps. It was Matron, I could tell by her stupid little feet — size three, navy-blue Kickers.

'I just heard about Emma Mills,' she said. 'I'm sincerely sorry.'

I stayed silent; I'd just managed to get hold of the bread between the very tips of my index and middle fingers.

'You're not to go blaming yourself,' she said, bending down to look at me.

I looked up at her. 'I don't,' I said. 'I blame you.'

Matron nodded and blinked for a while and then walked away.

I remained on that floor for a while, like a mad person. And then, because I couldn't face walking through the kitchen, I crept up to Room 9 and told Lady Briggs all about it.

PART TWO

Paradise Regained

14

Fiscal Confidence

Sister Saleem blew in on an east wind. Her little yellow Daf stalled on the cattle grid because she'd had no experience of cattle grids and imagined it best to slow right down instead of speeding right up. None of us knew who she was or why she had come because the owner had forgotten to mention it, and his forgetting — and Matron forgetting as well, or not having been told — was all the more reason to celebrate her arrival.

Sister Saleem didn't seem to mind having been forgotten, she just struggled along the narrow corridor with two suitcases, bumping the old paintwork, and a basket of fruit that her ex-colleagues had presented her with as a good-luck gift. She was all smiles and sweat patches. She'd come to make everything all right, but I was the only one who seemed to understand that then.

I began the introductions in the kitchen as if I were the oldest person there — everyone else was rendered speechless by her medical trouser suit (pale jade tunic and kick-slacks), her massive hair and the very fact of her.

'Hello, I'm Lizzie Vogel,' I said, holding out my hand, 'welcome to Paradise Lodge.'

'But you're only a baby,' said Sister Saleem,

taking my hand in both of hers.

'I'm an auxiliary nurse,' I said.

'I see,' said Sister Saleem, and looked at the assembly.

And after each of us had said who we were and what we did, Sister Saleem took a deep breath and said, 'It is very nice to meet you all. I'm Sister Saleem. I'm a trained nurse with a Masters in Business Administration gained at the European Centre for Continuing Education at INSEAD in Fontainebleau, France.' (I won't do her accent.)

'So, are you the new manager?' Matron asked, a bit defensive.

'Exactly, I am, and I have approximately three months to restore fiscal confidence and earn a loan from the Midland Bank.'

'Brillo Pads!' said Sally-Anne — which she'd picked up from me and sounded wrong in her mumbly voice.

It did seem like mostly good news, even though the unfamiliar words sounded extra foreign because of Sister Saleem's accent — which I couldn't place but might have been Ugandan or could have been German but was probably Dutch.

Straight away she started calling me 'Lis'. Not Lizzie, not even Liz, but Lis with an 's'. And I really liked it.

We all mucked in, getting Nurse Hilary's ex-room ready for Sister Saleem. Nurse Hilary had left some books and a Goblin Teasmade. Sister Saleem said Matron could take the Goblin Teasmade if she liked but hung on to the books

158

— two Agatha Christies, a book about owls and an illustrated book called *Missy Maidens and the Masked Spankers* with pictures of girls in stockings kissing each other while masked men with big hands stood by.

After that we had a coffee break and the owner joined us. Sister Saleem talked us briskly through her planned rehabilitation of the business as we leant over plates and ate the pineapple from her fruit basket — which she'd cut up with a meat cleaver. The owner's eyes were droopy and his nightshirt open to the navel; he didn't attempt the pineapple but smoked Gitanes to keep himself awake.

There were going to be different phases, Sister Saleem told us — probably five in all — and the phases would entail different remedial action, and by the end of the phases Paradise Lodge would be in better shape (she kept saying 'phases' but, as with my name, pronounced it not with a 'z' sound but an 's' — 'faces').

'And after twelve weeks, we might not be making a huge profit,' she said, 'but the downward trend will be corrected and there will be a solid base on which to build the future.' This is how she spoke. It was quite exhilarating but tiring as well — all the thinking you had to do.

⋆   ⋆   ⋆

On her first official morning Sister Saleem spent some time in the owner's nook going through the patients' medical notes.

159

The staff were called to a short meeting, before coffee, in which Sister Saleem berated us (Matron in particular) about the medical notes, which she declared 'inadequate and unhelpful' and gave us a short lesson in the management and use of these important documents.

Then, at coffee time, when the patients were sipping their morning beverages and murmuring among themselves, she appeared in the day room.

Ideally, Eileen or Matron would have issued a little warning beforehand but they hadn't known and Sister Saleem was suddenly there — in front of the fireplace — chin up, smiling, legs apart. No one — neither the staff nor the patients — had seen her enter the room and every single one of us jumped out of our skins when her voice boomed out: 'My Name is Sister Saleem.'

There were gasps and the sound of coffee being spat out, and chinking crockery as cups were hurriedly dropped on to saucers, and various coughing and choking and a sense of slight panic.

Sister wandered around the room, shaking hands and squatting in between the easy chairs to chat with the patients, and after lunch she had a series of more detailed interviews with selected patients — in a side room. And then, after tea, she went round the room and cut out every single foot corn with a sharp potato peeler. This was Sister's single most celebrated act and, if you've ever had a corn, you'll understand — and if you haven't, lucky you.

I can't deny that to begin with many of the patients were troubled by her foreignness. Mr

Blunt said something out loud about the Foreign that wasn't very kind and Eileen reminded him that Sister Saleem had left abroad to live here in England so she wasn't as bad as any ordinary foreign person (who just stayed abroad). Mr Blunt disagreed and said he'd prefer them to stay wherever it was they came from.

Miss Tyler asked Sister Saleem, out loud, what tribe she was from and everyone held their breath. Sister Saleem's reply sounded like elaborate tutting but was probably a joke because she doubled up laughing at herself.

It wasn't long, though, before the patients began to appreciate having a caring, intelligent, authoritative person in charge — they were dismayed by the ongoing chaos — and her qualities became the main thing about her. But however much they liked *her*, almost all of them disliked her trouser suit. Some said they couldn't even look at her bottom half.

At staff teatime on that first official day, Sister Saleem told us she'd had a 'super dooper day' and was very much on target. But then, after a few slurps of tea and the clearing of her sinuses, she shared important news about two of our gentlemen. Firstly, Mr Simmons had asked us to refuse any attempts by his stepdaughter to visit him — and, should he relent, Sister Saleem said he must be chaperoned.

Secondly, Mr Merryman, the convalescent patient in Room 7 would be leaving Paradise Lodge within the next few days. Nurse Eileen asked for an explanation in a slightly confrontational way — she was confused to hear that the upshot of Sister's first apparently triumphant day was the loss of one of our most profitable patients who had an en-suite bathroom and a subscription to two magazines.

Sister Saleem explained calmly that Mr Merryman wasn't happy at Paradise Lodge. 'Something has unsettled him and he is going to move on,' she said. That was all.

Matron hid her disappointment well but I knew it was a strike against her.

15

Eight Anadins

In spite of having settled into the chaos of Paradise Lodge, the arrival of Sister Saleem came as a relief to me. Things seemed exciting, on the up, and though there were some challenges — such as actually having to do some work and do it properly — I knew it to be necessary, and I'd been through this kind of change before when my stepfather, Mr Holt, had moved in with us and had insisted we clean our shoes and flush the toilet and so forth. And though these things had seemed like a faff at the time, we'd soon got used to them. Sister Saleem was having the same effect and we all knew that patients and staff alike would benefit and that things would be better. Things would be as wonderful as they'd been before the Owner's Wife had left. Maybe even more so.

Phase One began properly the following morning and entailed Sister Saleem sitting in the owner's nook and looking carefully at every single piece of paper in the building. The point being to gain a clear picture of the financial situation.

'I'm going to pick up the cat by its tail,' she said, meaning she was going to start with the paperwork, but the others didn't all get it and looked around on the floor for a cat.

163

For three whole days she sat on the owner's office chair reading paperwork in the semi-dark. Sometimes she swivelled right round and yawned out loud. They were authentic yawns, though, not the little fake yawns that Miranda used to do whenever she was showing off or lying. Sister Saleem's yawns were probably a consequence of her having entered a state of shallow breathing — probably out of boredom — and needing to get a blast of oxygen into her lungs. I knew all this from biology lessons and because I'm interested in the truth about yawning.

It was so bright outside that Sister Saleem had to have the blinds down with only slits of light coming through. We took turns taking her drinks of tea and coffee and lime cordial with ice cubes. One time she asked if I'd be so kind as to get her a milk and rum.

'Not the Bacardi rum,' she specified, 'use the Myers's from my basket.'

Cigarette smoke hung in the hot air. Paper dust and the smell of ink drifted through the house and reminded me of sitting against a radiator as a child in the Pork Pie Library, reading *The Wonderful Wizard of Oz* by Frank Baum, which was marvellous and took me one whole winter and I'd recommend to anyone, whether or not you like the film. Well, especially if you don't like the film.

At teatime on the third day Sister informed us that Mr Merryman's taxi was due. I was instructed to collect his cases and help him make his way to the hall. The car arrived to take him to

164

Newfields. Matron didn't say goodbye.

By the end of day four — or was it day five? — Sister had taken eight Anadins (four doses of two) and three rum and milks and she'd gone into spectacles. And we'd all had a glass of rum and milk — except Miranda, who didn't drink rum or milk (copying Mike Yu).

Sister Saleem had shown her stress via insulting the owner's Rembrandt self-portrait. 'Why would anyone want that puffed-up idiot hanging there?' she wondered. Eileen came to the rescue and draped it with a souvenir tea towel from a shopping centre in East Kilbride, where Matron had a pal.

Sister Saleem emerged from the nook briefly, from time to time, to telephone her cousin in private from the owner's sitting room. And one time she asked Matron to accompany her back into the nook. As you know, the nook wasn't very private and it was easy to lurk nearby and hear exactly what was being said. And that's what we did.

Sister's concerns about Matron were manifold. Firstly, she'd had numerous complaints — from staff, patients and the general public — about the inappropriately physical nature of Matron's conduct towards some of the male patients.

'I don't know what you mean,' said Matron. 'Who, where, when?'

'Mr Merryman, the Café Rialto in Leicester, where you had a three-course lunch at his expense, and former resident Mr Greenberg, robust cuddling in the car park at the Weetabix factory,' Sister went on, obviously reading from her notes, 'and Mr Freeman at a Gilbert and Sullivan concert at St James the Greater Church. Shall I go on?'

'No,' said Matron.

'I will tell you that I have had to let a patient go,' said Sister, 'for legal reasons, before his relatives involve their solicitor.' (Miranda mouthed 'Merryman' to the rest of us.)

Sister moved on. She told Matron she had searched the staff files with a fine-toothed comb and found absolutely no evidence whatsoever of her being qualified in any way whatsoever (she said 'whatsoever' twice). And, as far as Sister could tell, Matron had been recruited by the Owner's Wife in 1969 as chief bottle-washer. There was a pause then — when Matron might have defended herself — but she stayed quiet, which meant to us that she was guilty as charged. And though we weren't actually that surprised, we looked at each other — at first shocked, and then sad.

Matron was to be relegated to auxiliary — with immediate effect, Sister Saleem told her. Matron's response to that was a placid little, 'Right you are.'

She was no longer Queen Bee.

Shortly afterwards Matron joined us in the kitchen. She sniffed and, taking her tiny china teacup from its hiding place, helped herself to a measure of Myers's rum, drank it down quickly and said, 'C'est la vie,' in French.

Matron wasn't as devastated as you might think. The only noticeable difference in her demeanour being that she pontificated less. She continued to wear the Matron's dress and belt — and no other outfit. She did drastically and symbolically change her hair colour from obviously dyed black to a more natural (looking) straw colour. She did it herself in the staff bathroom using L'Oréal Preference, which I knew to be a good brand, and went from Gypsy Queen to Doris Speed in a matter of two hours.

One day soon after the relegation, as we were doing the beds in the ladies' ward, I mentioned it. It was an elephant in the room and I hate elephants in rooms.

'You seem to be getting on OK with Sister in spite of — everything,' I said.

'Yes, well, she has a job to do,' said Matron.

'And what about you — you know, your plans?' I asked.

'I'll have to try harder,' said Matron, and that could have meant a number of different things.

*　*　*

I shared the exciting developments with my family. My mother was most annoyed that I couldn't tell her where Sister Saleem was from (geographically). I explained that none of us had liked to ask — as if to ask such a question was rude. That made my mother even more annoyed.

'It's not rude to *ask*,' yelled my mother, exasperated, 'it's rude *not* to ask — she's your new work colleague, your boss, not a person in the street.'

My mother's world was part sonnet, part Bob

167

Dylan song and part boarding school dormitory. She thought everyone should share everything. She thought it was OK to buy a beggar a sandwich. She thought it was normal to jump into a river with nothing on and to chat to the girl on the checkout about instant mash and having better things to do than peel potatoes. She believed people should celebrate each other's exuberances and joys and stay up till midnight to share their pain. I think it came from being a certain age at a certain time in the 1960s and it feeling so wonderful to shake off the doom and gloom and disregard the rules. And she thought it was going to be like that forever.

Anyway, she considered it right and proper and absolutely imperative to ask a middle-aged black person where they came from — as if it had nothing attached.

I never did ask Sister any questions about her heritage or why she didn't eat certain meats or beetroot. And, apart from a few anxious enquiries from the most neurotic patients, neither did anyone else. No one asked which country she'd grown up in that had given her such a deep, Hitlerish accent and a love of cheese. No one asked about her family, her past or her friends. No one even liked to mention the weather — in case it led on to talk of hot countries. No one had asked if they could help her with the excruciating English on the medical notes she'd had to plough through. It seemed touchy and awkward — as if we were highlighting a defect, like Nurse Hilary's cow-hocks and pitted teeth, or a tragedy, like Sally-Anne's given-away twins.

Strangely, though, we all thought it perfectly acceptable to touch her bouncy hair. She told us it was water-repellent like a duck's feathers. But when we arrived for Gordon and Mindy Banks' charity fund-raising barbecue and dip she was already in the water, clinging to the ornamental bridge, and wearing a swim cap. So we were denied the chance to see it in action.

We thought it fine to look at her face preparations and discuss the pros and cons of differing nostril size. And to ask about the skin on her legs, which was shiny one minute and dusty like scorched earth the next.

★   ★   ★

All through Phase One, we came to dread Sister Saleem coming out of the owner's nook. Partly we wondered who'd be next for the chop, but also she kept noticing examples of bad practice. For instance, on the way to telephone her cousin in private she walked into a glass door that she hadn't realized was there and bashed her nose. She was furious at the lack of safety manifestations on the glass. She said even a dot of paint would be better than nothing.

Nurse Eileen took it personally and told her that no one had ever walked into the door before and maybe her eyes were unfocused due to being in the nook in the half-dark.

Eileen had taken slightly against Sister Saleem but, to be fair, she didn't try to influence anyone against her. Except to mimic her behind her back.

Sister Saleem had been trained in modern ways and she made changes on the spot, as and when, and she shifted things around in a most disruptive way. For example, she approached Miranda and me one morning in the day room.

'Why are the residents' chairs arranged thus?' she asked, gesturing at the circle of chairs around the edge of the room. Neither of us knew quite what 'thus' meant at the time.

Miranda began to babble and talk rubbish but I knew to be direct and honest, and said, 'What do you mean, 'thus'?' and Sister Saleem said, 'Like this, in a ring around the margin of the room — as if they are the audience of something that is going to happen in the middle of the floor.'

So I said, 'Because that's how it's always been.' And Sister Saleem's head went to the side while she translated it into Dutch, or whatever language she had in her mind, which gave me a further moment to think about it and quickly add, 'And the patients like it like this.'

For the next half-hour we rearranged the ring of chairs into little clusters of three or four with coffee tables dotted about, some by the windows and others by the fire and each with its own focus. The patients looked on, puzzled, and Nurse Eileen popped her head in and muttered 'ridiculous' under her breath. I must admit, the chair clusters looked attractive — like a coffee shop for hippies but with very ugly chairs. I wasn't sure it was right for the patients because it wasn't what they were used to and that was what they preferred. Always.

Nurse Eileen hit out at Sister one day, saying her father was a business manager and he knew never to make any changes in a new situation until week six — or later — by which time he'd have got the confidence of the entire workforce via trust-building chit-chat and cups of good old-fashioned tea. This didn't rattle Sister Saleem, she simply opened her eyes very wide, thanked Eileen for her ideas and said, 'Ah, if only we had the time for that palaver.'

It was unsettling, Sally-Anne said, meaning the atmosphere between Eileen and Sister. It was like having bickering parents. Miranda agreed, Mr and Mrs Longlady were constantly at each other's throats, apparently, trying to bankrupt each other on the Monopoly board and blaming each other for Melody going into punk after such a promising childhood.

One day, Nurse Eileen had thawed towards Sister Saleem, which was an all-round blessing. Sister Saleem seemed to know it even before Eileen did and gave Eileen a little pat, and somehow the little pat was the final thing that made Eileen like her. It was a curious circular situation. And then Sister Saleem was 100 per cent liked. Even Miranda, who found things to criticize in even the nicest person, liked Sister Saleem a lot — particularly, she said, on account of her arriving like Mary Poppins.

The owner liked her too. Except every now and again you might find him scratching his head and saying, 'Who is that curly-headed woman in the green trousers?' and Nurse Eileen or Matron would reply, 'It's Sister Saleem. You

171

recruited her.' And he'd say, 'Did I? I don't remember — I must have been in my cups.'

Sister Saleem's nursing trousers — the pale jade, drip-dry with patch pockets — had caused consternation from the off. The patients, you'll recall, having been aghast. The staff, on the other hand, had fallen for them when we'd seen her climb a stepladder, on the day she arrived, to unplug a portable telly and hadn't had to worry about anything silly — like showing her pants, or looking like Dick Emery.

Now Nurse Eileen and Sister Saleem had become friends, Eileen asked if she might order herself a pair of sea-green culottes and matching tabard from Alexander's, the workwear specialist, and we all joined in wanting them. Sister said she was sorry but the owner had enough unpaid bills. Then, only a couple of days later, she plonked a batch of the pale jade trouser suits on to the kitchen table.

It turned out that a hospital in Birmingham, where Sister had worked temporarily, had obsoleted them due to changing livery after merging with another hospital under the BUPA umbrella and going back to traditional all-white. Eileen was the first to change into the pale jade and looked superb. Actually, Nurse Eileen made the trouser suit look fashionable and attractive — she looked like a fashion plate (Mr Simmons' words).

I tried some but they were either too small or too big, and in the end I settled for a too-big top and too-short trousers. Miranda declined, saying one of the few nice things about working there was being dressed up as a nurse.

Next Sally-Anne tried on a trouser suit and, though it fitted well, I was dismayed to note that it looked all wrong on her. And I could see from the faces of everyone else that they thought the same. We didn't say anything until she was out of the kitchen and then we did. It was really sad, and I hate writing it, but Sally-Anne didn't suit trousers. It was to do with her stance (imagine an oldish man about to toss the caber). The trousers seemed to bunch up under her bottom. I felt so sorry for her — imagine not suiting trousers.

Matron said she would never fall for trousers. 'You see them in the catalogues, looking reasonable on a model with a perfect trouser-figure standing in a cornfield, but the truth is, they're going to look ridiculous on anyone who doesn't have the posture of a semi-ape.' The patients agreed and were appalled by the proliferation. Miss Boyd said trousers caused diseases and Miss Tyler said they were for deviants. The owner said it was vexing to see the staff going about like the crew of the Starship *Enterprise*. I felt very happy, though, seeing most of my colleagues in the pale jade, it seemed modern and sensible. In fact, the trouser suits gave us the sense that the place was changing for the better.

★   ★   ★

Sister Saleem very quickly instigated some other simple changes — such as the habit of taking our

173

coffee breaks sitting in garden chairs in the little orchard with our top buttons undone and a Labi Siffre cassette playing through the office window. Sister believed a lack of sunlight and decent music gave you the blues and that a dose of either perked you up no end. And some of the more daring nurses, including Eileen and a new nurse called Carla B (who I haven't mentioned yet), started wearing sarongs to go to the Piglet Inn and showing their tummy buttons. Not me, though — I went as far as a cheesecloth shirt with a tie waist but I was conservative when it came to clothing. I'm sorry to drop Carla B in like that. She was new around then, she had defected from Newfields and, though she had lots of gossip about it, was banned from sharing it with us for the time being. Nurse Carla was a year and a half older than me and seemed very grown up in some ways. She had a cowlick — and I felt it somehow unsuitable for a nurse to have a cowlick, the nurse's hats looking medically official but the cowlick looking like a disorderly little kid. Anyway, Carla B was there and she didn't mind showing her tummy button and tiny cleavage.

Sitting out in the garden was delightful and caused neighbours to wave and it helped us to appreciate our surroundings and Sister Saleem loved it. There were a few sunny days in a row and Sister Saleem commented on the patients not coming outside more often on warm days. It was true that when I first began at Paradise Lodge, back in May, the garden patio had been so pretty and inviting and a few of the patients did actually go out there and sit under a rug. But since then, the shrubbery had grown and become impenetrable, and it was true also that the patients couldn't see the bird bath from the windows — or the feeders, or the cows meandering along the lane back to Briars' barn.

Anyway, it was agreed that something must be done to make the garden more accessible to more of the patients. 'If the staff can come and sit outside and hear the birds and feel the sun on their skin, I think the residents should, don't you?' Sister asked us. And, not really needing an answer, she ranted about it until I butted in and said I'd do it.

'Ah, Lis, good.' She got up and announced to the patients in the day room that I was on the brink of renovating the garden and looking for volunteers to help. And I did do some gardening after that but it was too dull to describe in detail here, except to say it scratched my hands and, as with everything, it was the tidying up afterwards that took most of the time. And soon, thank God, Mr Simmons took over and seemed to love it more than anything else.

Talking further about the garden and the patients that lunch-time, I admitted that the patients weren't encouraged to sit in the garden due to the difficulty of getting them back inside in a hurry — to the comfort stations — should they need.

Sister looked up suddenly. 'What do you mean?' she said.

'It's tricky, getting them back inside, to the comfort stations,' I ventured.

'The comfort stations?' said Sister. 'What in the name of God Almighty are comfort stations, Lis?'

'The conveniences,' I said, 'the WC.'

'I know. But please, if you mean the toilets, then say the toilets,' said Sister. 'I can't keep translating.'

So I said, 'Yes, the toilets.'

And Sister Saleem said, 'Oh, if there's an accident — let the Lord judge us the way he sees fit.'

Sister Saleem's fury about the comfort stations/toilets provoked a rather aggressive and immediate ban on all euphemisms. You might imagine this was a good thing but it was unsettling and I actually thought it harsh.

'We can't talk like this,' she said, 'this is a medical establishment. We must call things by their proper name.'

I explained that the Owner's Wife had actually banned us from the real words and that it was the norm in England.

'But it is ludicrous,' said Sister Saleem, 'and confusing and unprofessional.'

And she told us of the wasted half-hour she'd had trying to help Miss Boyd find her bank book, because she was complaining of a problem with her ha'penny. 'This isn't even modern coinage,' she'd said and laughed, even though she didn't seem to find it funny, overall, and it was the nearest I came to a proper argument with her.

That evening I made her a euphemism translation card — to make up for the row — in

176

nice writing with tasteful but honest illustrations. It wasn't as easy as it sounds because some things I thought were proper terms were euphemisms and sometimes it was hard to find the real term.

Comfort station — toilet
Powder room — toilets
Cloakroom — toilets
Lavvy — toilet
WC — toilet
Powder my nose — go to the toilet
Spend a penny — urinate
Tinkle — urinate
Wee wee — urinate
Number two — open bowel
Do business — open bowel
Pass away — die
Pass on — die
Gone — died
Fallen asleep — died
Taken — died
Ha'penny — vagina
Tuppence — vagina
Twinkle — vagina
Downstairs — vagina
Sweetie — vagina
Place — vagina
Soldier — penis

I gave it to her and she read with a serious face and then she laughed. I've never seen anyone laugh so much. I felt silly for a moment but she thanked me and said I'd made her day.

She kept it in her pocket.

'Lis, this is wonderful,' she said, 'I love it, thank you.'

16

Harmony

While Sister Saleem was getting to grips with Paradise Lodge, a cloud on my horizon was the new school term and the question of 'O' Levels. I decided that within the parameters of continuing to work at Paradise Lodge (to use Sister Saleem's parlance) I would do my utmost to attend school. With hindsight, that seems unrealistic but, to be fair to my younger self, I had every intention of keeping up with my academic work at home. I was easily bright enough to manage both and I knew it was achievable because our neighbour, Lynda Good-child, had achieved a C grade in English 'O' Level and a diploma in Number at night school — in a year — while working at the Leicester Building Society and all the while shopping and cooking her husband's tea with home-made gravy. And she'd re-curtained the whole house and planted a row of tiny privets, which would one day be a screening hedge. Plus being pregnant half the time with baby Bobbi — and she wasn't a genius or anything.

Anyway, that was my plan (not the hedge or the hot meals, but the working-while-studying aspect). However, Sister Saleem's programme of change had hardly begun and I'd obviously not got the school-to-work ratio quite right because

Mrs Hargraves, the truant officer, pulled up beside me in the village on my way to work a late shift one day. School spent a lot of energy trying to keep pupils in school, such as sending Mrs Hargraves roaming the villages to pick up strays and bring them in — like the Disney dog-pound man.

I wasn't in school uniform but neither, thank God, was I in my nurse's dress. I told her I'd been to the dentist and that I hoped my mother had remembered to phone the school to report my lateness. Mrs Hargraves drove me home in her ugly white Ford and waited outside reading *Woman's Own* while I changed. Then she drove me to school. I was on her list of non-attendees, she told me. And could I explain my frequent absences? she asked.

I didn't tell her I had an important job and that I had no intention of going back to school full time, having become accustomed to a new standard of living. I said I'd simply been having the odd day off to help my mother who'd not long had a late baby and was finding it tough to manage everything since becoming addicted to short stories — reading them and writing them (which was true) — and it using up so much time she hardly got the baby fed. Which was half true. Mrs Hargraves responded sarcastically, saying she supposed we should be grateful it wasn't long stories my mother was addicted to.

At school, she walked with me to the Deputy Head's office, knocked twice and popped her head round the door. I could tell the two women were in bitchy cahoots. I heard a muffled conversation, including, 'Ooh, well done! Top marks, Jill.' And a lot of sniggering. Then Hargraves reappeared and told me to wait for Miss Pitt there in the corridor.

'Thanks for the lift,' I said.

'My pleasure,' she said, and winked. 'See you soon.'

'Not if I see you first,' I said.

Miss Pitt called me into her office and had another go at me about my erratic attendance. Her hair was a bit matted at the back, as if she'd been rolling her head about in bed with a troubling dream and hadn't had a hairwash since. I felt different towards her since I'd seen her being rough with Mr Simmons.

I felt superior. I hated her. And I was not going to let her beat me.

'So, Lizzie Vogel,' she said, 'here we are again.'

'Yes,' I said.

'Tell me please, Lizzie,' she was reading the back of a paperback while she spoke, 'that you do not have a burning ambition to wipe old people's backsides for a living for the rest of your life.'

'I might,' I said.

'A clever girl like you?' she said. 'Don't you think you should be aiming a bit higher than that?'

'I want to do my 'O' Levels,' I said, 'if that's what you mean.'

'Oh, good. So how about we help each other?' she said.

'What do you mean?' I asked.

'I agree to your coming back into the 'O' Level

group and you help me with my stepfather.'

'How?' I asked.

'Let me know what he's up to . . . when he's going to be in or out, or . . . at a concert,' she said, 'that kind of thing, just so I can keep tabs.'

'But he doesn't want to see you,' I said. 'You're barred from seeing him.'

'He says that, Lizzie, but I couldn't live with myself if I didn't make an effort,' she said.

'Mr Simmons barely knows you. But he knows you well enough to know you just want to control him,' I said.

I could see fury burning in her little eyes and though I felt strong, I blushed.

'Very well, Lizzie. Go back to your class now,' she said, 'and let me know if you come to your senses.'

I walked out of the office, out of the building, out of the school grounds and phoned Paradise Lodge from a tiny phone box near the Esso garage to apologize for being late. 'I've had an emergency dental appointment,' I said. 'I'm on my way.'

And then I jogged and walked and jogged again along the canal towpath. I walked past a pretty boat called *See More* and saw a kingfisher skim the water. And then, on the last bridge before mine, I saw Mike Yu standing, pointing things out to an old man leaning on the bridge. I waved.

'Lizzie!' he called, looking down at me.

'I've just seen a kingfisher,' I told him. I knew he'd be pleased.

And he turned straight away to the old man

182

and said in a loud voice, '*Pootong kew neow.*' And the old man looked out on to the water, breathing heavily through his mouth, and stared up and down. And then he looked down at me and smiled and bowed and thanked me with his eyes.

Mike began to help his grandfather into the passenger seat of the car. I called goodbye to them and walked on. Mike called out, 'Wait, Lizzie!' He spoke softly to his grandfather for a moment and joined me down on the towpath. We walked along and I asked how he was. 'I'm fine, thank you, Lizzie. How are you?' He was so polite and correct.

'I'm fine,' I said. And we walked in silence for a while.

We passed another boat, even prettier than *See More*. This one was called *Harmony*. Mike pointed to it. 'Harmony,' he said. We said how much we liked the boat, how smart the paintwork and how pretty the shutters, and how well-kept it was. And I said I'd love to float along in *Harmony* for a few days and forget all my cares and he said he would too and he wished we could.

'Harmony,' I said.

'Harmony,' he said.

And we smiled.

How could this day — that had started out so badly — suddenly be so nice? I wondered. How could I be watching the same dragonfly as a boy as lovely as Mike Yu, touching arms on the narrow towpath and talking about floating carefree in a boat called *Harmony*?

'Is your grandfather all right?' I asked.

'No, he's very unwell, I'm afraid,' he said. 'It has been most pleasant for him to come out here.'

'That's good,' I said.

'But I must go back to him,' he said. 'Thank you, Lizzie.' And he rushed back to the Datsun on the humpback bridge.

I reached Paradise Lodge and made my apologies for being late and in school uniform. I whistled as I worked. Miss Brixham complained and said I was no better than a crowing hen. But I couldn't help it. I was happy.

★ ★ ★

It had been a hot summer and was still hot. Though all of us liked the sunshine, we were all still a bit raw after the year before, when we'd been through the famous heatwave that people have never stopped talking and writing about. And though you'll be sick of hearing and reading stories built around it, I'll just tell you it was the year Mr Holt moved into our house and became our man at the helm and the heatwave caused no end of worry. It really started at the end of June and Mr Holt hadn't liked it. It wasn't so much the having to work in ridiculous hot weather but the frustration that he couldn't clean the Snowdrop Laundry vans due to the hosepipe ban that was soon in force. He liked things squeaky clean but he also understood the necessity for the ban. He said so and he'd never cheat it, like some neighbours did. As the heat continued, there was talk of extreme water conservation methods, which worried him even more, with laundry not being classed as essential. We'd had the elm trees chopped down earlier in the year and that had seemed symbolic, and now the freak weather made it seem that nature had turned against us.

And I was privately fretful, that hot summer, that being a step-parent was turning out badly for him, that somehow we three children were like the dusty vans he couldn't clean, the lawn that had perished away to hay and was then nothing but hard mud, and the beautiful, tall elm trees he couldn't save, and now the worry about future drought measures might be slowly tipping him over the edge, worry-wise. Mr Holt might leave, I thought, and we'd be back at square one, fatherless, which isn't as great as it sounds — back then, anyway.

Having a step-parent is stressful to start with — you always worry that the step-parent might change their mind and leave. If your real parent could leave and start again with another family, then why not the step-parent. That was how I saw it. But Mr Holt never did leave us and actually we stopped worrying after Danny was born because if he'd coped with having a surprise baby he was going to be fine with most things.

*   *   *

That's not to say there weren't problems and difficulties from time to time. And just about then — when Danny was around a year old and Sister Saleem was beginning to improve the situation at Paradise Lodge — my mother had a big argument with Mr Holt that she felt she'd never get over. She'd clipped a bollard at a complicated junction on the bypass, and to keep things simple she'd tried to make out that someone had hit the car while it was parked at Woolco. The problem being, a colleague of Mr Holt had seen her clip the bollard. In the row arising Mr Holt had called her a 'serial fantasist and compulsive liar' and then after that he'd said things that apparently couldn't be retracted.

She gave me the whole unabridged story as I washed out my new drip-dry uniform. It was so convenient — almost dry straight from the wash and not at all crumpled and no need to iron and such a fresh colour.

I felt strongly that the situation my mother found herself in was entirely her own fault and she'd made it worse by provoking Mr Holt into saying these non-retractable things. By saying, 'I suppose you regret taking up with me?' and that sort of thing. Anyway, she was going to leave, she said, if that was how he felt. Her plan was to go and rent a maisonette in town, near Gropecunt Lane so Danny could attend a Montessori nursery and become a better person than the rest of us. Not that that was how she put it, but that was the plan.

I was irritated by the whole thing. My life was here — a walkable distance to Paradise Lodge — and I didn't want to have to leave just so my mother could make Mr Holt regret being honest.

And have Danny become a better person than me into the bargain (the fate of the children of the first/failed marriage — constantly having to do things in order that the new, proper children can become better than their half-siblings).

'I'm not going with you,' I told my mother.

'Well, you can't stay here,' she said, 'not without me.'

Mr Holt was reasonable about it. He said we were welcome to go or stay as we pleased but that he'd like us to consider common sense and our mother's feelings — which, to be honest, was a tall order.

So she went. Not to a rental maisonette near Gropecunt Lane but to sleep on a Zedbed in Carrie Frost's titchy little flat near Leicester racecourse. Carrie wasn't a friend — as such — but actually an ex-employee. She'd been an au pair for us years before when she'd been gearing up for art school, and had taught us how to sing *London's Burning* in the round, which we still enjoy to this day. Anyway, my mother, Danny and Sue the dog went and we all just got on with our lives with Mr Holt. And though we missed her horribly, we didn't worry, as we might have, had she gone for the rental maisonette, which would have seemed permanent.

* * *

I was getting ready for work in the morning. Our mother had been gone a day and a night and the house didn't feel quite right. And though I wasn't desperately worried about her, I still had a nervousness in my throat that reminded me of all the awful things the world had done to her. All the men who'd had sex with her twice, even though she'd sobbed the first time, the man who'd punched her in the face with his elbow, the one who'd stolen all her money and the woman driver who called her a sissy because she daren't step on to the zebra crossing because a great fear had got hold of her. And the close relative who pretended he was going to strangle her when her mother wasn't looking, and called her an idiot because she'd believed him and cried.

Miranda appeared in the street opposite my house. We often found ourselves walking to and from Paradise Lodge together. I hated telling her anything personal. She had such a warped sense of things and might say, 'Typical of Mr Holt,' when she had no right thinking anything was typical of him because she didn't even know him. She had a way of extrapolating that was distorted and wrong.

I really didn't want to talk about my family with her, especially then. So, as usual, I brought up Mike. To be honest, if someone talked about my boyfriend as much as I talked about Mike Yu to Miranda, I think I'd feel a bit territorial or possessive. But Miranda didn't. She loved talking about him and suspected nothing.

I said, straight out, 'How's Mike Yu?' and that set her off on a wonderful ramble and I knew I needn't worry about it slipping out that my mother had run away with our baby and our dog.

That morning she told me that they'd been to see *Smokey and the Bandit* and how they'd devised a method of holding hands in a highly erotic way, squeezing and moving and wriggling and holding a single finger, touching fingertips on fingertips, stroking the other's palm with fingernails etc. Miranda said it was wonderful because no one could tell they were being erotic, and although it was unbelievably erotic she could still watch the film and take most of it in and eat sweets with her free hand.

'How is Mike's grandfather?' I asked, breaking the spell.

'Ugh,' she said, 'I don't know, but poor Mike's always having to cart him about.'

I didn't know what to say to that and we walked in silence until Miranda said, 'Mike's wonderful, though — he doesn't mind about me and Big Smig.'

'Mind what?' I asked.

'That I let Big Smig park his car in my garage,' she said. 'You know, when we were going out.'

'I thought Big Smig had a motorbike,' I said.

Miranda laughed then.

And I said, 'Oh, I see.' Because it was a metaphor.

★ ★ ★

Being at work didn't do much to occupy my mind. I managed to convince myself my mother was fine and would soon get fed up with Carrie's cramped conditions and poor taste in music and she'd come home. But other worries started crowding in. Firstly, Mike Yu. I felt sad, thinking of him not understanding Miranda's 'car and garage' metaphor — which he wouldn't, any more than I had — and probably thought the relationship between Miranda and Big Smig had involved the Longladys' car port. Not that it even mattered but I felt horrible knowing about it. And then, there was the whole 'O' Level thing and wondering if I should have been so combative with Pitt.

Lady Briggs said I looked pensive and asked me for my secrets. I didn't want to talk to Lady Briggs about my thoughts or secrets — she seemed too mad to understand any of it, or in fact to enjoy it — but I was sorry for her, having only me to talk to.

'I have nothing very interesting to tell you,' I said, 'except that I'm only fifteen and shouldn't really be doing this job and that my mother has left my stepdad because she's let herself down.'

'And will she come back?' asked Lady Briggs.

'Yes, I expect she's back already, she can't stand being away from home,' I said.

And Lady Briggs pointed to her secret telephone and asked if I'd like to give my mother a ring to see if she was home. I said no thank you. I knew I'd cry if she didn't answer or Jack answered it and then I'd have let myself down.

'She'll be back in no time. I'm not worried,' I said.

'So, why are you so sad?'

'I feel melancholy for some reason,' I said, and Lady Briggs held my elbow and stared into my eyes until her tagged eyelids twitched.

'I'm sad about Emma Mills,' I said and wished I hadn't said it.

'Emma Mills?' said Lady Briggs. 'What are you sad about her for?'

'I dropped her,' I said, 'remember, and she died.'

'Oh, yes, but I don't think worrying about that is a good idea, and neither do I think your mother's romantic entanglement should be uppermost in your mind. I'd guess that you are on the brink of falling in love, right now,' she said, clicking and spooky. 'And that's why you're melancholy.'

'I don't think so,' I said.

'Yes, yes, I'm certain of it. I'd say you are in love already,' she said, 'you just haven't realized.'

'Gosh,' I said (we weren't allowed to say 'God', or 'shit', in front of the patients). 'You sound like a witch.'

And she laughed. She was mad and spooky, and I vowed to stop talking to her as though she were normal.

17

In Love

The next day we had coffee break in the kitchen and Sister Saleem told us the Asian boy was outside in his car, either asleep or very sad. Miranda dashed out and appeared back in the kitchen with Mike Yu in tow. Mike had obviously been upset and was reluctant to come into the kitchen but there was no way Miranda was going to miss the opportunity to show him off in this romantic state — especially after the egg fu yung success — and she literally dragged him in and said, 'Erm, everyone, Mike's granddad has died and he's really upset.'

Sister Saleem offered her sincere condolences and a cup of tea. Mike dabbed his eyes with a proper hanky and Miranda answered for him, saying, 'Black, three sugars.'

I felt extremely sad. Too sad really.

'No milk?' Sister checked.

You could see how proud Miranda was of him not taking milk. It seemed so sophisticated and mature.

'He doesn't take milk,' she said, 'he has it black.'

The table was intrigued and Matron was irritated.

'The only milk he ever had was his mother's, wasn't it, hun?' said Miranda.

192

'I had some Angel Delight by accident once,' Mike said, being 100 per cent honest, as usual. And the table was delighted to hear such a charming thing.

He was holding it together and sipping his tea (black, three sugars) when the owner jangled in and said, 'Aha, hello, young sir.'

And Miranda said, 'This is my fiancé, Mike Yu. His granddad's just died.'

And the owner said, 'Condolences, condolences — he was a good Roman, I'm sure.'

And Mike broke down again and kept squeezing his eyes and saying, 'I'm sorry, I'm sorry.'

Miranda must have wished she'd persevered with learning the Chinese language and that she could say comforting Chinese things like, 'There, there, darling,' in Chinese, because all eyes were on her and Mike and it would have been impressive. But she couldn't and just said, 'It was a release, Mike, he'd had a good innings,' in English — and told us that the old man had been ill for some time.

The owner asked which nursing home he'd been in and how the fee tariff worked, and Mike said that his granddad had been at home with them all the time and that they'd taken turns to care for him. Miranda made a 'yuck' face behind Mike Yu's back and everyone felt extra sorry for him — knowing his life had been affected in this way.

'Jesus,' said Carla B, 'he was there, in your house, dying? Yuck.'

'Yeah, I know, and Mike had to feed him

mushed-up noodles,' said Miranda.

I kept waiting for a part of this to be a joke (or even a bizarre dream) but it wasn't. It was like something from J. B. Priestley — all these awful people, saying thoughtless things to this innocent boy in such grief and despair.

Mike Yu looked at me through his beautiful tears. It was as though he was thinking the same thing (that it was like something from J. B. Priestley) and I couldn't stop looking back.

'What was your grandfather's zodiac sign?' I asked, not that I was interested, but wanting to distance myself from the shallow madness of the others.

'He was born in the Year of the Rabbit,' said Mike, 'he was hospitable, graceful and sensitive.'

'And you know, Lizzie, down by the canal. Remember, the kingfisher? That was . . . ' he said, but couldn't finish what he was saying.

Miranda jolted to attention. 'When were you down by the canal?' she asked.

'Grandpapa and I met Lizzie, and she'd seen a kingfisher,' said Mike, and then to clarify for Sister who looked puzzled, 'a rare bird with some significance.'

'Did your grandpapa see this bird?' asked Sister Saleem.

'No, but he knew Lizzie had seen it,' said Mike, 'and that she had come to tell him he would soon be at peace.'

I had to get away. I mumbled something about hearing a bell, stubbed out my half-finished fag and dashed upstairs to Lady Briggs' room.

I was in love with Mike Yu.

18

Woman on the Edge of Time

My mother was still not home and I was missing her. And though I'd been feeling very mature in my new position in life (and in love) I'd still really, really hated her being away — probably sad and frightened and possibly having unwanted sex, though probably not (seeing as she was at Carrie Frost's).

I made a list of things to tell her about — including Matron's new straw-coloured hair, Sister Saleem's euphemism ban and the garden plan. I knew she'd wholeheartedly approve of everything and fall even more in love with Sister Saleem, whom she already loved for a variety of reasons.

I went to the phone box and rang Carrie Frost's number. Carrie Frost answered, which was inevitable but nevertheless irritating. She said our mother had that very minute left and was on her way home. Carrie was glad I'd rung because she wanted to give me some pointers about our mother's state of mind.

'Give her some acknowledgement,' said Carrie, 'she's just coming out of her post-natal slump.'

I had literally no idea what she was talking about — not knowing the term 'post-natal' — but I said, 'OK.' And drifted off while Carrie continued with some gibberish, which might have been useful except I couldn't concentrate, Carrie Frost was that kind of well-meaning idiot. I remembered an incident, years ago, when Carrie had been our au pair and Little Jack had wanted her to lift him up and had said, 'Carry!' and she'd said, 'Yes?' and he'd said, 'Carry!' again and I'd seen that there was a misunderstanding but hadn't the energy to explain. This was how my life felt at that moment. And then the pips went and Carrie called out, 'Be nice to her!'

By the time I got home, my mother was there, acting cool, and Danny was playing with a cloth octopus Carrie had run up for him with fabric scraps.

She apologized for having gone off but explained how easy it was for a woman to lose credibility and now she wanted the slate wiped clean and to make a fresh start with her credibility intact. And to read and discuss more contemporary writers and bake her own malt loaf to put in our packed lunches and not have to buy Soreen.

My sister told her that we loved her and didn't need her reviews of contemporary fiction or the malt loaf and I told her it had been utterly miserable while she was away, which was true.

'Did you have an OK time at Carrie's?' I asked.

'Of course not,' she said, 'but she did teach me how to draw people.'

And our mother demonstrated this new skill by sketching a quick person via a series of circular shapes. It was a fundamental tool of figurative drawing, she explained, promoted by all the great art schools and even the least arty people could get a decent result. I did notice that my mother's person had a very short neck but didn't say anything — remembering what Carrie had said on the phone — and I made a huge fuss of the sketch and so did my sister.

'Wow, that's brilliant,' I said.

'Thanks,' said our mother, proving how easy it is to please someone.

The feeling that she'd lost all credibility with Mr Holt was still uppermost in her mind. She knew as well as we did that this newly acquired drawing skill wouldn't count for much with Mr Holt, but for some reason she kept drawing people.

Credibility seemed a strange and intangible thing for her to dwell on. Ironically, none of us could be honest with her about it and had to tell her she'd not (lost all credibility) even though she most definitely had now lost the tiny shred she'd previously possessed. The thing we all knew — but which was difficult to say — was that she'd had barely any credibility to start with and none of us had ever minded. And that *realizing* she had none was actually a very promising thing — a sign of the beginnings of normality — after all her drugs and drink and terminated pregnancies etc. Though no one had the heart to put it quite like that.

My sister cleverly reminded her that credibility was ten-a-penny and that the village policeman had it in spades and what good did it do him? She had other things that most people could only dream of. Things you can only have (or be) if you're an extraordinary person. I said, 'You have art and music running through you like veins pumping blood to your heart.'

The mention of blood and veins gave me pangs momentarily about my biology lessons. Our new teacher had really brought it to life with beautiful illustrations on the board in pale pink chalk and said 'capillaries, oxygen and heart' as if they were poetry, not the workings of any old person. And I briefly regretted not being a dedicated scholar.

'You're an artist,' said my sister.

My mother responded by reciting William Shakespeare.

Alas! 'tis true, I have gone here and there,
And made myself a motley to the view,
Gor'd mine own thoughts, sold cheap what
    is most dear,
Made old offences of affections new.
Most true it is, that I have look'd on truth
Askance and strangely: but, by all above,
These blenches gave my heart another
    youth,
And worse essays proved thee my best of
    love.
Now all is done, have what shall have no
    end!
Mine appetite, I never more will grind
On newer proof, to try an older friend,
A god in love, to whom I am confin'd.
Then give me welcome, next my heaven
    the best,

Even to thy pure and most most loving
   breast.

'See,' said Jack, 'you've memorized that whole
poem.'

'Sonnet,' said my mother.

'Yes, not many people could just trot that out,'
said my sister, 'or want to.'

Mr Holt came in then and it was time for
dinner. We let our mother cook and, even though
we could see she was all over the place, none of
us dared help.

Afterwards the credibility thing came up
again, this time in front of Mr Holt, and you
could see he was a bit puzzled by it all. We tried
to tell her how extraordinary she was, that she
had a beautiful imagination and a conscience
that kept her up at night when she should be
sleeping. She had humour. She could see how
funny a thing was when no one else could see it
and when everyone else was frowning or tutting
or scared to death, there she'd be giggling and
gasping in a most imaginative way.

But she wouldn't hear it — the qualities we
listed counted for nothing in her eyes.

She wanted to *change*; she wanted us to be a
normal, happy family and her a normal mother
making malt loaf and hand-washing jumpers in
Stergene. We said we worried she'd throw away
her true self just to be like dynamic Mrs
Goodchild over the road.

Mrs Goodchild was nice and admirable with
her baby and job and home-made food and
curtains but had the habit of talking behind her

hand. One time she'd said to my mother (behind her hand) that I was looking pale. I knew what she'd said because I heard her, and even if I hadn't I'd have known because my mother responded, 'It's just her colouring, she tends to wanness.' Anyway, she and my mother had slightly fallen out when Mrs Goodchild took our washing in off the line one day — because the sky had clouded over and looked like rain — and took it into her house. But far from thanking Mrs Goodchild, my mother had told her, 'I'd rather you didn't do that again.' And then she'd seen my mother weeing in the kitchen sink, and told her she had, and it had become a much-mentioned thing in our house.

'I want to be like her,' our mother said, 'of course I do.'

'Why?' we asked.

'She talks behind her hand and has a miserable life,' I said.

We reminded her she could drive like a racer, turn on a sixpence and park in a shoebox (our mother, not Mrs Goodchild, who'd taken four driving tests but not passed yet). That she'd had simple, natural births and tanned easily, was a fabulous swimmer, a perfect diver and never felt the cold. She was green-fingered and good with animals. She had the voice of a nightingale and could sight-read and play the piano more beautifully than Bobby Crush. And she was brave. Brave like only the very alone can be.

My sister grew weary. 'Mother,' she said, 'none of us likes malt loaf.'

'But, I — ' my mother began.

'No, listen, Mum. You're worried because you're with Mr Holt and you've got Danny now and however happy the relationship is, the responsibility of being half of a couple is a big thing.'

'Yes, that's it,' she said, 'it's weakened me.'

'No, being with Mr Holt has *strengthened* you, but you have to stop acting as if you're on your own, stop misbehaving. Stop lying to him,' said my sister.

Mr Holt coughed to remind us he was there, behind his paper. And then made the very sensible decision to propose marriage.

'Elizabeth,' he said, letting his paper drop down so that he could look at her while he spoke, 'shall we just get married?'

And she said she was sorry to cry but being in a couple with such a straightforward machine of a man had really fucked her up, but yes, she would marry him.

And actually him wanting to marry her changed everything.

'I can finally get rid of the name Vogel,' she said.

My sister and Jack and I must have looked offended because she apologized. She'd been stuck with it since marrying our father. Her solicitor had suggested she go back to Benson but the thought horrified her and she'd rather be Mrs Vogel than Miss Benson. Now she was going to be Mrs Holt and saying it made us all laugh. Mrs Elizabeth Holt. That was when I first realized how utterly terrible marriage was. That only in being asked by someone could you truly value yourself and then it was all making gravy and curtains. I think I'd known it before but wasn't mature enough to put it like that. I vowed to marry only if I did the asking and if my sister could come, and no one else.

★   ★   ★

Mike Yu's college was still on its summer break. He had been helping at Paradise Lodge since he had a bit more time. Miranda must have found out that I'd been officially chucked off the 'O' Level course at school and brought it up in the kitchen in front of Mike.

'Lizzie's been chucked off the 'O' Level group, she's going to have to do the CSEs next summer,' said Miranda. Feigning nonchalance and doing one of her little yawns.

'Well, I'm not doing the CSEs,' I said.

'There's nothing wrong with the CSEs, they're legitimate qualifications,' said Miranda, 'for the less academic pupil.'

'Yeah, well I'm not the 'less academic' pupil, so I shan't be doing them,' I said.

Mike was aghast and said I must insist on being reinstated to the 'O' Level group as soon as possible. 'You must sort this out before next term begins,' he said, 'you must continue with your education at the highest level, Lizzie.'

'I don't know — ' I began.

'You're far, far too bright not to. You could do anything with your life,' he said. He was animated and passionate. 'If you drop out now, you'll be regretful and probably unhappy for the rest of your life,' he said.

202

Miranda butted in, jealously. 'She can go to Charles Keene College of Further Education and do a hairdressing diploma if she gets sick of being a nursing auxiliary,' she said.

'Hairdressing's a wonderful profession, but — ' said Mike.

'Yes,' Miranda interrupted him, 'imagine being able to cut and style someone's hair and change their life at the drop of a hat, literally.'

'But hairdressing's not for someone like Lizzie,' said Mike, 'Lizzie's an intellectual, she wouldn't be able to cut people's hair.'

Miranda reminded Mike that she was also under threat due to having already lost the best part of an academic year because of the glandular fever she'd had on and off throughout 1975.

'Lizzie's an intellectual,' Mike repeated.

'And I'm not?' said Miranda, hurt.

Mike said he was worried about both of us — but you could tell he really meant me and thought it would be fine for Miranda to drop out.

★   ★   ★

Later, Mike was still there, preparing a stew for the next day's lunch. The meat being such good value, the stew was going to have to be in the bottom Aga overnight.

'How come you're here so often?' I asked.

'I've been asked to lend a hand with the Aga and the cooking,' he said. 'It's not official,' he put a finger to his lips, 'but it's mutually beneficial.'

203

'You mean you like being here?'

'It's peaceful after the chaos of Good Luck House. The kitchen and the customers — who I respect — can be quite disruptive. With their noise and demands,' said Mike.

'I know what you mean,' I said, 'I like the quiet and being able to have a long hot bath on a split shift.'

'I like being here, especially I like the people,' he said.

'Especially Miranda,' I said.

'There's an energy here,' he said, 'a gentle energy and some love.'

'Yes,' I said, 'there is.'

'I think we have a lot in common,' he said, 'and that's another very nice thing.'

I got myself a glass of water.

'I meant what I said about school, Lizzie, you must put your education first.'

'I know,' I said.

'You might want to travel. And you don't want your husband to outflank you, do you?' he said, laughing playfully.

'How many 'O' Levels do you have?' I asked.

'I have ten, and eight of them As,' he said.

I left him to finish chopping the meat and was walking on air. I bumped into Matron who made a rude comment about him being there again.

'He's a sly one,' she said, 'surely he's needed at home. Bloody skiver.'

'No, he's not — he likes it here, the peace and quiet. It's mutually beneficial,' I said and marched off, blushing.

Everyone in my life felt strongly that I should straighten myself out, school-wise. My sister, my mother, my form tutor and Sister Saleem had all spoken to me on the subject, as had Miss Pitt and Mrs Hargraves the truant officer.

But hearing it from Mike Yu really made me think. He had absolutely nothing to gain from my actions. Mike Yu sensed something in me. And suddenly it felt as though my education should be a priority.

Mike had said so.

He'd called me an intellectual.

★   ★   ★

One result of my mother's running off to Carrie Frost's was that we almost missed Little Jack's birthday. Realizing this, close to the end of the actual day — the day Mr Holt had proposed — my mother rushed out and bought Jack some grown-up clothing and a book of poetry by Ted Hughes because it was all she could think of.

'It's poetry, but manly,' explained my mother.

And Mr Holt had tried to look neutral.

'But where were you?' asked Jack — no one ever told him anything. 'Where have you been?'

'She went to see Carrie Frost,' said my sister, 'and had an art lesson.'

Little Jack frowned. I knew his boy mind was whirring and he was remembering wanting Carrie to pick him up and her misunderstanding, thinking he was just saying her name. Not that it was her fault exactly, but it was frustrating and enough to make you mildly dislike her all the same. I could tell all that was going round in his mind. I knew him.

It annoyed me (the carry/Carrie thing) and I was annoyed further with Carrie Frost for spending two whole days teaching my mother how to draw people. Why couldn't she have taught her how to thread the needle on her Singer sewing machine? We all knew Carrie was a dab hand at dress-making and that our mother had the basics but lacked confidence on the needle-threading and casting off. Think what an enormous help it would have been had she come home from Carrie's saying, 'Let me alter that nursing tunic for you.'

There'd be no hunting for intangible credibility if she'd been able to say that. No need to make malt loaf or read Marge Piercy — unless she really wanted to.

Anyway, Jack seemed to like his clothing and Ted Hughes, and I gave him a Terry's Chocolate Orange and my sister gave him a PEACE badge — with a tiny dove and olive branch — and a bar of Golden Crisp. And our Granny Benson sent him a WHSmith token and our father sent him a cheque for double his age in pounds to put into the Leicester Building Society for a rainy day or driving lessons when he turned seventeen — whichever came first.

Mr Holt gave him the best gift of all. A Saturday/holiday job folding linens, sweeping the depot, cleaning vans, breaking or fixing pallets and oiling things. I should have been pleased for

Jack but the truth is, the luxury of sibling rivalry had come to us when Mr Holt had moved in and I was resentful of him having the perfect job handed to him on a plate — a job where he'd get a door-to-door lift into work and home again and was pretty much the boss's son and it didn't involve the general public or wearing a dress or a hat or Pop Sox or anything challenging at all.

19

Dream Topping

One day, as I entered the kitchen to help with the coffees, there was a note on the table that made my blood run cold. It had been written on one of Sister Saleem's official telephone message memorandum notes.

TELEPHONE MESSAGE
To: Lizzie Vogel
You Were Called By: Miss Pitt
From: Devlin's School
Re: 'O' Level examinations
Message: Please call back as soon as possible

It was horrible knowing Sister Saleem had had to write a message for me from this woman who was pretty much barred from the premises. On the other hand, I was certain I was about to get a full apology and be reinstated to the 'O' Level group — which was a good thing. I didn't phone Miss Pitt immediately because phoning was a big deal back then and not to be taken lightly and I needed to pluck up the nerve. I folded the note and put it in my pocket and imagined it coming in useful if any of this went to court.

When things had quietened down after milky coffees I went to make the call. Rather than use the phone on the special phone table in the hall with everyone around earwigging, I went up to Lady Briggs' room and asked if I could call from there. She said, 'By all means,' which meant yes.

Miss Pitt sounded nicer than usual. 'Can you speak?' she asked.

Can you speak? I'd never been asked that before. I have many times since, of course, but it was the first time and I couldn't think what she meant.

'I think so,' I said.

'Look, Lizzie, Dad's point-blank refusing to talk to me,' she said, 'I mean, Mr Simmons.'

'Yes, I heard about that,' I said.

'The thing is, Lizzie, I'd love to have a chat with him.'

'Right.'

'Yes, but in a neutral place and with our GP and maybe our solicitor.'

'What has this got to do with 'O' levels?' I said.

'Yes, well, I need you to lure the fox out of his hole, as it were.'

'You mean, lure Mr Simmons out,' I whispered.

'Precisely,' said Miss Pitt, 'lure Dad out.'

She had it all worked out. She was going to forward bundles of tickets to the free lunchtime piano and operatic recitals that took place in St James the Greater Church near Victoria Park and I was to let her know if and when one of them appealed to Mr Simmons so that she could 'bump into him' there — accidentally on purpose.

'What do I have to do?' I asked.

'Make sure he sees the tickets. Be enthusiastic and, I don't know, go with him if you can,' she said, 'and most importantly, let me know if he bites.'

Since Mike Yu had spoken so passionately about the need to continue my education, it seemed to me that Mr Simmons was quite capable of handling this situation with Miss Pitt — he was her father, after all, or stepfather. And now that I'd got him going on the garden revamp I couldn't see Miss Pitt finding it easy to lure him out on a permanent basis. He loved being at Paradise Lodge, and everyone was on to her.

And I really needed 'O' Levels, otherwise I'd be regretful and probably unhappy for the rest of my life — and I had a lot of life to be unhappy and regretful in (touch wood).

'And I'll be back on the 'O' Level courses?' I asked.

'Yes,' said Miss Pitt, emphatically.

'OK,' I said, 'I've got to go now.'

Miss Pitt said she was pleased we'd come to this mutually beneficial arrangement and that I should start reading the 'O' Level texts straight away. Starting with *Animal Farm* by George Orwell.

'*Animal Farm*,' I said.

'Yes, George Orwell,' said Miss Pitt.

'I know who wrote *Animal Farm*,' I said.

The call ended.

'Is everything all right?' Lady Briggs asked.

'Yes, I'm back on the 'O' Level course at school,' I said.

'*School?*' said Lady Briggs.

'I'm fifteen, remember,' I said.

And Lady Briggs said, 'Oh, is that you? I get you all so muddled.'

'Have you got a copy of *Animal Farm* by George Orwell?' I asked her, on the off chance — her having a pile of books in the corner of the room — and to my delight, she said she had, somewhere, she'd find it and I could borrow it as long as I promised not to dog-ear the pages.

A day or so later, she handed it to me. It had been downstairs in the library, she said, all muddled with her other twentieth-century novels — someone had had it sent up with the housekeeper. I laughed and promised I wouldn't dog-ear the pages. Lady Briggs talked beautifully about her books. She talked about *Mrs Dalloway* and *Ulysses*, *Of Human Bondage* and her favourite play *Time and the Conways*. She invited me to go downstairs and look at the books any time and borrow them if it would help. I wondered where all those books really were now. The ones in the corner were all Ulverscroft Large Prints and not a classic among them, except for *All Creatures Great and Small*.

Mr Simmons spotted me reading *Animal Farm* shortly after that and was very interested in my new allegorical reading material and kept quoting from it — which made me feel doubly guilty and awful. I kept reminding myself, 'Mr Simmons is tough — he's from the modern age. He's come through a world war on the winning side and worked for the BBC.'

$\star$ $\star$ $\star$

My sister had worked hard at school and I'd had to suffer teachers telling me how well they remembered her — meaning, I compared badly. Since my sister's failed smoking ban in our shared bedroom and subsequent move to the living room we'd not got along very well and we'd annoyed each other. But that summer, while she hung around waiting to go off and study thinkers from the dawn of civilization to the modern day and across the globe and what it meant to be human, something happened to her that brought us close again. I'm not sure what exactly, but I know it started when she went on a camping holiday to Scarborough with her boyfriend, Eric Carter, and his family.

A few days into the trip we received a postcard from her, which read:

> Having a nice time. Rode a Bucking Bronco at the rodeo yesterday — won £5 for being the only lady contestant. The campsite is a microcosm. This morning, we had a walk through splendid woodland to the remains of a glacial lake — except for Eric's mother who spent all morning cooking a full Sunday roast on the camping stove — including trifle.

She sounded typically philosophical.

I was still in bed when she got home from the camping trip. Eric Carter's dad had driven home through the night to avoid the traffic because he was towing a trailer with the camping equipment on it and he preferred the B roads. My sister came into our bedroom, got into her old bed and pulled the bedclothes over her head.

It was strange — not only because she'd moved out of our room on account of the health risk posed by my cigarette smoke but because it was getting-up time in anyone's book.

'Oh, you're back, are you?' I said, but my sister didn't answer. She just hid her face in her duvet and cried. I asked her what was wrong and even tugged the duvet off her.

'How was the trip?' I asked, but she didn't answer and I could tell there was something wrong. I asked her to tell me what, but she couldn't. I wondered if she'd had sex with Eric and hated it. Or had sex with Eric and he'd hated it. Or she'd heard Mr and Mrs Carter having sex in the tent next door. Or something embarrassing had happened with the chemical toilet.

I was suddenly worried that something really bad had happened, so I called our mother and she came up.

It wasn't anything bad or really bad. It was an 'epiphany', which would usually be a good thing but, on this occasion, wasn't — or maybe it was, she couldn't decide. The camping trip with the Carters had made my sister terrified of a future in which she'd have to try to exist outside of our mad, smoky little family and get to grips with the greatest thinkers in the world and at the same time be normal and cook roasts and choose the B roads (so to speak).

Seeing the family take for granted that Mrs Carter would miss the splendid woodlands and the glacial lake in order that she could cook a roast, and Mr Carter plumping to miss a whole night's camping so that they could travel at a sensible time and on the B roads on account of the trailer rendering them a 'slow vehicle' (and even affixing a 'slow vehicle' notice to the back of the trailer alongside the spare registration plate), she suddenly felt blind panic about interacting with normal, sensible people — who were, of course, not normal because everything is relative.

And she worried that people like her — who couldn't cope in the real world — often ended up reclusive and institutionalized. And I thought to myself 'like Lady Briggs' plus, I felt, it seemed quite similar to our mother's anxiety about malt loaf and trying to be like Mrs Goodchild across the road but I didn't say anything. It wouldn't have helped. You don't want to feel unoriginal.

Over the next few days my sister deferred her place at Durham University and instead enrolled on a nursing course at Leicester Royal Infirmary so that she could at least have a career and do some good, and practical things would fill her mind and block out any troubling thoughts. She was suffering from tiny, infrequent panic attacks. Every now and then she'd do something like scrape the marmalade jar, and I'd wonder if she was having another one. Other times, I'd try and cause one by pretending I'd electrocuted myself or had seen something horrible in the hedges.

Our mother spoke to me about my sister's

214

change of direction. She was very disappointed — she'd always believed my sister would become a modern-day philosopher (like, say, Judith Hann or Iris Murdoch) and be able to show us metaphorically where to go or, failing that, a vet. She thought every family, ideally, should have a doctor for when you're sick, a vet for when your dog is, and a philosopher for when you're confused. I had to remind my mother that neither I nor Little Jack was planning to become a doctor. My mother said she had hopes for Danny — hence putting his name on the Montessori waiting list and buying him educational toys.

My mother wrote a short story entitled 'Bird's Trifle', in which the mother of a family accidentally burns her chest area while heating milk for a trifle on a camping stove while the rest of the family visits an ancient penis-shaped monument. They return to the campsite to find the mother all decorated with Dream Topping, hundreds and thousands and glacé cherries. It was meant to be a tragedy but it really cheered my sister up.

* * *

Not long after the proposal, my sister and I went with our mother in the Snowdrop van to Market Harborough Registry Office to book the marriage. The lady there told my mother she must bring the groom-to-be (Mr Holt) into the office before the actual day. My mother said she needn't worry, he'd definitely turn up on the day, but the lady said she needed to see him — in the flesh — beforehand to check it wasn't a bogus wedding. We were allowed to provisionally book the date, though, and my mother said she'd take the first available slot — whatever day of the week — as long as it was before ten if it was a weekday. I wished she hadn't said that. It made it seem bogus.

The lady went through the ledger, she turned page after page and then looked over her spectacles at us. 'Here,' she said, 'nine-thirty.'

My mother peered at the date and said, 'Yes, fine, we'll take it.'

My sister and I looked at each other. This date was the anniversary of one of the saddest events in our mother's life. A few years had passed but on that day every year since she had been quiet and deeply unhappy — sunk in regret and pain. And we were too. Had she really forgotten it? Had this forthcoming marriage buried it? Maybe it had, maybe that's what a nice wedding could do. I felt my eyes fill with tears with the thought of the sad thing and knew that a marriage — however happy — would never cover the memory of the sad thing for me. I looked at my sister and I could see by the way she jiggled her leg and by the slight tremble in her lip that she'd remembered too. Neither of us said anything, though. If our mother had forgotten and the pain was gone, that was only a good thing.

The marriage was scheduled to take place on this particular date, nice and early in the morning before Danny got crotchety — not that he often did get crotchety but he was definitely at his best early. And we sped off in the van.

'Just think, girls,' said our mother — and she said the date — 'on that day I'll be Mrs Harry Holt.'

'Yes,' we said.

It hit her then and she pulled in abruptly on to a gravelly bit of verge by Gartree Prison. She got out of the van and stumbled along with the wind whipping her hair about. And we got out too and stood beside her on the roadside, together in a little tripod, gripping each other's arms, and cried for a few moments. If a prison guard had peered out they might have thought we were plotting to spring a murderer.

'How could we have forgotten?' our mother said through her tears. 'How did we forget?' And looking at us, she knew that we hadn't. And then Danny banged his cloth octopus on the windscreen and we clambered back into the van.

We talked about the sad thing, our baby brother, who we had all longed to meet and get to know. But who'd died, almost four — or was it five? — years previously, just before he was supposed to be born. We talked about how awful things had been then, and how we'd pinned all our hopes on him, as if he was the answer to all our woes. And how we were trying to keep the pregnancy quiet for a while but because we were so excited we gave him the code name 'Bluebell the baby donkey' so we could talk about him. And how our mother wanted to call him Jack even though our little brother was already called Jack and would have to go back to being called James or Jimmy. We remembered how Bluebell

217

dying like that had made our mother want to die herself and she'd drunk from the bottle and shouted and cursed God. And there wasn't a soul in the world who cared about our mother — our loving her didn't count — and we'd felt a mix of fear and uselessness because nothing was going to stop us falling down and down.

And I found suddenly my sister and our mother had stopped crying and it was only me speaking, and I heard myself say the saddest things and cried into my open palms. And our mother said, 'Lizzie, Lizzie.'

My sister said how wonderfully things had turned out (considering) and how lucky we were now that Mr Holt had put a stop to the falling and our mother had cleverly tricked him into having another baby. And that baby being as beautiful as Bluebell would have been. None of us said Bluebell was in Heaven or anything spooky or weird, but we all knew the grief had faded. We sniffed and wiped our noses and eyes and I finished my crying.

'Will you be able to go through with it,' my sister asked, 'on the anniversary?'

'No,' said our mother, 'I shan't.'

So we went back to Market Harborough — all red-faced and wretched — to book the next available slot which was a few days later. And we were lucky to get it — it being the only one for weeks and weeks and, due to cancellation, a much sought-after Saturday morning.

★　★　★

Mr Holt left it entirely up to my mother re all the arrangements and the wedding guest list. Just as long as she kept it minimal and didn't invite his parents because they'd feel obliged and didn't travel well out of Norfolk. My mother couldn't decide who to invite and took about an hour and two cups of econo-coffee to come up with a list of approx eight people, including a nice couple from across the road called Alistair and Sarah (the only Liberals in a ten-mile radius), a couple called Jeff and Betty from the Snowdrop depot who weren't Liberals but nice in other ways, Deano the van boy and Miss Kellogg, our ex-au pair Carrie Frost, and my mother's much younger brother — who we all liked immensely.

It didn't seem to me to be enough people and I tried to add names. 'Just invite your friends,' I advised. And my mother said she hadn't really got any since Celia Watson had gone into the menopause and could no longer be trusted.

'What about Mrs Goodchild, across the road, and her husband and baby Bobbi?' my sister said.

This was a red rag to a bull. My mother shouted, 'What is your fucking obsession with that woman?'

It was strange her yelling at my sister like that because it was she who had the obsession.

I suggested Melody Longlady but her punkishness seemed to fly in the face of a wedding and also, I'd then have to invite Miranda. And then the floodgates would be open — if Miranda, why not Sally-Anne, or (God forbid) Matron and Sister Saleem and then Carla bloody B with her navel showing? And though the idea of them all was quite cheering, the thought of them all *at my house* — looking at my mother's drawings of horse's heads (and now people) and pulling books off the bookshelves and throwing darts at the dartboard and commenting on the unusual patchwork carpet — was unbearable and to be avoided.

Then there was the planning of the bunfight. My mother and sister and I called in at the Copper Kettle on the bypass to ask for a quotation and when the proprietor told us the cost for their most basic cold finger buffet for fourteen — with a glass of Blue Nun or a bottle of Pony — was over a hundred pounds we almost fainted and my mother called it 'preposterous'. Then my sister and I imagined we'd do the food ourselves and have it at home, and ask the Liberal woman across the road to do the meringue Pavlova she was always boasting about, but my mother groaned and said no, she couldn't bear it. I toyed with the idea of asking Mike Yu to deliver sufficient egg fu yung and making a home-made juice and whisky-based punch with floating apple chunks but that seemed inappropriate and actually just imagining it gave me butterflies.

20

The Liquid Cosh

Sister Saleem went through the patients' notes with Eileen and Sally-Anne. She questioned them about prescriptions, symptoms, pill dosages and contraindications, opioids, opiate antagonism, vasodilation and risk of overdose in patients with high blood pressure. It became clear that neither nurse knew much about the drugs — or, in fact, the patients, medically speaking.

And then, when Sister Saleem saw the drug trolley under the stair bend, with brown pill bottles and canisters, just there — in the open — loose pills scattered like Smarties on a birthday cake, she exploded.

Never in all her life had she seen such an unprofessional mess, she said. And she didn't just mean the drug trolley, she meant the whole place, 'the whole ruddy ball of wax' — a phrase she'd learned from Mr Simmons.

She stood and looked up to the heavens and took a deep breath. Then the owner came shuffling round the corner and she had a go at him. 'How could you let this happen?' she asked, shouting.

'I don't know, Nurse Goolagong,' he said, trembling, 'it all got out of hand when my life left.'

We all looked at each other and, thinking Sister Saleem must have noticed the Freudian slip, hoped she might go a bit easier on him — realizing the extent of his madness.

'You've no right calling this place a nursing home,' said Sister Saleem. 'And stop calling me Nurse Goolagong.'

Sister immediately instigated a modern drug-handling procedure, which required the pills to be kept in a locked cabinet and the key pinned to her belt (or Eileen's), and gave us a crash course in drugs commonly prescribed to the elderly. There would be an official drug round at breakfast and just before coffee and again with bedtime drinks.

Matron took it badly about the drugs. She'd been tolerant of Sister Saleem up to then — as mentioned — but this rattled her. 'For the love of God, we're not a great big, huge, bleddy hospital, we're a residential home with a few poorly old folk on water tablets.'

★   ★   ★

Thankfully, Sister Saleem had some happy news at the team talk the next morning. A new patient was coming. Mr Godrich (a GP referral) would be with us in approx a fortnight's time to convalesce after a simple surgical procedure.

'How long will he be staying?' asked Matron, with a forced nonchalance.

'Until he's fully convalesced,' said Sister Saleem, giving Matron a hard look. 'If we manage not to give him an opiate overdose.'

'How long is that likely to be?' asked Eileen.

'A couple of months at least,' said Sister Saleem.

It was good news, said Sister Saleem, and would almost single-handedly take us to where she wanted us to be, business-wise, and if Mr Godrich stayed longer, then that would really help turn our fortunes around, especially now some of the residents were helping and there was now no urgency in finding a cook or laundry lady.

'And,' added Sister, with a slight grimace, 'we are entitled to charge slightly above the advertised tariff since he'll be bringing a little dog.'

We all squealed with delight. Sister Saleem was touched by our enthusiasm — failing to appreciate it was the little dog we were pleased about and not turning a profit. We clanked coffee cups and congratulated Sister Saleem on her successful negotiation. Matron gazed out of the window, in a world of her own.

There was a slight issue that needed addressing before Mr Godrich arrived. And that was where to put him. Mr Godrich wanted peace and quiet in an upstairs room and needed an en-suite bathroom because of an incapacitation.

'Some beds are worth more than others,' Sister reminded us.

'Which would you say,' she asked, looking at Eileen, 'is the best room in the place?'

We all chipped in. Eileen said she thought probably the little drawing room which had been turned into a two-bedded male ward. It had

223

views of the garden and was a level walk to the day room. Miranda said she thought Room 8 with its bathroom and fireplace and view of the reservoir.

'What about Room 9?' said Sister Saleem.

And we went silent. Room 9 was Lady Briggs' room. It was a lovely room but it wasn't to be thought of as a possible room. It was Lady Briggs' room.

'It's Lady Briggs' room,' we all said.

'Yes, but theoretically, is it the best room in the home?' persisted Sister Saleem.

'Yes,' we all said, 'it is.'

And then Sister told us how much Lady Briggs was paying.

'According to the paperwork,' said Sister Saleem, 'Lady Briggs is paying absolutely nothing.'

'That can't be right — ' said Nurse Eileen.

'Yes,' interrupted Matron, 'the first patients came on advance payment programmes and she'll have paid up, she's been here years.'

'Well, in that case, I don't think we have any choice. We're going to have to move Lady Briggs out,' announced Sister. 'She can go in the ladies' ward, in the bed in the corner.'

'Oh, Emma Mills' old bed,' said Miranda, looking at me and pulling a sad face.

There was some mumbling and grimacing.

'So, which member of staff will break the news to her?' asked Sister Saleem.

No one said anything. It was too awful a thought — Lady Briggs had that condition where you can't leave the room for fear of something intangible.

'Well, who gets along with Lady Briggs?' Sister Saleem persisted.

And the others said, all at once, 'Lizzie.'

'Lis, it seems you know her best,' said Sister Saleem, 'can you break the news?'

★   ★   ★

Some tickets arrived for a Chopin piano recital and my stomach churned just seeing them. I put them on the hall console so that the ladies and gentlemen could see them as they passed on their way to the toilet. Nothing happened.

A day or so later, I fanned them out and presented them at tea-time. 'This looks interesting,' I said, 'a free piano recital at St James's.'

I faked an interest but Mr Simmons seemed to suddenly smell a rat and wondered where the tickets had come from and then said, 'Actually, I'm not sure I fancy it.' Meaning the Chopin.

I had to ring Miss Pitt again. I told her the tickets were much appreciated but that Mr Simmons hadn't fallen for the lure.

Miss Pitt said she'd put her thinking cap on and that I should be poised to respond with my catch off. I was beginning to dislike all the hunting and war metaphors. It showed a lack of tact on Miss Pitt's part and reminded me of her lack of rapport with pupils at school.

★   ★   ★

The new drug and pill procedure wasn't

225

difficult. The pills were sorted into little pots and arranged on a tray laid with a map of the patients. This would then be checked by a second nurse and then the pots would be distributed prior to the coffees at coffee time and then again at bedtime, for those who needed further doses. There was also a breakfast round but that was purely the business of the night nurse. This was how it had been done in the Owner's Wife's time and although it seemed unnecessarily official, it was obviously the correct way.

One morning, as I was going round the day room with the milky coffees, I noticed Matron shadowing me, behaving oddly. I pretended not to look at her but watched via the mantel mirror and was shocked to see that she was taking pills from the little dose cups on the patients' trays. I watched her do it a few times before I could really believe it. She'd approach a patient and begin a little chat and then, with her hand slightly behind her, she'd feel for the pot and tip it into the pocket of her uniform. I watched Matron a lot after that and noticed that she'd rescue pills from the floor and search for them down the side of the easy chairs where the patients let them fall. And then, one day, I saw her hook a pill out of Miss Lawson's mouth with her tiny little finger before she could swallow it down, and she glugged down her syrupy stuff.

I found myself angry with Matron mostly for living up to the bad opinion Sister Saleem had of her and doing something that would certainly result in her being sacked if she got caught. And being in the very situation she so dreaded — jobless and homeless. I knew I should probably do something — confront her or tell someone — but I hadn't the energy or the heart straight away.

Then, not long after that, Miss Lawson bit me. She bit me because she was confused and deranged, due to not having taken the tablets and syrup she'd been prescribed to prevent it.

It was teatime on Miss Lawson's birthday, I'd fed her two whole Primula Cheese and chive sandwiches and a mushed-up peach and was feeling pleased with myself. I'd lit the candle on her little birthday cake, we'd sung Happy Birthday and I'd taken her bony little hands and held them with both of mine. 'Happy birthday,' I said, 'let's blow out this candle.' And I smiled at her. She seemed to smile back but then yanked my hand up and sank her gums into the flesh just above the thumb.

She gripped tight and wouldn't let go. I tried to pull my hand away, but she still wouldn't let go. I pulled so hard at one point she almost fell off the chair (she wasn't very heavy — approx six stone). It was frightening and embarrassing — and painful, though that was neither here nor there — and all the time she stared up at me with manic eyes. I tried and tried to shake her off without disturbing the other patients but her jaw seemed to have locked shut.

There was something horrific about the tremulous grip, the jumble of our four hands all by her bony head and the strings of saliva hanging down. It seemed like something very dark and bad and demonic. Miranda stood by, bent double laughing, saying it was like the time Melody fed grapes to a tortoise in Chapel and it had bitten her in exactly the same way and they'd had to call the police.

Miss Boyd noticed and tried to intervene. 'You vicious little woman,' she shouted, and tried to hit Miss Lawson with her stick. I had to fend off the stick to protect Miss Lawson. Miss Boyd yelled down the table, 'Miss Lawson has got the little nurse in a gum bite and she won't leave off of her.'

And Miss Moody, sitting on the opposite side, burst into tears and then said, 'Oh dear, oh dear, oh dearie, dearie me,' and then called out that she'd had an accident and needed assistance.

Soon Sister Saleem arrived and evacuated the table so that there was only Miss Lawson and me sitting there. Sister asked me what had happened. I explained and she looked at us for a moment and said, 'Annie Lawson, I am here now.' And she put her hands softly around Miss Lawson's face. 'Annie, you haven't been taking your medication, have you? That's why you're feeling unwell,' she said. 'If you'll let go of Lizzie's hand we can get you into bed and help you.'

And Sister held Miss Lawson's face like that for some time. My hand was still in Miss Lawson's mouth, and the three of us were all huddled together with the little candle burning out and a tiny trail of smoke giving off that burnt-wax birthday cake smell. Sister spoke to Miss Lawson about how the doctor would find out what was hurting, because she knew there must be something, and continued talking about her aches and pains and so forth until, after a few minutes, Miss Lawson let go of my hand.

Sister Saleem didn't fuss about it. She checked there'd been no puncture of the skin (Miss Lawson's gums or my hand) and sent me to the kitchen to eat some cucumber, which she said was calming, and have a cigarette, which was also calming. With the help of Nurse Eileen, Sister Saleem took Miss Lawson to bed and was soon back in the kitchen — with Miss Lawson's notes — ranting about the dangers of patients not taking their medication properly.

'What's she on?' She handed the notes to Eileen. 'I can't read this.'

'The liquid cosh and a water tablet,' said Eileen.

'The what?' said Sister Saleem.

'Largactil,' said Eileen.

'Patients like Miss Lawson must have the syrup and you must make sure they take it,' she said.

Matron nodded, wiped her teacup dry, put it in the cupboard and left the room. I followed her. She started trotting up the stairs, but I caught up with her.

'Can't you get tablets from the doctor like any normal person?' I asked.

'You know I can't,' she said, looking around to check no one was listening.

'No, I don't,' I said. 'Why can't you?'

She rushed up the stairs to get away but was soon out of puff and leaning on the banister on the halfway landing. 'I'm not registered,' she said, breathing hard.

'So what?' I said. 'Go and register. What are you — a killer on the run?'

She was affronted and waddled off. I followed her to her room and, when she unlocked the door, I barged in and sat on the only chair.

'Don't report me, Lizzie,' she said.

'I will unless you tell me the truth,' I said, and I held my throbbing thumb joint.

Matron blamed everyone else but herself. It was Sister Saleem's new lockable drug cabinet, before which she'd been able to help herself to sleeping pills, painkillers and the liquid cosh. It was Nurse Eileen, who kept the drug-trolley key pinned to her tabard. It was the National Health Service and its prying eyes. It was her mother who'd caused problems years ago, it was her monster of a father and it was the Owner's Wife's fault — for leaving.

'And now Miss Lawson's bitten you,' she said, as if it had nothing to do with her.

'It's your fault Miss Lawson bit me, you stole her antipsychotic medication — which you don't even need, you lunatic,' I shouted.

'I *do* need it,' she said. 'I need it more than Lawson does.'

'No, you don't,' I said. I knew all about prescription drug-takers, my mother having been hooked for years, and I'd seen her top up with Lemsips, dog aspirins and Fisherman's Friends, baby medicine, you name it — anything to prolong the feeling of being medicated, rather than face the world.

230

'Please don't report me!' she said, and she ran her hands through her hair dramatically. The gesture was weak now that her hair was straw-coloured, and I recalled the drama of her previous shade 'Raven's Wing', which was almost black with a glint of bloody red, and which made you not mind her being such a bad person — having the right hair for it, especially with her little snub nose.

'I *am* going to report you,' I said.

'I'll be gone soon.'

'I'm going to report you today,' I said.

'The world's changed, Lizzie. It's all regulations. It wasn't like that in my day.'

'What's that got to do with stealing the patients' medicines?' I asked.

'I can't help myself since she came and locked everything up.'

'But that's the normal, correct procedure,' I said.

'And she's more a fake than I am. The owner has no memory of taking her on — she's just turned up, on the make,' said Matron, 'she's been tipped off by some scoundrel selling coal or in the pub.'

'This isn't about Sister Saleem, it's about *you*,' I said.

To my astonishment she then asked if *I'd* go to the doctor and pretend I had severe chronic back pain and insomnia — and pass on whatever was prescribed.

'Just say you're totally knackered all the time but when it comes to bedtime, you can't get off to sleep and your head's buzzing and if you do

231

drop off, you're awake again in no time with your heart thumping in your ribs.'

'NO!' I said.

'Well, then I have no choice but to keep stealing the pills,' she said.

'But the patients need them. They're their pills,' I said.

'I have the greater need,' said Matron. 'I have work to do. I can't sit in the window reading a large-print romance or snoozing the afternoon away.'

'Just go and register with Dr Gurley in Flatstone,' I said.

'I can't,' she said, 'I'm under an assumed name because I fled here with a fugitive.'

'What fugitive?' I asked.

'My mother — she smothered my father with a goose-down pillow,' she said.

'Was he ill?' I asked.

'No,' said Matron, 'he was a beast.'

'How did she have the strength to smother a healthy, full-grown man?' I asked.

'It's easier than you think — with goose down,' said Matron.

'Well, that was your mother, not you,' I said. 'Just go and register under your true name.'

Then her excuses became ridiculous. She told me a whole yarn about taking a wrongly labelled chocolate cake instead of award-winning coffee cake in a self-service café and then, in some kind of disappointed trance, strangling a nun.

'I strangled a nun,' she said.

'I'm not colluding with you,' I said.

I didn't care about the dad-smothering or the

nun-strangling, I told her if I saw her taking the patients' pills ever again I'd report her to Sister Saleem. And she just sniffed. She didn't care. Or she didn't think I'd do it.

'Anyway,' she said, 'I expect I'll be leaving with Mr Godrich.'

'Mr Godrich?' I said. 'He's not even here yet.'

'I'm hoping to become his live-in companion,' said the poor, deluded old woman.

I didn't believe a word of the cake-and-nun story — mainly because cafés weren't self-service back then. But I did believe she was frightened, and I felt merciful. I let her talk about Mr Godrich and I wished he'd hurry up and arrive, get better and then leave — with Matron.

And then, thinking that, I remembered I still had to tell Lady Briggs about the move.

21

The Purcell Medley

One day, my sister telephoned. She never usually telephoned because of the lock on the phone and because she hated phone boxes because of the smell of old windowpanes and all the urine.

I knew something awful must have happened because she was all whispery and said 'Hi, Lizzie, how are you?'

So I said, 'Why are you ringing?'

And she tried to speak through her tears and I had a horrible moment thinking Sue had died. But it wasn't Sue, it was Marc Bolan — which was terrible, but certainly less bad (for me) than it being Sue.

Marc Bolan was a big favourite at Paradise Lodge. Not among the patients, of course — I don't think they were aware of him — but among the staff he was definitely number one, pop star-wise. Partly because he'd remained important after they'd grown out of David Cassidy and The Osmonds. Also, he was known to be just up the M1 in London messing around being a star and sexy and probably a bit druggy, not all the way over in California being American and out of reach and married to the Church.

Once the full story was known — Marc died when a Mini driven by his girlfriend, Gloria Jones, hit a tree — I felt sorry for Gloria Jones.

People were pointing the finger of blame — as they always do when you're the driver, especially if you survive. I knew from bitter experience how Gloria Jones felt. Bereft and to blame and yet probably not to blame. In my version of events Marc Bolan had been messing about in the passenger seat — grabbing the wheel as a joke — high on the excitement of being a pop star etc. Not that we can ever know for sure that he was, but you have to assume.

But Gloria Jones couldn't say any of this. Marc had died and she knew the country would be in mourning — she couldn't go blaming him for causing the crash with his crazy behaviour. It was exactly the same as when Miss Mills had died. I couldn't blame her, I couldn't say, 'She kept shouting and making a fuss and disturbing all the other ladies in the ward,' or, 'I'd lifted her on to the bed fine, but she wouldn't shuffle back and toppled forward.' I had to take the blame, 100 per cent.

Anyway, Marc Bolan had died and it felt strange. I have to compare it to the day — exactly one calendar month earlier — when the catering grocer had given us an ultimatum about the unpaid bill and Elvis had died and the owner said he didn't know if he wanted to exist in a world without Elvis. And one of the barmaids at the Piglet Inn had sat and sobbed on the bench outside the bar saying her 'hunka hunka burning love' had died on the toilet and she was just going to sit there and think about him and if anyone wanted a pint, they'd have to pull their own.

The owner and the older staff had been devastated by the death of Elvis, but in general the nurses hadn't. They'd been saddened but not devastated.

Marc Bolan was different. Granted he'd had fewer albums and hadn't brought rock 'n' roll to a whole generation but he was ours and we'd got used to him and he had his own telly show, smoky eyes and girlish good looks. And you couldn't imagine him eating two whole burgers or not wanting to have sex. You could imagine him having sex twice and not wanting a burger. That was the difference. I didn't adore him myself. But the others — including my sister — did. And they wailed and sobbed. Melody got the London bus — even though she'd entered a punk phase — and went to put flowers and glitter by the crash tree and there'd been thousands there (people and flowers).

Mike Yu turned up with a box of cabbages and carrots that were on the turn for us to use for a stew dinner. And, since practically everyone was in a sad daze about Marc or — in Miranda's case — on the brink of weeping, Mike ended up making the stew himself.

Miranda 'cried' on Mike Yu's shoulder in front of everyone in the kitchen as he chopped the carrots.

Sally-Anne was sad too but she didn't show it. 'You don't look bothered at all, Sally-Anne,' said Miranda. Sally-Anne calmly replied that she was sad but she couldn't cry because she was dead inside. And the thought of Sally-Anne being dead inside seemed sadder to me than Marc.

My sadness about Sally-Anne's deadness inside meant I must have, momentarily, looked sad and Mike said to me, over Miranda's shoulder, 'I'm so sorry the T. Rex guy has died, Lizzie, I know you all really liked him.'

And, for some reason I can't fathom, I replied, 'Oh, he wasn't really my favourite.'

Everyone looked surprised. It was a terrible thing to say about a 29-year-old person who'd died and I tried to make amends by saying how dreadful it was when anyone died — especially a young person, and so on. But the damage was done and I seemed so cold — colder even than Sally-Anne, who at least had the excuse of being dead inside.

Maria Callas's death, which we heard about later that day, was of course very sad too. The owner shuffled into the kitchen, in floods, and noisily plugged in his Panasonic. And after a lot of rewinding and the sound of operatic music being fast-forwarded, he then played the most God-awful racket anyone had ever heard (the late Maria Callas singing an opera).

'Music is an illusion of a better world,' he said. 'Ah, La Divina Maria!'

Mike Yu popped back in to check on the stew and asked what was the matter with the owner.

'His favourite singer has died,' I said.

'I thought Elvis was his favourite,' said Mike.

'That was just for sex with his ex,' said Miranda, shouting to be heard above the music.

'Who's this, then?' asked Mike.

'It's Maria Callas — she died,' I said, and I began to cry. I wiped the little tears that ran down my cheek and that very thing was enough to make me cry a bit more. I don't know what made me cry — it might have been Maria Callas and the rising music or the owner dabbing his tears away with a great big white handkerchief, or it might have been Mike standing there in a cloud of steam and stripy oven gloves.

Mike gave me a brotherly pat and I felt relieved to have shown some emotion.

★   ★   ★

The tickets for a Purcell medley that arrived the next day were more appealing to Mr Simmons than the Chopin recital. Miss Boyd also fancied it and I said I'd go too. The concert was in the Haymarket Theatre which was more modern but had fewer parking opportunities so we took the bus there and had a taxi booked for the return, with time built in for refreshments at the Swiss Cottage just over the road — where Miss Pitt would presumably turn up unexpectedly and have a chat with her stepfather. I telephoned her to let her know we'd be going. Speaking to her on the phone felt disgusting. She was all pleased and cooperative, treating me like an accomplice.

'I shall arrive afterwards,' she said, 'and Dad and I will probably go and have a cup of tea somewhere and then I'll drive him back to Paradise Lodge.'

'Just as long as you're not going to kidnap him,' I said.

Miss Pitt laughed. 'No, no, don't worry, I shan't kidnap my own father.'

'Stepfather,' I said.

The concert was unexpectedly moving, due to it being partly like a very sad funeral — in which the songs were sad and slow and very affecting. The main female singer — dressed in black feathers and a black net veil — was not only a fantastic singer but a brilliant actor too and seemed to be singing about her own imminent death. And partly about the composer's own life and his journey through it, including royal and sacred themes. The concert ended with these words, narrated by a young man from the choir:

And in 1695, at the height of his fame, aged just thirty-five years, Henry caught a chill after returning home one night late from the theatre to find that his wife had locked him out. His body is buried next to the organ in Westminster Abbey and the music he composed for Queen Mary's funeral was performed at his own.

It was all quite heartbreaking (imagine being the wife who locked him out). Mr Simmons and Miss Boyd both clutched their handkerchiefs. I was already miserable at my treachery and churning in trepidation about what was going to take place after the concert. I regretted the whole thing and was on the brink of telling Mr Simmons to hide in the gents until I gave him the all-clear when I saw my Granny Benson ahead in a little gaggle of posh old women and I hurried my companions out of the foyer.

'Let's go for a quick cup of tea,' I said, breezily.

'If you like,' said Mr Simmons, 'but I have my flask so I'll not need any.'

And then, as we went to cross the busy road, Miss Pitt's distinctive pale blue Dolomite pulled up at the kerb a few yards ahead of us. Two blokes got out, grabbed Mr Simmons by the elbows and marched him to the car quicker than his little feet could go. His tartan flask dropped to the ground and rolled away down the street.

He struggled and looked round at me. 'Nurse!' he shouted.

And I shouted, 'Hey, no, let go of him,' and pulled at the sleeve of the nearest bloke. 'Get off him!' I yelled again.

But they pushed him into the car, jumped in themselves and the car drove off.

In the taxi on the way home Miss Boyd kept mithering me about the incident. 'Who was that? Why did they take Mr Simmons?' and so on.

'It was his stepdaughter,' I told her, 'she's taken him for a cup of tea.'

'Oh, that's nice,' said Miss Boyd.

I had to keep my face turned away from her so she wouldn't see I was upset, but when we got back to Paradise Lodge I collapsed into Sister Saleem's arms.

'What's happened?' she asked. 'Where's Mr Simmons?'

'We bumped into his stepdaughter and she's taken him off — probably to try and keep him at home,' I said.

'Was she aggressive, unpleasant, violent?'

asked Sister. 'What was she like?'

'Well, she was quite assertive,' I said.

As soon as I could, I ran up to Lady Briggs and told her the whole awful truth — including my treachery. She didn't seem surprised and wasn't at all cross.

'She'll have taken him back to live at Plum Tree Cottage — what shall I do?' I cried.

'There, there, dear,' said Lady Briggs, 'let me see what I can do.'

And though there was nothing she could do, I felt better for having poured my heart out.

*　*　*

Mr Simmons still wasn't back a couple of days later and though I was genuinely devastated, I had to face up to the truth that this was exactly what I'd planned to happen. Plus it occurred to me that should Miss Pitt successfully prevent Mr Simmons from returning to Paradise Lodge, then Mr Godrich, the imminent convalescent patient and his little dog, could have Room 8 and Lady Briggs needn't move out of hers. On the other hand, Mr Simmons had been almost single-handedly running the place.

I felt bad about it — and selfish and all those awful things — but I was more worried about Lady Briggs having to move into Ward 2 than Mr Simmons having to live with a controlling woman with bad taste.

Then, as I was justifying myself (to myself), Mr Simmons appeared with a pot of cream in his hand.

'You're back,' I said, 'thank God.'

And Mr Simmons said, 'Yes, and I must apologize most sincerely that you were dragged into the incident at the Haymarket. I am sorry.'

'That's OK,' I said, 'but how did you get away?'

'That's the curious thing, the milkman called at the cottage and said he'd heard I needed a lift back here — so I just walked out and got into the float.'

'How marvellous,' I said.

I couldn't work out where this left me, 'O' Level-wise. I guessed the deal was off.

Mr Simmons made himself two rounds of bread and butter and a cup of tea.

Matron watched him eat it, smiling. 'Thank God you're back,' she said.

Later I spoke to Matron. 'Don't pin your hopes on Mr Simmons,' I said. 'You won't beat the Deputy Head.'

'No, no, indeed not,' she said. 'I'm hoping to leave with this fella Mr Godrich, when he's ready.'

'Fantastic,' I said, wearily.

'Have you told Lady B that he needs her room yet?' asked Matron.

★ ★ ★

It was true I did know Lady Briggs a bit better than the others but only because every single break time, every lunchtime and teatime and many times in between, her bell would ring and ring and everyone would ignore it — except to call out, 'Lizzie, her ladyship's ringing.' And I'd go up.

Occasionally Lady Briggs' bell-ringing would be to ask for one of her stationery boxes to be lifted out of her tallboy and given to her. She had work to do, she claimed, but mostly it was that she needed the commode, and then, nine times out of ten, there'd be nothing in the pot at the end of it — even though she'd make a point of visibly 'trying' which involved tensing up, holding her breath and bearing down and sometimes asking you to whistle.

There was no point leaving and coming back, her room being at the end of the corridor and miles away from everything else. So I'd stay and we'd chat about the goings-on at Paradise Lodge and she'd feign an interest in the administrative side of things just to keep me there. And then she'd say, 'Oh, I give up,' and I'd sometimes say, 'There you sit, broken-hearted, paid a penny but only farted,' and she'd laugh.

It was during one of those five-minute interludes — her on the commode, trying to go — that I was supposed to introduce the idea of her leaving the quiet and pretty solitude she loved, and moving downstairs to a shared, rather chilly ward with a bunch of lunatics and a hospital bed with a chipboard cabinet beside it and no space for her nice bevel-edged nightstand and Chinese ablutions jug and basin.

But there was no immediate rush. Mr Godrich wasn't due for a week or two.

★ ★ ★

I began to enjoy chatting with Lady Briggs about Mike Yu. Her memory was poor enough not to worry overmuch about her bringing it up again. And I couldn't stop being impressed that she'd quite rightly known I was in love — before I even had.

One time I'd gone up there determined to tell her about the room move but ended up confiding in her my concerns about Mike and Miranda's zodiacal compatibility — Miranda having been born in the Year of the Ox and therefore being either a perfect match for him or, more likely, a sworn enemy in the long run and might even murder him. The thing was, I was an ox too and so the same applied to myself and Mike. But I just knew which one of us would be the perfect match (me) and which one would end up stabbing him to death over a minor disagreement (Miranda).

Mike Yu was much more my type than Miranda's. I have to be quite honest here, Miranda was shallow. Openly shallow. She didn't even want to not be. She liked Mike because he was a company director and had a car and was attentive. It was annoying because she pretty much admitted it. I said she had a father who ticked all those boxes (and hoped she'd see what I was getting at).

And I was much more Mike's type than Miranda. Mike was strange and beautiful and born in the Year of the Rabbit like his gentle grandfather — who he'd jointly nursed to death with his strong-bonded family. Even though both Miranda and I were oxen, we were different types of oxen. She seemed to have the most disadvantageous traits in oxen e.g., poor communication skills and stubbornness.

I had a feeling Mike Yu and I would end up together and that I would probably have to face Miranda in some kind of fight. I didn't want a physical fight because I knew she'd win — she'd do anything to beat me — but I couldn't think of any other fight where I'd win. My only hope was that she would dump Mike Yu and break his heart and then I could come in as a soothing friend and one thing could lead to another. I knew one thing; I wanted to lie down and go to sleep with Mike and wake up before him and look at his face. I'd imagined it so many times, it was almost as though it had already happened.

There was only one thing I didn't love about Mike Yu and that was his strong family bond. I didn't mind that we were going to have his elderly parents living with us in 2020 when they reached eighty-five and needed live-in care. I was anxious that they might expect me to pamper Mike in the years between now and then, and I wasn't that kind of girlfriend/wife. I was going to expect certain freedoms and wanted to be able to go pony-trekking and generally do lots of things with my sister and I'd be happy for him to go on long holidays to China and Hong Kong and go pony-trekking or whatever with all the Chinese cousins that he was bound to have. I'd pop over for a week just to see his heritage and see the sights, and then I'd leave him to it. But I didn't want his closely bonded parents thinking badly of me.

I told Lady Briggs snippets of this and though she was very kind about it — saying I mustn't worry about the oxen or the rabbits and that she was certain they'd sort it out between them — I could tell she didn't really get it, so I changed the subject.

Then one day Lady Briggs almost dropped me in it with Miranda.

Lady Briggs suffered with crusty blepharitis and Miranda and I had been asked to give her an eyebath before bed — and run a bicarb-soaked cotton bud round her lashes. It was a horrible job because the person whose eyes they were would always flinch away and you needed a second nurse just to hold the patient's head still. And it was all too easy to jab them in the eyeball because telling an old lady to hold still is like telling a canary. Anyway, suddenly and apropos of nothing and in front of Miranda who was gripping her head, Lady Briggs grabbed my arm and said, 'Are you still in love with that beautiful boy from the next village?' and I said, 'Wah? No, who, me, no?'

And she continued, 'The one who comes into the drive in his car with the music playing?'

And Miranda butted in and said, 'Oh, yes, that's me, he's my boyfriend. Lizzie hasn't got a boyfriend.'

'And are you in love with him?' asked Lady Briggs.

'Yes,' said Miranda.

After the eyebath Lady Briggs blinked a lot, took hold of Miranda's hand and turned it over and looked at her and beckoned her closer. 'Let me see you, dear,' she said, and stared Miranda full in the eyes. 'But you're not in love, my dear, you're not in love at all, with anyone.'

*   *   *

After her mental collapse after the camping trip my sister needed to patch up her ruined life and, with absolutely no encouragement from me, she presented herself at Paradise Lodge and offered to become a full-time volunteer with a view to gaining experience before embarking on nurse training at Leicester Royal Infirmary.

And, to my annoyance, she was snapped up by Sister Saleem and came in slightly above me as 'Nursing Carer'. Which meant that while I'd be hoovering the stairs or lumbering around with the mountains of laundry, she'd be doing something more skilled, like cutting toenails or applying egg white and oxygen to a bedsore.

Sister Saleem was thrilled, of course, to have another whole extra pair of hands — for free — and she thought my sister commendable and Christian.

My sister didn't seem to be suffering with a ruined life. She seemed fully on top of everything and turned up at Paradise Lodge on her first day with a box of mini-rolls for the staff and a bunch of wild flowers for the patients. They were just grasses really with the odd flower but they did look nice in the jug and she was straight into their good books, unlike everyone else who arrived and had to slog at it for weeks.

She straight away began doing what older

sisters do. She became quite popular with the staff and told funny stories about me. About my romantic correspondence with Dave Cassidy of Alice Springs and my brief belief in ghosts and the time I winded myself on a steep slide and couldn't speak for a day. And the time I rescued a kitten from dogs on one side and a swimming pool on the other and it scratched me half to death. And the time a handsome Spanish man offered me a puff of his cigarette only to turn it round so that I closed my lips on the burning end. And an awful story about the time we ran out of toilet paper.

None of these stories were particularly funny or interesting, I'm only writing them here to illustrate how and why I came to dread coffee breaks. My sister wasn't trying to undermine me. She really wasn't. She was the new girl and was trying to squeeze into a space that wasn't actually there and join in a world which wasn't as she'd imagined it — partly because I'd not explained it properly. It's a thing friends and siblings do — either that, or they're all reserved and coy (and that's worse because you're embarrassed about them) — I have been guilty of it myself.

I did one time retaliate and told about the time my sister had run away from the dentist because she was scared of the little mirror. And Sister Saleem had said, 'Your sister is a good Christian and a very caring girl.' And I said, 'No, she's only here because she had a faked mental breakdown in Scarborough so she doesn't have to leave home.' And I felt the whole room turn against me.

22

I Dreamt I Dwelt In Marble Halls

I had a lot on my mind. Mr Simmons and Miss Pitt, for a start, and Matron's pill-stealing. But I worried most about telling Lady Briggs she was going to have to move from Room 9. I worried about that so fiercely that sometimes I'd have to go to the bathroom for a cry. And I'd not get to sleep at night.

It got ridiculous. I was dreading it so much, I considered leaving Paradise Lodge completely and becoming a dedicated scholar who only reads and studies. Or, getting a job in Saxone. I even wondered briefly if the whole 'moving rooms' thing hadn't been cooked up to get me back to school, by my mother, in cahoots with Sister Saleem.

It was time to speak to my mother — who knew all about dealing with problems, and was as kind and compassionate as you get in an English person.

The thing about having a flawed but kind mother is that you don't have to be afraid to tell them things. You can be yourself and everybody else can be just as they are. And you don't owe them anything, you just love them and they love you and you're in it together — for life. That's how it's always been with mine anyway.

First I told her I had some worries and began

with Matron and the patients' pills. I thought she might be a bit cross (you know, an old bitch like Matron nicking the pills out of the old people's mouths etc.) but she wasn't. She was deeply sad and affected. Sad for Matron.

'Christ, Lizzie, that could be you,' she said.

'Me?' I asked.

'Taking them for me!' she said, referring back to her years as a prescription pill addict.

And I said, 'I suppose so.' But I didn't think I'd have stooped that low, even for her.

'The thing is, should I tell Sister Saleem?' I asked her.

'I don't know,' said my mother, 'maybe you should tell Dr Gurley.'

Dr Gurley being the local doctor who'd helped my mother stop being such a prescription pill head and throwing her life away. And we had great faith in her. 'Yeah, maybe I should,' I said, knowing I never would.

My mother settled down then, in the nicest chair in our sitting area, as if everything was sorted out. But I'd hardly begun.

I let her have a moment then told her how worried I was about telling Lady Briggs. Though she felt negotiating with a reclusive almost-ninety-year-old over accommodation was a tough assignment for a fifteen-year-old, she used the situation to serve her own agenda and asked whether I ever spent a fraction of this energy on my schoolwork or worrying about my own future.

She could see I was genuinely anxious, though, and after a short discussion about getting one's priorities right, we examined the Room 9 situation and looked for the best way forward. Best for Lady Briggs and easiest for me. We decided I should focus on the convenience aspect of being downstairs — it being the main concern for the elderly (inconvenience could be lethal). I would tell Lady Briggs how very convenient being downstairs would be — for the toilet and for meals and for any kind of attention — and it would be true.

I'd tell her that the distance, the stairs, the corridor all made the coming up to her a real pain in the neck and that she'd be much better attended to downstairs and, more to the point, she'd be able to sit in the day room with all the other patients and gaze out of the window at the bird table and birds in general, which she didn't get to see upstairs, apart from birds flying around, which weren't so appealing and charismatic as the ones fluffing their feathers in a shell-shaped bird bath. And she'd be taken to the toilet in the main sluice on the comfort rounds and be part of the great toileting half-hours — when everyone went to the toilet and talked about going to the toilet and there was much talk of the toilet (the successes and the failures, the issues, the related medication and symptoms) — and she herself might offer her new neighbours nuggets of her own wisdom and tricks pertaining to the whole prickly subject (from the whistling of 'To Be A Pilgrim' to the little puffs). She'd be able to wave goodbye to the old commode and become acquainted with Thomas Twyford's grand old porcelain and rediscover the charms of beautifully crafted Victorian plumbing — the old chain flushes, the cascading of the water from the elevated water cisterns and the much-admired wall tiles which, according to the owner, rivalled the ones in Grand Central Station. Here, also, I was going to give her a toilet tip of my own which she could share with her new friends and neighbours to prevent needing the toilet again soon after going. Toilet Tip: just when you've finished weeing, turn as far as you can to one side and then to the other and then do two big coughs.

And, if all that didn't work, I was going to suggest that her constant need to go on the commode might be partly psychological and really because she needed to see another human being, to break the boredom of just sitting there staring at her knuckles in her lap. I wouldn't put it quite like that. I didn't want to humiliate her — after all, that's what she'd been doing for the last seven years. Literally, that's all. I was simply going to suggest she might not really need to go to the toilet at all and that was why she had so much trouble actually going and that she might just long for human interaction. It was my mother who'd come up with the 'longing for human interaction' thing, having longed for it herself a few times before she'd met Mr Holt.

We talked it through and rehearsed it enough times I could have winkled a hermit out of a cave.

★ ★ ★

It was time to grasp the nettle and on my next duty I went straight upstairs to Room 9 and, after helping Lady Briggs on to the commode, I began.

'There's a new patient coming next week, a fussy fellow with a small dog — to convalesce but hopefully stay forever,' I said.

'That's good,' said Lady Briggs — she seemed genuinely thrilled with this news — 'very good for the business.'

'Yes, but he needs a private room and his own convenience, and Sister Saleem is struggling to find one.'

'But he could have my room, couldn't he?' suggested Lady Briggs.

'Well, yes,' I said, 'yes, that would be perfect. But how would you feel, going downstairs to a shared ward?'

'I have been waiting to move closer to everything,' said Lady Briggs.

'Have you?'

'Yes, she was going to move me,' said Lady Briggs, 'Ingrid, the Owner's Wife, as soon as a place became available, but nothing came up.'

She'd been the very first patient at Paradise Lodge, she told me, and had been put in an out-of-the-way place to avoid all the noise and dust of the builders. It had always been the plan to move her to a better place, maybe a downstairs room with access to the garden, once the house was fully refurbished, but that hadn't happened for some reason. And quite some time had gone by.

'So you'd be happy to move,' I said, astonished.

'Nothing would make me happier,' said Lady Briggs, smiling and thinking and clicking like mad.

As I left Room 9, I checked, one more time, I'd understood correctly.

'So, you'll be happy to move downstairs — to a shared ward?' I said.

'Yes,' she said, 'is there room downstairs for me?'

'Yes,' I said, 'a bed has just become available.'

⋆　⋆　⋆

Moving day was strange. For a start, Lady Briggs had a bath — usually she'd just have a flannel wash unless the doctor was coming. So I had to help her into it, lurk in case she drowned, and then help her out of it. During the bath we chatted in exactly the same way as when she was on the commode, except I was outside the little bathroom and plucking my eyebrows in her magnifying mirror. I asked her if she felt ready for the move.

'Oh, yes,' she said, 'it was always the plan when my son brought me up here.'

'Seven years ago,' I said.

'It's not seven years, is it?' said Lady Briggs. 'Please don't tell me it's as long as that.'

'Oh, maybe not,' I said.

The nurses had celebrated downstairs when I'd told them of Lady Briggs' eagerness to move and that she wasn't going to resist or be unhappy. They'd seen it as a good outcome. And I had too, really, because it had been so much

254

easier than I'd expected and with no wailing or woes. But actually knowing she'd been waiting to move all this time — not a recluse at all, but lonely and longing to be with everyone — was very sad. Too sad to think about really.

I helped her out of the bath and dried her feet and chucked a tub of Johnson's all over her and rang the bell for some help in getting her downstairs.

'I did just want to say to you, Lizzie,' said Lady Briggs, 'I think you really should get yourself an education and not spend all your time here, now I'll be downstairs and shan't need you so much.'

'I know, I should,' I said. 'I'm doing my best, but I've come to hate school.'

'*Hate?*' said Lady Briggs, admonishingly.

'Dislike,' I corrected.

'You'll regret it later if you don't get your certificates, I guarantee it.' She went on, 'It'll come back to roost.'

'My stepdad is an autodidact, I could always go that route if necessary,' I said.

'A what?'

'Self-taught with dictionaries and encyclopaedias and books in general,' I said, 'and he's easily a match for any graduate.'

'Golly, I hope it won't come to that,' said Lady Briggs, 'but if it does, I have many, many books and you are very welcome to borrow them, you must help yourself.'

It was very kind of her. I thanked her and helped her with her stockings and Nurse Carla B arrived.

The three of us made our way to the top of the stairs and Lady Briggs rested on the chaise that was there especially for resting old ladies. And then we descended. It was very moving. Lady Briggs sang 'I Dreamt I Dwelt In Marble Halls' in her warbly voice and everyone gathered in the hall below and looked up, cheering gently as she took each step.

'You know, I thought for a long time I might be in an asylum,' she called down, and a roar of laughter went up. 'No, no, I'm not being flippant, I truly believed I had been incarcerated — you know, a sort of prison where one is punished for one's strangeness.'

And then she continued with her song and took the last tentative steps downstairs.

★ ★ ★

Lady Briggs had been allocated space in the communal wardrobes along one side of Ward 2. We brought down her stationery boxes and put them in her bedside cabinet, and her clothing and Chinese jug and bowl. But we threw away the twenty-odd bars of Cadbury's Old Jamaica we'd found in her tallboy.

That night I fished out her medical notes from the cabinet in the owner's nook.

Lady Briggs was admitted in 1969 after a small procedure at Kettering cottage hospital. She had varicose veins and a history of constipation for which she self-administered senna. In 1975 she was diagnosed with conjunctivitis and was given antibiotic eye drops.

She'd requested a room with a view over the farm — not the reservoir. Her interests were listed as reading, theology and horticulture. She declined a portable television.

Her next of kin was listed as 'Harald T. Anderssen — son'.

I thought I'd try to track down Harald Anderssen and arrange for him to come to visit now it turned out she wasn't a recluse. But the notes were patchy and there was no address or telephone number listed, save those of Paradise Lodge.

'Would you like us to invite your son to visit you?' I asked her as we arranged her things in the bedside cabinet.

'Where?' she asked, 'in here, no, I shall see him later, I expect.'

'Do you have his telephone number?' I asked. 'I can't find it on your notes.'

'You'll find him in the sitting room, dear,' she said.

★   ★   ★

In honour of Lady Briggs coming downstairs, Gordon Banks finally brought his video machine and played us *The Sound of Music* on telly during the afternoon. It was a big deal, not just because of us watching telly during the daytime but because Gordon couldn't carry the machine on his own and Sally-Anne had to help and was too shy to be so close to a person, especially Gordon Banks, who might or might not have been *the* Gordon Banks — but probably wasn't,

257

I'd decided by then (having seen the real one in a newspaper saying he was settling well in the USA).

I think it was an early VHS but it might have been Betamax. No one remembers. But we had it anyway and the ladies were thrilled to bits (not so much the gentlemen). Even the nurses on duty were allowed to sit down and watch. I sat in Emma Mills' old spot and what made it doubly sad was that I sat in her wheelchair and could smell the 4711 they all used to mask the smell of wee.

I'd seen *The Sound of Music* a few times and never thought much to it, but that day my heart was breaking. It wasn't just Lady Briggs being down among us — it wasn't Lady Briggs at all, actually — it was that Mike Yu was affecting me and changing me. I'd been a straightforward thinker before I'd looked into his tear-filled eyes when Grandpa Yu had passed. Now I was just an idiot full of stupid dreams and ridiculous fantasies, such as this recurring fantasy that evolved over a matter of weeks and went something like: I am in a big, scary warehouse and the leccy has blown, and I'm on my own and I'm terrified. There's someone or something in the warehouse with me and I can't see anything because I don't have a torch. Mike Yu drives by in his Datsun Cherry and senses something wrong (maybe he sees my bike outside). He does a safe three-point turn and pulls up outside the warehouse and by chance has a torch on him. He makes his way inside the building and finds me — slightly injured and very scared — and he lifts me up into his arms and carries me to his Datsun. I don't know what I was doing in the dark old warehouse, but there you are.

And that day, watching *The Sound of Music*, when it got to the really awful bit where Liesl sings with Rolf and Rolf is so hideous and anyone with an ounce of sense can see he's going to turn out to be a Nazi and Liesl is putting herself down saying what a flibbertigibbet she is. But still, I could hardly stop myself crying, watching them in the gazebo and wishing it was me singing that I was sixteen going on seventeen and Mike Yu responding that he was seventeen going on eighteen, and would take care of me — except I was fifteen going on sixteen and Mike was twenty and he was a colleague's boyfriend and definitely not a Nazi. I began to get a bit fed up with ordinary things being hijacked by my love for Mike Yu. Every book I read, every song and every film I saw. It was all-encompassing.

Lady Briggs was overwhelmed too but not because of an illegal romantic obsession. For her it was seeing the film and hearing the songs that she remembered and being part of this whole vibrant event. She sat quite close to the screen and kept talking and the other ladies didn't hold back on their disapproval. Miss Brixham told her to 'belt up or go back upstairs'.

At the end, numerous folk were in tears and Lady Briggs was fast asleep with her mouth open and, because I hadn't got her to the toilet in time, she'd wet the chair.

23

Kawasaki ZIB 900

An ambulance clattered into the drive.

'It must be Mr Godrich,' said Eileen.

'Since when do convalescent patients travel by ambulance?' asked Sister Saleem, and she went out to assess him before he was brought in. She then came back inside and telephoned the cottage hospital to ask about his condition. The sister in charge there told Sister Saleem that Mr Godrich's operation had gone fairly well, but he'd picked up something afterwards and had coughed so hard he'd broken a rib and it had gone a bit downhill from there. But he showed every sign of being on the mend now, and his family had wanted him to move on so that he could have Rick the dog with him and be that bit closer for their visits. Sister got off the phone to confer with Nurse Eileen. Neither of them wanted his lurgy coming to us and agreed he should not be admitted until he was off the antibiotics.

Sister spoke to the ambulance men and told them to take him back to hospital. And then phoned the hospital to let them know he was on his way back.

Shortly after that, the relatives arrived with Rick the dog. And began arguing politely with Sister Saleem. She told them she was very keen to welcome Mr Godrich, but not until he was a bit better.

'We don't take patients as poorly as your uncle,' she said, 'we're not a hospital, or hospice.'

'No,' said Nurse Eileen, 'patients come here to live, not to die.'

'But, the dog?' said Mr Godrich's nephew, holding Rick up for all to see.

'We're not a dog kennels either,' said Sister Saleem.

The owner butted in and said we'd be happy to take Rick while we waited for Mr Godrich, for a small fee — to be agreed with Sister Saleem. And so Rick moved into the owner's quarters. And we all clamoured for sightings of Rick. It turned out that Rick stank to high heaven, as if he'd rolled in something rotten. The owner was immune to it, for some reason, but the all-over smell made it difficult for the rest of us to pet Rick and in the end my sister gave him a Badedas bath and cleaned his teeth with Pearl Drops until he was like a Hollywood star.

It was lovely having a dog around. It always is — even a small, nervy one with minty breath. Rick brought the owner to life. He would pop him in the pocket of his dressing gown and take him for visits to the day room. And he would talk to him and say how sweet he was and how handsome. He was a huge hit, especially with Lady Briggs and Miss Brixham.

Sister Saleem felt differently. She had nothing against Rick, per se, but thought it indulgent to have dogs inside as pets. 'Is he going to guard us against intruders?' she asked and, because it was rhetorical, answered herself, 'No, he is not.' She tolerated Rick, though, because she was charging him £3 a week plus food.

Mr Godrich arrived finally, one morning, in a taxi this time, and Matron quickly asserted herself as a dog specialist and reclaimed Rick from the owner and told Mr Godrich she'd see to his feeding and toileting (Rick's) — thinking it the quickest way to Mr Godrich's heart. Which it probably would have been under normal circumstances, but I wasn't actually sure Mr Godrich was hearing her.

Mr Godrich, the man himself, was a bit of a disappointment. He had absolutely no vim in him. And apart from occasionally hawking up and spitting into a dish, he did nothing but lie in bed staring at the ceiling, propped up by a special catarrh pillow.

There was much discussion about his condition. Matron considered him to be on the mend, and truly believed he'd bounce back after one of her back rubs, but Sister Saleem began to suspect that he was much worse, health-wise, than his relatives had made out. And, if that was the case, there'd have to be a meeting with them and a recalculation — the fees having been calculated on the basis of him being in basic good health and with no extraordinary medical needs. Nevertheless, here he was at death's door — or so it seemed — and we'd banked on two months' money minimum and forced Lady Briggs into moving. Although, as it turned out, that was a good thing. And Sister said she didn't want Matron to give him, or anyone, a back rub.

At team talk one day Sister Saleem told us that Mr Godrich would never recover sufficiently to live independently. 'That man will never be able to look after himself and a dog,' she said. And in all likelihood, he'd remain at Paradise Lodge.

I watched Matron taking all this in as she buffed up her china teacup and saucer.

'He needs round-the-clock care,' said Sister Saleem.

* * *

Sister Saleem wanted us to make the most of ourselves. Not just regarding our looks, but professionally too. She'd often ask if we were satisfied with our work or whether we thought we could improve etc.

Sister Saleem wasn't afraid to tackle even the thorniest of issues. She was disappointed that our love lives were so immature and there were no wedding plans. No one asked her for her status, we thought of her as neutral.

'You girls are all swollen and fat because of your contraceptive pills and drinking so much alcohol.' It was true, the nurses were all chubby due to being on the pill — except for Carla B who was on a low dose specially devised to not cause weight gain. But she didn't tell everyone — it giving her the advantage, figure-wise.

'What medications are you taking?' she asked Matron.

Matron looked mortified at this. 'I beg your pardon,' she said.

'I have been wondering what you are taking, I notice your skin is sensitive to sunlight and you have some muscle twitching,' said Sister Saleem.

'That's none of your business,' said Matron, and she bustled out of the room.

⋆ ⋆ ⋆

I was thrilled one day when the talk turned to facial features and Sister Saleem said I had nice eyes. Having nice eyes, she said, was a great thing and could make up for awful defects.

'If you have pretty eyes,' she said, 'you can get away with a flat behind or hairy arms or even spots — but having not very nice eyes is a curse.'

We all discussed this and agreed, the worst kind of eyes being dead eyes which don't sparkle. The deadest I knew of were Nurse Hilary's, which looked like a fish's eyes, or Miss Pitt's — who looked like she'd poisoned you but you didn't know it yet. The nicest eyes were almond-shaped, but not like Sister Saleem's which, although almond-shaped, had purple skin all around — which my sister said was the colour of a man's resting genitals, but not in front of her.

Anyway, even with mediocre eyes you could improve them with care and a bit of make-up and putting your chin down, said Sister Saleem, and not looking down your cheeks at someone.

Sister Saleem said the most alluring look for any type of eyes was the 'on the brink of weeping' look but not with actual tears, just the facial expression. Smiling was nice but could be

264

off-putting and look crazy.

I vowed not to smile quite so much at Mike Yu. I didn't want him to think I was crazy, but then again I didn't entirely like the idea of looking as though I was 'on the brink of weeping' — especially as I often was when looking at him and could easily tip over.

It wasn't my style to linger, try to get into a conversation or angle for a lift or in any way do anything treacherous or flirty. But I can't deny I did look at Mike Yu too often and for too long and hard and full in the eyes and I knew he knew. I thought he looked at me a bit too hard as well. Although it's always difficult when you think someone's staring at you and makes you stare at them and then they think you started it, or they might think that. Ditto with people in general. So I was going to try this weepy look the next time I saw him, and I knew exactly what time he pulled up into the drive every day to collect Miranda in his Datsun. I might find an excuse to wander out into the courtyard and go, 'Oh, hi, Mike, how are you?' and look as if I was on the brink of tears and look at his face while he answered something like, 'Hi, Lizzie, how are you?'

★ ★ ★

Miranda and Lady Briggs had an altercation. Lady Briggs had become quite outspoken since coming downstairs and she'd told Miranda, again, that she actually *wasn't* in love with Mike Yu and wasn't in love with anyone — she could

265

tell by her eyes (like everyone else, she was obsessed with a person's eyes). Miranda had been annoyed by Lady Briggs poking her nose in and called her a gormless old idiot.

Later, Miranda told me the reason she'd been so upset by it was that it was true. She *had* cooled off towards Mike Yu and found herself pulling away from his barely-there kisses and not finding his hand-holding and finger-squeezing so erotic, or erotic at all, and it was just fucking weird.

'Are you going to drop him?' I asked.

'God, no,' she said, 'but I am going to get this other boy out of my system and I know I'll go back on to Mike Yu.'

'What other boy?' I said, furious.

'Just some boy,' she said. 'I'm just using him for the sex because Mike won't.'

She confided in me that she had started seeing her ex, Big Smig, the boy from Market Harborough who her parents really liked. Big Smig was a nickname. His real name was something like Rupert Smith-Browne. There was also a *Little* Smig in Market Harborough — Miranda was at pains to make clear that her Smig was the big one. Big Smig had a Kawasaki ZIB 900 and though it wasn't as convenient as Mike Yu's Datsun, especially in rainy weather, the Kawasaki was much sexier in Miranda's eyes. Big Smig had taken the baffles out of the exhaust to make it that bit louder than it already was and it meant everyone looked at him as he roared by, in fact it was so loud everyone looked at him as soon as he started it up. Miranda explained that

266

taking baffles out of a Kawasaki exhaust was the male equivalent of wearing a very enticing outfit — say, a low-cut blouse or a bum-skimming mini. Or a bird having colourful plumage or an interesting call. And Miranda found that exciting. He was the exact opposite of Mike Yu, who was modest and dignified and whose ambition wasn't to turn heads but to live a happy and fulfilled life and do no harm and to start a foil container business and employ over one hundred people and breed sighthounds.

I realized then that dignity was what I admired most in a man — that, and a love of dogs. It did slightly worry me that Mike Yu might be planning to cook and eat the dogs he hoped to breed, but that was just a horrible racist thought of the type that everyone had back then. Even decent people, and I'm ashamed of thinking it.

The news about Big Smig was troubling and thrilling. While undoubtedly bad for Mike Yu it made my feelings for him slightly less wrong and illegal, and that was good for me. And I felt it took me a tiny step closer to Mike being my boyfriend, and thinking that was incredible. I'd only ever had one boyfriend and it hadn't gone well. I'd realized pretty quickly that this boy and I were incompatible (because of everything he said and did), so I told him it was over. It took months for him to get the message. It was so excruciating, I thought I was going to have to pay someone to kill him.

But I was normal and neither a nympho, like the Owner's Wife, nor asexual, like poor Carla B who never got the urge or imagined sex except to

267

ward off car sickness — it is such a good warder-off of car sickness, better even than imagining winning the pools (for me anyway). But you have to start thinking about it as soon as you start your journey. There's no point waiting until you're a mile down the road and feeling queasy, you can't then suddenly try to get in the mood for sexual thoughts. If you feel sick, it's already too late and your best bet is to look out of the front window.

Anyway, Mike was semi-free of Miranda and that was overall a very happy-making thing.

24

Wedding Rings

I went into town on the County Travel with Miranda and Sally-Anne, who were going to look at clothing, but I had to leave them at lunchtime to meet my mother and sister at Green's the Jeweller on Church Gate — to look at wedding rings. I was to represent Mr Holt and choose a ring for him. 'Shouldn't Jack choose?' I'd asked but Jack had said, 'No, thanks, I hate choosing other people's wedding rings.' Which was one of the funniest things Jack had ever said and made us all die.

And Mr Holt made it nice by saying, 'In any case, Jack's needed at the Snowdrop depot.'

I interviewed Mr Holt to find out his taste in wedding rings and he said all sorts of witty things that I wouldn't be able to repeat to my mother. And in the end he just said, 'No nonsense, love.' Which made my job easy but boring.

My mother and sister were already in the shop when I got there. They were looking at the pendants — my mother was holding a great ugly cross up to her throat, with a thorn-crowned Jesus on it.

I got straight down to business and approached the shop assistant — a little fellow with an onyx ring on his right-hand ring finger, which seemed too big for his delicate hand and I thought must mean he was homosexual but could equally have meant he got a discount. 'We're choosing wedding rings,' I told him, 'for a man and a woman. The woman,' and I pointed to my mother, 'will want one of the nicest ones but the man wants something very plain, no nonsense.'

The shop assistant went to the glass cabinets flanking the walls and returned. 'These are the plainest gentlemen's,' he said, placing a velvet-covered tray on to the table in front of me. 'And these,' he said, placing another, 'are the nicest ladies' rings.'

I called my mother over. The chunky crucifix was now resting on her sternum. We gazed at the gentlemen's rings. 'They're very plain,' she said.

'He doesn't want any nonsense,' I reminded her.

We looked at the ladies' tray — a collection of diamond-cut, engraved and fussy rings in different colour golds. 'This one is yellow gold — a golden gold — and this is rose gold. This is pink gold and this, this is lovely, it's rhodium-coated white gold.'

We picked up certain rings and tried them on and after a short while my sister said she had to go on an errand and she'd be back in a few minutes. I secretly knew she was looking at a second-hand wedding dress in the War on Want on Granby Street and we gave each other a sisterly look. The minute my sister had stepped out of the shop, Miranda and Sally-Anne appeared. I wished to God I hadn't told Miranda that we'd be there because she completely took

270

over the event and, though my mother had never thought much of Miranda, she very much enjoyed the way she conducted the whole thing, saying, 'Look at the way it catches the light,' and, 'You'll only have one wedding ring,' and, 'It's a symbol of your love,' and all that kind of thing that I imagined my mother was beyond.

It was easy to see how much time all this was taking since clocks kept chiming the quarter-hour and Miranda was not for speeding things up but kept asking for different trays to be brought out and saying which wedding ring she liked best — not that she was planning to buy hers there at Green's but at Mappin's of Bond Street, London, or even Tiffany's in the US of A (her words) — and also that she was planning to get her dinner service from there, a replica of the one 'Lady Bird' Johnson commissioned Tiffany to design for the White House, featuring ninety flowers and all sorts of fronds and leaves.

This sickened me. Not only because it was supposed to be my mother's wedding ring event but because it made me feel funny about her trapping Mike Yu with yet more disgusting plans and status symbols.

In the end, there was no wedding ring my mother liked. Not a single one. The main problem being she hated the idea of marriage but truly loved her husband-to-be and no ring the shop assistant showed us (or Miranda chirruped about) no matter how it 'caught the light' quite matched my mother's feelings and though I'd seen a nice plain band for Mr Holt, she thought it bad form to buy his and not hers.

So, we decided to call it a day and Miranda and Sally-Anne left.

My mother took off the crucifix, we thanked the assistant (who had been extraordinarily nice) and started to leave. On our way out my mother's eye was caught by a tray of mixed trinkets in the porch window.

'What are these?' she asked the fellow.

'That tray is entirely second-hand,' said the assistant, 'but there are a couple of handsome rings amongst it.' And there were.

My mother fell in love with a traditional Irish Claddagh ring — a crown with two hands holding a heart and which represented love, loyalty and friendship (the hands: friendship, the heart: love, and the crown: loyalty). This ring had come from Galway and had a mark on it to say so. This appealed. My mother adored Ireland, especially the west, and said it had all the best creative minds and that for every brilliant writer there was a sister who could paint like anything and an even better poet cousin and that they could all build canoes and tame animals to boot, and then the assistant said he was from County Kildare and had raced horses at the Curragh and my mother pretended to know it and then changed the subject.

Sitting quite close to the Claddagh on the second-hand tray was a plain gold ring. 'What's this one?' asked my mother.

'It's a nine-carat utility ring from the war years,' said the assistant, picking it off the velvet and peering at it with his tiny telescope, 'so called because it weighs less than two pennyweights.

The two rings came together.'

'You mean that these rings were married to one another?' my mother asked.

'I believe they were, madam,' said the assistant.

'Oh, my God,' said my mother, 'that's incredible, don't you think, Lizzie?' and I said I supposed it was.

'Don't you think that's the most romantic thing in the world?' she asked the assistant, and he said it really was very romantic indeed. And my mother had to dab her eyes.

My mother couldn't fully decide until my sister came back. 'I must just check with my daughter,' she said. 'I always need her seal of approval.'

I was stunned. She'd had *my* seal of approval, why did she need my sister's? I thought I was the top seal of approval. I was the one most like her, who understood her. I'd said I thought the rings were romantic etc. And she herself fucking loved them and had cried real tears over the idea of them and now we had to wait for my sister to come back and give the final seal.

And when she did, two minutes later — with a bag — the assistant showed her the Claddagh and the utility ring and she said they were so perfect and meaningful she might cry, even though she wasn't the type, and the assistant looked relieved.

'Wait a minute,' I said, 'I'm not sure about the ladies' ring, I'm not sure I like the little hands, they're a bit monkey-like.' But the assistant and my mother and my sister didn't even hear me.

Anyway, my mother paid for them with cash and left Mr Holt's there to be engraved with a secret message. Before we left the shop my mother asked what was in the bag and my sister took out a silky dress and it was as though someone had thrown a jug of cream across the carpet. She held it up and there were embroidered vines and twisted silk for straps and the bottom was fluted like a slim, cream lily.

'What's that?' asked our mother.

'It cost one pound-fifty,' said my sister, which didn't answer the question but seemed like good value.

25

The Fight Back

Even though Newfields were getting all the available patients, Sister Saleem never indulged in badmouthing them — the rest of us did, though. We called it ugly, modern and soulless, and said the nurses looked like clapped-out old prossers. How could the patients be happy, we wondered, when there wasn't a tree or a leaf in sight, let alone a reservoir view? It was all wipe-clean and plastic, nothing was antique or unique (not counting the patients themselves) and the nurses were only there for the money. Sister Saleem's attitude was, if GPs were recommending the place and patients choosing to go there, they must like what Newfields had to offer. It was a free market and instead of childish name-calling and envy, we should take note and make our home more attractive and get it noticed. We should fight back.

And when Newfields put out a brand-new, glossy eight-page brochure packed with activities, amenities, facilities (including their new 'Stair-levator' stair-mounted lift) and smiling 65-year-olds sniffing sweet williams, Sister Saleem just leafed calmly through it and used it to gently motivate us.

'Look here,' she said, 'they have daily chairobics to improve flexibility — we can do that. They have goldfish, bingo, games after-noons and Vicar visits — we can do all that.'

And then, after a long talk with the owner, Sister Saleem announced that Paradise Lodge was going to fight back with a full-colour illustrated advertising leaflet which would be distributed to appropriate places throughout the county and really get the Paradise Lodge name 'out there'. It was important news, but without the actual leaflet there to admire, it was difficult to get excited.

Also, we were to have the builders in to make a series of small but important and very visible improvements to the place.

Carla B, who'd worked at Newfields, talked us through the Newfields brochure. She said the people in the pictures weren't bona fide patients but models from the ABC School of Dancing where the Owner's Wife and Dee-Anna were taking lessons, and the tropical fish tank had been on loan from the Red Rickshaw for the shoot, and she told us that there was a secret plan to throw Newfields open to the public the following Whitsun holiday (by which time the grass and saplings would have grown a bit), when they'd offer tours of the home, with entertainments, local celebrities, Radio Leicester and refreshments. And it would become an annual event — maybe even the highlight of Whitsun.

'She's going to invite everyone and it will all be free and fun,' said Carla B.

'Why don't we have an open day,' I shouted, 'but sooner?'

'Brillo, Lis!' said Sister Saleem. 'We will beat them to it.'

Then we did get excited. We all chattered like mad about what we might do at our open day until Sister Saleem shut us up and scheduled a meeting for the following week where we could all share ideas and suggestions sensibly. We talked of almost nothing else all week.

Sister wondered if we should get a local choir to sing — maybe even her church — but we all said no. The patients and villagers were up to their necks in choirs and would prefer some amusing and interesting turns, like Miranda's moving dance to 'Young Hearts Run Free' or Carla B's cancan, which showed her pants, but fleetingly (that being the point). Sister agreed but drew the line at Big Smig reciting 'Mary had a little lamb' in burps. I couldn't think of anything to do.

My sister suggested bringing Sue the dog to do her jumping out of the window trick, which she loved doing and for some reason looked hilarious, especially after being told, 'Stay, Sue, do not go out of that door, Sue.' It doesn't sound much but I was certain the patients would love it, it being just their kind of silly humour.

Sally-Anne was too shy and awkward to perform any act but agreed, in theory, to wear a coat backwards for Eileen's 'two drunken men' act. But Sister Saleem had misgivings and felt it might offend the owner.

Gordon Banks' wife, Mindy, wanted her ten-year-old nephew to sing Allegri's *Miserere mei, Deus*, but we all groaned and said we didn't want anything gloomy or serious. Mindy said he was double-jointed and could bend his thumbs back horribly at the end. I knew the *Miserere* and said it would be sacrilege to bend his thumbs back at the end and Mindy said she was just trying to add a comedy note. In the end we said he could sing 'Mother Of Mine' or 'Wings Of A Dove' and she was happy. The cook wanted to bring her dog, Brandy, in and have it attack the Hoover, which was apparently great fun to watch, but we'd already got Sue's window leap to look forward to so asked the cook for a boiled ham instead.

Carla B talked endlessly about the importance of bunting and tried to recruit people to help her sew the necessary yards of it but no one volunteered, and she was on her own. I couldn't help but wonder if this was somehow connected to her being asexual and wanting some kind of elaborate physical activity.

I haven't said much about Carla B (apart from her being asexual). But I'd like to add here that I started liking her (or rather sympathizing) when she'd said one day, 'I used to love Mondays and longed for school to start again,' meaning she hated being at home at weekends. It made me think she must've had a miserable home life. In my opinion, having a miserable home life is the worst thing to have — whoever you are — because it should be where you're able to rush in and go to the toilet and flop on the sofa and cry at the horror of the world, or laugh at the silliness of it, and not dread being there. God. And thinking that made me realize how nice my own home was and, even more so, how nice Paradise Lodge was and how much we all, patients and nurses alike, loved to be there — crying or laughing or on the toilet. And that was a huge deal and I considered offering to speak along these lines at the open day. I might have said that I liked being there so much that on my split shifts, in the break between 1 p.m. and 5 p.m. when I could have jumped on a bus to somewhere exciting or gone upstairs to the off-duty nurses' quarters and listened to records or gone for a walk in the pretty countryside, I preferred to hang about, sitting on the arm of an easy chair, showing a lady how well the Norwegian hand cream rubs in compared to Nivea and doesn't leave a greasy residue, although I'd have had to admit to preferring the smell of Nivea for a general body lotion. Still do. I didn't offer to speak, though, because the sad fact is that ideas of this kind just don't come across, you can't tell it, you have to feel it for yourself. But to me it was a huge revelation.

By the time the official open day meeting came we had a thousand wonderful ideas between us. Some of the best things were rejected for safety or financial reasons, including the donkey derby and the hot-air balloon. Sister Saleem had to keep emphasizing and re-emphasizing how little cash we had to spend and that the entertainments must be home-made, and she reminded us that the whole point was to showcase the home and the idea of living there. By the end of the planning meeting everyone had been given their duties and jobs in the run-up to the event and for the actual day, and we had a provisional schedule including the following:

Gordon Banks to head a balloon
Guests welcomed in with a glass of sherry
  or squash
House tours offered throughout the after-
  noon (guided by the owner and Carla B)
Talks entitled 'My Life at Paradise Lodge'
  (Miss Tyler and Matron)
Hand and foot care, nail cutting and hand
  cream application (Deb-on-Hair)
Talk entitled 'Constipation: Causes, Cures
  and Common Sense' (in a side room
  with Nurse Eileen)
Afternoon tea
'Young Hearts Run Free' — dance on the
  patio (Miranda Longlady)
Sue the dog
The thumb piano demonstration (Mike Yu)
'I Dreamt I Dwelt In Marble Halls' (Lady
  Briggs)
'Wings Of A Dove' sung by Wesley Banks
Sketching lesson (Nurse Eileen)
Chairobics session
Miss Tyler's 'Oh! Oh! Antonio' (which no
  one had actually heard but she'd do on
  the day)
Kung fu demonstration and *The Weaver
  Girl and the Cowherd* story-dance (Mike
  Yu and Miranda Longlady)
Barry Sheene demo on gravel path (Big
  Smig)

We spent a good many team talks focusing on the open day — the activities, talks, tours and entertainments. Also, what refreshments? Sister had wondered about roasting a kid but we all agreed that the patients and guests would prefer egg and cress sandwiches and cakes.

Sister Saleem was keen to have a leaflet in time for the open day, and there was much talk about what to feature in it. And once we'd decided between us, Sister Saleem and my sister made a rough and took some photographs and hired Mr Costello — of Costello & Son Printers from Northampton — to produce a trifold advertising leaflet.

⋆   ⋆   ⋆

And then one day, at coffee break, Mr Costello called in and delivered five fat bundles of leaflets, and they looked wonderful. They weren't as glossy and thick as the Newfields brochure but they were a start and Paradise Lodge already felt better and improved.

The words across the front read: 'Paradise Lodge — *Come Here to Live*'.

'Come Here to Live' had been Nurse Eileen's idea. She'd said it to Mr Godrich's relatives when they'd wanted him to be admitted too soon, before he was well enough, and it turned out they couldn't stand looking after Rick the dog.

'Come Here to Live' implied you'd have a fun time and that you hadn't just been dumped there to die. Even though you probably, eventually would.

There were three colour photographs on the leaflet. One was of Miranda in her white dress, smiling at Miss Tyler in her turban. There was a fold across Miranda's face, which gave her a big chin. Another was of Mr Simmons' hand — with clean, short nails and a signet ring — resting on the arm of Mr Freeman's corduroy Parker Knoll with just a hint of a garden view. The last was of Rick the Yorkshire terrier sitting in Miss Boyd's lap and Miss Boyd laughing but looking dignified in a smart blouse. It was only right that Rick should feature, him being a dog and us having a 'well-behaved dogs welcome' policy and him indirectly causing the slogan 'Come Here to Live'.

There was also a small extra bundle of leaflets which advertised our *Open Day* with a trendy 'stop press' stamp, as if we'd just remembered it. 'All Welcome', 'Refreshments', 'Entertainments', 'Talks', 'Games' it said, and it listed all the fun things on offer. The date was Saturday the 15th.

What? Hang on!

I was stunned to see the date was Saturday the 15th. I almost choked. The 15th was the date for my mother and Mr Holt's wedding day. I froze with confused and troubled thoughts. I checked the date. It was the 15th, both things were happening on the 15th, and neither could be changed.

Which was more important — the open day or the wedding? The wedding, of course, but somehow the open day was important too. Privately, secretly, the open day was *much* more important to me. The open day was a huge thing

282

for me. I was involved. It had been my idea. I had suggested Mike Yu perform on his thumb piano and do a kung fu story-dance and it was me who'd planned Marguerite Patten's skyscraper club sandwiches and two types of tea in separate catering teapots, which were big but had two handles and were easy to carry, even by a steady eighty-year-old (Mr Simmons).

Now it was all going to happen without me there. Mike Yu would do his kung fu while I was stuck at my house, wearing culottes and borrowed high sandals or a home-made bridesmaid's dress (if I let Carrie Frost twist my arm) eating mini cheese flans and sipping a home-made punch and making small talk with two Liberals, two laundry workers and my overexcited mother in a War on Want dress.

I ran up to my sister who was giving a patient a bath. I apologized and interrupted with the bad news. And I gabbled on and on about the social clash. She thought as she rinsed the patient's hair with a jug and then shampooed again.

'You rinse and repeat?' I said.

'Sometimes,' she said.

'We can't miss the open day,' I said, wanting some wisdom and guidance from her.

'We can't miss the wedding,' she said, which was what I was expecting.

'I know,' I said. 'But what about the open day?'

She thought about it. I could tell she was thinking because she rinsed the patient's hair again and shampooed again (a third time). And as she let a thin trickle of water fall gently on to the patient's waxy head she said, 'The wedding party could take place here — at the open day.'

'Oh, God,' I said, 'I mean, gosh.'

And the patient said, 'Amen.'

I ran down the stairs and found Sister Saleem in the owner's nook.

'I have a huge favour to ask you,' I said.

★   ★   ★

The Paradise Lodge open day was going to appeal to the whole community. Mainly, though, to middle-aged people who might want to have an elderly relative housed there. In addition to that, it was going to be the venue for my mother and Mr Holt's wedding tea because Sister Saleem had been thrilled at the idea.

This combining of private and community events was perfectly normal where Sister Saleem came from and since it suited us, no one mentioned it being slightly unusual here. Sister Saleem had only stressed that my mother should wear a proper dress and at least hold a bouquet — knowing how unorthodox she could be at times.

I was to be in charge of the tea — the planning and serving on the day — even though I was also second bridesmaid. I had asked various reliable people, and my mother, for cake and tart donations.

My mum was very pleased to be involved and promised an almond cake which was extremely tricky to make but looked nothing — even though it would be in the run-up to her wedding day and she'd be busy doing what brides do in the run-up. I wondered if she might be better off making something easy that looked stunning — like when you buy a cake and tinker with the icing and pass it off as home-made — but she was adamant the almond cake was the best-tasting cake ever made. It was strange to hear her talking like that about cakes, her being borderline anorexic and never touching a crumb since piling on three stone during her pregnancy with baby Danny due to denying herself drugs.

Mrs Longlady was going to bring the famous secret recipe, Longlady Chocca-Chocca cake, which I knew the patients would hate. They weren't as keen on chocolate as the next generation and they hated silly names. Gordon Banks had promised a Dundee and I was going to buy some mini Bakewells.

⋆ ⋆ ⋆

The improvements and the open day — and in fact everything Sister Saleem had been striving for — were all about happiness, she told us one day.

'It's *all* about happiness,' she said, with her arms outstretched.

This was a Sunday and she always talked like this on a Sunday because she'd have been to church and it was her way of spreading the Lord's joy. Not to miserable St Edmund's or St Nicholas in the next village — where you'd be gloomy as hell afterwards and just relieved to have it over with for another week — but a happy-clappy church by the brook where they sang modern songs and acted out being happy for an hour, even though they'd made total idiots of themselves, grinning and waving, clasping each other's hands, clapping and singing childish songs. We knew all about it because one by one she'd asked us to go. 'Just see what it's like,' she'd said. And we had and none of us had ever returned.

It was nice to hear, though (that everything we were striving for was about making the patients happy), it made sense and seemed the right thing and better than it just being a business to make money for the owner and his nieces — or whoever would inherit.

'I want to see the ladies and gentlemen laughing and singing and never, never crying,' said Sister Saleem as she tucked into her roast lamb that day. The roasts had been reinstated due to the cook agreeing to come in on Sundays to do them — on the condition that she was paid up front and got to take the leftovers home for her husband who'd got a disease and couldn't digest shop-bought food.

The ladies did seem happy. They laughed a lot and they never cried, even when they were sad. You sometimes wished they would. I mean, even as Miss Mills had lain on the linoleum with a fractured femur saying, 'I'm a goner, Fanny-Jane,' she wasn't crying, as such. She was just saying. And Miss Geltmeyer hadn't cried when the chiropodist slipped off his stool and almost had her toe off.

Matron was the one female who seemed unhappy — even Sally-Anne had a bright future, albeit with twin-shaped ghosts forever lurking. Matron was the most likely to cry. She'd often hark back to her childhood or early adulthood and tell all sorts of sad tales and quite often she'd cry, even when the others had stopped listening. She'd be telling a story in which she was the victim of an injustice — from 1920-something — and she'd have to go scrabbling around in her pocket for her handkerchief at the memory of it. She'd made me cry once. Her mother had forgotten to pick her up from the dentist, or never intended to. Matron (though she wasn't a matron then — not even a bogus one — being only seven or eight years old) had caught a horse and cart into the nearest town, which I think might have been Dublin or Limerick, and had had a whole load of teeth taken out by a cruel old dentist who just pulled out people's teeth for money and didn't even try not to. She'd been given the cocaine gas and was all woozy and upset and walking home with bloody dribble on her chin. She'd had enough money for the horse and cart but was too woozy to be sensible. The memory made her lips tremble and her hand came wavering up and she dabbed her hanky under her spectacles and the whole thing was too sad to watch. A dalek would've cried.

It was difficult to tell with the old men, crying-wise, mainly because the obvious ones always had watery eyes all the time and the less obvious ones were just lying there not awake enough to be crying or not crying. The only unhappy male was the owner, who had been diagnosed with a sprained heart (and alcoholism). The owner having a sprained heart proved the theory I'd heard a few times — that a break is better than a sprain. A sprain leaving a weakness forever, whereas a break mending and leaving only a hairline scar — imperceptible except by X-ray. A sprain just keeps spraining, just as you trust it to be strong and you put weight on it, it goes again and you're on the floor (that's a sprained ankle, but it must be the same with a sprained heart). Unlike Matron, though, the owner would never dream of crying. He was one of those posh folk who speak in slurred baby talk and pretend everything's jolly and walk around with ice cubes clanking around in a chunky tumbler. Like my mum used to be, except she never had ice cubes.

We talked about crying at the kitchen table over the roast. Nurse Eileen told of her aunt who had never let herself cry, even when awful things happened, which they did a lot, but the aunt just got on with life and in the end she'd exploded with pent-up grief. Not exploded like a bomb but like a rancid Kia-Ora carton. And had ended up in The Towers for a spell. She was taught how to cry after that, by a special crying therapist who would shout at her, 'Cry Nora, cry!' And the aunt (Nora) would cry. And she became like any normal person, crying at the Hovis ad and so forth, and when very good or very bad things occurred in life or on telly.

26

Baby-Face Finlayson

My wedding present to my mother and Mr Holt was that I was turning over a new leaf attendance-wise at school. I hadn't told them about it in case it came to nothing. Anyway, I'd gone into school with a clean shirt and even had my sister's smart satchel-type bag. I looked as if I meant business.

My first lesson was double French but I was advised by Madame Perry to go instead to the European Studies class — the CSE alternative.

'*Quoi?*' I said.

'*Tu es dans la classe inférieure,*' said Madame Perry, looking sorry.

I went to see Miss Pitt.

'I seem to have been moved into the CSE classes,' I said.

'Yes, correct, you have been,' she said. 'You can move into the 'O' Level groups as soon as I've had another meeting with my stepfather.' She said it straight out.

'But I arranged a meeting — it wasn't my fault the milkman brought him back to Paradise Lodge.'

'Ach!' she clicked her fingers. 'It was the milkman, was it?'

'Well, I don't know, I heard it was,' I said, kicking myself.

'Get me that meeting, in church, at a concert, in a tea room, it's up to you. Just do it, and then you can move groups, do you understand, Lizzie?'

'Yes,' I said, 'I'll try.'

★ ★ ★

On Miranda's sixteenth birthday Mike gave her a C60 cassette of himself singing Paul McCartney's 'Silly Love Songs'. It was the most wonderful, romantic, heartbreaking thing I'd heard, sadder even than the Purcell. Miranda played it on the owner's Panasonic at coffee break. I felt she should have kept it private.

I gave her a card and a bamboo back-scratcher that I'd got from the Very Bazaar on Silver Street. Everyone had a little go with it. It was generally agreed to be blissful and everyone wanted one.

Sister Saleem gave her a copy of *The Diary of Anne Frank* which, she said, every teenager in the world should read and ponder on their good fortune. (Unless they lived under siege or hostile occupation.) Miranda was thrilled to get *The Diary of Anne Frank*. She turned it over and over in her hands.

I could tell she'd never even heard of Anne Frank because she said, 'I can't wait to read Anne's adventures.' And when she got some looks she deflected them by saying, 'Bloody hell, Anne Frank's the spitting image of Lizzie.'

And that caused everyone to look at the photograph of Anne Frank and then at me and then back at Anne Frank. It was awkward because no one wanted to agree — because of her tragic fate and not wanting to seem shallow talking about Anne Frank's looks — but it was undeniable.

I regretted giving her the back-scratcher and wished I'd only given her a card.

★   ★   ★

Sally-Anne came looking for me one day. I was in the laundry folding ladies' dresses. She told me Matron needed me urgently in Room 9 — Mr Godrich's room. I trotted up there hoping they were going to tell me the three of them — Matron, Mr Godrich and Rick — were planning to run off together at the end of his convalescence. But when I got there Matron was clanking about with ghoulish instruments and a kidney dish, in desperate tears. She needed me to help her lay out Mr Godrich, she said. I wasn't sure what it meant.

'What do you mean, lay him out?' I asked.

'I mean, he's dead, he's gone and fucking died,' she said, pointing to the bed, 'look.'

And there he was — dead.

'So, we've to lay him out,' she said.

'I don't think you should carry out this procedure in your current upset state,' I said, firmly. Also, I didn't want to do it. I'd never laid out a dead body before (and don't even know if it's laid or layed) and I really didn't want to do it or be part of it — even under normal circumstances.

291

Soon Matron was sitting on the bed — squashing the deceased — and telling me all about how she and Mr Godrich had been planning to move out to his home in Stoneygate where she'd be his companion-cum-cleaner-cum-cook-cum-dog-walker. And it had been thoroughly thrashed out and they'd been on the brink of telling Sister Saleem and the owner and handing in her notice when she'd got the call from Nurse Carla B that Mr Godrich looked funny and she'd dashed up the stairs and into his room to find him dead and with his little travel case packed and Rick the Yorkshire terrier trying to revive him with little yaps and digging frantically at his bed sheets. She said it in one long breath and then collapsed down beside the dead man.

'He died, Lizzie,' she said, all muffled.

Rick lay on a cushion in the window seat with his frilly little ears pricked up, alert.

'I know,' I said, of course I knew. To be honest I was worried about poor Rick but knew not to say so.

'And now I've to lay him out,' she said.

The thing was, Matron usually quite liked laying people out. It was a known fact. Not that it was morbid (apparently), she felt it was one of life's rituals and an honour and all of that kind of thing that people might have actually thought in olden times. The staff used to call her 'Mrs Gamp' behind her back. To begin with I thought it was because she always carried an umbrella — even in drought weather — but I found out later it was because she had a penchant for laying out the dead like the grim midwife from *Martin Chuzzlewit*. Anyway, however much of an honour and a privilege the laying out was under normal circumstances, Matron was very sad at this particular laying out and could hardly keep her composure. But she began it anyway. She seemed bad-tempered and it felt wrong. It's best that I don't go into detail except to say that Mr Godrich's mouth wouldn't stay closed and Matron got very cross and swore at him and in the end she put a bandage round his head and tied it under his chin in a great big bow. He looked like Baby-Face Finlayson.

'We were that close, he and I,' she said, holding her gloved finger and thumb close together.

Matron blathered on about what a total let-down it all was, her high hopes for a decent recovery — their talk about a possible cruise around Asia Minor.

It was less awful than I'd imagined — the laying out — it being a preliminary thing rather than the actual real undertaking procedure. But it was still affecting and gave me cause to imagine it being my grandmother, mother or me lying there all creamy with chubby little Matron clanging around, swearing and forcing cotton-wool balls into my cavities.

Finally, she chucked the instruments into the kidney dish, signalled me to close my eyes, and muttered a prayer. In the quietness, we could hear Bruce Forsyth's voice — or was it Val Doonican's? — drifting up from the telly, which was always on high volume because of the hard

293

of hearing, and Matron sped up a bit, said Amen and sloped off to catch the end of whatever it was. On my own with Mr Godrich I tried to feel the importance of being beside a dead person without being silly, but the feeling of wanting to watch the telly took over, like it had with Matron. I picked up Rick and trotted off too.

* * *

Later that day, Matron — in a very sad mood — told us all about a life-changing incident. It was the early 1960s when she was recovering from a disease that had 'pained her beyond endurance' and her parents — themselves quite elderly and decrepit — had gathered all their money and bought her a telly. One of the very first tellies in her village (it was so early I don't think they even called it a telly). And they wired it up and got the aerial sorted so Matron could watch it from her recovery bed, even though there wasn't much on — it being so new — except the news, and the odd cartoon. And that one day when she had nipped out to see the doctor — because it was cheaper than the doctor calling in — and returned and was getting her nightie back on, she realized someone had burgled her telly.

It was bad enough losing the telly, but what made it a life-changing experience and so deeply affecting was that the burglars had simply thrown the telly into the river. They hadn't wanted it for themselves — they'd just not wanted *her* to have it. And not only that, the local council had charged her father to have it removed from the river.

'That's awful,' we all said and meant it. I thought it a rather good and thought-provoking story and a cut above her usual lies and fantasies.

Later Matron seemed a bit better and we chatted in the kitchen.

'What are your plans now, vis-à-vis leaving to take up a live-in companion job?' I asked.

'Oh, I'm looking in *The Lady* magazine, and keeping my ear to the ground,' she said. 'And if you really must know, I'm thinking about Mr Simmons,' she added.

'NO!' I said. 'You can't. He's got that horrible stepdaughter, you'd never inherit, plus, she'd make your life hell.'

I didn't want Matron getting involved with Mr Simmons while I was still trying to secure my place in the 'O' Level group. I was struggling with *Animal Farm* and now Matron was going to lure Mr Simmons away from me luring him away. I couldn't see how it was going to end well — either thing.

Matron looked at me for a moment, saddened.

'I'm sorry,' I said, 'it's just that she's my Deputy Head at school, I know her, and she really is a total cunt.'

I had to put it in the strongest terms, talking to Matron.

'I'm desperate, Lizzie, I need a job and a home. This place is going to go to the dogs, Saleem doesn't believe in me, and what'll become of me?' she said. 'I'm sixty-five.'

'Sixty-five?' I said. 'Crikey, I thought you were at least seventy-five.' It was the new straw-coloured hair, it made her look ancient.

'I'm going to have to try for Mr Simmons,' she said, 'I've no choice; there's no one else.'

★ ★ ★

Early one morning I went to the cemetery with Mr Simmons in his Rover. It was a thing he really wanted to do — it being his late wife's birthday — and the others were too squeamish to go. I thought it'd be a bit of a skive. The normal thing to do, apparently, was to drop the patient off at the warden's post with a few details and wait in the car. I could have let Miss Pitt know about the outing, I suppose I was contractually obliged to, but I hadn't the heart on this particular day.

Mr Simmons' driving was awful and I had to keep saying, 'Keep to the left,' because he constantly veered over into the middle of the road. I realized he really shouldn't be driving when he turned into a gateway for no reason and had to reverse out again and couldn't see in the mirror because he couldn't move his head in that direction. When we finally arrived at the cemetery I could tell the drive had stressed him too much for me to simply dump him with the warden — especially as the warden looked quite grumpy.

'We're very popular today,' said the warden, nodding towards a group of visitors. And he offered us a map of the graves. Mr Simmons said he knew the way but he took the map for reference.

We walked along a few paths and it did seem to be busy. Clusters of people and single figures stood beside graves and sat on benches and the place was alive with activity.

We reached Mrs Simmons' grave. I expected Mr Simmons to lay the flowers down and cross himself but he stood and looked at the stone. I lit a fag, more out of self-consciousness than actually wanting one, and walked away a bit in case he burst into tears. But he didn't, he spoke quite formally, his feet planted on the tiny, gravelly garden with his hands by his sides. I didn't hear it all, only, ' . . . I didn't make you happy, but I remarried, you know.' It was quite conversational, and like a play where people say things they'd never say in real life just to explain to the audience what's going on.

' . . . and I was happy. I think you'd be pleased about that.'

And then he saluted the stone and began to walk away. I thought we were going back to the car but Mr Simmons said, 'No, hang about, I need to see my other wife.'

'How many wives have you had?' I asked.

'Two,' he said, and we chatted as we strolled. His first marriage had been twenty years of mild misery. His second, only three of near bliss until his wife had died stupidly from flu because they'd not realized how bad she was and not wanted to bother the doctor. And now Miss Pitt — who he barely knew and had seen probably twice all the time his wife had been alive — had swooped in and spoilt his already broken life with her voice, her bossiness, her leotards, her awful taste and a mirror with a rainbow surround that made him sick to look at.

He was all tangled up with her now because the will pretty much made him a caretaker — until he died, when everything became hers — and she would badger him about the state of the paintwork on the window frames. 'She doesn't want to inherit a wreck,' said Mr Simmons.

We had some difficulty locating the second wife's plot on the map and when we worked it out (K_{45}), it was quite a walk up a long slope and past the baby graves which were little toadstools and bunnies and I couldn't help wondering whether or not Bluebell had qualified for a toadstool or a bunny or whether he'd been too premature. And by the time we got to K_{45} Mr Simmons was exhausted and we both felt wretched. It was obviously a less expensive plot with no view — except of a grey stretch of the railway just before it reaches the station — and no trees, no benches and no glassy green gravel, just the dead stems of something in an ugly square vase in a rectangle of stubbly grass, and a hundred similar plots. It was where the newest graves and most of the visitors were and it felt strangely crowded and desperate.

Mr Simmons started speaking to K_{45}. Here his hands, rather than hanging by his sides, flapped around expressively as he spoke. I walked away again so as not to hear. But caught this.

'Well, happy birthday, lovey. I've been to see

Floss and she's fine.'

And I saw his hanky come out and suddenly understood why no one else could face coming here. I lit another fag and watched a train stop for a signal and, turning to see if I could make out the university, I saw a figure rushing towards us.

'Well, well, Lizzie,' said Miss Pitt, 'I wish you'd told me Dad was coming out, I could have given him a lift and saved him the petrol.'

'Dad!' she called. He didn't look round but she began walking towards him. 'I've come to say happy birthday to Mum too.'

I grabbed her arm, 'Please let him have a moment,' I said, impressed at my mature tone.

She pulled her arm away and went to walk again but I blocked the path. She tried to dodge to the side but I stood in front of her. She put her whole hand in my face. I shoved her backwards. 'Leave him alone,' I hissed, and I went to push her again but she was too quick and grabbed my arm, wrenching it to the side expertly until I'd fallen to my knees — she'd probably had a lifetime of trying to break children's wrists — then she shoved me and I fell on to the grave of someone called Rose Wilston who'd fallen asleep in 1974.

She was now walking towards Mr Simmons. I crawled after her and grabbed the hem of her coat and, with all my might, pulled until she was on the ground, on her back. I sat on her and held my forearm against her throat. We looked at each other. It was the most extraordinary moment of my life so far — even more extraordinary than my breaking the telephone dial just to hear Mike Yu's voice. I still had a cigarette in my hand, and for some reason I took a puff.

'Lizzie Vogel, get off me right now,' she said, and somehow knocked me off balance, but I wasn't long out of childhood and instinctively pulled her with me. We rolled around, she shouted, 'Get off me, you little devil!' And I shouted back, 'You get back to school and leave us alone — you money-grabbing cow!'

At that, Miss Pitt grabbed the decorative cross that marked Rose Wilston's grave and started hitting me with it. I wrestled it out of her hands and jabbed the pointed end at her in a threatening way. She screamed, grabbed it and held it to my throat as if she was going to throttle me with it.

Everyone for yards around, including Mr Simmons, was looking at us as we rolled about. Someone must have alerted the warden because he suddenly appeared on a scooter.

We got up and brushed the dried grass off our clothing.

'I don't know why you're making such a fuss, Lizzie,' Miss Pitt hissed, 'you made the deal.' And she clipped off.

'What's going on?' asked the warden.

'That woman was trying to interfere with that man,' I said, pointing to Mr Simmons. And Mr Simmons looked suitably shaken. In fact, he was trembling violently with his mouth open — you might describe it as 'hyperventilating noisily'.

The warden jumped off his scooter, stood it beside the dull, cream headstone of Mrs Melitta

Simmons who'd been called to God in 1973 and administered sips of water from his emergency first-aid kit — which was needed, he said, 'every single day on some poor bugger'.

We had a sit down on the nearest bench and I told the warden it had been a domestic incident and nothing criminal. The warden said he'd seen plenty of it — especially by the Ks and Ls and Ms — and he walked us to the car park. Mr Simmons had trouble locating his car. It was a whitish Rover — that was all I knew. And the car park seemed full of white cars.

'What's the registration?' asked the warden.

'You Jolly Fucker 264G,' said Mr Simmons.

We scanned the vehicles and I walked away to get a different angle, until the warden shouted, 'You Jolly Fucker — over there.'

Mr Simmons didn't feel up to driving. That's the thing with old people, it doesn't take much to put them off and then you're stuck. The warden had lingered and when I told him this, he said he'd thought it would be the case and asked if I'd like to telephone someone from his post. I phoned my mother and she must've driven like the clappers because she was with us in less than twenty minutes in the Snowdrop van. She'd been allowed to hold on to the van due to not fully resigning and making odd laundry deliveries as and when necessary for the company, and covering sick leave. She'd agreed to this because she loved her Leyland van — the height, the noise and driving with the door open, which you couldn't do in an ordinary car — and she needed the capacity for carting stuff about

301

for her pine-stripping business. Plus, I think she imagined she could live in it — if the worst came to the worst (that's what I thought anyway). The warden was still lurking and came to join in.

'What's happened?' my mother asked as she strode towards us.

'The girl's had a scrap with a lady at the graveside,' he tipped my mother off, 'very nasty, like something out of *The Exorcist*.'

The incident at the cemetery caused me to have to tell my mother something about my tacit arrangement with Miss Pitt. She'd driven us back to Paradise Lodge. Mr Simmons had got out of the van and I was about to. 'No, wait,' she said, 'what's this all about?'

I gave her the barest bones and she hit the roof. I mean, she actually punched the roof of the van and screamed at me, 'You *fucking* idiot, all you have to do is go to school, what the fuck do you think this is? A story, a play, television? Jesus, Lizzie, just GO TO FUCKING SCHOOL.'

And, later, at home I had to go through it step by step.

'I'll sort this,' my mother said.

302

27

Sale of the Century

Our mother started to sell her last remaining heirlooms. Knowing this made me feel a bit guilty. Not that I could have paid our utility bills with the bits of money I was earning — but it was an irony that I was so well-off and splashing out on various hair products and assorted coffees and teas when she and Mr Holt had such profound financial worries.

She'd first got a taste for selling heirlooms when she'd sold a four-poster bed a few years before — but not the mattress, which she was ashamed for anyone to even see and had to take to the council dump secretly, at dusk, when no one else was around. She wasn't able to lift it on her own and had to ask my sister and brother and me to help. And the shedding of that mattress left its mark on all of us.

We'd been too young to be subtle about it and had asked and asked what was wrong with the mattress and why she couldn't just leave it on the bed for Dr Gurley — who'd bought the bed and was sending someone round to collect it. Finally, she'd had to tell us the mattress was badly stained and that Dr Gurley would buy a new mattress for her and Sheela. 'What stains?' we asked. And then we clambered around in the back of the van as our mother drove and, with

Little Jack's key-ring torch, we located the stains on the mattress and drew round them with our fingers and noticed one was in the shape of a dog with fat legs and another was like a pumpkin. And eventually she'd told us they were bloodstains from some terrible times and my poor little brother cried — imagining someone had been murdered on it (probably someone blameless like Maid Marion's father). And my sister told him it wasn't that. My sister and I realized that it was just the usual women's stuff, just the outpourings of things going right or wrong. And that these things, if they happened to a guinea pig or a dog, would have been all right, but happening to a woman, they were deeply shaming and to be hidden and thrown away at dusk. We didn't feel revolted, we felt frightened.

Anyway, the time had come to sell her last remaining valuable possessions so that she could catch up with some private bills — about which she hadn't been entirely honest with Mr Holt. And so she buffed up some jewellery and polished some wood. She'd inherited a dressing table from somewhere on her mother's side. It was beautiful — if you liked that kind of thing — walnut with a hinged triptych mirror and wavy piecrust edging. She advertised it for sale in the *Longston Advertiser* and hoped her sister-in-law wouldn't notice (it being a family heirloom). Her plan was to accept a price in the region of £35 (nowhere near its real worth — but just to get the quick cash). However, and this is the whole point of writing about this, the person who answered the advert was Miss Pitt and when I saw her standing there on the doorstep, in her hound's-tooth ski pants with her pal the fat doctor, I panicked.

'Oh, shit, don't answer the door, no, tell her it's sold.'

And my mother said, 'No, Lizzie, this is perfect.'

My mother showed her in, sat her at the dressing table and, like the girl off *Sale of the Century*, began demonstrating its features. She slid the long slim sorting drawer out over Miss Pitt's lap so she could appreciate the handy compartments for eyeshadows, lipsticks, powders and so forth. She angled the three mirrors so that Miss Pitt could see her face from every angle and even the back of her head, and showed her that the snug little stool could be tucked away when not in use. And when she was sure Miss Pitt couldn't live without it, she put the price up to £60. And after the fat doctor had loaded it into the back of his Land Rover and Miss Pitt had counted the notes out into her hand and she'd put them into her back pocket my mother said, 'And by the way, if Lizzie isn't reinstated immediately into the 'O' Level classes, I shall report you to the board of education for misconduct.'

I went to registration at school the next possible day and, like magic, Mr Mayne passed me a note telling me to go into the 'O' Level groups for all subjects. He was pleased. 'Now, just make sure you keep up,' he said.

As the days went by, Sister Saleem was very keen to know how Miranda was getting on with *The Diary of Anne Frank* and would ask occasionally, 'How are you getting on with Anne Frank?' And, for a while, Miranda would say, 'I haven't started it yet.'

And then, eventually, she said, 'Yeah, I'm getting through it slowly, it's not the most riveting read — especially after *The World is Full of Married Men* by Jackie Collins.'

One time she said that Anne Frank seemed like a 'right little madam' and Sister winced.

Miranda took ages to read a book. Days. You'd see her at break times reading the same book day after day. Whereas I'd read *Girl From the Outback* in a day and was now rattling through *Animal Farm* by George Orwell even though it was highly allegorical. I mentioned this and Miranda retorted, 'You try reading *The Diary of Anne Frank* and having a full-time boyfriend and rehearsing for the open day.'

One day Miranda was at the kitchen table reading Anne Frank's diary and she cried out in anguish.

Sister Saleem looked concerned. 'Are you all right?' she asked.

Miranda slammed down the book and put her head in her hands. Everyone stopped what they were doing and it was a solemn moment. 'Finally,' we all thought, 'the significance of the book has struck her.'

'I've been following this girl's life, day after

306

day after day,' said Miranda, gloomily 'and she just completely misses my birthday. She goes the 22nd blah-di-blah, 23rd blah-di-blah, 24th blah-di-blah, then the 26th. She totally ignores the 25th.'

Sister Saleem looked stunned.

★　★　★

Mike Yu had a secret. He'd told Miranda and sworn her to secrecy because his parents mustn't find out. He'd had to tell Miranda, though, because it involved her. It was his ambition to move to the USA. He was allowed because he'd lived there slightly as a baby, or maybe he was born there, and that qualified him to go back for as long as he wanted.

Miranda told me, obviously, that's how I knew. The idea captivated her and she couldn't stop talking about it. She'd had a visit to America in 1972 when her family had gone to see Boston in the Fall and it had been the holiday of a lifetime. I remembered this trip well because her sister Melody had given a talk to the class when they got back and had made it sound terrific.

'The funny thing is,' said Miranda, 'I had this feeling when I was there, that I sort of belonged somehow.'

'Oh, well, that's handy,' I said.

'Mike says he's planning to go in 1980, when he's finished his degree and his parents have paid off their mortgage. He wants me to go with him,' she said, doing a fake grimace and gripping my hand.

I was smoking on an empty stomach and hearing this awful news made me nauseous. 'Fantastic,' I said.

And even though it was a secret, the subject of America and moving there and the American dream and so forth began to crop up all over the place.

Mr Simmons said we, as a nation, became envious of the Americans. It had started in the Second World War. And only got worse in the 1950s when things were so bleak here but looking attractive over there and they seemed to do things better. And people would go there and come back full of it. Like the Longladys — when they'd been to see Boston in the Fall and came back talking like they'd never seen a leaf go yellow and die before, or had too much to eat.

Mr Simmons had himself been there and been impressed by the place — the attitude and the confidence and the idea that a man could get on. They'd cracked it, he said, because there was an equality you'd never get here. And Sister Saleem had laughed. She'd been there too. A black woman. And Mr Simmons had apologized for his statement and backed away.

'Will Mike be OK over there?' I asked Miranda, later, privately.

'Why shouldn't he be?' asked Miranda.

Miranda didn't care about equality for Mike, she just wanted an exciting adventure and to snub her mother into the bargain. Mike was just a vehicle.

★   ★   ★

The owner still mourned his marriage and, even though he'd adopted Rick the Yorkshire terrier, he missed Lazarus — the retriever his wife had got custody of. And he missed the children he might have had but hadn't because of his ex-wife despairing of the awfulness of the world. And though they'd been in full agreement about it, he'd begun to worry that she might now have a child, with a new lover — because the world probably didn't seem so awful any more. Not that it had become any better than it was, but because she might be in love — and being in love clouds your perceptions.

'Who'd want to bring children into this awful world — where you can be abandoned and have your dog taken from you, not to mention all the muggings on short cuts and the bombings and the way Venice is overrun with tourists?' the owner kept wondering. And the cook kept agreeing — she'd come in for a chat and a drink but wasn't working because of the money she was owed.

Of course I thought of Danny and all the babies I was planning to have later on and hoped the world would get better — but I felt a bit disheartened. And then Matron piped up with one of her long rambles about how the world was a damned sight better than it used to be and if ever there was a time for hope and babies and for women, it was now and we'd got Paul McCartney to thank for it. And I wondered if the world getting better for Matron was the same thing as it getting awful for the owner but decided it probably wasn't that neat.

Although the cook fully agreed with the owner about the awful state of the world (her being, like him, from the upper classes fallen on hard times), she did have one child now aged twenty-something. The cook defended her decision to bring Anthony into the world.

'I've always been open and frank about how fucking awful the world is,' she said, 'and he is suitably cynical.'

'That's good to hear,' said the owner.

'He rages against the establishment in satirical artworks,' said the cook, 'and he's changed his name to 'Blue'.'

'Bravo,' said the owner.

★ ★ ★

The change in Lady Briggs was striking and occasionally alarming. For a start, she'd stopped eating all her meals from a small bone dessertspoon and had begun using a knife and fork and had even complained that the forks had only three tines, not four.

She'd become sociable. She'd gone from recluse to life and soul of the party within a matter of days. I felt it was like a starving person eating too much cake, too soon and if she didn't slow down, she'd overdose (on metaphorical cake).

She was considerably more mobile than we'd given her credit for and because she'd got hold of one of the Paradise Lodge leaflets (and believed every printed word) it meant we actually had to do some of the things listed, including chairobics, bingo and window bird-spotting and Nurse Eileen had to give the short talk that was advertised as an example of the pastoral care offered ('Constipation: Causes, Cures and Common Sense'). Also, because the leaflet advertised 'interesting excursions' — a thing people would like the idea of but not many would actually want to do — Lady Briggs stirred up an interest where previously there'd been none and formed an excursion committee with a few of the more able ladies and gents. Inevitably, an excursion to a farm in a nearby village was planned.

Matron fell out with Lady Briggs. The two argued like a sitcom, with Lady Briggs as the nice old girl and Matron as the spiteful old harridan.

'Now she's given up being a recluse, she's become a show-off,' said Matron, right in front of Lady Briggs.

'No, she's just enjoying life,' said Eileen. 'She's an ambassador for Paradise Lodge, aren't you, Lady B?'

Matron didn't agree. 'She's gone like a man,' she said, 'bossing everyone around and demanding adventures, just because she's down here being listened to — I preferred her shut up there.'

Lady Briggs had chummed up with Mr Simmons, which was the real problem, now Matron had him in reserve.

Lady Briggs broadcast the possible farm excursion and recruited so many patients we needed to borrow a larger-than-average vehicle from Zodiac Cabs. A minibus was organized and the trip to Burrows' farm was confirmed and arranged. Lady Briggs herself had suggested Burrows' farm because they had a flock of Bluefaced Leicesters — a breed she'd wanted to look at, having heard the fascinating history of it. No one else knew what a Bluefaced Leicester was, except we supposed it was an animal of some sort — but it might have been a turnip for all we knew.

Anyway, the trip was on and we discovered that a Bluefaced Leicester was a sheep and this farm not only had some, they had over a hundred and they'd just been shorn. And that was just the beginning of it.

I hadn't planned to go on the trip but changed my mind when Mike Yu was drafted in to drive at the last minute because Matron's feet wouldn't reach the minibus controls without the steering wheel digging into her 18-hour girdle.

Anyway, off we went with Mike at the wheel and Matron in the passenger seat and six patients and me in the back.

Lady Briggs started off on a lecture. 'Bluefaced Leicesters are a longwool breed of sheep which evolved from a breeding scheme here in Leicestershire in the eighteenth century. Recognizable through their Roman noses and dark blue skin which can be seen through the white hair, hence the name. They are related to the original Leicester longwool breed, and commonly used as sires for mules.' She droned on, reading from a book. 'Fully grown Bluefaced rams can weigh as much as . . . and they have curly threadlike wool, yes, which is lighter than other breeds. They have no wool on the head or neck . . . '

She'd run out of breath and had to pause and Matron put the radio on. 'The Price Of Love' by Roxy Music blared out and I suspect the urgent beat made Mike Yu drive a little faster than was sensible on the undulating lanes.

'Our trip today,' shouted Lady Briggs, like a tour guide, 'will include a close-up experience with a very famous ram — stud name 'Gunner Graham' — the most prolific breeding ram in the county.'

Mike turned into a farmyard and after a few words with the farmer we bumped slowly across a field and stopped. A large flock of sheep started walking towards the minibus. I can't explain what happened next but it was something to do with Lady Briggs opening the window to take a photograph of Gunner Graham and dropping the camera out of the bus.

Lady Briggs shrieked and Matron swore at Lady Briggs, 'You stupid old fucker,' and the patients gasped at the curses. Mr Simmons gallantly got out of the bus to retrieve the camera. Matron then got out, slid the side door shut, jumped back into the passenger seat and ordered Mike Yu to drive away.

'But, Mr Simmons?' said Mike.

'Drive on!' she shouted. 'I said, drive on.'

So Mike started the engine and drove away — leaving Mr Simmons out in the field surrounded by Bluefaced Leicesters. Mike drove slowly and protested, trying to reason with

Matron, but she yelled at Mike again, 'I said, drive on.'

Mr Simmons was now sitting on the grass.

'Hang on,' I said, 'Mike, wait!'

But Matron shouted, 'Drive on, I'm the superior here — '

And I butted in, 'No, you're not.'

And Lady Briggs just stared out of the back window at a sheep removing Mr Simmons' Ascot cap with its mouth.

★   ★   ★

Sister Saleem was surprised to see us back so soon and questions were asked as the patients — most of whom were shaken and upset — filed back into the day room. Matron took herself off and sat in the owner's nook, like a dog waiting to be whipped.

Sister Saleem told Mike and me to go back and collect Mr Simmons. As we set off Sister asked, 'Why did she do it?'

And I said, 'I don't know.' But I did know. She was jealous and mad and I suddenly believed she *had* strangled that nun over the award-winning coffee cake.

Mike Yu was a bit freaked out by what had happened and he likened himself to a young German officer doing what he was told even though he was a decent person at heart etc.

There was no sign of Mr Simmons at the farm — not in the field and not in the farmyard. We'd been told not to ask the farmer but just to find him. He wasn't on the roads between Paradise

Lodge and the farm — about three miles of country lanes.

We walked along the canal towpath.

It'll sound terrible now but no amount of worry for Mr Simmons could stop my romantic feelings for Mike. I was worried and acting worried at the same time, and trying to chat with Mike. Mike himself was very worried, and perfect. He kept thinking of sensible things, like, 'Perhaps someone stopped and offered him a lift,' and I'd say, 'He did talk about the canal, though, so I think we might find him along here.' Just to prolong our walk.

A thought occurred to me and I gasped. I'd realized that Mr Simmons' actual home, Plum Tree Cottage, was in the next village and that he would obviously have walked back there.

I didn't tell Mike my thought, though, because I wanted the joy of strolling with him and maybe seeing a kingfisher and remembering the last time we'd been on the towpath together and I'd brought peace to Grandpapa Yu. It was selfish and awful. I'm not going to try to justify it.

'What?' Mike Yu asked.

'What?' I said.

'You gasped,' said Mike Yu.

'I thought I saw a kingfisher,' I lied.

We ambled on. Mike Yu kept squinting into the distance, around the curves of the towpath, hoping to see the shuffling figure of an old man.

'What do you make of Sally-Anne?' he asked.

'Sally-Anne?'

'Yes, what's she like, you know, as a person?' asked Mike.

'She's dead inside,' I said, and then I pointed out our narrow-boat, *Harmony*, which was either back for another visit or, less romantically, had been parked there all this time, meaning the inhabitants lived on that bit of canal, and never floated along forgetting their cares and spent all their time simply keeping the boat spick and span and admirable for passers-by.

'*Harmony*!' I pointed.

Mike was preoccupied and seemed desperately worried about Mr Simmons. We walked for a while, but there was no sign of him so we turned round.

Back in the Datsun, Mike asked if I knew what had caused Sally-Anne to be dead inside. I didn't mention the twins and her baggy downstairs and numb heels — due to a fast and multiple birth, and never being able to marry royalty. I suspected Miranda had already told him all that, plus I didn't want to spoil our walk with gossip of that kind. Instead, I said she suffered with a difficult past.

'Oh, God!' I yelled. 'I've just realized where Mr Simmons is.'

Mike looked at me. 'Where?'

'He'll be at his cottage, I'll show you.'

I directed Mike and soon we pulled up outside Plum Tree Cottage. Mr Simmons was shuffling up the path and, at that moment, the front door opened and there stood the Deputy Head.

I leapt out of the car. 'Mr Simmons!' I called.

He didn't hear and, after ushering him inside, Miss Pitt looked at us and gave me that hand signal that means 'OK' to an adult (but can also indicate 'vagina' if used concurrently with a prodding index finger). Miss Pitt thought I'd delivered Mr Simmons home as per our tacit agreement in spite of our fight at the cemetery. It was unbelievable but that was teachers for you. No grudges.

* * *

Sister Saleem hadn't decided whether or not to sack Matron for leaving a patient in the sheep field — she suspended her from duty while she thought it through and spoke to her church minister.

Matron popped up when Sister Saleem wasn't around. Just to say what a know-it-all monster Lady Briggs had become and what a love-struck idiot Mr Simmons was and how she didn't care what happened and she was all packed and ready for St Mungo's in case Sister Saleem sacked her. And what was Mr Simmons saying about the incident?

'Mr Simmons isn't here,' I told her.

'Where is he?' asked Matron.

'At home,' I said.

'Home?'

'Plum Tree Cottage,' I said.

* * *

I spoke to Lady Briggs. It wasn't as natural to chat now she didn't spend hours on the commode and was living in communal areas, but we did have a very meaningful talk about the

317

sheep field incident.

'Lizzie,' she said, 'what made Matron behave in such a peculiar way?'

'What?' I said.

'Leaving Mr Simmons in that field of Bluefaced Leicesters.'

'She's turning into a monster,' I said, 'because she's facing a frightening and uncertain future.'

'How so?' asked Lady Briggs.

'Her mother smothered her father with a pillow and they had to run away and now she has no pension coming and believes she'll end up in a homeless shelter near the prison,' I said.

'Good grief,' said Lady Briggs. 'But why did that cause her to leave Mr Simmons in the sheep field?'

I told her about Matron's quest to find a live-in companion position and her fear of other women encroaching, like Nurse Hilary had done with Mr Greenberg.

'But she could be my live-in companion,' said Lady Briggs, clapping her hands.

'No,' I said wearily, 'it has to be someone who can leave her a bungalow to live in — after they've died.'

'I see,' she said, 'how very quaint.'

28

Punk

I got to work a few days later and discovered a lot had happened. Serious things. Firstly, Mr Simmons was back. Matron had rescued him. Mr Simmons told me all about it. Matron had knocked at the door of Plum Tree Cottage and Miss Pitt, thinking she was there to return Mr Simmons' car, opened the door to thank her, but Matron pushed her aside, told Mr Simmons to get his stuff together, helped herself to the spare car key — which was helpfully hanging on a car-shaped hook — and brought him back to Paradise Lodge.

She told Mr Simmons it was the least she could do after leaving him in the field and him ending up back at home. Mr Simmons had said she shouldn't worry about the sheep field incident, he hadn't minded at all, plus he was getting used to being kidnapped and rescued and abandoned and had since then armed himself with an Acme Thunderer, which I thought might be a weapon but turned out to be a police whistle.

Secondly, Matron had been sacked and she was gone. Sister Saleem refused to discuss the ins and outs of this to begin with. All we knew was that Jeremy Hughes, the owner's solicitor, had come and spoken to him (presumably about the sheep field incident) and it was presumed that he and Sister Saleem had had no choice but to sack her for gross negligence etc.

And thirdly, You Jolly Fucker, Mr Simmons' car, had gone — presumed stolen by Matron. No one else had the ignition keys and no one even tried to defend her.

No one knew for sure where she'd gone but everyone doubted it would have been St Mungo's.

'Where did she say she was going?' I asked.

'St Mungo's,' said Eileen.

I telephoned St Mungo's on the phone, in the hall, without batting an eyelid. It answered after about fifty rings. I told a nice man I was trying to track down a relative (I knew to say relative since the Emma Mills at the Royal incident) and described Matron in great detail. The man at St Mungo's had no knowledge of a Maria Moran (which was apparently her name, according to the paperwork Sister Saleem had found) and advised me to call the police. They'd had only one new resident in a month and she was from outside the county and definitely not called Moran and not in a nurse's dress. I took this to be good news but the others reminded me that the Midlands had many such shelters and Matron might have gone to any of them. She had a car, after all.

It should have been a relief to be rid of Matron really — especially as we were trying to make improvements, and her always being so awful — but everyone was terribly upset about it. Paradise Lodge was poorer without her. The patients, who we'd kept in the dark regarding the Owner's Wife's departure, knew straight away she was gone. We couldn't possibly have kept it from them because they missed her being there and felt the loss of her too keenly.

Mr Simmons worried that his chivalrous act over the camera had sparked everything and Lady Briggs felt it was her fault — for dropping the camera and not being sensitive to Matron's state of mind. Sister Saleem wrung her hands over not making it clear that sacking her didn't mean she was throwing her out with immediate effect. We all blamed ourselves but no one more than me. I counted a hundred things I could have done — people I could have spoken to about Matron — to get her some help and understanding, instead of colluding with her and half protecting her when I should have turned her in to get the help she needed.

Lady Briggs kept asking where Matron might be living. I told her it seemed she *hadn't* gone to St Mungo's, even though she'd repeatedly said that that was where she was going. Lady Briggs understood that Matron's unreliability and vulnerability were one and the same thing and asked if I couldn't help her find more reliable details about Matron. For instance, was her name really Moran? Lady Briggs thought not. She remembered her from years before, and didn't recall that name. She had a book, somewhere, that Matron had lent her years ago with her name written on the flyleaf. Could I help her find it perhaps, when I had time?

Eileen and I searched Matron's old room for

clues. There was nothing there, not even the Goblin Teasmade.

'Would you take a Goblin Teasmade to a homeless shelter?' I asked.

'Matron would,' said Eileen.

We got used to Matron not being around but no one liked it. It was like when the Owner's Wife was suddenly not there — but a hundred times worse. The patients didn't stop asking about her.

★ ★ ★

It wasn't Mike's fault but I started to hate him. I was fed up with being in love and feeling so on edge all the time. I tried to tell myself I was kicking out at him because I was feeling low about various things. But it wasn't that — that only happened in an actual relationship.

It was that he started to seem *too* good-looking. I felt shallow for loving his beauty and felt inferior and not worthy. It was like the time my mother had driven us to Dorset to join a family holiday and it had been an embarrassing misunderstanding and we'd sat in the beach car park having a cheese cob while our mother summoned the strength to drive all the way home again. Even from the car, the beach had seemed too beautiful for us and we hadn't been welcome and I just longed for the muddy ruts of a Leicestershire field or the messy verges of the motorway. It was all we deserved.

Plus I'd begun to feel furtive and sleazy at my deviousness. My manipulating Miranda into divulging personal things about him, running into the drive just to say hello and look as if I were on the brink of weeping. And my betrayal of Mr Simmons in return for getting back into the 'O' Level group — which had been very much under Mike's influence.

I imagined married life and having to see his face all the time and how its niceness would soon become sickly, like winning by cheating or eating too much pudding. Like when I'd begged for another slice of strudel and cream and Granny Benson had finally agreed and made me eat every last flake until I was sick.

Why did I love him anyway? Probably just because Miranda had paraded him and his love for her. She'd worn his love like a new mohair jumper and we'd all wanted its softness. It was probably nothing to do with his being so good-looking, so good and philosophical.

*　*　*

The planning of the wedding was well under way. We'd booked the registry office and would be having the wedding party at the Paradise Lodge open day. But we still couldn't decide who to invite.

I never really understood my mother's friendlessness. She was funny and nice to be around. Still is. She was unshockable — pretty much (not counting overpriced lunch buffets and cruelty) — and very jolly and not too serious and didn't mind when awful things happened.

But because of a faraway boarding school, an

323

early marriage and move to London and then back and then a long bout of druggy drunkenness and a slide into poverty, she'd ended up quite alone, friend-wise.

After she started cohabiting with Mr Holt and began her rehabilitation, she met Mrs Goodchild across the road. Though Mrs Goodchild was friendly and supportive, I wouldn't have called her a friend exactly — my mother didn't like her very much and I don't suppose Mrs Goodchild liked my mother. But they were thrown together due to virtually being able to see each other from their kitchen windows and having babies around the same time. But then my mother started weeing in the sink and Mrs Goodchild ruined everything by mentioning it.

My mother's only other friends were Carrie Frost and a woman called Celia whose husband my mother had had sex with in 1972 but Celia hadn't minded until 1975 when the menopause sent her round the twist due to sleeplessness and hormone headaches and her husband had come clean about some affairs on his deathbed.

My mother had been at the husband's funeral and had spoken to Celia and had said how selfish of him, coming clean like that just to get into Heaven, but Celia wanted the drama and told her to fuck off.

★   ★   ★

My mother's lack of good friends reminded me that I'd let my best friend Melody slip away. Not because she'd seen me weeing in the kitchen sink or anything serious, but because I'd pretty much stopped going to school. Melody Longlady, Miranda's sister, had been the prettier twin all through childhood but things had switched for the twins during puberty (as previously mentioned) plus Melody hadn't taken care of her skin and drank insufficiently diluted cordials. Melody had had a miserable year coming to terms with being judged for not being pretty after a lifetime of being admired. Going punk hadn't occurred to Melody until one day she went babysitting with another friend and the friend suggested it (punk) and gave her a glass of orange liqueur and by the time the people came home (for whom they were babysitting) Melody had pierced her own ear and had literally become a punk.

All of a sudden she looked fabulous and exciting, like something in a magazine. And Miranda, her non-punk twin, in gipsy skirt and fluffy bolero, looked nothing next to Melody in a plastic mini-dress.

During Silver Jubilee week, everyone got cross with Melody about her punk attitude but Melody stuck up for herself.

'I'm not really saying I hate the Queen. I'm glad she's made it to twenty-five years. I just don't suit any other fashion and it's who I am for the time being,' she said, cleverly keeping her options open.

Melody's punkishness really brought out the best in her — for instance, in the inevitable arguments with her parents, she called her mother a 'waste of space'. A phrase I'd never heard before, but was so accurate.

In the run-up to the ~~open day~~ wedding day I'd felt slightly nervous about meeting Melody now she was a full punk and so comfortable with it. I had the same ridiculous preconceptions as other people and thought it conceivable she might beat me up for not being a punk. That was because the press always tried to show punks in a bad light doing awful stuff and saying upsetting things. But the truth was they were just people, like Melody, who happened to like wearing a bin liner and hanging around in a group with others who hated the mainstream.

I missed Melody and our friendship but wondered if I could be fully friends with her now she'd committed so strongly to punkhood. I worried that she might dredge up something from our past and want to get even with me — I'd heard punks bore grudges. Like the time I wouldn't help her with her European studies project even though I knew a hell of a lot about Denmark and Holland and the Low Countries. And in the end she wrote a load of nonsense about Belgium and Belgian artists being only interested in patterns and not realism. But she got a B for it because of her good vocabulary and knowledge of chocolate.

29

The Joy of Sex

The building work began. All staff had annoying extra jobs so that the owner didn't have to pay the builders to do things we could do. Having the builders around was most inconvenient. For instance, no cars could park in the courtyard because the paving stones were being levelled and fixed on the drive. And the builders constantly needed cups of coffee and cigarettes and made the nurses feel uncomfortable. None of us wanted to go anywhere on our own because of the feeling of embarrassment when they said things and laughed.

One day I was given the job of moving the contents of the larder into the morgue, along the corridor — it had to be done *that* day as the dry-lining of the larder was due to start the next morning. I began but, because the builders were in and out and couldn't help but shout things at me ('Nurse, Nurse, prick my boil' etc.), I decided I'd do it after 5 p.m. when they'd gone home.

Then at 5 p.m. we were all called to the kitchen to have pancakes with lemon juice and sugar to celebrate Eileen's birthday. Sister Saleem gave her an eyelash- and brow-tinting kit and someone gave her Tweed by Lenthéric, which she was spraying around. Carla B gave her

327

a strawberry pendant because she was known to love strawberries and I gave her a tiny tin of La Sirena anchovies with a beautiful mermaid illustration and foreign writing that I'd found in the larder. I knew it was worth having because my mother had bought an identical tin from Casa Iberica in Leicester and displayed it like an ornament even though it only cost 20p. Mike Yu was there — peeling vegetables and doing odd jobs to prepare for the builders — and he was embarrassed not to have a gift for Eileen.

'You do so much for us, Mike, it's more important than any gift.'

After the pancakes most of us — though not Mike or the owner — went to the Piglet Inn for vodka and gin drinks. As we left, I heard Mike quietly ask Miranda what time she'd be back and should he wait for her — to do some kung fu practice.

Her response, 'For the last time, Mike, I'm not fucking doing it,' made Mike look so sad.

I never liked going into the pub. I was always questioned by the landlord about my age and had to swear on my mother's deathbed, out loud, in front of all the blokes at the bar, that I was eighteen, and then he'd burst out laughing. I hated the pressure to have vodka and lime and how, even though I sipped it really slowly, it made me red in the face and unable to think straight.

A few of Eileen's old friends turned up, including Nurse Gwen. Feeling out of my depth, I turned and chatted to Miranda even though I hated her for being so mean to Mike.

'How's the kung fu demo coming along?' I asked.

'I'm not doing it. I'm sick of Mike,' said Miranda, taking a swig of her vodka, 'and all that Chinese stuff.'

I shrugged.

'He'll have to find someone else,' she said.

'Have you dropped him?' I asked.

'Yeah, probably, I don't know, I'm torn between him and Smig,' she admitted. She scrabbled about in her bag. 'Look, I've made a pros and cons list, because honestly, Lizzie, I just don't know which way to jump.'

Even though I was mildly drunk, Big Smig came out yards ahead of Mike on the pros and cons front. Mike only having his future foil container business and a possible life in America going for him (Miranda, like me, was wary of his strong family bond). Big Smig had, first and foremost, a love of sexual intercourse and all types of sex, a sense of adventure, humour, an interest in reggae music, motorbikes, skiing and amateur dramatics, plus a wealthy family (with weak family bonds) and an unusually attractive penis.

'I don't know what to do,' Miranda whined.

Then, with perfect timing, Big Smig appeared at the door with his helmet on and she went off with him.

I left the pub quickly before anyone could engage me in conversation. And I went back to finish clearing the larder — running, so that I wouldn't miss Mike Yu. I'd decided that if Mike was still there, I'd offer to stand in and do the kung fu dance instead of Miranda. I had to dash, so as not to miss him and then change my mind. The drive was out of action so it was difficult to know whether or not he was there, but scanning the street outside Paradise Lodge, I couldn't see his car.

I shuffled into the back corridor and gazed into the larder at all the giant tins and jars I had to move. I wasn't in the mood to finish the job but I had to — the builders would arrive at eight in the morning. Now I'd had the vodka, the job seemed almost insurmountable. I wandered out to the kitchen and asked the night nurse if she'd seen Mike. And if not, to see if she might be able to give me a hand. And if not, if Mr Simmons might be around.

Mike had been around, she said, but she hadn't seen him for a while. Mr Simmons was watching a drama and the night nurse was doing her nails. I went back to the larder and moved a few 10lb tins of apricot jam and some marrowfat peas into the morgue. I put the sweet things (tinned fruit, grapefruit segments, fruit pie fillers and jams) along one wall. And savoury things (tinned stew and mince to the left, and then soups) along another, and the things in-between (like flour and rice) in the corner.

If Mike was still here, waiting for Miranda, he'd soon give up and leave and when he left, he'd have to walk past the morgue door. I stopped caring about doing a good job and just waited to see Mike, and the more he didn't walk past, the more I wanted him to, and the more I daren't turn away from the corridor. I kept

330

nipping to the kitchen to see if he was there, but he never was.

After a while, I heard 'Kung Fu Fighting' — the track for Mike and Miranda's story-dance — faintly playing, drifting down the backstairs. When it finished, it started again. It made me feel really sad for Mike. He must be upstairs in the nurses' quarters, rehearsing on his own, waiting for Miranda to turn up, not realizing she'd sped off on the back of Big Smig's Kawasaki ZIB900 and wouldn't be seen again until the next morning, with today's eyeliner still on.

Mike's ordinary, everyday expressions made me want to sob; his hopes and dreams, his tenderness towards his grandfather made me want to sob; his hair made me want to sob. He had the nicest hair I'd ever seen on a man. It was straight but had a spring in it that meant it didn't flop down over his forehead but stood away and danced around his face in clean wisps. And strands of it reached down his neck. It was cut into a sort of kung fu feather cut, but because he had such good face bones it looked wonderful. His eyes were black and his lips were like an elongated heart. He was a work of art that you could just look at and look at. He was like a teenager's drawing of a boy. He was actually rather like David Cassidy — a calm, smiling, Chinese David Cassidy who'd never pose in a cowboy outfit or with his shirt off.

And sitting there, on a tin of marmalade, in the morgue thinking about Mike's unusual hair — knowing that Miranda wasn't going to do the

331

dance with him at the open day because she was going to do a Barry Sheene demo in hot pants with Big Smig — I did *actually* sob.

I went to the kitchen to blow my nose on some kitchen paper and make myself a cup of coffee. The night nurse was fiddling with the breakfast trays. I asked her if Miranda had come in. 'No,' she said, 'the day nurses are all at the pub.'

I went to the sluice and checked my face. I looked perfectly normal and actually the drunken pinkness was a good look on me and I seemed on the brink of weeping. I crept into Ward 2 and saw Lady Briggs sitting up in bed looking at her papers with a torch.

'Miranda has gone off with another boy,' I told her, in a whisper.

'I think you told me this already,' said Lady Briggs.

'Yes, but she has actually dropped him now,' I said.

'Is this about the Chinese horoscopes again, dear?'

'Not really, well, yes, sort of.'

'I suppose it was inevitable,' said Lady Briggs, 'and good for you, since you like him, hmm?'

'I'm going to offer to do the dance with him,' I said.

'The what, dear?'

'The kung fu dance,' I said, 'at the open day.'

'Oh, yes, I see,' she said.

'What do you think?' I asked.

'He won't be surprised,' she said, smiling and taking my hand, 'I've told him all about you, how much you care about him and how well suited you are, and he was thrilled.'

And though her words were ridiculous, they gave me a real boost.

'Oh, you know Mike, do you?' I laughed.

'We've spoken on the telephone,' she said.

'Well, thanks,' I said, 'wish me luck.'

I knew the kung fu dance was a love story involving a girl and a boy and a flock of magpies. And I knew the soundtrack off by heart. I was going to step in and I was going up to tell Mike, now.

Giggling quietly, I followed the soft music upstairs to the nurses' quarters. It was coming from the spare room, as I expected. I didn't want to burst in, mid-song, and embarrass Mike (mid-kick) so stood outside and waited for the song to fade out — which, if you know the song, you can imagine now. I giggled again slightly at the thought of Mike and, as the song faded away, I knocked gently on the door.

The song started again straight away and I realized Mike wouldn't hear the knock, so I opened the door. It took a while to understand what I was seeing.

It was Mike and Sally-Anne.

'But she's dead inside,' I thought.

'Sorry,' I said, 'I was looking for volunteers to help with the larder clearance.'

'Bad luck,' said Mike, and Sally-Anne giggled.

★   ★   ★

Walking home along the lane, I noticed the hedge was as thick as it had been all year. Still in

333

full leaf and with some berries. I loved this hedge — over a mile of blackthorn, hawthorn and some elder. The ditch on the field side was like an empty stream with a single strand of rusty barbed wire — unneeded now since the hedge had done so well. Nothing would get through it. Unless a speeding car swerved to avoid a collision with an oncoming vehicle and came off the road. That would go through it.

At home I cried, which my mother said was only natural after such an ordeal.

'What exactly were they doing?' asked my sister.

'Oh, God, they were in some kind of cross-legged, facing-each-other thing,' I said.

'Naked?' asked my sister.

'Yes, completely naked,' I groaned and grimaced and relived the whole fucking thing, 'naked, except for all her hair and his bandanna.'

'Definitely having sex?' she asked.

'Yes, *definitely*,' I said.

'Like this?' My mother showed us a sketch she'd done using Carrie Frost's fail-safe people-sketching method.

I looked closely. 'Yes.'

'The lotus,' she said, 'it's in *The Joy of Sex*, very middle-aged.'

I had a couple of days off work and school and read the rest of the George Orwell and started and gave up on *Julius Caesar*.

I had a long talk with my mother and sister. I decided it was time to start making an effort.

30

Coffee-Mate

What happened then was odd and yet obvious. Lady Briggs had gone to bed early one night and hadn't drunk her Horlicks. The night nurse — on that occasion Carla B with her cowlick, cleavage and clompy shoes — found her dead on the 9 o'clock round. I was shocked to hear it. I thought about our last conversation — when I'd been tipsy and planning to approach Mike Yu about the kung fu dance.

Carla B was upset and full of self-recrimination at not having picked up on Lady Briggs being poorly. She'd seen her at eight and had asked if she'd like to have her Horlicks warmed up and Lady Briggs had declined, saying she 'hadn't the puff to sit up' and then at half past eight she'd told Carla B she felt as though she'd danced the tarantella and maybe she should return to Room 9, and half an hour later she was dead.

'Well, she's in the morgue now, with all the tins and jam jars,' said Eileen, who had come to take Carla B off for a private pep talk. I sat in the kitchen and rested my head on the table. The owner came in — I could tell it was him because of his jangling buckles — but I was too embarrassed to look up. A chair scraped and a lighter clicked.

'I'm sorry you're upset,' he drawled.

'Well, she wasn't paying any fees, so I suppose it's not that bad for the business,' I mumbled, 'but I really, really liked her. I didn't realize how much until now.'

'I can't say I liked her, but I'm bloody sad the old girl's gone,' said the owner.

'I liked her a lot,' I said. 'It's like when a very important dog has died long ago and you know you'll never have such a glorious dog and you take other, subsequent dogs for granted and don't realize just how much they've come to mean to you.'

I told him how the memory of our dog Debbie had eclipsed poor living Sue until the night she ate the sock and might have died. And we all felt differently about her after that.

'Except Lady Briggs didn't sick up a sock and come back to life,' I said. 'She died, full stop.'

'Well put,' said the owner.

The solicitor arrived then and the owner patted my arm and went to speak to him in private. Eileen came back and told me the owner's mother had also died, the day before. I wished I'd known and could have offered my condolences.

★ ★ ★

Paradise Lodge felt strange now with no Matron and no Lady Briggs and Mike having done the lotus sex-position with Sally-Anne. Sister Saleem did the morning routines almost single-handedly and at coffee break said the kindest, nicest things

336

about Lady Briggs. 'She was a marvellous lady,' she said, 'and we must be very happy that she made it downstairs before she died.'

'She was up there all that time, though,' I said, 'just waiting to come down but taken for a recluse.'

'Yes,' said Sister Saleem, 'it was awful, but let's remember that she made it down and she had a fine time at the end.'

The staff treated me slightly as if she'd been my relative — I suppose because I'd always answered her bell. Even Mike Yu approached me to offer his condolences.

'She was a great lady,' he said, 'and very intelligent and caring.'

'Yeah, she was great,' I said, rather snappily, and went to walk away.

'You know, Lizzie, it was Lady Briggs who told me that Miranda and I weren't compatible,' he said, 'and that Sally-Anne was in love with me.'

'*Sally-Anne?*' I said. 'How did she even know Sally-Anne?'

'Well, she called her the quiet little nurse,' he said.

★   ★   ★

Approx one week after Lady Briggs had died, it seemed like an ordinary day but Jeremy Hughes, the owner's solicitor, arrived and went into a meeting with the owner.

Sister Saleem made a tray of hot drinks to take through but the milk had gone off and went into globules on the surface of the coffee and no

337

amount of frantic stirring disguised it. She made another round of coffees but found that every bottle of milk had turned because the fridge had been accidentally unplugged for the Philishave and no one had noticed. So I had to run over to the Piglet Inn. They couldn't give me a pint but gave me some sachets of Coffee-Mate.

The moment I got back I was sent into the owner's sitting room with four cups of coffee/Coffee-Mate. I put the tray down on the low table and was about to leave when the owner asked me to stay and told me to take a cup of coffee. I turned and saw then that the Owner's Wife was also there, taller than ever in sling-backs with heels and piled-up hair and tendrils.

'Hello, Lizzie — ' she said, and she went to introduce herself.

But I interrupted. 'Yes, I remember, hello.'

She touched the back of her hair and told me she'd used Linco Beer shampoo ever since I'd put her on to it. She said it to break the ice really — but I must say, her hair did look healthy.

'It looks very healthy,' I said.

'Are you still using Linco?' she asked.

'No, I've switched to Silvikrin lemon and lime for greasy hair,' I said, which wasn't true but I didn't want to use the same shampoo as her any more.

She looked crestfallen. I felt guilty.

I took a sip of coffee. God, the Coffee-Mate was good. It had transformed the slightly stale catering granules into a strong but creamy cup. It was gorgeous.

'Isn't the Coffee-Mate delicious?' I said.

The Owner's Wife pointed to Jeremy Hughes; he was trying to get our attention.

'So, your mother,' he began, nodding towards the owner, and then, looking at me, 'that is, Lady Briggs, has made her wishes very clear in her will.'

And that was when I first knew that Lady Briggs was the owner's mother. No one said it like that but I put two and two together and then asked, just to make sure.

'Are you saying that Lady Briggs is — was — the owner's mother?'

And the Owner's Wife, with a puzzled little laugh, said, 'Yes, of course she was — but you knew that, surely?'

And I said, 'No, I didn't, I don't think anyone knew that.'

And the Owner's Wife laughed again and the owner looked sad.

'I'm sure everyone knew — didn't they?' said the owner, grimacing.

'They didn't,' I said, 'they really didn't. I wouldn't have said all that about it being like loving a dog, and sicking up a sock, if I'd known she was your mother,' I added.

The Owner's Wife gasped.

'No! It was a lovely thing to say,' declared the owner, and him saying that made me want to cry.

The solicitor began his talk. I looked around the room, to keep my tears at bay. It must have been built and furnished according to the highest aesthetic law. It was so perfect. The shape (a chubby rectangle) and the central fireplace, with three long settees in a horseshoe around a low table in front of it. The high ceiling with pretty plasterwork and a central thing from which the loveliest chandelier hung. Glass droplets, not diamond-cut, not fancy-looking but like water, and not grand but just beautiful. Tall panelled doors, diagonally opposite each other. The dual aspect giving the room pretty light and French windows, closed now for privacy, leading out on to a secret glade. The wobbly old glass slicing the view, of fifty different greens and yellows and oranges, into segments.

'*Did* everyone know?' the owner asked his ex-wife.

'I'm sure they did, Thor,' said the Owner's Wife.

'Does it really matter?' asked Jeremy Hughes.

'I don't know,' said the owner.

'No, it doesn't matter, she's dead now,' said the Owner's Wife.

'She told me she was the first patient here?' I said.

'That's it,' said the owner, 'she was the bellwether, she helped us get patients in the beginning.'

'Oh, yes, she did,' said the Owner's Wife, 'she showed prospective patients around and said how super it was, dear Allegra.'

The couple had a little talk about her and I gleaned that Lady Briggs had been the first patient at Paradise Lodge because she'd already lived there. It had been her house. It was her money that started the business. It was she who executed the trust fund that later denied the business money when it was being run badly. It was Lady Briggs who denied the Owner's Wife the right to modernize. And then, it was she who'd demanded a business manager be taken on after the Owner's Wife had left and things had hit the skids. It was she who'd taken on Sister Saleem. And it was she who'd put Mike Yu off Miranda and told him about the quiet little nurse who liked him.

Jeremy Hughes was eager to get on with the business in hand and coughed.

'I just want to run through your late mother's — Lady Briggs' — wishes as specified here.' He held a wodge of papers. 'Firstly, as far as they pertain to Lizzie Vogel.'

I blushed.

'Lizzie, Lady Briggs wished for you to have her collection of books to help with your studies — a marvellous collection of novels and a rare Audubon. She also left you fifty pounds towards your education — should you still be in education at the time of execution — or to be used as you wish.'

'I hope you love novels?' said the owner.

'I'm actually reading the second novel ever to be written at the moment.'

'Oh, what is it?' asked the Owner's Wife.

'*Moll Flanders*,' I said, 'by Daniel Defoe.'

'Oh, didn't he also write *Robinson Crusoe*?'

'No,' I said, 'he didn't.'

The Owner's Wife smiled at me but I'd really gone off her now, so didn't smile back.

'Thank you,' I said, looking at the owner, 'I

don't really know what else to say.'

'The books are mostly here, in the sitting room,' Jeremy Hughes gestured behind us to a wall of bookshelves, 'and on the shelves in the drawing room.'

I gazed at the books. I should have been grateful but I only felt panic and embarrassment at the thought of lugging them all home in a bin liner in Danny's pram and then, I don't know, shoving them in the garage.

It must have shown in my face and Jeremy Hughes said I didn't have to take them immediately, or in fact ever, and that Lady Briggs had written that I should choose the books I wanted and not feel obliged to take them all, or any. The disappointing (for them) truth was that my mother owned a similar collection — to which I had full and free access — but I didn't say anything and let them enjoy the gesture.

The solicitor turned away from me then and spoke to the owner. It seemed Lady Briggs had left some money plus two flats in Leicester and a house in Norfolk, most of which went straight to him, Harald Anderssen, and some bits and bobs went to the Owner's Wife, including a tiny watch that she'd already been given and a special painting of some fruit, which I had previously assumed Nurse Eileen had done, it being so out of proportion and wrong-looking.

Lady Briggs had left a small cottage in the next village, 'Myrtle Cottage', to Bridget Marie Monaghan, a distant cousin, who the owner said he'd have a heck of a job tracking down. 'I doubt her name is even Monaghan these days.'

The Owner's Wife had never heard the name before. 'Bridget Monaghan,' she said. 'I didn't know you had a distant cousin called Bridget, Thor.'

The three of us stood about while Jeremy Hughes talked us through the ins and outs of the will in the most boring way and asked for my postal address and then said I could go back to work. I went back to the kitchen and told Sister Saleem about my inheritance.

'What a lovely thing,' she said and stroked my head.

Afterwards, while Jeremy Hughes talked more with the owner, the Owner's Wife popped into the kitchen to say hello to Sister Saleem and Eileen. Eileen was frosty, which was fair enough.

'Have you been into the day room to say hello to the patients?' Sister Saleem asked her.

'Er, no, I wasn't sure I should,' said the Owner's Wife.

'Oh, yes, please do,' said Sister Saleem.

The Owner's Wife seemed so reduced suddenly. I realized I didn't like her one tiny bit but because I felt sorry for her I went with her to the day room. The patients were having their coffee and biscuits. I could see from the colour, they'd got the Coffee-Mate too.

'We've got a visitor,' I said, quietly, and braced myself for a whoop or two, but none of them seemed to remember her, except Miss Tyler.

'Oh, hello, are you back now?' she asked.

'No, no, just a flying visit,' said the Owner's Wife.

It was so embarrassing I couldn't stay and watch and I scuttled back to the kitchen. Sister Saleem sent me back with another cup of coffee for the Owner's Wife. But when I got through there, she'd gone.

Later, I questioned Eileen and the others. Had they known that Lady Briggs was the Owner's Mother? And not a single one of them had. They were as shocked and troubled by it as I was.

★ ★ ★

The day before the wedding day, my mother and sister dashed into town to Green's the Jeweller to collect Mr Holt's wedding ring, which had been engraved with a secret love message. And, according to my sister, my mother had forgotten what the message was and it was a total surprise when she read it.

It was this: 'Shall we?' Which I thought a bit much and obviously sexual and therefore private.

And on the way home they'd called in at 'Fresh Blooms' and bought tons of orange and yellow chrysanthemums and kaffir lilies and picked armfuls of foliage from a railway siding.

31

The Big Day Dawns

I'd set my alarm for 6 a.m. My sister and I had a bowl of Ricicles and went over our plans. She was to be based at home getting everyone ready for the wedding — especially our mother, who wanted to look bridey but not as if she was being sold into patriarchy. My duties were all Paradise Lodge-based and included preparing the buffet, decorating the rooms and setting the others to work. Mr Holt very kindly drove me up there since he was nipping into the depot early to get started on the autumn stocktake.

It was a lovely day with milky sunshine and Mr Holt commented on it.

'Nice day for a wedding,' he said. And I agreed.

Cheryl, the new night nurse, hadn't quite finished the breakfasts when I arrived so I helped her for ten minutes before I started preparing the wedding buffet. I was already in the bridesmaid's dress that Carrie Frost had run up for me with an apron over the top to protect it from splashes of salad cream, beetroot and so forth. The dress was simple, pink and rather ugly, with a high neck and a line of daisies at the hem. I could see Cheryl noticing it and told her about the open-cum-wedding day and I could see the bewilderment on her face.

'So, your mum's getting married today and the party's going to be here — with all the old people?'

It did seem unusual — hearing it like that — and I felt a wave of anxiety.

'Yes, it's going to be marvellous, feel free to come along.'

'I spend enough time here, thank you very much,' she said. 'In any case, I'll be in bed. I'm on nights again tonight.'

'OK,' I said, 'but if you change your mind . . . '

'I won't,' said Cheryl.

I'd decided to call the wedding tea a 'buffet' to distinguish it from an ordinary tea. I'd changed my mind about skyscrapers and was making the sandwiches heart-shaped instead — using a tart cutter and hammer. This would leave some wastage, but tasty wastage that would soon be eaten. I was also doing ham horns with the ex-cook's boiled ham. I hadn't wanted to get it ready the night before because I hated people who did things the night before for convenience sake when everything would be much nicer freshly made on the day. I never wanted to become that kind of person — not for a wedding anyway.

I cracked on and tried not to think about Mike Yu. Cheryl watched me cut the sandwiches as she ate her breakfast and asked awkward questions. And then, thank God, Nurse Eileen came down with a curler in her fringe and a Consulate in her fingers and everything was safe and jolly. Soon Mr Simmons and assorted others appeared and sat smoking at the kitchen table. They all looked smart. Deb-on-Hair had been the day before — all day — and done almost everyone's hair, including all the staff — except Sally-Anne, who hadn't had her hair cut for years. Carla B said it looked like something from a shampoo advert when it was down. I could vouch for that. I didn't say anything but glanced at Sally-Anne.

Deb-on-Hair had done Sister Saleem a 'Syreeta' and it had taken till 10 p.m. I couldn't take to it — the beads looked clumsy, all clacking together, and I suspected Deb-on-Hair had bitten off more than she could chew — and some of the pieces, round the back, were a bit on the thick side. Deb-on-Hair was proud of it, though, and according to Sister Saleem, had said she wanted to photograph it for a hair competition.

The only patient who'd not been done was Miss Boyd who'd had a headache while Deb-on-Hair had been there, brought on by the fumes of the Amami setting lotion. Nurse Eileen did it for her on the actual day, and gave her full Farrah flicks.

Carla B disappeared to put the decorations up in the hall and day room — and when she'd done it she called us all to come and look. We went into the day room first and it looked very pretty and festive and we all congratulated her and said what a very good eye she had for bunting placement.

Then we saw the hall. For this she had sewn some special bunting with the words: 'PARA-DISE LODGE — Come Here to Live!'

And it was so moving and such an amazing thing to have sewn by hand we all just stared at it. Sister Saleem stood there with her mouth open.

And Eileen said, 'Carla B, you genius, it's gorgeous.'

And then, just when I thought I couldn't love bunting more, Carla B unfurled a silver and white banner which read 'THE HAPPY COUPLE' and had wedding rings and horse-shoes.

★ ★ ★

The plan was that the drama and musical entertainments (except for Mike Yu's thumb piano demo) would take place outside on the patio with the audience either watching from the day room — through the French windows — or, for those wanting a closer view, seated around the patio in the garden furniture which had been tarted up by Eileen and Gordon Banks. The wisteria hung down around the 'stage' in pretty loops, like an alfresco theatre-set in a picture book. It was glorious and the weather was set fair.

Eileen and Miranda were to prepare the patients, and the cook and Gordon's wife, Mindy Banks, had been in the day before and plumped all the cushions and sprayed a lot of Haze around. The umbrella-and-walking-stick urn was in place, with ladies' and gents' wellingtons, and there were assorted plants borrowed from Fresh Blooms — two cheese plants, a weeping fig and

348

some African violets — dotted around, looking lovely. All on sale or return.

It should have been a morning of calm before the big day unfolded but it turned out to be quite strange and eventful in itself.

The owner appeared, which was miraculous, him having been in a coma for days — in mourning for his mother and still missing Matron. He even began picking at the leftovers from the heart-shaped sandwiches, which was unlike him. He said he'd woken up from an exciting coma-dream in which he was fighting with a badger.

He got hold of Sister Saleem to show us what he'd done in the dream and shouted, 'You're not stripy, you're plain brown, damn you!' Sister Saleem loved the attention and they had a right old wrestle that almost ended in a kiss, and actually the beady hair looked quite nice swishing about. Plus, it was really pleasing that the owner had come round from his coma and was going to join in the day.

Everyone started telling their dreams. Mr Simmons said he'd dreamt that a man had telephoned from a phone box in Market Harborough to say that he and his brother were on their way to visit him, and would that be convenient? Then the pips had gone and he'd woken up.

Eileen had dreamt that someone kept offering her Polo Mints and when she put them into her mouth they'd turned out to be Polo *Fruits*. I thought it was symbolic and horrible.

The owner went and changed into his riding

togs and a few minutes later waved at the window as he clopped past on Daybreak. It was a big deal as he'd been too depressed to ride for weeks and poor Daybreak had been bored to distraction and had kicked at his stable door like a forgotten prisoner and only got one or two hacks out per week with the catering grocer's wife — who liked lone riding.

Then the doorbell rang and it was two visitors to see Mr Simmons — it was the Attenboroughs (but we didn't know that at the time). They explained that they'd tried to call ahead from a phone box in Market Harborough. Sister Saleem left them in the hall with Eileen and came back to the kitchen.

'Quick, Nurse,' she said to Carla B, 'two visitors for Mr Simmons. Run up to his room, make the bed and clean the toilet.'

'Who is it?' asked Mr Simmons.

'I don't know, they rang ahead from Market Harborough,' said Sister Saleem.

Mr Simmons looked up in surprise and said, 'Good heavens, my dream's come true.'

'Nurse Eileen will keep them talking in the hall,' said Sister to Mr Simmons, 'you go up the backstairs and get dressed.'

Eventually, the Attenboroughs were allowed up to see Mr Simmons in his room and Sister Saleem took a tray of tea and Lincolns up. The rest of us wondered who the visitors were while I plated up the array of cakes donated for the wedding (including a tin of sickly-looking butterfly cakes from Sally-Anne). I found I was a little afraid of Sally-Anne nowadays, when I put it all together — the twins, the uncut hair, the deadness inside, and now the lotus position with Mike Yu.

We knew the visitors were very famous but none of us could place them. I thought they might be local MPs. Sister Saleem sent Sally-Anne to get their autographs so we could analyse the signatures, but Sally-Anne chickened out just in case they weren't famous — like all shy people, her main objective was not to seem an idiot.

The visit was brief because Mr Simmons wasn't very good at being visited — which was a shame because he got all sorts of exciting visitors, being ex-BBC. When the Attenboroughs came back down to the hallway and Eileen was helping them into their rustly mackintoshes I was sent out to get their autographs. Nurse Eileen was telling them that she was an artist in her spare time and showing them a little oil painting (done by her) on the wall by the front door.

'Tuscany?' one Attenborough asked.

'Kirby Muxloe,' replied Nurse Eileen.

And I realized, for the first time, the painting was of a little house. Until that moment I'd seen it as an Aston Villa player (framed by an open goal). I was amazed and blurted this out to Eileen and the Attenboroughs. The Attenboroughs found this — me seeing the little house as a football player — more interesting than the painting itself.

'It's a fascinating yet common phenomenon,' said the smaller one, 'you perceive only one image at any one time.' And he squinted at the painting. 'Aha, I'm seeing the footballer — now I look away and look back and I'm seeing the house again — look again, aha, and there's the footballer.'

'Wittgenstein's rabbit,' said the taller.

'It is whatever you see it as. You see a football player, who's to say it isn't a football player?' said the smaller one, to me.

'It's a cottage,' said Eileen, butting in.

'Ah, but who's to say it is?' asked the taller one.

'I am,' said Eileen, 'my Nan lived in it.'

'He's saying the painting, any painting, is whatever we see it as,' I said, and surprised myself.

'Precisely — it is what we see,' said the smaller one.

Eileen seemed a bit hurt, but hung around while they peered at the picture, just in case they came back round to the subject of her (the artist).

The phenomenon happened to me a lot. I hadn't even realized it was a phenomenon; I thought it was just me seeing the wrong thing. I supposed it was further evidence of my being an intellectual. But I didn't dwell on it further — enough was enough.

As they neared the front door, the smaller one commented on my bridesmaid's dress and the bunting about the place. I told them about the open-cum-wedding day and what a doubly huge day it was going to be and that in less than three hours my mother and stepfather would be man and wife and returning here for their party and so forth. I described all the wonderful entertainments on offer, including their friend, Mr

Simmons, leading the Gilbert and Sullivan recital on the harmonica, Gordon Banks' balloon header, the kung fu demo and dance, and Big Smig's Barry Sheene look-alike act, and I firmly invited them to join us. They seemed pleased and said they'd try to pop back.

'We'll try to pop back,' said the small one, who, it turned out, was a huge Bruce Lee fan and could do an impression. They got into their car and Eileen and I stood on the drive and waved them off.

The owner and Daybreak appeared at the cattle grid, having finished their hack just as the Attenboroughs' Peugeot turned into the lane. 'Who was that?' he asked.

And I told him all about the Attenboroughs and that they were going to try to pop back for the open day. And then I went back inside to put the parsley garnishes on my sandwich platters. Soon I'd fully prepared the tea and there were sixteen Bacofoil-covered plates. The balloons and bunting were up and the patients were all in their nicest clothes and looking forward to lots of fun. Miranda was going to be in charge of music and Sally-Anne was going to make sure the kettle went on in time — it taking almost a half-hour to come to the boil.

Then Mike Yu arrived to reheat a stew for lunch and to fill the air with wholesome smells. And, presumably, to see Sally-Anne, or Miranda — or both. I didn't care.

I hated Mike Yu now, even though he was still wonderful, sweet and kind and just about the most beautiful person you'd ever see.

32

The Battenberg Heart

The Snowdrop van clattered over the cattle grid mid-morning and I shuffled out in my ballet shoes. It was time to go with my family to the registry office. Carla B beat me to the van and quickly strung some white ribbon across the windscreen and laughed and ran away again. Mr Holt got out of the van and rearranged it.

My sister had got our mother ready and she was wearing the lily dress that had come from War on Want. She looked beautiful with soft, wavy hair and greeny-blue eyeshadow. She was wearing flip-flops but hadn't painted her toenails, which I thought a shame. Mr Holt had on a brown suit that I'd seen a couple of times before, and he couldn't help himself but push the sleeves up. Danny was in a cowboy suit and Jack was in jeans and black sweater and looked like a Frenchman.

My sister looked much nicer than I did because she'd had the guts to reject Carrie Frost's grotty bridesmaid's dress and had worn a wraparound silk thing and had her hair all swept up and dangly earrings. She'd spent quite a bit of time on herself, hence my mother's lack of toenail paint.

Anyway, we were a well-dressed family off out to get married and it felt very nice. It was a sunny autumn day, as previously noted, and winding through the villages on our way to Market Harborough registry office, I felt the countryside must surely rival New England for leaf colour. Not that I'd been there.

My mother had wanted Jack to give her away but it wasn't that kind of wedding and in the end she just went and stood beside Mr Holt and they nodded at each other as if they'd bumped into each other outside Wilkinson's hardware. The registrar droned on and it was dull until the couple faced each other and tried to repeat what the registrar had told them to say regarding marrying each other. My mother said it a bit wrong and giggled and tried again and giggled again. And Mr Holt, when it was his turn, said it perfectly, but very cautiously — and that summed the two of them up. That was when I felt emotional and so glad about Mr Holt. I mean, my mother was my mother and that was that but we'd somehow got this man, this unusual man who was never going to say the wrong thing. Who was going to slow everything down and get it right. The antidote.

★   ★   ★

We arrived back at Paradise Lodge a bit later than expected because we hadn't factored in needing some lunch, Danny falling asleep, and having to collect Sue the dog so that she could come and jump out of the window.

And by the time we got there, the open day was in full swing and going well.

We'd missed Gordon Banks heading the balloon. But Mr Simmons was playing a doleful tune on the harmonica with his mouth and hand. The French windows were open on to the stage — as planned — and the big umbrella was up and there were jugs of drink everywhere with cucumber bobbing about. And although it was October and only a few days after the anniversary of the saddest day in our lives, everything was perfect — apart from the Mike thing, Matron not being there and Lady Briggs being dead and unable to sing 'I Dreamt I Dwelt In Marble Halls'. Apart from all that, it was very nice.

Sister Saleem dazzled in a bright yellow two-piece and Eileen was in the pale jade uniform (which had been optional for the day). Carla B was in check capri pants and a bra-top and I can't even remember what Sally-Anne wore except she looked grim and strange and I hated her.

I thought we'd slipped in unnoticed but Sister Saleem suddenly shouted, 'The bridal party!'

And the staff and some of the patients made an archway and whooped as we all came underneath. The official wedding guests — the Liberal couple, Miss Kellogg, Deano the van boy and Carrie Frost — were already there. Jeff and Betty from Snowdrop had been and gone and were probably at the depot working on the autumn stocktake.

The owner played the piano rather beautifully in honour of our arrival but ruined it at the end by calling out, 'Are the fucking Attenboroughs here yet?'

Little Jack welcomed Mr Holt to our family, which he'd seen various in-laws do at family weddings, and Mr Holt nodded and thanked him. My mother said she'd intended to read a poem by John Keats but now the moment had come she wanted to talk briefly instead about my sister. She started by saying she'd taken her 'A' Levels a year early (which I thought tactless), and then that she'd been brave enough — in spite of a life-changing anxiety attack — to enrol for training at the Royal. And that we should all take care of ourselves, our hearts and minds as much as our bodies. This went on for about two minutes. Most of the gathering had no idea what she was on about. Then, when it ended, Miranda Longlady did a short dance routine to 'Heaven Must Be Missing An Angel'. My sister looked horrified but held up well considering.

Truthfully, the rest of the day was partly spoilt by what was going on in my heart and mind. I'd been fine during the preparations and the actual wedding, having been occupied and busy. But once we'd settled into the 'open day' part of the day, especially with Mike actually being there and Lady Briggs not, I grappled with notions of truth and understanding — what is the truth? And how do you know?

Should I have known Lady Briggs was the owner's mother? Did it matter that I didn't?

If Lady Briggs hadn't intervened, would I now be limbering up to do the kung fu dance with Mike? What made Mike assume the nurse who liked him was Sally-Anne, when it should have been obvious it was me?

And, on a grander scale, what actually makes a thing true or not true, and can you believe a thing into truth? All the kind of things my sister had been so keen on before her camping collapse. At one point I approached her and tried to start a conversation about it all.

'What's bothering you?' she asked. 'Mike Yu or Lady Briggs?'

'Both — shattered illusions have made me doubt myself,' I told her. 'I'm in turmoil.'

I told her I'd not only been robbed of my reality but also forced into an ongoing hunt for retrospective meaning in every past exchange. And that every brief comment that had seemed at the time to offer a hint of romance to come (Mike) or of senile dementia (Lady Briggs) was actually a clue to a different truth, a truth in which I was a tiny player. It was a troubling and time-consuming realization.

My sister couldn't have been less interested or curious and her response was as sad and perfunctory as a lazy vicar addressing a group. 'Peace will come with acceptance, Lizzie,' she said, 'we only know what we know, and the rest is anybody's guess.'

And then she asked if I'd liked the dainty buttonhole corsages she'd made from sprigs of fern and tiny autumn daisies.

I didn't want the peace that comes with acceptance, I wanted the ongoing chronic joy that came with ignorance and fantasy — I'd rather go back to not knowing about Mike and Sally-Anne, and thinking that Lady Briggs was just a weird recluse.

I felt better when I was busy; rushing around offering newcomers a heart-shaped sandwich, topping up teacups, guiding Miss Brixham to the toilet or fixing a fallen stocking.

The Vicar ignored everyone and sat with a glass of Winfield sherry, reading the *Leicester Mercury* classifieds. He was looking for a second-hand hostess trolley, he told my mother, it being a long way from the kitchen to the dining room at the vicarage. 'I'm fed up with lukewarm béchamel on cold plates,' he said.

'Ooh, how very Barbara Pym!' my mother chuckled.

Mr Holt tapped me on the shoulder and said he was going to have to leave now, to finish the paperwork for the autumn stocktake.

'But you'll miss seeing Sue jumping out of the window,' I said.

'I've seen it before and I dare say I shall see it again,' he said, and it was true that there'd be many opportunities, Sue being our dog.

'Happy Wedding Day,' I said and gave him a pat on the arm.

'Thanks for everything, love,' he said.

★   ★   ★

Mrs Longlady arrived with her secret recipe Chocca-Chocca cake and, to my surprise, I saw it was decorated with tiny bride and groom figures and had 'Mr & Mrs' piped in curly white letters across the top — as if it were THE wedding cake, which it wasn't (my sister having fashioned a heart out of four Battenbergs). My mother came over and was suitably grateful and Mrs Longlady seized the agenda and invited her to cut the Chocca-Chocca cake and make a wish for the future.

'Where's the groom?' shouted Mrs Longlady, as if she were a firm friend of the couple. 'He's needed to cut the cake and make a joint wish for the future.'

'He's popped away to the laundry depot,' said my sister.

'Popped away,' said Mrs Longlady, 'from his new bride, for the cutting of the cake? It's a most significant ceremony.'

'Yes,' said my sister, 'but yours isn't the official wedding cake anyway, so don't worry.'

My mother did the honours with Mrs Longlady's cake and made the first cut with Little Jack — who was glad to step in, seeing as he'd been denied giving her away — and our mother made a wish on behalf of herself and Mr Holt but ruined it by blurting it out, which made it unlikely to come true because it should have remained a secret in their hearts, apparently.

'I've wished for harmony,' she said and hearing the word I glanced at Mike Yu, *Harmony* being the name of the narrowboat we'd admired on our romantic towpath walks — and I'd gone as far as imagining us navigating Foxton Locks and photographing each other struggling with the heavy mechanisms. Mike Yu didn't glance at me. Harmony meant nothing to him.

I helped Mrs Longlady cut the Chocca-Chocca cake into tiny cubes and wrap each one in kitchen paper to hand out to guests. And though it was a cheek — putting her cake up as the official wedding cake when my sister's Battenberg heart was there on the table surrounded by Sally-Anne's sickly cupcakes — it felt good, someone that horrible being nice and taking the marriage seriously, and we took the Battenberg heart home to have as a family.

And then Melody was there and to my relief was exactly as nice as she'd always been. And even though she was wearing a genuine dog's collar that she'd got from the pet shop near the Odeon, she looked quite nice with eyeliner and black lipstick and she'd bought my mother a lovely wedding present of a book of love poems written by a Chilean politician. She told my mother she remembered her and Mr Holt first meeting and said things that were both romantic and sensible at the same time and then she told my mother she admired her. I felt proud to be friends with Melody that day and vowed to fix our friendship asap.

33

The Entertainers

At 3 p.m. precisely — as per the agreed schedule — Mike Yu appeared in white pyjamas and a black belt ready to begin his kung fu demo and dance. Eileen banged a cup with a spoon and announced that Mike Yu and Miranda Longlady — senior nursing auxiliary — would perform an ancient Chinese folk tale, and that anyone who'd rather hear her talk on bowel health should go next door to the morning room. There was some mumbling but no one moved, guests and patients alike were intrigued by Mike — in his outfit — standing there, trancelike, with such dignity, looking like a warrior of peace.

It was about to begin — Sally-Anne was just about to press 'Play' on the Panasonic — when the rumble of Big Smig's Kawasaki ZIB900 broke the mood and Miranda rushed from the room.

'Hang on,' she called back, 'don't start the demo yet, it's Big Smig.'

The Kawasaki appeared on the patio and its throbbing engine made some of the ladies tremble and put their hands to their lips in fear.

'What is it?' they asked. 'Who is it?'

And Sally-Anne spoke, 'It's Miranda's boyfriend, Big Smig.'

Mr Simmons said, 'Sounds like a Hell's Angel.'

362

'Oh, no, he's a smashing lad,' said Mrs Longlady.

But the words 'Hell's Angel' hung in the room and we all looked at Mike Yu, who seemed ready to defend us.

'Switch the fucking engine off!' Carla B shouted. 'We're waiting for the kung fu dance.'

Big Smig cut the engine after a flourish. He dismounted and, leaving the Kawasaki centre-stage, strode through the French windows into the day room wearing Belstaffs and a full-face helmet. He looked like an alien intruder who wanted to force us all into his spaceship and the room was silent and terrified. Even Mrs Longlady looked perturbed.

He took the helmet off and tousled his hair with his free hand and suddenly he was just a handsome young man with freckles and a chipped front tooth, not unlike Huckleberry Finn or Tom Sawyer or some other nice American boy who you can probably trust. Miranda rushed up to greet him and it was easy to see that he'd parked his car in her garage and Mike Yu stood there, feet slightly apart in the position of readiness.

'Sorry,' said Big Smig, 'silly me — I thought it was time for us.'

Miranda stood beside Smig. 'I'm not doing the kung fu dance, Mike,' she said.

Mike Yu looked downcast but seemed to accept it. The room groaned. Mike nodded and stepped forward. 'I will give you a modern, kung fu interpretation of *The Weaver Girl and the Cowherd* — a Chinese folk tale about the love between Zhinü, the weaver girl, and Niulang, the cowherd. Their love was not allowed, and they were banished to opposite sides of the Silver River. But once a year hundreds of magpies would flock together, wing-to-wing, to form a bridge to reunite the lovers for one day.' He paused, then said, 'I will do my best on my own.'

Before he could begin Miss Tyler interrupted excitedly to tell the audience she had a serving platter depicting this very tale.

Sally-Anne pressed 'Play' and 'Kung Fu Fighting' filled the room. Mike Yu began, there in the middle of the day room, a routine of kung fu moves perfectly in time with the music. And after a bit of a nervous start, the audience were soon clapping to the beat.

Mike performed alone until Sally-Anne joined in. The audience made noises of approval. Biting her lip from shyness, she sort of karate-chopped the air and you might have thought she was a terrific actor, looking all modest and anxious like a weaver girl might have and glancing over at Mr and Mrs Yu who were sitting in a corner, but I knew she was just being herself and it was a lucky coincidence. And I'm not being mean when I state that Mike would have been better off alone, looking the part and doing very good moves.

The kung fu demo and dance was a huge success, though, and the whole room clapped like mad. Even Miranda, who rushed to take over the Panasonic, was clapping and smiling. Then there was much clanking and whirring as she searched for the music track she wanted.

'That was great,' said Eileen, banging a cup with a spoon again. 'Thank you, thank you, Mike and Sally-Anne.'

Sally-Anne stood beside Eileen and, speaking clearly, said, 'His name is Jiao-Long.'

'Oh, righto,' said Eileen, 'thank you to *Jiao-Long* and Sally-Anne.' And, then, consulting her schedule, 'Now, I think Miranda Longlady, senior nursing auxiliary here at Paradise Lodge, will perform 'Motor Biking' with Big Smig.'

Big Smig remounted the Kawasaki and started it up, 'Motor Biking' blasted out of the Panasonic and Big Smig sped off towards the summer house. He then performed a turn so sharp, gravel cascaded from his sliding rear tyre and his knee almost touched the ground. Everyone gasped.

He came past the French windows again and did a small wheelie and was then out of sight briefly. To everyone's delight, he reappeared and rolled slowly past with Miranda, in hot pants, riding pillion, kneeling behind him, waggling her feet. Again they went out of sight and then reappeared, this time with Miranda standing up behind Big Smig. This caused gasps and clapping. The motorbike disappeared again for quite some time, finally reappearing with Miranda standing on her head behind Big Smig. She then jumped down and into a cartwheel and Big Smig roared off at high speed and didn't come back. The effect was slightly spoilt by the fact that the audience kept thinking he was about to reappear, and then a car would drive past in the lane and you'd hear Miss Boyd say, 'Here he is.' And so that went on until Eileen suggested it was time for Carla B's party games.

Musical chairs was set up and played but lacked the enthusiasm and chaos usually associated with the game and Carla B moved swiftly on to 'pin the tail on the donkey'. And then it was time for another cup of tea and a talk from Miss Tyler entitled 'My Life at Paradise Lodge'.

Mike Yu played his thumb piano and explained the workings of it to some of the more technically minded patients. I was scheduled to do a backbend into crab and kick-over but the length and narrowness of my bridesmaid's dress made it impractical so we went straight to Sue jumping out of the window and Mindy Banks' nephew singing 'Wings Of A Dove' rather beautifully. I wished he were going to sing the *Miserere mei, Deus* after all, the mood I was in.

The open day drew to a close and there were only a few patients still awake, and a couple of stragglers, when Miranda entered the day room and gave Sally-Anne a bitchy look. Sally-Anne, unusually bold, asked Miranda what her problem was. Miranda replied that she didn't have a problem — and what was her problem?

Sally-Anne said she didn't have a problem and reminded Miranda that she'd asked her first. There was a lot of loud talking about which one of them might or might not have a problem when Miranda suddenly remembered she did have a problem.

'Oh, yes, I do have a problem,' she said, 'that you stole my boyfriend.'

366

'I didn't mean to steal Jiao-Long,' said Sally-Anne, 'he came to me.'

'Bollocks,' said Miranda.

'He doesn't fancy you.'

There were gasps at that.

'You *what*?' said Miranda.

'He's never fancied you,' said Sally-Anne, in her quiet voice.

'Yes, he has,' said Miranda, furious.

'So, how come you never had intercourse?' said Sally-Anne.

'Who says we never?' asked Miranda.

'*You* did,' I said, wearily, 'you said Mike wanted to walk through the forest on foot, remember, and see all the dewdrops etc.'

Miranda stormed out of the room.

★ ★ ★

A few of us, including my mother, sat chatting in the kitchen. Sister Saleem came in, flopped into a chair dramatically and beamed. It had been a very successful afternoon.

'I think that went well,' she said.

The owner said he supposed so, except he'd been on tenterhooks all afternoon waiting for the Attenboroughs to pop back — he'd been longing to speak to Dickie about *The Bridge on the River Kwai*. And Sister Saleem put her hand out and told him not to be silly and he put his hand on her hand.

'We didn't need the Attenboroughs,' she said, and put her other hand on top of his hand, and we all stared at their hands. 'We're on the map.'

Mr Holt arrived in the van to take us home and tooted outside. Jack got up to go and my mother told him we'd be out in a minute. She thanked Sister Saleem and the owner for sharing the open day with her and Mr Holt, and then she added her hand to the pile of their hands and it was all very affectionate. Sister Saleem said some things about my sister and me — praising our niceness and our invaluable contribution to Paradise Lodge etc. — and my mother said it was lovely to hear but she wished I wouldn't work there quite so often and that I'd go to school more. I basked in these two women talking and worrying about me — as any normal fifteen-year-old would.

Then, as we got up to go, my mother told Sister Saleem how she'd very nearly not recognized Matron when she'd delivered towels to St Mungo's shelter, because she'd been wearing slacks.

Sister Saleem and I leapt up in shock.

34

The Travellin' Man

We drove into Leicester in Sister Saleem's Daf Variomatic. It was slow and had no radio but the highest-pitched engine I'd ever known, so that by the time we'd reached our destination we were all on edge. Sister and I went into the hostel and the owner waited in the car because of the parking situation. Sister, still in her yellow ensemble, and me, in my bridesmaid's dress and tiara.

Inside, Sister Saleem spoke to a staff member.

'My name is Sister Saleem and this is my colleague. We're looking for Maria Moran, she's a nursing matron and may be wearing uniform,' she said, 'navy blue.'

'Or possibly slacks,' I added.

The staff member said they'd had a number of enquiries regarding a Maria Moran and I said, 'Yes, that was me enquiring — we still haven't found her.'

'I'm sorry, we can't help you. According to our records, Maria Moran isn't here and never has been,' said the staff member.

Sister Saleem was forceful. 'Actually, someone saw her here a couple of days ago.'

'Really?' said the staff member. 'We've had only two new residents recently — one, a male, from Nottingham and the other, a female, from London, I believe.' He consulted a ledger and whispered, 'a Bridget Monaghan.'

'Oh, my God, Bridget Monaghan! She's the owner's distant cousin,' I shouted.

* * *

The staff member said he'd go and tell Bridget we were here, but it was up to her whether or not she wanted to see us — in his experience these situations could be difficult. As he walked away, Sister whispered that we should say nothing about the Bridget Monaghan thing for the time being and leave it to the solicitor.

'We shouldn't jump the gun, Lis,' she said.

Her English was really coming on, I thought.

Matron appeared in the foyer looking grumpy and self-conscious. She was wearing slacks and a St Michael blouse I recognized as Miss Brixham's.

'Wow,' I said, 'I hardly recognized you.'

Matron made a joke about Sister Saleem's Syreeta hairstyle. Sister told her gently that Lady Briggs had died. Matron paused for a moment, 'So, is that what you've come for? To tell me that Lady Briggs has died?'

'We've come to take you home, Matron,' said Sister.

Matron reminded Sister that she'd sacked her and she was no longer Matron. And Sister Saleem reminded Matron that she had *never* been Matron, if she was going be argumentative.

'I sacked you for gross negligence,' said Sister. 'You left a vulnerable patient in a sheep field, remember.'

The member of staff looked up from his desk.

'He isn't *vulnerable*, he's a spoilt old bastard,' said Matron.

'I sacked you, but I didn't throw you out into the street,' said Sister. 'I made it clear you were entitled to keep your room until you sorted out somewhere to live.'

'Yes, and I sorted out here,' said Matron, 'and it's fine.'

'Are you coming home?' asked Sister Saleem.

Matron shrugged. The member of staff looked up again.

'Are you coming or not?' I asked. 'I want to see my mum off on her honeymoon.'

Matron toddled off and reappeared, struggling with her Teasmade and a small bag. I travelled with her and Sister Saleem back to Paradise Lodge in You Jolly Fucker, which had two parking tickets on the windscreen and a note saying the car was in danger of being towed away unless it was moved within forty-eight hours. Sister asked me to go with the owner in the Daf because he was on his own. I refused, saying I never wanted to go in the Daf ever again.

⋆ ⋆ ⋆

Back at Paradise Lodge, the owner phoned to ask Jeremy Hughes if he'd mind popping in, to speak to Matron/Bridget Monaghan.

I'd missed seeing my mother and Mr Holt off, so I rang The Bell Inn, Moreton-in-Marsh, where they were staying the night and having

371

dinner. Miraculously I was put through to their room and had a chat with my mother while Mr Holt had a bath. I told her we'd got Matron back and hurriedly explained about Matron turning out to (possibly, probably) be the woman to whom Lady Briggs had willed a cottage. My mother was very excited and sent a message of congratulations.

'We haven't told her yet,' I said, 'just in case.'

My mother understood and said also it might come as a huge shock and that we should be prepared for ructions. 'It'll be like winning a competition she didn't know she'd entered,' she said, 'she could have a heart attack.'

When Jeremy Hughes the solicitor arrived that evening, he went straight into the owner's nook with the owner and Matron and broke the news about Lady Briggs bequeathing the cottage. No messing about or coffee and Coffee-Mate. You could tell he wanted to get it over with and get home for his dinner, and fair enough — it was Saturday night and I bet they were having a steak. He was the type.

Sister Saleem, Eileen and I eavesdropped and were ready for ructions.

' . . . to live in for your lifetime, after which it will revert back to the Anderssen estate, and furthermore you may live on the proceeds therefrom, should you need further accommodation,' rambled Jeremy Hughes in legal jargon.

'So, I can live in it, and then what?' asked Matron.

'You can move out and live somewhere else on the rental proceeds — a nursing home, for instance — should you so wish,' said the owner, 'or need.'

'Do you think I could have one of the flats instead?' Matron asked. And Jeremy Hughes said no, he didn't think she could.

I broke away from the other eavesdroppers and went into the nook with the three of them. I wanted to sort something out.

'Matron,' I said, 'did you know Lady Briggs was the owner's mother?'

I said it very clearly because I was certain Matron would not be able to comprehend the question.

'Of course I did,' she said, 'didn't you?'

'No, I didn't.'

'What was all that grovelling for, then?' she said.

Jeremy Hughes looked at his watch and I left them to it. I hated Matron.

★   ★   ★

Afterwards, when Jeremy Hughes had gone, we celebrated Matron's return and her good news with a cup of coffee and rum. Staff and patients (some in their nightgowns) wandered in to welcome her home and hear her tales of running away, which had apparently started when she was a teenager. We had to listen to quite a bit of historical stuff and some obvious lies before she reached the most recent adventure.

It felt as though the day had gone on and on forever — even writing it, it seems impossible — and I longed to get home but Gordon and

Mindy Banks had called in and Gordon was quite emotional so I stayed. 'Paradise Lodge wasn't the same without you,' he said, with great meaning. But Matron still had no respect since seeing him washing his car in the Marigolds, and she just shrugged.

'I heard you stole old Bert's car,' chuckled Gordon, meaning You Jolly Fucker.

'I borrowed it,' said Matron. She told us then that her original plan had been to actually *live* in You Jolly Fucker, opposite the fire station, and use Longston Library as her sitting room and get breakfast from The Travellin' Man — where she had a discount — and keep a permanent wash flannel on a hot pipe and a bar of Camay in the ladies' toilet there. But, in the end, she hadn't been able to get the front seat of the Rover flat enough to make a comfy bed and she presented herself as a homeless Londoner at St Mungo's.

Mr Simmons laughed. 'Oh, yes, that lever's a devil, you need to give it a really good yank.'

'Did you find that friend of yours at St Mungo's?' I asked.

'What friend?' asked Matron.

'Your dear friend who ended up there — she owned nothing but her name — but whose name you couldn't remember?' I asked.

'Oh her, I forgot about her,' said Matron.

She was surprisingly complimentary about St Mungo's and reported only one awkward moment — when someone mistook her soft toy for a rat and threw a fire extinguisher at it.

I watched Matron's face in all its expressions and her chubby arms gesticulating as she continued with her tales, and I went into a kind of reverie. It was easily a match for *The Fortunes and Misfortunes of the Famous Moll Flanders*, I thought.

. . . Born in Newgate, and during a Life of continu'd Variety for Threescore Years, besides her Childhood, was Twelve Year a Whore, five times a Wife (whereof once to her own Brother), Twelve Year a Thief, Eight Year a Transported Felon in Virginia, at last grew Rich, liv'd Honest, and dies a Penitent. Written from her own Memorandums . . .

I smiled at my own cleverness and the brilliance of Moll herself. And planned to tell Matron to start writing her memoirs asap.

'The open day went *very* well today,' said Mindy Banks, and though Matron showed little interest in our big day, we couldn't help ourselves but tell her all about it.

Sister Saleem described my heart-shaped sandwiches and Carla B's amazing bunting. Eileen told her about the Attenboroughs and their nice voices and maroon car and how they'd loved her paintings. Carla B remembered my mother's pretty wedding dress and Sue jumping out of the window. Mr Simmons told her that he'd been banned from doing his magic tricks because Sister had said it was against God. Sister Saleem protested and said she'd meant against nature. Matron's attention was only caught, though, when Miranda described Sally-Anne stepping in and snatching Mike Yu away from her.

'Where is Sally-Anne?' asked Matron.

'She's gone for a Chinese lesson with Mrs Yu,' said Eileen.

'I don't care,' said Miranda, 'I'm back with Smig.'

It was getting late and the night nurse was making the bedtime drinks. We all rejoiced at the various happy endings, as well as regretting the less happy ones, and raised our coffee mugs to Lady Briggs.

'And we were thrilled to hear that you've inherited a lovely home to live in,' chirped Mindy, 'weren't we, Gordon?'

'Yes,' said Gordon, 'congratulations.'

'It's not a *lovely home* actually,' said Matron, 'it's a tiny cottage in the middle of nowhere with a hippy bloke living in it.'

'It's a short-term let,' said the owner. 'Blue will move out in January if you need him to.'

'You don't seem very pleased about it,' said Miranda.

'Yeah,' agreed Eileen, 'you've just inherited a cottage with two outhouses and a myrtle tree — bloody hell!'

'Yeah, considering *everything* and all the fuss,' I said, pointedly, 'Jesus!'

'Of course I'm pleased,' protested Matron, 'but I want my job back.' And her voice cracked a bit.

'Do you?' said Sister Saleem. 'But can you behave yourself? That's the question.'

'Of course I can behave myself,' said Matron, indignantly.

'She can now she's got the cottage,' I added helpfully.

'In that case, yes, we *do* need an auxiliary nurse,' said Sister Saleem.

'A live-in position?' asked Matron.

'If you like,' said Sister Saleem.

'But we don't *need* an auxiliary — *do* we?' said Eileen.

'Yes, we do,' said Sister Saleem, 'to replace Lis.'

'What?' I said.

'Yes, Lis, you're sacked,' said Sister.

'What?' I cried. 'Why?'

'You have to go to school,' Sister said. 'We're going to do things properly now, Lis, and that means we can't employ you.' She looked sad. 'I'm sorry.'

Everyone was staring at me and as I gazed from face to face, trying to make sense of the situation, it dawned on me that everything was sorted. The owner now had enough money to get Paradise Lodge properly back on its feet (and seemed to have Sister Saleem by his side — literally and metaphorically — and Rick in his pocket). I'd taught Sister Saleem all the euphemisms she'd ever need. Matron was safe and sound forever. Mr Simmons was where he wanted to be. Mike had been rescued from Miranda. Miranda was back with sex-loving Smig. Sally-Anne was learning Chinese at the Yus'. My sister was about to start a career in nursing and my mother, though lacking credibility, was at least married.

'You'll fly through your exams now you've got all those books,' said Eileen, helpfully.

For a moment I couldn't decide whether to be

moody or dignified, and then Miranda piped up, 'It's like what Mike always said, Lizzie — you're an intellect.'

'An intellect-*ual*,' I said.

Acknowledgements

I would like to thank my brilliant editor, Mary Mount, for being a total joy to work with — since the beginning (and without whom etc.).

Thanks also to Jo Unwin — my top-notch agent and minder — constant source of fun and sage advice.

I'm happy and proud that once again Reagan Arthur is my US publisher.

Thanks to Stella Heath and Jon Reed for utter marvellousness, enthusiasm and wise words.

Thanks to my family, especially my fantastic mum, Elspeth Allison, and A. J. Allison, John Allison, Victoria Goldberg, Alfred Nunney, Eva Nunney, Jeremy Stibbe, Tom Stibbe.

Thanks to Shân Morley Jones, Chantal Noel, Poppy North, Sarah Scarlett, Keith Taylor and Isabel Wall at Penguin Books.

I remember with great affection my time working at The Grange Nursing Home in Saddington, Leicestershire, in the 1970s. Though it was nothing like Paradise Lodge, happy times there — under the leadership of the wonderful Meena Ackbarally and Rafick Ackbarally — inspired me to write this novel. I'm indebted also to Victoria Goldberg and Fiona Holman for sharing memories with me and for their nursing expertise.

Finally, huge thanks and love to Mark Nunney.

We do hope that you have enjoyed reading this large print book.

Did you know that all of our titles are available for purchase?

We publish a wide range of high quality large print books including:
Romances, Mysteries, Classics
General Fiction
Non Fiction and Westerns

Special interest titles available in large print are:
The Little Oxford Dictionary
Music Book
Song Book
Hymn Book
Service Book

Also available from us courtesy of Oxford University Press:
Young Readers' Dictionary
(large print edition)
Young Readers' Thesaurus
(large print edition)

For further information or a free brochure, please contact us at:
Ulverscroft Large Print Books Ltd.,
The Green, Bradgate Road, Anstey,
Leicester, LE7 7FU, England.
Tel: (00 44) 0116 236 4325
Fax: (00 44) 0116 234 0205

MAN AT THE HELM

Nina Stibbe

Not long after her parents' divorce, heralded by an awkward scene involving a wet *Daily Telegraph* and a pan of cold eggs, nine-year-old Lizzie Vogel and her sister and little brother are packed off to a small, slightly hostile village in the English countryside. Their mother is all alone, only thirty-one years of age, with three young children and a Labrador. It is no wonder that she becomes a menace, a drunk — and a playwright. Worried about the bad plays — though more about becoming wards of court and being sent to the infamous Crescent Home for Children — Lizzie and her sister decide to contact, by letter, suitable men in the area. In order to stave off the local social worker they urgently need to find someone to be the new man at the helm.

WHAT SHE NEVER TOLD ME

Kate McQuaile

Louise Redmond left Ireland for London before she was twenty. Now, two decades later, her heart already breaking from a failing marriage, she is summoned home. Her mother Marjorie is on her deathbed, and it is Louise's last chance to learn the whereabouts of the father she never knew. Stubborn to the end, however, Marjorie refuses to fill in the pieces of her daughter's fragmented past. Then Louise unexpectedly finds a lead: a man called David Prescott — but is he really the father she's been trying to find? And who is the mysterious little girl who appears so often in her dreams? As each new discovery leads to another question, Louise begins to suspect that the memories she most treasures could be a delicate web of lies . . .

BLIND

Cath Weeks

Twyla Ridley — resourceful, optimistic — has just had her first child. It's what she and her husband, Dylan, have always wished for. However, Charlie is blind. For the first time in her adult life, Twyla feels truly tested. She cherishes her son, showering him with love and boundless affection — but there's a part of her that aches for him to see. So Twyla throws herself into motherhood with a very private agenda, because maybe, if she strives hard enough, she'll be able to find a way to fix him. But is it a risk worth taking?